LARA GIESBERS

BALBOA.
PRESS

A DIVISION OF HAY HOUSE

Scripture taken from the Holy Bible, NEW INTERNATIONAL VERSION®. Copyright © 1973, 1978, 1984 by Biblica, Inc. All rights reserved worldwide. Used by permission. NEW INTERNATIONAL VERSION® and NIV® are registered trademarks of Biblica, Inc. Use of either trademark for the offering of goods or services requires the prior written consent of Biblica US, Inc.

Balboa Press books may be ordered through booksellers or by contacting:

Balboa Press
A Division of Hay House
1663 Liberty Drive
Bloomington, IN 47403
www.balboapress.com
1 (877) 407-4847

Because of the dynamic nature of the Internet, any web addresses or links contained in this book may have changed since publication and may no longer be valid. The views expressed in this work are solely those of the author and do not necessarily reflect the views of the publisher, and the publisher hereby disclaims any responsibility for them.

The author of this book does not dispense medical advice or prescribe the use of any technique as a form of treatment for physical, emotional, or medical problems without the advice of a physician, either directly or indirectly. The intent of the author is only to offer information of a general nature to help you in your quest for emotional and spiritual well-being. In the event you use any of the information in this book for yourself, which is your constitutional right, the author and the publisher assume no responsibility for your actions.

Any people depicted in stock imagery provided by Thinkstock are models, and such images are being used for illustrative purposes only. Certain stock imagery © Thinkstock.

Print information available on the last page.

ISBN: 978-1-5043-5311-3 (sc)
ISBN: 978-1-5043-5313-7 (hc)
ISBN: 978-1-5043-5312-0 (e)
Library of Congress Control Number: 2016903902

Balboa Press rev. date: 06/03/2016

Part 1

THE BIRTH OF WISDOM

"The Fear of the Lord is the beginning of wisdom, and the knowledge of the Holy One is understanding" Proverbs 9:10

In the year AD 29 Jesus of Nazareth, whom Pilate pronounced King of the Jews, was crucified on Golgotha between two thieves. He rose from the grave three days later as he said he would. His disciples became apostles and went into the entire world and preached the gospel of this great king who gave life to all who seek it.

There was war and unrest in the world. The last apostles who laid hands on others to bestow spiritual gifts also laid hands on a few whom the Spirit passed supernatural gifts to. These people were to protect mankind from itself until the return of the king. They were governed by the word of YAHWEH and were taught from birth to uphold all his laws. By doing so, they were charged to protect their fellow man from the evil men visit upon one another. They lived their lives, passing on their vast wisdom with mortals as they saw fit.

Some were given gifts of healing. Others were given great wisdom to guide leaders who would seek out their counsel. Others still were given acute awareness, foresight, and great understanding of arcane knowledge both light and dark. These people came to be known as those of the Craft. For wisdom molds and shapes minds and hearts as a fine craftsman molds and shapes precious metals. Those of the Craft also made choices to use their precious knowledge and power for the good of all, and fulfill YAHWEH'S will. Or they chose to walk in darkness and use their gift and power to suppress those less powerful; using their gifts for themselves. These turned to the god of blood and lies who was cast out of heaven and forced to wander the earth causing chaos and unrest in his wake.

As the darkness covered the lands of the earth, darkness grew in the hearts of men. Honest men began to distrust his brothers who were of the Craft. People came to fear the strange people of YAHWEH. Soon this fear turned to action against the very people YAHWEH entrusted to help all of his children, forcing those of the Craft to make difficult choices. One of the Craft who chose to walk with YAHWEH was a man named Marcus. In the year AD 166, he settled in a land that would come to be called Nereheim and built a family. He sought to help the king of Nereheim rule with wisdom and justice. His family and ancestors grew as Nereheim grew. This is their story…

1359

THE BLACK MIDNIGHT SKY WAS studded with stars. Orion aims his bow as Libra balances its scales of justice. A flurry of attention is given to a group of travelers outside the manor of a large vineyard. The Lord of the manor watches with apprehension as a small child, a little girl, is placed delicately in a wagon. His son places a soft kiss on her forehead and gently brushes her cheek. He looks up at his father with tears in his eyes.

"She is all we have left of mother," whispers the little boy. He kneels down and looks his son in the eye and brushes the tears aside.

"I know. Lord Lucerne will take excellent care of her. She will be safe from harm," he says. The boy nods and puts his arms around his father. After a moment, another man bends down to him.

"Your father is a great friend among the gypsies. We will guard her with our lives," he says to reassure the boy.

Both men rise and face each other. "Thank you for taking this risk. Are the borders being checked?" asked the Lord of manor. The other man's face is grim.

"We can only assume so. Many women and young girls are fleeing Nereheim at this time," he replied.

"How will you get to North Agea?" asked the father.

"I have given thought to that. We will cross into North Agea by way of Herron," replied the gypsy.

"Herron? Surely that is a treacherous road?" he asked. The boy's eyes widen at the name.

"It may be. However, the way will be no more treacherous than if we were found in Burnea with your daughter," replied the gypsy.

"So be it. Our fates are in YAHWEH'S hands," replied the Lord of the manor.

Father and son watch as the caravan pulls away from the manor. It is only when the last lantern is out of sight when the father speaks again.

"Jason, you must not let this evil time sway you from the path YAHWEH has marked out for you...

Jason Mauldon holds his little girl in his hands. Already he can see the shadow of dark hair on her head. Her eyes shine like beautiful bright sapphires. As he gazes into her innocent face, he remembers his father's words.

Part 1

CHAPTER 1

"WHAT ABOUT THIS ONE?"

Nafaria looked intently at the red flower her mother held before her. Her long dark curls fell in waves around her face as she continued to peer at the flower. Her blue eyes sparkled and a slight smile crossed her lips. The flower had a brown center, like a sunflower.

Lady Thena Mauldon sat next to her holding the flower. Her hair was golden with just enough red in it to make it dazzling in the sun. Though her light features were very different from Nafaria's dark, they still held one thing in common. Lady Thena loved nature and the intricacies of plants, flowers and herbs. That love of nature seemed to be completely passed on to her youngest child. Her oldest son Philip loved the woods, but was not willing to pay attention to the details that made up those woods. Her middle son Michael was willing to read everything there was to know about plants and herbs, but not as willing to spend his time gathering them. Nafaria was the one child who treated a small plant as tenderly as she would treat a living animal. To her, nature was sacred.

The green hillside overlooking the village of Denholm Glen was breathtaking today. The grass seemed to sway with the breeze that came and went. The village was engrossed in sounds of midday bustle. Horses came and went along the paths that led to and from long roads and into the woods. Various songs and laughter rose up to meet them.

"Coneflower," Nafaria said proudly. The flower moved in the wind of a gentle breeze.

"What is the other name for this flower?" asked Thena patiently.

Nafaria thought for a second. Her mother often asked her to name the roots and flowers of the healing herbs two ways. The name was almost there.

"Ech-Echin, I cannot remember," she finally said.

Thena smiled as she looked at Nafaria.

"Echinacea. It is important to know both names. There may come a time when you need someone's aid and they know one name for an herb but not another. You must be very knowledgeable," said Thena.

"Yes mother," replied Nafaria.

She looked down the slope. A group of children played in the sunlight. The girls danced around in a circle. Garlands of coneflowers sat on their heads. Boys ran around them laughing as they danced. Nafaria sighed. Thena put her arm around her daughter.

"I know it is hard. I grew up without playmates too. However, you will make friends in time. Those of the Craft will be your confidants," said Thena.

"All I wish to do is play with them, mother. Why do I have to be separated all the time?" asked Nafaria.

"You will not always be separate. The destiny of those of the Craft is different from that of a common woman. As a wielder of the Craft, you must possess great wisdom and discretion. Next year, I may send you into the village for your schooling like your brothers. I am confident that Lord Luxton will make sure your schooling will not be lacking," said Thena. She touched Nafaria's cheek.

"Yes mother," replied Nafaria. Her gaze traveled back to the children below.

"That will be enough for today. With each day, your memorization of the healing herbs is growing. Very soon I will be teaching you the poisonous herbs and how to counteract their effects," said Thena. Nafaria smiled.

"Nathaniel and father help me every day. Father tells me that one day I may shape history with my studies. If I work hard, that is," said Nafaria.

"So you might very well. Remember one of our most important proverbs. Always be prepared to give an answer[1]. Your answer must be wise. Wisdom comes from careful study, like you are learning now. It also comes from applying your knowledge, as you grow older. Wisdom is everyone's responsibility," said Thena.

"Can we go into the village and buy some yeast rolls?" asked Nafaria.

"I suppose we could. But you must make sure that Sylvia does not find out. She would be crushed," said Thena with a wink.

Sylvia was the cook of the manor. Nafaria loved her cooking. Her simple stews were fit for kings. Any bread she made melted as it touched a human tongue. Nafaria well believed that God himself blessed her food each morning before mere mortals lay hand on it. Though her food was unmatched, Nafaria felt herself drawn to the bustle in the village.

"Let us go. Perhaps we can find some Epimedium," said Thena.

"I do not know that plant, mother. What is it used for?" asked Nafaria.

"I will teach you the use for that plant when you are betrothed," replied Thena with a mischievous smile. She rose from her seat on the hill and pulled her daughter to her feet. Nafaria followed Thena down the hill to the clamor of the village below.

* * *

The sky was beginning to cloud overhead. A teenage boy about sixteen years of age was lurking through the woods. His bow was in his hand, but he was not concentrating on the hunt quite yet. He continued through the woods, treading lightly over brush and leaves. His aim was to be as quiet as possible. His senses were sharp. He was quickly becoming aware of every animal around him. There was a rustle in the trees, and a medium sized buck came out into sight.

He crouched down, about to put his hand on the mound of dirt in front of him, when he felt himself being jerked backward. He was

---

[1] 1 Peter 3:15

silent as he quickly turned around to see a girl his own age standing behind him. She put her fingers to her lips then pointed her own bow at the mound. He saw a few bees buzzing around the sod that he was unaware of before.

The girl crouched down next to him, following his sight on the buck. She pointed to him and then off to her right, and looked at him. He nodded once and crept through the brush heading toward the buck's path to head him off.

She crept around the back, keeping watch on the buck as well as where the boy was. She knocked an arrow on the bowstring and took aim. Her arrow hit its mark, into the side of the buck. It took off heading straight toward the boy. He let an arrow fly from his bow and hit the animal through his left eye. The buck thrashed through the forest with the boy and girl running after it. They watched it fall on the forest path twenty feet before them. He reached the animal first and found it still breathing. He put another arrow into it, through its heart. She came up behind him. She walked around to the head and looked at the arrow protruding from the animal's eye.

"I will never be able to match that skill, Philip," she said with a sigh.

"You will never really need to. It is not like your family is starving for fresh meat, Viscountess," said Philip. She looked him in the eye.

"My sister is Viscountess, thankfully. I am sure your household is just as well off," she replied with a smile.

"Your skill is as fine as any man's, Alana. Do not look down on yourself because I had a good shot. It is not healthy," replied Philip.

"I suppose not. I wonder what my father would think if he knew I spent many of my days hunting in the woods. What he would say if he did?" said Alana.

"How could your father not know?" asked Philip. "My father knows how good you are."

"Your father knows we hunt together?" asked Alana.

"I have told my father everything I have taught you," replied Philip.

"Why would you do that?" asked Alana.

"He saw us in the woods one day. It was on a day when we each brought down a wild turkey. He asked me about it, so I told him," replied Philip.

"So what does he think about a girl who would choose to spend her days hunting?" asked Alana.

"I told him that we have been hunting together a long time and about the things that I have taught you about being in the woods. He is happy that I will gladly teach what I learn to others," said Philip.

"I am glad as well. I shudder to think what lessons of etiquette I would have to endure if it was not for this time in the woods that we have together," replied Alana. Philip laughed aloud as he bent over the buck. He removed the arrows and pulled out his knife.

"You may be Count Deveraux's daughter, but a courtier's life I could not fathom you tolerating," said Philip. He proceeded to clean the buck. "You are not like your sister at all."

Alana pulled out her knife to help. "No, I am not. A courtier's life is the last form of torture I would wish upon anyone. I am neither sadist nor masochist," said Alana.

"That may be true, but you are an excellent hunter," replied Philip. "By the way, thank you for saving me from the bees."

"You are welcome. I am just surprised you did not see them yourself," replied Alana.

'My focus was on the buck," said Philip.

"You need to remember to be aware of everything around you. You must even respect the air you breathe, so I am told," replied Alana. Philip stopped his work and looked up into her eyes.

"That is good advice," replied Philip quietly. They both looked back at the buck and continued their task. After a few moments Alana spoke again.

"Do you think you will go to visit Lord Saintclaire this summer?" she asked.

"I have not visited him since I was thirteen. I am quite content here," said Philip.

"You may feel content in the woods, but I can tell there is something haunting you, Philip. Sometimes it is as if there is a ghost here in the woods with us," said Alana. Her voice had an uneasy tone.

"What could possibly be haunting me?" asked Philip.

"Love is following you. I think you never really got over your childhood crush on Nadia Saintclaire," replied Alana.

"What of it? If I choose to stay in Denholm Glen, what difference does it really make?" asked Philip. Alana looked up at him.

"You remind me of what an unhealthy thought is. I am merely doing the same. There are times when I think there is a specter following you. I think the only thing you can do is confront your true feelings and let nature take its course," replied Alana.

"Have you had experience with this sort of thing?" asked Philip dryly. Alana smiled.

"No, I have not. However it unnerves me when I think you are slipping into territory that separates me from you when we hunt. When we are in the woods, you are my partner. It becomes dangerous when either of us loses our focus," said Alana.

Philip looked at Alana again. Her eyes were large, and bold, but a hint of sadness lurked there as well. He sighed as he sat down next to her. "You are right. Nadia is someone I have missed greatly. When I would go visit, we spent many hours in the afternoon and early evening riding the horses. She showed me the finer points of mastering a horse. I showed her how to survive in the woods. I still hear her gentle and carefree laugh in my mind sometimes."

Alana smiled a sad smile at him. "I felt it was so. Nadia Saintclaire is a very capable young woman. I can understand why you admire her so."

"What of you? We have been friends for so long, and I treasure our time together in the woods. Will you not miss me if I were gone?" asked Philip. Alana shrugged.

"However I may feel is inconsequential. You must make the decision your heart is in," replied Alana.

"Once again, you have spoken wise words. Perhaps I should take some time to think about where my future lies," replied Philip. They continued the remainder of the task in silence.

* * *

Philip came into the kitchen with a side of meat he put on the counter in front of the cook. She took one look at the boy and took in the blood under his nails and the mud on his boots. "Your skill is improving," she said as she looked at the meat.

"We were lucky today, Sylvia. We brought down a nice sized buck," replied Philip.

"You and Alana were out in the woods again today?" asked Sylvia.

"Yes. She has become a very good hunter," replied Philip.

"Does Count Deveraux know what his younger daughter does in the woods from day to day?" asked Sylvia.

"She has not told him. I think she fears he would forbid her," replied Philip.

"He is sure to find out sooner or later," said Sylvia. She looked at the meat again. "We shall save the chickens I found in the market this morning and cook this deer meat for dinner tonight. I can dry the rest of it and we will have it in the pantry this week," said Sylvia. She looked at Philip. "Why is it you hunt?" she asked.

"It helps me stay alert. It also teaches me to have respect for the world around me. I do not hunt for sport. That was a promise I made to father years ago. I hunt to learn about life," replied Philip. He turned and walked outside.

Philip found a bucket half full of water. Dipping his hands into it, he proceeded to wash the rest of the blood from his hands and fingernails.

"Sylvia tells me we are having deer meat for dinner this evening," said a quiet male voice behind him. Philip looked over his shoulder and saw his father standing there. Jason stood sharp and alert.

Lord Jason Mauldon was the youngest land baron in the region outside Denholm Glen. He respectfully declined the title of "Baron" or

"Lord", but everyone in the village referred to him as Lord Jason and his mother Lady Thena anyway.

"Yes father. We were very lucky today. We brought down a nice sized buck," replied Philip.

"Alana was with you?" asked Jason.

"Yes father. We always meet in the woods. Since I started teaching her to hunt, she has become a valuable partner. She is very skilled," replied Philip.

"She is also the Count's daughter," replied Jason gently. Philip continued to wash his hands in the water. Jason squatted down to his son's level. "She is also not of the Craft." At his father's last remark, Philip felt his shoulders stiffen. He turned his head and looked at his father.

"I know father. She is not acceptable as a mate for me, but she is my friend. She respects me and the knowledge she has gained. I know I have a responsibility to the Craft to marry within it, but if I had my own way…" said Philip. His voice trailed off as a sigh escaped his lips. He stared down at the bucket again.

"What would you do if you had your way?" asked Jason gently. He paused for a moment and waited for his oldest son to speak.

"I just might choose Alana," he whispered. Jason sighed.

"Is there someone of the Craft that captures your attention? Perhaps Nadia Saintclaire?" asked Jason. Philip stifled a laugh as he continued to clean his hands.

"Nadia Saintclaire is beyond my reach," said Philip quietly. Jason furrowed his brow.

"I would invite you never to speak those words in my presence again," replied Jason quietly. Philip looked at his father.

"You are a very capable young man, and the woman you finally marry will be very lucky to have found you," replied Jason.

"I know how betrothal works father. I will choose whoever you choose for me," replied Philip. Jason shook his head.

"Perhaps that is the way it has always been, but it will not be in your case or Michael's or Nafaria's. Your mother and I decided long ago that we would help you find a match. The final decision is to be yours," replied Jason. Philip looked down at the ground again.

"Why do you think Nadia is beyond your reach? You two were always so close," said Jason. "You never told me what happened the last time you went to stay with Lord Saintclaire," he said quietly.

Philip felt his father's eyes on him. He knew Jason wanted an answer to something that however far in the past, it was still painful to think of. Perhaps it was time to talk about it.

"That summer, when I was thirteen, I was doing many different tasks that Lord Saintclaire needed done. He and his men were very busy, and Lord Saintclaire seemed to always be shorthanded for menial jobs. I did whatever was asked of me, and some things that were not. It is one reason why I am so good at shoeing a horse.

One day I was cleaning out the stable area when a nobleman's son happened upon me. He was looking for Nadia. He mistook me for a hired hand. Throughout that week, he would see me with Nadia, whenever I was free. One day, while we were in the village, he sought me out. He told me to 'look elsewhere for a mate, because Nadia was a rare jewel. She would never fall for a mere stable boy.' I came back home as soon as Lord Saintclaire had no need of me," said Philip.

Jason shook his head as he sighed. "Philip, how many times have I told you that nobility shows its ignorance through arrogant boasts? It is one reason why I have always taught you and your brother especially how important it is to be humble. Patience, gentleness, and humility; these are all great attributes the sacred writings teach us are necessary in strong leaders. Did you ever mention this to Lord Saintclaire?" asked Jason.

"No. Nadia is a year older than I am and she always seemed to attract the attention of those older still. Besides, I did not wish to be thought of as a mere helper," said Philip.

"There is no such thing as a 'mere helper' Philip. Lord Saintclaire needed you that summer, and you did the right thing by relieving his mind of baser things so he could concentrate on greater. If I remember correctly, he had quite a few foals to look after that year?" said Jason.

"Yes, he was quite busy," replied Philip.

"He never would have been able to concentrate on the work he needed to get done without you. I know Lord Saintclaire has missed you these last few years. He always mentions what an accomplished rider you became. He is always interested to hear about what you are doing," replied Jason.

"He is?" asked Philip.

"Yes. Perhaps it is time for you to spend a few days with him. It might put your heart at ease," replied Jason.

"Perhaps you are right. Alana gave me the same advice just today," replied Philip. He watched as Jason rose to stand up and turned to leave.

"Father," said Philip. He looked up from the bucket. Jason turned around and faced his son.

"How did you know mother was right for you?" asked Philip. Jason laughed.

"I did not. One greater than I chose her for me," replied Jason.

"Who?" asked Philip.

"My father did," replied Jason.

"He chose well," replied Philip.

"He did indeed. Please trust me to help you do the same when the time is right. The time may be soon, but maybe not just yet," replied Jason with confidence.

"Yes, father," said Philip as he continued to wash his hands.

* * *

The late afternoon sun was still hidden in the cloudy sky as Thena and Nafaria returned from the village. Thena was carrying a small sack with special herbs that she found in the market.

When the fountain came into view, a smile lit Nafaria's face as she caught sight of her brother Michael with a friend. He was about the same size as Michael, but with light brown hair instead of Michael's golden blond. Nathaniel Stone's blue eyes sparkled when he looked up and saw her coming toward him.

"Nathaniel!" Nafaria exclaimed as she scampered up to him. She collapsed into his arms and he hugged her tight.

"Well, what a great surprise. I thought I would miss a chance to see my most favorite little one," said Nathaniel with a smile. He pulled her away from him and put his hand out to measure her height. "What a relief, I am still taller," he said with a laugh. Michael rolled his eyes then cleared his throat.

"This is disgusting, Nathaniel. Did you come here to see me or my sister?" said Michael.

Nathaniel's eyes narrowed. "Of course I came to see you, but I like to make the most of every opportunity[2]," he winked at Nafaria. She smiled broadly, pleased that Nathaniel would not shy away from her, even when he was being teased.

"Now Michael, just because Nafaria has a healthy relationship with your friend, it does not mean you need to be jealous. Nathaniel has a heart big enough for both of you," replied Thena.

"Is your father here too, Nathaniel?" asked Thena.

"Yes Lady Thena. I know he brought the Angelica you requested and he dropped some Roman Chamomile with Sylvia. He was also very interested to show Lord Jason a formula for a new elixir he has been perfecting," replied Nathaniel.

"Well, that should be interesting to hear about," said Thena.

"Do you have time to play?" asked Nafaria. She looked at Nathaniel, her eyes wide with the question. He smiled back at her then glanced at Michael.

"I think I will spend time with Michael today. I would not want to upset my friend. He is smarter than me, you know. However, I will come back tomorrow and see you. We can go into the meadow and hunt coneflowers together," replied Nathaniel. He reached out and touched her lightly on her rosy cheek.

She smiled brightly and said, "I cannot wait!" She turned and skipped toward the house with Thena flowing gracefully behind her.

"Why do you encourage her like that? She talks of you constantly," said Michael.

---

[2] Ephesians 5:16

"I like her. She is so sweet and always talks, but the everyday things she does seem like an adventure to her." Nathaniel lowered his voice. "I guess it is the same kind of preference you have for Lillia," said Nathaniel quietly. Michael looked at him in horror. His head turned sharply to the manor.

"Do not ever say such a thing again! My father can never know," replied Michael fiercely. His voice was almost a whisper.

Nathaniel smiled as he put his arm around his friend. They started up the path that led into the vineyards that began in the back of the manor.

"I understand what you face, but it will pass. We will both be betrothed each to some great wizard's daughter. Perhaps she will mean even more to you than Lillia. We are only thirteen, who knows what the future will hold for us?" said Nathaniel.

Michael sighed. "If we moved away and it would be a memory that I have to hold on to, it would be one thing. If we stay here and grow up together, I am afraid my heart will break when I am betrothed to another."

"In a way, I envy you that. I have never been able to feel as close to anyone as you are to her. Perhaps that is why being with Nafaria is so comforting. With her, I can be as silly as I want to be. I can be myself," said Nathaniel.

Michael rolled his eyes. "Maybe if you stopped putting frogs in girls' hair, you would find one that actually likes you," he replied.

"Maybe, but it is a funny thing to watch," laughed Nathaniel. Michael laughed with his friend as he nodded his head in agreement.

* * *

Nafaria came into the kitchen from the servant's entrance. The shadows began to grow longer. She looked forward to a night beside a cozy fire in the main hall with a cup of tea in hand.

The kitchen was alive with servants preparing the evening meal. Sylvia stood over the stove stirring a giant pot. After sniffing the steam that rose from the pot, she grabbed a ladle and poured a thick hot liquid into little jars sitting next to the stove.

"What is that?" asked Nafaria.

Sylvia looked up from her task. She saw Nafaria standing in the kitchen. "It is elderberry jam, very sweet. Would you like to try some?" asked Sylvia.

"Elderberry is a dangerous berry. It is very poisonous," replied Nafaria. She looked warily at the jars of red liquid.

"It is if the berries are eaten raw. When cooked properly, elderberry has a sweet taste. I have baked some yeast rolls for dinner. Would you like to try some jam with one?" asked Sylvia.

Nafaria's eyes brightened. The thought of Sylvia's light and fluffy yeast rolls still warm from the oven allayed her suspicions of the jam. She took one of the rolls from the breadbasket and handed it to Sylvia. She watched as the cook smoothed the jam heavily onto the roll.

"This recipe has been in my family a long time. I do not know why I have never thought to make it before. Elderberry runs rampant in Denholm Glen," said Sylvia.

"You always think of creative ways to feed us," replied Nafaria as she took the roll. She took a bite and smiled. "This reminds me of mulberries or grapes."

"Yes, it is often called the Englishman's grape. Would you like some more?" asked Sylvia.

"I had better wait. I would not want to spoil my dinner," replied Nafaria. She turned and scampered out of the kitchen.

The family sat in the main dining hall and ate their dinner. Sylvia prepared the deer that Philip provided. She also made sure there was an ample supply of wild rice. Nafaria eagerly dug into her meat as her brothers talked about their lessons in the village.

"So has anyone learned anything of use from the schoolmaster?" asked Jason.

"We have been studying healing herbs and plants found in the wild, father. Our master's knowledge is quite lacking," replied Philip. Jason chuckled at his oldest son's remark.

"I do hope you have kept that to yourselves. I want you to remember to show proper respect to your elders. Lord Luxton has not had the benefit of growing up learning about plants and herbs," said Jason.

"Yes father, we have been very quiet," answered Michael.

Thena looked over at Nafaria. She was almost through her third slice of deer meat. Her rice and vegetables were gone. Her face looked a little more pale than usual. She reached for the water pitcher.

"My, you are hungry tonight. Would you like some more?" asked Thena.

"No thank you mother, but I would like some more water. I am terribly thirsty," replied Nafaria.

"Yes, of course. Did you not eat enough for lunch today?" asked Thena.

"I ate a little, but I had a yeast roll and some jam before dinner," replied Nafaria.

"You ate jam before dinner? I am surprised you could eat at all," said Thena.

"I could not resist. It looked so good, and Sylvia offered," replied Nafaria.

"Well, it seems to have made no difference tonight," replied Thena.

"May I be excused? I feel a little tired," said Nafaria.

"Yes, you may go," said Thena.

Nafaria rose from her seat. She came over to her mother and embraced her. She then walked over to Jason and wrapped her arms around him.

"Good night father, I love you," said Nafaria.

"And I love you, my sweet daughter," replied Jason as he kissed her forehead. Michael watched as Nafaria left the room. He pushed his chair away from the table.

"May I be excused as well? I need to get back to my studies," said Michael.

"I suppose so. What are you studying tonight?" asked Jason.

"Something puzzling I found written in the family annals. It had to do with alchemy," replied Michael.

"Be careful of too much study in that discipline. It can become an obsession," replied Jason. Michael turned and looked at his father.

"Too much study in any discipline can become an obsession father," replied Michael. He turned and left the room. Jason watched him go.

"One day he is going to be wiser than I would ever hope to be," replied Jason with a smile.

"I wonder why it is that Michael spends so much time in study," said Thena. She looked at the table as she sat back in her chair.

"Sometimes careful study can be a great distraction," replied Philip. He rose and left the room. Thena watched him leave as she considered his comment.

"If we ever wanted to raise children to be wiser than we are, I think we have succeeded," said Jason with a smile.

"Only time will tell if we have succeeded in teaching wisdom. However, each one is very bright. Nafaria is getting along well in her own study with me. Philip could live as a wild man in the mountains with everything he knows about the woods and hunting at his disposal. Michael knows the content of each book in our library by its placement on the shelves. Sometimes I think our children do not need us," replied Thena with a sigh.

"For that, we should be very happy and satisfied. Each one of our children has their own path to follow, and they seem to be steadily walking it. I think that we should celebrate by taking the evening to relax," replied Jason. He leaned forward and reached across the table for his wife's hand. "Spend time with me tonight?" he asked. Thena smiled at him.

"I will find you. I found some herbs in the village today that I wish to make use of," replied Thena.

"Go then, and I will look forward to retiring for the evening," replied Jason.

* * *

Jason sat on the terrace that was immediately outside their bedroom. The sky was ebony with millions of pinpricks of light darting out toward him. They shone as bright twinkles and formed the familiar patterns of constellations in the sky.

He held a glass of wine and watched it in the glow of the candle sitting on the table. This was a most favorite ritual for him. Sitting on the terrace, watching the moon rise, Jason was at peace. Somewhere in the house, Thena was mixing an exotic elixir for him to sample. He smiled at the thought. One look at Thena was enough to intoxicate him, but Jason was also deeply in love with the inventiveness of his wife. He knew what she was working on would be special.

As he thought about her, his mind drifted to his father. A conversation from his eighteenth birthday floated back through his mind.

"Jason, it pleases me to tell you that I have found your match in every way. I have just had a very intricate discussion with Lord Briton. If you wish it, you will marry Thena Briton at the end of the summer."

"Father, Thena is not of the Craft," replied Jason. His father smiled broadly, but then became serious again.

"Thena is indeed of the Craft, for she was adopted by Lord and Lady Briton. They have hidden her knowledge for her protection," replied Jason's father.

"Who is she?" asked Jason.

"That will be for Thena to tell you herself, when and if she is ready," replied his father. "I have watched you two together since you were children, Jason. I believe she is ideal for you."

"I would love nothing more," replied Jason in a whisper. He felt his eyes begin to moisten.

"You will need great patience, but if you take care, you will help Thena succeed in finding the path YAHWEH has for her. Who knows what treasures you will unearth," replied his father.

Indeed, so many years later, he sat waiting eagerly for his wife and the fruit borne of that patience. He heard the soft pad of footfalls and turned around. He could make out her form as Thena approached in the mixture of candle and moonlight that filled the room. She wore a silken gown that fell to the floor. The light sage color complemented her green eyes and blended with her soft gold hair. She carried a chalice in her hand and a grin on her face. Her eyes spoke of mischief as she handed him the chalice.

"The last time you wore that gown, we produced a daughter," he said as he took the chalice.

"Who knows what tonight will produce," replied Thena. She kissed him on the forehead.

"So, what is it that you have made for me this evening?" asked Jason. He put the chalice to his nose and breathed in the elixir's aroma.

"Nothing that I did not drink myself," replied Thena.

"I smell horny goat weed and saw palmetto," replied Jason. "You have concocted a dangerous brew, my lady."

"I hope so," replied Thena. She dipped her finger in the chalice and traced his lips with it. Jason licked his lips eagerly and kissed her palm.

He took the chalice and drank deep. The sweet elixir had a heady feel to it. The taste was sweet and very full. Thena's elixirs had a body like wine. Many times people wished to be ill just so that she could make one of her tisanes for them.

He drew her into his arms and kissed her. The smell of coneflowers drifted around her from the flower crown she wore on her head. Her scent mixed with the flowers entranced him. Jason felt the elixir's effect as he kissed her on the neck. Thena's body shuddered at his touch, and she let out a groan. He picked her up and carried her to bed.

It was long after midnight when Thena woke. She heard Nafaria whimpering in the darkness. She sat up quickly.

"Jason, there is something wrong. I can hear Nafaria crying," whispered Thena. Jason stirred at his wife's touch.

"What is it?" asked Jason.

"Something is wrong with Nafaria," replied Thena. She got out of bed and pulled her robe over her sleeping gown. She followed the whimpers down the hall until she found Nafaria slumped against the wall. Sweat dripped from her body. She shook as she sat in the hallway. A pool of vomit and blood was around her.

"Oh child," whispered Thena. She then shouted out, "Jason, Nafaria's sick!"

Jason quickly appeared in the hallway. "My God!" he exclaimed when he saw the mess on the floor. He ran over to mother and daughter. He scooped Nafaria into his arms. "We need to get her into a cool bath. She is burning up!"

They quickly hurried downstairs and out into the garden. The moonlight provided adequate light for Jason to see the path. "Go grab some fresh linen," said Jason. Thena ran back into the house. He turned his attention back to Nafaria. "Stay with us, child," he whispered.

Jason plunged Nafaria into the cold pool. The shock of the temperature on his bare arms made him cry out. "Nafaria wake up!" he shouted. He continued to pour the cool water over her face and neck as she sat in the pool.

"How is she?" cried Thena. He looked up and saw her crouch down next to him.

"What did she have that made her so sick? Did you eat anything from the meadow yesterday?" asked Jason.

"No. The only thing we ate were a couple yeast rolls when we went to the village," replied Thena. Fear was in her eyes. She looked at her daughter. Nafaria whispered something.

"What is it child?" asked Thena.

"Elderberry," Nafaria whispered very faintly.

"What? Where did she get that?" exclaimed Jason.

"From Sylvia," replied Thena. She remembered Nafaria's comment about the jam at dinner.

"Sylvia gave her elderberry?" asked Jason.

"Stay with her Jason. I will find out from Sylvia what happened," replied Thena. She jumped up and ran to the servant's quarters.

"Sylvia!" shouted Thena. She burst through the cook's bedroom door and rushed over to her bed.

"My Lady, what is wrong?" asked Sylvia. She was slowly rousing from her sleep. She saw the fear in Thena's eyes from the moonlight coming through the window. Her face was ghostly pale.

"Nafaria is very sick. She has a fever and has coughed up blood. She said she had some elderberry jam before dinner tonight," said Thena.

"Well, yes my Lady. I put the jam on the dinner table with the rolls as well. Is anyone else sick?" asked Sylvia with alarm in her voice.

"No Sylvia, only Nafaria. What did you do to cook the jam? Was there anything special?" asked Thena.

"No, I only added honey and some nutmeg. I cooked it until it was thick," replied Sylvia. Thena nodded her head, relief swept over her face.

"That is very good. A tisane of peppermint, milk thistle and aloe should do the trick. She will require fresh fruits for a couple of days and plenty of water mixed with a little gingerroot. Nafaria appears to be very allergic to elderberry. See to it that she has no more of that jam," replied Thena with a weak smile.

"I will give it away to one of the women who sell in the market. There are a few who could use the extra money from the sale," said Sylvia.

"Thank you Sylvia," said Thena as she turned to walk out of the room.

"My Lady, I would never do anything intentional," Thena turned around and looked at the cook.

"Sylvia, you have been our cook as long as Jason and I have been married. I hope I can judge your character better than that," replied Thena. "There was no way you could have known. We will speak no more of this. Go back to sleep. I have a tisane to make for my daughter."

Thena came into Nafaria's bedroom carrying a tray with a kettle full of hot liquid, a pitcher of water, a cup and a glass. Jason looked over at her as she entered. The relief she saw on his face gave her added confidence.

"How is she doing?" asked Thena.

"Mother, is that you?" asked Nafaria. She turned her head and looked at her. "Where have you been?"

"I have been making something that will help you get well," said Thena with a smile.

"Oh. That is what father said," replied Nafaria. She sat up slowly.

Jason helped Thena put the tray on the table next to the bed. She poured a cup of the liquid and sat on the bed next to Nafaria.

"I wanted to be at your side, but it was more important for me to make this. It will help heal the effects of the elderberry jam," said Thena.

"Thank you mother," said Nafaria as she took the cup. She held it beneath her nose and took a deep breath. She smiled.

"I smell milk thistle," said Nafaria.

"You smell milk thistle in everything, even over the peppermint!" exclaimed Thena.

"It is my favorite," said Nafaria with a weak smile. She drank the liquid. After a few sips, she felt her stomach settle.

"I feel better," said Nafaria.

"Good. Get some sleep. I will leave this drink on your table. Have one more cup of the tisane when you wake up. Sylvia has been instructed to give you only fresh fruit and water for the next couple days. No yeast rolls," said Thena.

"Yes mother," replied Nafaria. She settled back into her quilts and closed her eyes.

Jason followed Thena out of the bedroom and shut the door behind them. They went back to their room. A servant had already cleaned up the mess in the hall.

"Do you have any aversion to elderberry?" asked Jason.

"Only what the average person might encounter, do you?" asked Thena.

"No, I do not. It must be an Achilles heel she was born with," said Jason.

"It is strange. She cannot even eat cooked elderberry, which is supposed to be very healthy. A very dark Achilles heel to have," replied Thena.

"It must be a secret she takes to her grave. When she marries, she cannot even tell her husband. It could be used against her. Make sure the recipe for the tisane you made finds its way into her Diary when the time comes," said Jason.

"I will record it in my book. She will record it when she gets hers. I will make sure of that," replied Thena.

"Good. You will teach her the importance of keeping the book secret?" asked Jason.

"Of course," replied Thena. She pulled back the quilts on the bed and slipped inside. She held her arms out to Jason as he slipped into bed next to her.

"I was afraid we would lose her," said Jason quietly.

"Tonight is a night of thanksgiving. We have been spared the cruelty of burying one of our children," replied Thena quietly. She sighed as she drifted off to sleep in her husband's arms.

* * *

The next morning Nathaniel came with his father, Malcom Stone, to the manor. The sun was shining brightly as they walked up the path toward the kitchen entrance. Malcom was almost ten years older than Jason. His black cloak fell to the ground. His hood was down around his shoulder to reveal dark auburn hair. Sylvia smiled at them as she returned from the garden. "Good morning gentlemen. It is early, but I am sure Michael and Jason are awake," said Sylvia.

"Actually, I came to see Nafaria this morning. I promised to take her to the meadow," said Nathaniel.

Malcom looked at his son with interest. "What do you intend to do there?" he asked.

"I promised her we would play today. We will probably go looking for coneflowers," replied Nathaniel.

"What an interesting idea," replied Malcom.

"We will have to ask Lady Thena about that. Nafaria was very sick last night and may still be weak," replied Sylvia.

"What happened?" asked Malcom. A look of concern came across both their faces.

"Nafaria had something to eat that did not agree with her. She was very sick most of the night," said Sylvia. She did not give specific details, as she did not feel it was her duty. She decided to let Jason and Thena tell Malcom what happened if they chose. Malcom and Nathaniel followed Sylvia into the manor. Nathaniel followed his father down the familiar hallway toward Jason's library.

Almost every wall of the large room had bookcases from floor to ceiling. The only wall that did not have a bookcase had a fireplace in the center. Two large padded chairs sat in front of the fire. Malcom smiled as he saw Jason at his desk, bent over a book, and looking from time to time at a sheet of paper next to him. He looked up and his face brightened.

"Malcom, I did not expect you so early. Welcome," said Jason.

"Thank you," replied Malcom. He pulled a chair from the corner to Jason's desk.

"Good morning Nathaniel. I did not expect to see you so early either," said Jason.

"I came to play with Nafaria today, but Sylvia said she may not be able to. Is she well?" asked Nathaniel. There was genuine concern in his voice. Jason smiled at him.

"I think we should let Nafaria decide if she is well enough. Why not wait in the kitchen for her? She was feeling much better when she finally went back to sleep," said Jason.

"Thank you. I will be in the kitchen," said Nathaniel. He turned and left the room.

Malcom watched Nathaniel leave and then looked down at the floor for a moment. "Do you know what Nathaniel and Nafaria are up to today?" asked Malcom.

"I was under the impression they were playing in the meadow today," said Jason. "It was all Nafaria could talk of before dinner last night."

"I have noticed that they seem to have a very strong friendship, for being so young," said Malcom.

"I would not worry about them. They get along well together. That is cause to be grateful, not suspicious," said Jason with a smile.

"Yes, you are right of course. I just have never seen two children at that particular age get along the way they do. If it were not for their ages, I would swear they have crushes on each other," said Malcom. After a moment Malcom asked another question.

"Jason, have you been giving any thought to betrothing Nafaria?" asked Malcom.

Jason laughed out loud. "No, I have been so busy with training the boys, I have not had it even cross my mind. Besides, Thena would kill me," replied Jason.

"I do not think that is possible. Thena adores you too much," said Malcom.

"I am not ready to think of that yet. She is still my little girl," replied Jason.

"Well, when you are, please consider Nathaniel. It may be strange to think of, but perhaps the reason they get on so well is that they are true soul mates. Maybe they really do belong together," said Malcom.

"Maybe they do. However, I think I should betroth my sons first," said Jason with a smile.

"When the time is right, please promise to think about it. Nothing would make me happier than to see our families become even closer," said Malcom.

"I will think about it," replied Jason.

Malcom nodded his head. "That is where we will leave that conversation. Now, I was thinking about some of your suggestions for the elixir we talked about yesterday," said Malcom. From there, the conversation turned to the purpose of Malcom's visit.

Nathaniel waited in the kitchen with Sylvia. It was only a few minutes when Nafaria came in, and noticed he was there.

"Good morning, little one," Nathaniel smiled as he spoke.

"Nathaniel! You are here so soon!" exclaimed Nafaria. She dove into his arms when she saw him.

"I promised you a trip to the meadow. However, your father told me that you were sick last night. Do you think you feel up to it?" asked Nathaniel.

Nafaria smiled broadly. Her eyes twinkled like little stars. "I feel just fine this morning. Will we look for coneflowers?" asked Nafaria.

"If you wish," replied Nathaniel.

"Nafaria, you need something for breakfast before you go anywhere. Your mother has said only fresh fruits and water for the next couple days. No wild berries while you are out," said Sylvia. She began to fill a small bowl with fresh strawberries and slices of apple.

Nafaria happily ate the fruit while Sylvia poured her a glass of water. "Would you like something, Nathaniel?" she asked.

"No thank you. Maia also made sure I did not leave without breakfast," said Nathaniel. He sat and waited patiently for Nafaria to finish her food. When she was finished he picked up the cloak that was draped over her chair and put it on her shoulders.

"It is a little cool out, but I suspect it will warm up," said Nathaniel to Nafaria.

"Thank you," replied Nafaria with a smile.

Sylvia watched them leave the kitchen. She thought it strange that Nathaniel made time to have a special friendship with Nafaria. She was three years younger than he was. She reminded herself that those of the Craft raised their children differently than most people. They were taught to respect each other in a very tender way. Nathaniel was a good friend to Nafaria, and that pleased Sylvia greatly.

Nathaniel and Nafaria spent the morning and into the afternoon running through the meadow picking flowers, chasing butterflies, or anything else she desired to do, no matter how silly. She treasured these times with Nathaniel, as it was Nafaria's only time to be with a friend. Her brothers were kind to her and spent time with her, but they were still her brothers. She liked being with people who did not live under her roof once in a while.

They took off their cloaks and lay in the grass looking up at the clouds in the sky. "Look, a rabbit," said Nafaria as she pointed off to her left. Nathaniel looked where she pointed and saw the shape.

"I see a lion," he said as he pointed. She followed his hand. Then she looked over at him.

"Thank you," Nafaria said.

"For what?" asked Nathaniel.

"You are the only real friend I have. People may think it strange, but I think you are nice and I like playing with you," said Nafaria.

"Good. I like playing with you too," said Nathaniel with a smile.

After a moment, Nathaniel put his hand inside his pocket. When he drew it out, he opened his palm. In his hand was a tiny silver ring.

A very delicate heart shape sat in the center. He handed it to Nafaria. Her eyes grew wide as she looked at the tiny ring.

"Is this for me?" she gasped.

"Yes. Your birthday is in a couple days. I made it for you," replied Nathaniel.

"You made it?" she asked. She looked even more closely at the ring. "I love it, and I will always wear it!" exclaimed Nafaria as she gave Nathaniel a big hug. "You are so sweet to me. You are like a big brother only nicer," said Nafaria.

"Who could refuse to be nice to such a wonderful little creature?" replied Nathaniel with a smile.

They both lay back in the grass, enjoying the afternoon sunshine and looking for pictures in the sky.

* * *

The nearly full moon lit the ground as Lya Bernard wandered out of the village and across the field to the brook that ran alongside the main road into Denholm Glen. The Bernard family lived in the village, but situated in a place where the fields began. Her mother used to say it was a convenient place to live; nearer the village, but still wild enough to enjoy the beauty of the woods and streams that wound its way through the western parts of Nereheim.

Lya felt something nagging at her spirit, a restless voice calling her in the night. She looked up into the imperfect sphere of the moon. Soon it would be full. The light it gave off was still bright enough to see by, even in this black night. She sorted through her troubled mind to make sense of what was keeping her from her dreams.

One face kept recurring as she walked through the open land. It was a perfect face; rugged yet angelic at the same time. Soft brown eyes, the color of warm caramel floated before her. Young Nathan Bowman had invaded her thoughts very often of late. What was so fantastic about him that made her senses quiver? She was not accustomed to this feeling of inadequacy. Lya was one of the Craft, with power at her disposal to use as she deemed necessary. She was not given to such trivial displays of emotion as this. Nathan was not of the Craft, yet he invaded her mind constantly.

For the past several months, Lya had taken to wandering in the night. She felt clarity come to her in the darkness. Her study of the Craft had taken a darker turn, but it thrilled Lya to see that YAHWEH'S word held so much power for those not afraid to use it. Lya was not afraid.

Her mother warned her of the uses of the herbs she gathered and what they could be used for. There were plants and roots that were not only poison but could influence the weak minded or unprepared. This was the kind of knowledge a Court Adviser would have. She thought of the king of Nereheim. Would he ever consider a woman of the Craft to be Court Adviser?

Her thought flickered back to Nathan and another face came to light. The soft fair features of Ana Deveraux floated before her eyes. Lya saw Nathan steal glances in her direction often. Did he really fancy such a frail and fragile creature? She was a foolish girl who thought only of etiquette and fine dresses. Would he really prefer Ana to someone like her? Someone who could be a true match of wit?

Eliminate the useless. Take what is yours. Lya heard a whisper in the night as plainly as her mother calling her. She looked around and saw she was quite alone. She saw only the darkness and heard the rushing of the brook. She felt her feet move toward the sound of the water. As she came nearer the water, she noticed a patch of belladonna plants she had not seen before. Her mind had been going over the uses of belladonna as of late. She knew Lady Thena often used small doses of the plant as a balm to help those in pain sleep. It was a very potent plant that had other potential as well. Her mother told her it could be used as a poison as well as sedative. What if combined with another potent plant? What would happen?

Lya sat down next to the brook. She reached out and carefully took pieces of the plant from its branches. A moment later, Lya heard the voice again. *Use your knowledge to make your own destiny.* The words worked into Lya's mind a little at a time; massaging her brain. Her knowledge had grown so much over this past year. She could have whatever she wanted. A light breeze blew the scent of honeysuckle in her direction. She sat next to the brook, and breathed in the scent. It was very common in Denholm Glen, and very soothing. Her eyes grew wide as she looked down at the plant in her hand. Lya had the tools before her. She also had the courage to use them. She could take whatever she chose. Lya quickly rose from her place at the brook with the plant still in her hand. She had to get back home right away. There was much to prepare; for her time would soon come.

***

It was very early morning, but the sun was bright and warm for the hour. Jason walked through his vineyards to survey the progress of his crop. He left his servants to their duties. They worked well and very hard when not under vigorous surveillance. Jason was never one to flaunt authority of any kind.

His inspection was more an excuse to walk his land, take in the crisp morning air and be thankful for all YAHWEH provided for him. From his thriving land to the health of his family, Jason was thankful indeed. He breathed in the fragrant sweetness of the grapes that hung from the vines. Closing his eyes for just a moment, he let a smile cross his face. "YAHWEH, you have blessed me greatly. For this I am content," whispered Jason.

He stopped at the little herb garden Thena and Nafaria kept. What started as an exercise in botanical knowledge and responsibility for Nafaria grew into a place of peace for his youngest child. Nafaria spent much of her precious free time in the garden alone weeding, or with Nathaniel learning how to harvest the plants she grew.

He stopped amid the plants and looked at the neat little rows. Each one was clearly labeled, for the benefit of Sylvia and the other servants. Jason knew that Nafaria knew the look of each plant without the benefit of a label. Nathaniel spent as much time as he did quizzing her on the plants she grew and what they could be used for.

He thought about the idea of Nathaniel and Nafaria betrothed. They were so very similar indeed. Nathaniel was not given to tenderheartedness of any kind; he had a reputation of being quite a prankster. However, Jason saw such gentleness and compassion emanate from him whenever he was with Nafaria. He did not know why she would mean so much to Nathaniel, only that he understood it. Nafaria was a rare jewel in Jason's mind as well.

The sound of horse's hooves rattling against the cobblestones near his manor roused him from his thoughts. He walked out of the little herb garden toward the sound and his face brightened considerably when he saw the figure of Lord Bryant Saintclaire walking toward him. Jason quickened his steps to meet his friend.

"To what do I owe a visit from the horse master of Illith?" asked Jason. He embraced his friend with a hearty bear hug.

"Jason, you are too old a friend to address me with such airs," replied Bryant.

"What brings you to Denholm Glen?" asked Jason. "Certainly you have important tasks to take care of." Lord Bryant laughed.

"That is what I have apprentices for. Ian is minding the horses and training today," replied Bryant. "Incidentally, the filly you wanted for Nafaria will not be ready in time for her birthday. She will be a day or two late."

"Well, that is no matter, Nafaria will still be thrilled when she arrives," said Jason. He looked at Bryant carefully. "However, I suspect you did not come here to give me a progress report."

"No, I did not. I had a single most important task in mind. However, Cassandra made certain that I did not leave Illith with only one thing to do. She has given me a list of items she needs from Malcom, a letter to drop to her sister, and a healthy bunch of fresh lavender for Thena. I have left that with Sylvia," said Bryant.

"So, I am to be your first task of the day," replied Jason. Bryant smiled.

"The first, and most important task," said Bryant. Jason looked at him intently. "I have weighed very carefully the proposal I give to you this morning. As you know, Nadia is seventeen years old. I have considered men for her that are her age, but I am not satisfied with the candidates. I had always hoped to find someone who will help Nadia mind the horses. She is my only heir. I want her to have help," said Bryant. He looked carefully at Jason. "Up to three summers ago, Philip has spent time with me and eagerly learned all that I have to teach him. He was always a great help to Ian when he visited, and a great encouragement to Nadia. I know he is a year younger than she is, but I would offer her to Philip in betrothal."

Jason's eyes grew wide. "Lord Bryant, I do not know what to say. It is an honor to me to have Philip chosen for Nadia," he said quietly.

"I have watched them together many times. Their tempers and thirst for adventure seem to run together. They would be a good match," said Bryant.

"Of that I have no doubt. I am very certain Philip will find working with horses very suitable indeed," replied Jason. Bryant smiled again.

"I think it would be best if we talk to Philip about this. It has been some time since he has been to Illith. He may not be receptive to the idea," replied Bryant. He clapped his hand on Jason's back. "However, I hope that soon we will be brothers of yet another sort," he said merrily. They turned and walked together back toward the manor.

Philip started quietly down the hall toward the kitchen. He knew perhaps his father was awake, but Nafaria was a late sleeper and Michael probably fell asleep at his desk. There were many times when either he or his father picked him up and carried him to bed in the late night. Philip typically walked silently through the house as a form of respect to his family.

As he passed the library, his father called to him. "Philip, could you come here please?" Philip sighed and turned to go into the library.

He noticed immediately that Jason was not alone. In the chair near the fireplace was the stocky figure of Lord Bryant. Philip's eyes brightened. "Lord Saintclaire," he said with a smile. He kept his bow in his hand as he approached Lord Bryant.

"Good morning, my son; heading out to hunt already?" said Lord Bryant as he embraced Philip.

"The morning is the best time to be alone in the woods," replied Philip.

"Indeed it is," replied Bryant thoughtfully. He looked Philip in the eye. "You have grown much since we last met. You are now taller than me. I told you it would only be a matter of time."

Philip smiled again. "I remember you saying that patience is earned with every inch of stature; you must learn to wait on it so," said Philip. Lord Bryant smiled again.

"Philip, I will not keep you long, but there is something I wish to discuss with you. I brought it to your father's attention, but now I think it is time to see what your thoughts may be. If my proposal is agreeable to you, a vocation change will happen very quickly for you," said Lord Bryant thoughtfully.

"A proposal?" said Philip. He looked at Bryant carefully. Bryant nodded his head.

"I greatly desire to betroth Nadia to you. Of all the young men I have come in contact with, you are the only one I can ever consider a son. You are not only a steady worker, but you have the temperament for working with horses. Nadia and I can help you learn even more in that area. You would be a great asset to her in the future. Besides, your skill with a bow is quite legendary; even in Illith," said Bryant.

Philip was truly stunned. He held onto his bow, but paced the room for a few moments. Finally, he stopped and looked at Bryant. "What does Nadia think of this arrangement? Surely she has her heart set on someone already," said Philip.

"She has had her heart set on the wild boy who hunts from Denholm Glen since she was ten years old. Young men come to visit, but she never takes them seriously. Not even those of the Craft," replied Bryant. He moved closer to Philip. "She has loved you her entire life. What has troubled her the last three years is that you have not come back to Illith. She misses you greatly."

"Then why has she never visited herself?" asked Philip.

"Out of respect for you, she has let you to yourself. I must say, it has not been easy for her to do so. You know how impulsive she can be. She has mastered restraint in giving you your solitude. Which is why she never even wrote a letter," replied Bryant.

Philip felt his eyes mist. "She was my greatest childhood friend. I have missed you all so much," replied Philip.

Lord Bryant laid his hands on Philip's shoulders and looked him in the eyes. "Then say you will marry Nadia and come to Illith and help me raise my horses. You will become the greatest horse master in Nereheim," said Bryant proudly.

"Nereheim already has a great horse master, Lord Bryant. I would count it great fortune to marry Nadia and learn from you," said Philip. He wrapped his arms around Lord Bryant. Jason watched them embrace.

"It is fortunate for me, that I have such efficient managers for the vineyard. For the day is coming when they will be the ones to oversee it," replied Jason with a smile. He moved toward Philip and Lord Bryant and put his arms around them both.

***

Later that morning, Thena and Nafaria walked hand in hand through the marketplace. The sounds of the merchants peddling their wares reached Nafaria's ears. She smiled at Thena as they happily wove their way through the crowd that gathered. They stopped at a man who sold different animals. Nafaria picked up a rabbit and began cuddling it.

"Be careful, Nafaria. This rabbit is going to be a family's dinner. You do not want to grow attached to it," said Thena gently.

"Oh, sorry," replied Nafaria as she gently put the animal back. "I hope Sylvia does not make rabbit stew for dinner tonight."

"Let us hope," laughed Thena.

Thena felt a tap at her shoulder. She turned to see a petite woman with black hair and ice blue eyes standing before her. Her skin was as pure as milk with enough pink in her cheeks to make her desired of any male who saw her. Indeed, all the village men knew Analia Bernard was happily married; yet she almost always had at least one man approach her. Thena smiled when she recognized her friend.

"What, no suitors today?" said Thena as she hugged Analia.

"Lya is with me today. They are following her around," said Analia.

"How is she doing? You must be getting ready to betroth her," said Thena.

"We are hoping it will be very soon. It can be a task to find a suitable candidate for someone as spirited as Lya," replied Analia.

Analia looked up and caught sight of her daughter. A small group of young men clustered around her. Lya's playful laughter cut above the dull buzz of the marketplace.

"I worry about her, Thena. I remember when Lya was Nafaria's age. She was so gentle and easy to teach and correct. Now, adolescence has reared its ugly head. She is becoming more headstrong with every day. Her thirst for power grows with it. I fear that it will bring her ruin," said Analia.

"It is a phase, nothing more. Were you so different? I know I felt frustration toward my parents, especially before I was betrothed to Jason. In so many ways he saved me from the despair that comes with being of the Craft. If not for him, I might have pursued the darkest parts of the Craft to prove myself capable of real power," replied Thena.

"How so?" asked Analia.

"He believed in me. From the beginning, he was interested in what I had to say. He has always sought my counsel. Rarely does he make a decision without it," said Thena.

"I do not know if Lya's problem is so easily solved," said Analia.

"All will be well in time. Just keep belladonna out of the house for a while," replied Thena with a smile.

"Oh, that will not stop Lya. Unfortunately, she finds that herb easily enough in the wild," replied Analia with a weak smile.

Nafaria kept her mother in sight but saw a couple children playing. They looked to be her own age or a little younger. They had wandered away from the busy market to where some wild flowers grew. She quickly walked up to them. She stopped one from picking a white, bell shaped flower.

"Do not touch this flower. It is very dangerous," said Nafaria as firmly as she could. The girl looked at her with a questioning glance.

"But it is so pretty. How can it be dangerous?" asked the girl.

"Things are not always as they seem. This flower causes your skin to burn wherever you touch it," said Nafaria.

She looked at the coneflowers growing in a small patch not far from where they stood. She walked over and picked one. "This flower is a good flower. If you want, I can show you how to make a crown for your hair." The little girl smiled. They walked over to the patch of coneflowers and sat down.

Thena looked out and saw Nafaria with two girls laughing as they made coneflower crowns to wear on their heads. Thena smiled. She allowed her daughter the moment to be a little girl.

"I need to go find old Martha. There are some herbs I need, though hemlock is not one of them," said Analia with a laugh.

"Let me get Nafaria and we will come with you," replied Thena. Analia looked over to where Nafaria was playing with the little girls.

"Oh, let them play. We will not be far," said Analia. Thena looked back at Nafaria, and then nodded her head.

"I will just let her know where we are going," said Thena. She walked over to her daughter. "Nafaria; Analia and I are going to see old Martha," said Thena.

"May I please stay, mother?" asked Nafaria. She looked up from the flowers in her hands.

"Yes, you may stay. I will not be gone long," said Thena.

"Thank you mother," said Nafaria. Thena smiled and left with Analia.

Ten minutes after Thena left Nafaria, the girls finished their projects. Each one put on their crowns.

"There, now you are both fit for kings," said Nafaria with a smile. One of the little girls leaned over and kissed her cheek.

"I must go. Thank you," said the little girl. Nafaria gave her a hug. She sat a moment and watched them both leave together. Finally, she stood up and went in search of her mother.

She walked through the market toward the baker, where old Martha's cart usually stood, but Nafaria did not see her mother or Analia. Her heart beat a little faster as she looked around for her mother. She had never been in the village alone.

Nafaria made her way back to where her mother left her, hoping Thena was waiting for her. She saw the same bell shaped flowers and knew she was in the right place. Then she heard a boy's voice behind her.

"Well, what do we have here?" he asked as he stepped toward Nafaria. Two other boys stepped toward her, forming a ring around her.

"I am Nafaria," replied Nafaria. Her tone was simple and fearless.

"Such a pretty little girl to be left all alone," replied the boy. He moved toward her and snatched the coneflower crown from her head.

"Please give it back," said Nafaria as she reached for it. The boy held it over her head, laughing as she reached for it.

"Make me," he said. His eyes gleamed mischievously. Nafaria's eyes narrowed. She dropped her gaze to his shins and kicked with all her might.

The boy let out a yell, and looked at her with blazing eyes. Her bravado turned to fear, and she backed into the other two boys, who held her fast.

"I will teach you to kick me, you little shrew," spat the boy. He lunged at her, grabbing her wrists.

"Mother!" shouted Nafaria as she thrashed around in the boys' grip. She tried desperately to free herself.

"Gentlemen." The boys holding Nafaria looked up and shuddered. The boy who was facing Nafaria tensed his shoulders at the sound of the male voice behind them. It was only one word, but it filled him with dread.

"Please be so kind as to remove your hands from this little girl," said the boy. His voice held a very authoritative tone. The leader turned and faced the newcomer.

"I do not think this is any business of yours, Nathaniel," replied the boy.

"She is a friend, Dominic, therefore it is very much my business," replied Nathaniel with a smile. His eyes narrowed. "Let her go."

The boys felt the piercing gaze directed at them. They lowered their hands. Nafaria stepped away from them toward Nathaniel. He looked at her. "I think it would be best if you stay with me until we find your mother," said Nathaniel to her. She gave him a grateful smile.

He returned the smile and looked back at Dominic and the other two bullies. He walked toward them. "Now, what shall we talk about?" asked Nathaniel.

Dominic looked at Nathaniel with disdain. "Who do you think you are to talk to us like you are better than we are?" he demanded. He was an inch taller than Nathaniel, but the nervousness in his eyes told Nafaria the bully was afraid of him.

Nathaniel ignored the question and looked down at the ground. Seeing the bell shaped flowers there, his face brightened. "I have it," he said. He walked over to the flowers and picked a few. He held them by the stems with his fingers. He handed them to Dominic.

"What is this?" asked Dominic.

"It is a flower. I dare you to hold it in your hand," replied Nathaniel with a smile. The boy looked uneasily at the flower in Nathaniel's hand. "Come now; you are willing to pick on a girl three years younger than you. Surely you are not afraid of a simple flower?" taunted Nathaniel.

The boy's eyes narrowed as he took the flower from Nathaniel's hand.

"Now, close it in your fist and crush it," said Nathaniel. The boy looked at him questioningly. Nathaniel narrowed his eyes. "Do it," he snarled.

Dominic closed his fingers into a fist, crushing the flower in his hand. He cried out a moment later and opened his hand. It was full of red blisters, and burned with pain. He looked at Nathaniel, his eyes widening. "How, how did you do that?" stammered Dominic.

Nathaniel moved closer to him. "YAHWEH has given me the power to exact vengeance for those who cannot defend themselves. Pray I do not have to exact it on you again," said Nathaniel quietly. "Now go."

Nafaria watched the boys quickly disappear into the crowd of the market. Dominic looked over his shoulder at them as he left. She put her arms around Nathaniel and hugged him.

"Thank you, Nathaniel," she whispered. He smiled back at her.

"I do not think they will bother you again, but do not give them opportunity," said Nathaniel. "Now, how about if we find your mother?"

"She and Analia were going to find old Martha. I went looking for her, but did not find her at the usual spot, so I came back here," said Nafaria. She pointed to where Lya stood in the same circle of young men. "Lya is still here with them."

Nathaniel followed her gaze to the young woman standing in the center of a small crowd of young men. As she half-heartedly listened to them, she caught sight of a fair haired young man walking with a blond haired girl about her own age. They stood in one corner of the market making conversation. Something the young man said sent her into a fit of giggles. Lya's eyes narrowed as she watched them. After a few minutes, he took her hand, kissed it, and went on his way with the girl watching him as he left. Lya broke from the group and quickly walked up to the girl.

"I think he fancies you, Ana." The girl jumped as she turned to look at the speaker.

"Oh, Lya, you startled me," said Ana.

"Nathan is quite handsome," said Lya as she looked in the direction the young man had gone. Ana smiled, her cheeks turning a few shades rosier than before.

"Yes, he is," replied Ana quietly. "It is hard to say if he prefers me or my father's title,"

"Oh, I am sure he would prefer you, Viscountess," said Lya. She paused for a moment then spoke again. "Perhaps I can help ensure that Nathan really does prefer you to your father's title."

"How could you do that?" asked Ana.

"I could give you an elixir, an old family recipe that might bring out his more amorous side," replied Lya with a wink. Ana looked at Lya suspiciously. "I can help you," Lya whispered in return. "May I visit you later this afternoon?"

"My father does not trust those of the Craft," replied Ana.

"Your father need never know. It is your choice how you choose to live, Ana," replied Lya. "I will visit you later today."

"I do not think it is a good idea," replied Ana. "Father thinks those of the Craft keep dangerous secrets."

"Perhaps some do. We have grown up together, Ana. The sacred writings say to seek the Lord while he may be found.[3] This is good advice. YAHWEH has provided this opportunity. It would be a shame to waste it," replied Lya softly.

After a moment, Ana nodded her head. "Perhaps you are right. It is only a harmless potion after all," said Ana.

"Indeed," replied Lya. She turned and walked away from Ana.

Philip was searching through the market place until he finally found his mother talking with Analia. He delivered a message from his father when he noticed Ana and Lya in conversation. He watched them for a few moments, before Lya walked away. As he watched the two part company, he felt a tap on his shoulder. He turned and smiled when he saw Alana standing behind him.

"Good afternoon. It is nice to be able to see you in a place not surrounded by forest," said Alana with a smile. Her smile faded a little when she saw the cautious expression in his eyes. It was an expression she was familiar with. It usually showed itself when Philip was puzzling through something of great importance.

"What is wrong?" asked Alana.

"I was watching Lya and your sister together, Alana," replied Philip.

"They are the same age, Philip. Perhaps Ana was getting some advice from her," replied Alana.

"Alana, you cannot trust Lya. I have overheard my parents in the past talking about some fears that her parents have. She is not someone you should gather advice from," replied Philip.

"Has she done something wrong?" asked Alana.

"Not that I have heard," replied Philip.

"Then I think perhaps you should not judge her. How is it said 'Do not judge, and you will not be judged[4]," replied Alana. Philip looked at her carefully.

"You are right, of course. I just wish you to promise me one thing," replied Philip.

---

[3] Isaiah 55:6
[4] Luke 6:37

"What is that?" asked Alana.

"Be wary of Lya," said Philip. He looked around to see Nafaria coming toward them with Nathaniel.

"If you think I should be cautious around her, I will," replied Alana. Philip nodded his head.

"Thank you. I will see you again another time," said Philip.

"I will look for you in the woods tomorrow," said Alana with a smile. He smiled back as he walked toward his little sister Nafaria, and Nathaniel Stone. The three headed away from the market place.

Alana walked home from the village alone, and in thought. Why would Philip warn her about Lya? Raymond and Analia Bernard were known in Denholm Glen for their use of the Craft, but they were very noble people. Lady Analia always used her knowledge to help others. She was someone to be respected, not feared. Was Lya like her parents, or was she driven toward another purpose? Alana had no use for anything Lya might offer her, but Ana was not as judicious with her common sense. She was so good and pure that she only saw the best in people. Ana would mistake jealousy in Lya for passion and be unsuspecting of any design against her. Alana wondered if Lya would go so far as to harm another person such as her sister with her knowledge. She considered this as she walked on.

As she neared the house, Alana passed the gardener who was trimming rose bushes in the front just outside their great room window. She rounded the corner and saw Ana sitting on a stone bench in the small courtyard off the back entrance of the house. She sat with a rose in her hand and was idly picking the petals from the stem. She looked up when she heard footsteps coming her way.

"Alana, you made it home, I see," replied Ana. She looked back down at the flower in her hand. Alana sat down on the bench next to her sister.

"I took my time coming from the village. There were some things I needed to consider," replied Alana.

"Such as how you might win the favor of the hunter in the woods?" asked Ana. She looked over at Alana.

Alana smiled, but shook her head. "Philip is just a good friend, and has been for a long time now. I do not think he even considers me in that fashion," replied Alana. She looked up at the windows of their house. "You must not tell father about my hunting. I have managed to keep it a secret this long, as far as I know. I cannot bear to lose the one thing that makes me feel whole."

"You always were so free spirited, but yet practical. If father has not found out for himself yet, he will not find out from me," replied Ana.

Alana smiled and took her sister's hands in hers. "Ana, you must promise me that you will not follow Lya's advice, whatever it may be. I have seen the way she watches Nathan Bowman. Her expression darkens whenever she sees him around you. If Nathan truly loves you, it will be a genuine love that will come from his heart, not from any potion she might concoct," said Alana. Ana looked at her sister questioningly, so Alana went on. "I fear that Lya's designs may not be in friendship, Ana. You do not see how she watches Nathan when his back is turned. I do not wish harm to come to you over a man."

Ana laughed out loud. "Alana, that is very sweet, but I do not think Lya would go so far as to hurt someone over Nathan. I am afraid your imagination has run away with you," said Ana.

"I merely wish you to be cautious, Ana. Please consider what you are doing if you see her," replied Alana. She rose from her spot on the bench and went into the house, leaving Ana to gaze at the petals on the ground at her feet.

* * *

Nathaniel said goodbye to Philip and Nafaria, then watched them walk away for a few minutes before starting home. He and his father lived in the village square. Malcom Stone owned an apothecary and herb shop. They had enough land behind the shop to be able to grow wild herbs and sell to the villagers. Malcom also sold spices and oils that were not easy to find in the western part of Nereheim.

Nathaniel walked through the gate that led to the back entrance and the garden area. There his father stood among the rows of plants, making assessments of each one. He thought it strange that his father did not label each row as other gardeners did. However, he knew his father knew each and every plant by sight. As he continued to the house, his father called to him.

"Nathaniel?" said Malcom. Nathaniel looked up at his father and walked toward the garden.

"Yes father?" asked Nathaniel.

"I heard that you had a conversation with Dominic Cavanaugh earlier this afternoon," said Malcom. His gaze shifted from the plants to his son.

"Yes father. He and a couple of his friends thought it would be amusing to pick on Nafaria while she was alone," said Nathaniel.

Malcom raised an eyebrow at Nafaria's name. "This I did not hear. However, you decided to have a little fun of your own with the Lily of the Valley?" asked Malcom.

Nathaniel broke his gaze from his father and stared at the rows of plants surrounding his father. "Yes father," said Nathaniel after a moment.

"Dominic's mother came to see me, wondering if there was something I could recommend for the pain her son is in. She told me about the flower and I assured her that the effects of burning will diminish by morning. I am afraid Dominic is in for a long night," said Malcom. He looked at Nathaniel closely. "I have stressed so many times before, Nathaniel, how important it is never to treat the knowledge of the Craft lightly. We are meant to serve and protect those around us with our knowledge. We must never abuse that knowledge by being vengeful," said Malcom.

Nathaniel looked up at his father. The look on his face told Malcom that his son was struggling to control his anger. Nathaniel took a deep breath.

"Father, they thought nothing of picking on Nafaria when she was lost in the village looking for Lady Thena. Am I supposed to just let them hurt her?" demanded Nathaniel.

Malcom saw the tears forming in his son's eyes. He was beginning to see just how sensitive Nathaniel really was when it came to Nafaria.

He sighed and shook his head. "No, you did the right thing to intervene. However, next time try and use a kinder approach to make your point," said Malcom gently. He waited a moment then asked, "What is it about Nafaria that makes you act this way?"

Nathaniel thought a moment then shook his head. "I do not know father. Every time I am with her, I am reminded of all that is good and pure in this world. She holds no hatred of any form, and is always so happy. When I am with her, I just want to protect her from evil."

"Just like you protected her from Dominic," said Malcom. Nathaniel nodded.

"Well, at least I can understand that. Just be careful, Nathaniel. You may not realize it, but you are getting quite a reputation as someone to be feared," said Malcom.

"It is only because I refuse to back down. I am willing to show people like Dominic that I will fight for the things I hold sacred," said Nathaniel. He stood up from his seat. "If I caused any problem, father, I am sorry. I just wanted to teach him a lesson."

"I am sure the lesson is quite learned, Nathaniel. As I am also quite sure it will be a while before Dominic reaches on a dare for any wildflowers," replied Malcom with a laugh. "Maia tells me that dinner will be soon. Go get ready."

Maia was the housekeeper and cook. Malcom hired her when they first came to Denholm Glen to help him manage Nathaniel and the housekeeping so that Malcom could build a new life for them as an apothecary. Now, she was just as much a part of the family as the mother he only heard about from his father.

"Yes father," said Nathaniel with a smile. He turned to go into the house, when he paused. "There is something else about Nafaria that I just cannot forget," said Nathaniel.

"What is that?" asked Malcom.

"There is something in her eyes that reminds me of mother," said Nathaniel. He took a step toward the house.

At that moment, Count Deveraux burst through the back door, followed by Maia. She was protesting his intrusion to no avail. His eyes were wide, and his face was red with anger. In his hand was a little glass vial with a cork in the top. Malcom and Nathaniel both stared at him. The Count held out the vial to Malcom.

"Malcom, Ana is dead. I found this vial in the pocket of her dress. I think she may have been poisoned," said the Count. He could barely get the words out.

Malcom took the vial, and then looked at Maia. "I will see to the Count, Maia, thank you," he said. She dipped her head and returned to the house.

Malcom looked at the vial carefully and opened the cork. He waved it under his nose a moment, and then his face went pale. He handed it to Nathaniel who also sniffed the contents of the vial. Nathaniel's expression turned to horror as he handed the vial back to his father.

"Father," whispered Nathaniel.

"What is it?" shouted the Count. Malcom looked at the Count uneasily.

"The mixture is belladonna and hemlock. Those are the two most deadly herbs of the Craft. The two mixed together form a poison that will kill within minutes," said Malcom quietly.

"Who would have given this to my daughter?" shouted the Count. "Ana has never hurt anyone in her life!"

"Someone of the Craft did this. That is all I can say for sure. Knowledge of poisonous herbs is not common to the villagers of Denholm Glen," said Malcom. "I am truly sorry for your loss." Malcom looked at the Count with sadness in his eyes.

The Count took the vial. "I will find who is responsible," fumed the Count. He stormed out of the back yard area. Nathaniel looked at Malcom with a worried expression.

"Father, there is only one person who would do such an impulsive thing," said Nathaniel. Malcom held up his hand and refused to let his son say anything more.

"We cannot accuse each other, Nathaniel. Count Deveraux will know more as facts come to light. Let us not cast suspicion on each other. If you are wrong, you would never be able to tolerate the guilt associated with ruining an innocent person," said Malcom. After a moment, Nathaniel nodded his head.

"Yes father," replied Nathaniel.

At that moment Maia opened the door and announced dinner, but neither Nathaniel nor Malcom had any appetite.

***

The evening sun became a memory and the stars popped out in the clear night sky. Lya sat at a table in the great room while her parents sat on a couch to the side, in quiet conversation. A thick book lay before her and she was busy scrawling notes on a sheet of paper. She held a concentrated gaze on her writing. She paused for a moment to look up at her parents. They sat so peacefully with one another. She smiled as she looked at them, wondering what it would be like when she finally married. After a moment, she looked back down at the writing in front of her.

Suddenly, there was a loud knock at the door, then Count Deveraux, with four other men walked into the room. Raymond rose from his seat at the sight of them.

"To what do we owe this visit, Count Deveraux?" asked Raymond. His eyes were steady, but he struggled to hold his composure under such unprecedented circumstances. The Count, after all, was the king's representative of justice in Denholm Glen.

Lya looked at her parents, then at the Count. The Count addressed Raymond.

"Your daughter is responsible for a despicable crime against my family. She poisoned Ana earlier this afternoon," said the Count sternly. He glared at Lya.

"That is a wild accusation, Count Deveraux. You had better be able to prove it," said Raymond. Anger quickly replaced uneasiness.

The Count held out a small glass vial with a cork in the top. "I have already shown this vial to Malcom Stone. He confirmed that it contained a poison made of two of the most deadly plants in this region. Only one of the Craft could have known this," said the Count.

"So you accuse Lya? Anyone of the Craft in Denholm Glen could have done this," exclaimed Analia.

"When I arrived back home from visiting Malcom, my gardener came forward and told me of a conversation between my daughter and Lya earlier in the afternoon. He saw Lya give Ana the vial. He said she told Ana it was a love potion!" shouted Count Deveraux.

The color drained from Analia's face. Raymond turned and looked at his daughter with the same horror-stricken expression.

"Is this true Lya?" whispered Raymond.

Lya looked from her parents to the Count. She knew she was caught; there was no way to deny it. "Yes father," she replied.

"Oh child, what have you done?" whispered Analia. She sank to her knees and sobbed. Raymond looked at the Count fearfully.

"What will you do to her?" asked Raymond.

"Lya will be hanged in the Village Square tomorrow at noon, for the murder of my daughter. Your wife shares the blame in this atrocity for not teaching her to be disciplined with her knowledge. Analia will be hanged as well for her lack of ability to teach her daughter temperance," said the Count.

"You cannot do that! Analia cannot be held responsible for Lya's indiscretion. It is unjust!" shouted Raymond.

"Both mother and daughter will be hanged tomorrow!" shouted the Count.

"I will not let you!" shouted Raymond. He lunged at the Count.

At that moment, the other men pounced on Raymond and began beating him. Two other men appeared in the door and grabbed Lya. They threw a rope around her and carried her out of the house while Analia watched them beat her husband.

"Enough! Take Analia. We will keep them both bound in ropes until noon tomorrow," said the Count. The men moved toward Analia who thrashed about screaming her husband's name over and over as she was carried out of the room.

***

Malcom sat before the fire, troubled by Count Deveraux's news. He felt as if something terrible was about to happen. He watched the flames dance about in their bright orange and yellow hues. He had never known anyone of the Craft to do such a wicked thing as murder another human being. He was sure it happened before, and that it would perhaps always happen, that is the nature of abuse. Now that it visited Denholm Glen, how would he react to it? That was the question before Malcom now. Was Lya so cold as to seek the death of an innocent young girl? Why would she? He pondered this as Nathaniel came into the room and sat down across from him.

"Is there anything wrong Nathaniel? You are usually wrapped up in study of one sort or another at this time of night," said Malcom.

"I wondered if you would tell me about mother," said Nathaniel. Malcom raised an eyebrow. It was not often that Nathaniel would ask about his mother.

"What would you like to know?" asked Malcom.

"What was she like?" asked Nathaniel.

Malcom smiled wistfully as he looked at his son. "Your mother was captivating. Whenever she walked into the room, my eyes instantly went to her. I could be in mid-sentence on a very important topic of discussion and I would forget my train of thought entirely. She held a very strong sense of innocence, but for all her naiveté, she was extremely intelligent. She spent most of her days in the royal library. She thirsted for knowledge the way your friend Michael does.

I would find her in the garden with Susanna learning everything there was to know about roses and how to care for them. Eventually, I made sure our paths crossed outside and I began to teach her about the flowers and plants that grew near the castle. She was so charming. The day finally came when I made the decision to put away the rule of marrying within the Craft because I loved her so. I have not regretted a single moment of my life since I made that choice," said Malcom.

"Mother was not of the Craft?" asked Nathaniel.

"Your mother was Princess Sasha, little sister of King Rohn Catalane," replied Malcom. Nathaniel looked down at the floor.

"You met mother when you were Court Adviser," whispered Nathaniel.

"Yes," replied Malcom.

"If you were Court Adviser to the king, why did you leave?" asked Nathaniel.

"King Rohn loved his little sister also. You were not even a year old when she took ill of a plague that began in Burnea and spread through the royal city before it could be stopped. He was distraught and in his grief, his anger came through. He cursed me, and told me to leave Wildemere. So I took you and left. I did not wish to leave Nereheim, so I went to the western part of the country. I settled us in Denholm Glen when I saw the need for an apothecary. Jason and Raymond became like younger brothers to me," said Malcom.

"Would you have married mother if you knew what would happen?" asked Nathaniel.

"I would have done it as naturally as I breathe. Your mother was a rare jewel that YAHWEH blessed me with. She gave me you as a son. Even though you are of mortal descent as well as of the Craft, you are brilliant. I am very proud of you," said Malcom. Nathaniel reached over to his father and grabbed his arm.

"I am very proud of you as well, father," replied Nathaniel.

At that moment, both heard a loud thump on the doorstep. "I wonder what that could be?" asked Malcom. He got up from his chair and went outside, with Nathaniel right behind him.

Both were shocked to see Raymond lying at the entrance to the house, his body bruised and bloody from head to foot. His left eye was swollen shut, and his breathing was labored.

"Raymond! What happened?" exclaimed Malcom. He knelt next to his friend.

Raymond struggled to respond. His voice was raspy and no more than a whisper. "He took Lya and Analia. Lya killed Ana with poison," gasped Raymond.

"Raymond, do not speak, let me get you into the house," said Malcom.

"He is going to execute Analia too, at noon tomorrow," whispered Raymond. His breathing was even more labored than before.

Malcom's face was horror-struck. "He cannot do that!" said Malcom.

"An example," whispered Raymond. He clutched Malcom's hand. "Get our books, they must be kept safe." Then he stopped breathing.

"Raymond!" shouted Malcom. He shook the bleeding figure in his arms. "Raymond!" he shouted again. He sat on the ground holding the man's head in his hands.

"Father?" whispered Nathaniel. Malcom wiped his eyes with the sleeve of his shirt. He looked at Nathaniel.

"We need to build a pyre and burn his body," said Malcom.

Nathaniel felt tears burn hot on his cheek as he helped his father organize wood from the wood pile and gently laid Raymond on it. Malcom lit the wood on fire and watched as it consumed the body of his old friend. He turned to Nathaniel.

"I need you to go to Raymond's home and look for their diaries. Get Maia to tend the fire until you return. Make haste, Nathaniel. I will find the answer to this puzzle," said Malcom. He spurred his horse and took off into the night.

Malcom quickly rode up the winding drive toward Count Deveraux's manor. He stopped his horse in the courtyard near the rear entrance and looped his horse's reins over the branches of a small flowering tree.

"Stay," he whispered to the horse. Malcom then turned his gaze toward the house and burst into the rear entrance.

The cook and a maid were busy cleaning up the kitchen when Malcom came into the room. The maid jumped.

"Where is the Count?" demanded Malcom.

"He is in the sitting room, sir," replied the cook nervously. She had never heard Malcom Stone raise his voice before.

Malcom stalked into the sitting room and found the Count, his wife, and Alana all sitting together on a large couch. The expression on the Countess's face caused Malcom to soften his own expression. He directed his gaze at the Count.

"Count Deveraux, I need a word with you," said Malcom coldly.

Alana looked at Malcom, but she did not register his anger. The only fact she could register was that her older sister was dead. She rose from her seat and exited the room. The Countess followed after her.

When they left, Count Deveraux spoke. "What is the meaning of this intrusion?" asked the Count.

"You have unjustly imprisoned an innocent party in your pursuit of justice. Lya was obviously at fault, yet you took Analia as well. Why?" demanded Malcom.

"I wish to make an example of her. In the future, those of the Craft will be more careful of what they teach their children," replied Count Deveraux.

"What happened to Ana is not Analia's fault. Lya was warned repeatedly by Analia and Raymond of the importance of discretion. Analia does not deserve death," said Malcom.

"My daughter did not deserve death, yet she is buried in the ground as we speak. I will see justice served!" shouted the Count.

"You seek vengeance, not justice! Your vengeance has already killed Raymond. Do not execute Analia too!" shouted Malcom. The Count looked at Malcom.

"Raymond is dead?" he asked.

"He died in my arms after crawling to my doorstep. He was severely beaten," said Malcom coldly. He moved closer to the Count so they were less than a foot apart. "I should make an appeal to higher authorities. They may not see justice the same way you do."

The Count's anger burned. "To whom would you make an appeal? The king perhaps?" he shouted. Malcom stared at the Count.

"No, perhaps not," said the Count. He moved even closer to Malcom. "Do not threaten me. The king no longer cares for those of the Craft, and I will have whatever justice seems right to me for my daughter's death," said the Count bitterly.

"Death always comes full circle, Count Deveraux. What you begin with murder often ends in murder at your doorstep," replied Malcom. He turned and walked out of the room.

***

Nathaniel quickly rode to Raymond's house. He saw the door wide open, with the household servants rushing about. He slowed his horse and climbed down. After securing his horse by a tree, he moved with swiftness through the front door.

The servants seemed to be in a quandary, rushing about, searching rooms, calling their masters' names. One of them stopped when he saw Nathaniel standing in the doorway.

"We cannot find Master Raymond, Analia or Lya anywhere! We heard a great commotion, but they are all gone. Do you know what happened?" he asked Nathaniel.

"Raymond is dead. He died in my father's arms on our doorstep," said Nathaniel quietly. The servant looked at him.

"Why are you here? Where is your father?" asked the servant.

"My father instructed me to come and find something Raymond wished him to have. We are burning his body on a pyre at our home," said Nathaniel.

The servant hung his head. "I will take care of the household responsibilities. Gather what you need to take," said the servant quietly. The servant left him to tell the others in the house what happened.

Nathaniel looked around the room. He found a large book sitting on the table. A candle was burned down about halfway, a pool of wax gathering below it. He turned the book to the front page. It was Lya's diary.

He quickly panned through the pages and what he saw made him gasp. Lya had very meticulously copied the most dangerous herbs into her diary, with their effects and what they could be used for. He read one of the last entries in the book. It was an elixir made of belladonna and hemlock, along with a few other ingredients. He had no doubt that this was what killed Ana. He closed the book and picked it up off the table. A few minutes later, he found the other two books he was in search of and left the house.

Nathaniel was troubled by what he read in the pages of Lya's book. However, he was also intrigued by the ingenuity she showed. He would ask his father about her entries at another time.

***

Nafaria awoke as the morning sun's light fell on her face. Her eyes fluttered open when she felt the warmth kiss her cheeks. Her mother's smile came into focus.

"Good morning little one; happy birthday," said Thena. She kissed Nafaria on the cheek.

"Good morning mother," replied Nafaria. She wrapped her arms around Thena and hugged her tightly. "What are we going to do today?"

"No study today. Maybe we can pack a basket and have a picnic in the meadow," replied Thena.

A knock on the door interrupted them. The door pushed open and Jason entered.

"Good morning, Nafaria, and happy birthday. Please allow me to present you with your first birthday gift." He held out a leather parcel. Nafaria smiled.

"Thank you, father, but you are too late. Nathaniel gave me a gift a couple days ago," she said as she took the package from her father's hand.

"Is that so? I shall have to be quicker next year," replied Jason with a laugh.

Nafaria opened the leather and lifted up a long green crystal about two inches in length. It was encased in a delicate gold frame. A long chain was threaded through the top. She held up the chain and watched the green color as it reflected the sunlight. Her eyes widened in wonder.

"Can you tell me what stone this is?" asked Jason.

"It is emerald," replied Nafaria.

"You know much for one who is only ten years old. Your mother has done her job well," replied Jason.

"The ancients once ascribed this stone as your birthstone," said Thena. She smiled at Jason. Nafaria put the chain over her head. She let the stone fall against her gown.

"Thank you," she replied. She hugged Thena again, then Jason.

"You are welcome, little one. Enjoy your special day," said Jason. He rose and left the bedroom.

"Get dressed. We will have breakfast," said Thena. She got up off the bed.

"Mother, is it possible to have too much knowledge?" asked Nafaria.

"Only if it is not used or if it is gained to hurt others. Never fear your heritage. As one of the Craft, you have the ability to help so many people. You have a good heart, Nafaria. I know that you will be wise with your knowledge. This is why I push so hard. I wish to help you be strong," said Thena.

"Yesterday, I stopped some girls from playing with a dangerous plant. Was that wrong?" asked Nafaria. Thena smiled.

"No. You used your knowledge to help others. That is never wrong. The only thing I beg you to remember is to not draw attention to your knowledge of the Craft. People fear what they neither possess nor understand," said Thena.

"Yes mother," replied Nafaria. Thena left the room with those words, shutting the door behind her.

A little while later, Nafaria skipped into the kitchen holding a basket lined with a cotton cloth. She wore a soft green dress that complemented her emerald. Her dark hair was bound in a single braid flowing down her back.

"Child, you look wonderful today," said Sylvia.

"Thank you, Sylvia. Mother asked me to pack a basket. We are going to have a picnic in the meadow," said Nafaria.

"Well, there is some chicken left over from dinner last night. I also have these," said Sylvia. She held up a bowl of ripe strawberries.

"My favorite!" smiled Nafaria.

"We will have berries and sweet cream for dessert tonight, but I can part with a pint for you to take on your picnic," replied Sylvia.

"I think mother would like some cheese also. Do we have cheddar? That is her favorite," said Nafaria.

"Yes, I believe we do. I also baked some yeast rolls for lunch today," said Sylvia.

"That will be perfect. A flask of wine for our drink will round out lunch," replied Nafaria. She packed the items one by one in the basket and left the kitchen.

"Mother, I have our lunch ready," said Nafaria as she entered the hallway.

"Perfect. I found a book of Denholm Glen folklore. We can read stories while we sit in the meadow," said Thena.

Mother and daughter headed out the door. The sun was bright in the courtyard. They passed the fountain Nafaria had been bathed in earlier that week. Jason approached them.

"Have a good picnic. Tell me what pictures you see in the clouds," he said as he hugged Nafaria.

"When will you be back?" he asked Thena.

"Before twilight, but who can to tell on the longest day of the year?" said Thena smiling.

At that moment, the air was noisy with the sound of hooves. Jason turned around and saw Sebastian Cavanaugh riding toward them. The look on his face was very serious.

"Lord Jason, everyone in your manor is summoned to the Village Square at once. Count Deveraux is demanding everyone in the village be in attendance."

"What has happened, Sebastian?" asked Jason. The messenger looked uneasily at Thena and Nafaria.

"You will find out when you get there," replied Sebastian.

"Not everyone in the manor can come. Some have tasks that cannot be stilled for petty gossip masquerading as news," replied Jason.

"Unfortunately, it is much more than that. The cook and two others may stay," replied Sebastian. He pulled the reins on the horse. The horse turned and the young man galloped back the way he came.

"What do you suppose has happened?" asked Thena.

"I do not know, but the sooner we get to the village, the sooner the riddle will be solved. I will let one of the servants know to spread the word, and then we may go," said Jason.

Ten minutes later, Jason, the boys, Thena and Nafaria strolled into the middle of the Village Square. A gallows was set up on a raised platform and two ropes hung down. Thena's eyes widened at the sight.

"Mother, what is that?" asked Nafaria.

Thena's mind raced. What did she say to her ten-year-old daughter? She was still so innocent. She wanted to call down a curse at that moment on the monsters that decided a child needed to witness such an event.

"Tell her the truth. Do not try to hide it," whispered Jason in her ear.

Thena turned and looked into her husband's face. The grief she knew was in her own, she found in his blue eyes. She nodded and looked back at Nafaria.

"Nafaria, listen to me. There is going to be an execution today. Someone is going to die," said Thena.

"But why?" asked Nafaria.

"I do not know," said Thena quietly. She felt a tap on her shoulder. Thena turned to see Philip trying for her attention.

"Mother, father said to tell you he was going to find Malcom," said Philip.

"Then he will find out what is happening. Where is Michael?" asked Thena.

"Michael went with him. Father wanted me to stay with you," replied Philip.

Jason and Michael threaded their way through the crowd. Sebastian did his job well. It indeed looked as though the entire village was in attendance.

"Father, I saw him over by the blacksmith's cottage," said Michael. Jason followed his son's direction and saw Malcom in his black cloak. His mahogany eyes caught Jason's gaze and he raised his hand to beckon him. Jason quickly shuffled Michael alongside him over to where Malcom stood. He placed a hand on Jason's shoulder. He led them into the blacksmith's cottage.

"It grieves me to bring greeting on such a black day," said Malcom.

"What has happened? Who is going to be executed?" asked Jason.

"One of our own, I am afraid. An error in judgment was made and the penalty is death for one of the Craft," replied Malcom.

"Death?" asked Michael.

"Yesterday, Ana, the Count Deveraux's daughter, was found dead. She was poisoned. She was given an elixir of hemlock and belladonna. Count Deveraux brought a half empty vial found in her pocket to me to verify what the elixir was made of," said Malcom.

"Did someone see what happened?" asked Jason. Malcom nodded.

"The gardener overheard a conversation between Ana and Lya when they were outside. He was out of sight, so they must have thought they were alone. Lya told Ana that the elixir was a love potion. If she drank it, then she would draw the attention of one of the men she was interested in. Ana drank it without question. A couple hours later, the Count found her lying on the floor in the library. She was already dead. When the gardener heard of this, he told the Count what he had seen and heard. The Count went to Raymond's house and questioned Lya. She confessed when she knew she had no other choice.

It was suspected that this whole thing came about because Lya was interested in the same man Ana was. Lya's jealousy caused her to abuse her knowledge. She has been sentenced to death," said Malcom.

"But there are two ropes on the gallows," said Jason. Malcom looked at the ground uneasily.

"The Count demanded an example be made of both mother and daughter," Malcom sighed.

"An example made of Analia? But why?" gasped Jason.

"Lya was reckless, she is a murderess. Analia was her mother. She was responsible for teaching Lya discretion. She failed," said Malcom quietly. Jason heard the disdain in his words.

"Where is Raymond?" asked Jason. Malcom looked at the ground.

"He is dead. When the Count came for Lya and Analia, Raymond resisted. He was beaten to within an inch of his life. I shudder to think of how he made his way to my house. He died on my doorstep after telling me what happened," said Malcom.

"So now the mother dies for the sins of the daughter. Not even God is so cruel, and we boast that we are made in his image," replied Jason bitterly. "I have to get to Thena. She and Analia were so close."

"Be careful what you say in public. People fear what they do not understand. Thena's life could be in danger," replied Malcom. Jason put a hand on his mentor's shoulder.

"Be careful as well. We may be entering an evil time for our kind," replied Jason.

Jason and Michael left the cottage with Malcom and found the rest of their family. Nathaniel was standing nearby. He had Nafaria's hand in his and looked uneasily at his father.

Philip looked around the square. Alana stood with her mother and father off to the side of the platform. She glanced around and caught his gaze. Her eyes were puffy and red. She looked as though she spent the entire night crying. Philip felt his eyes water just looking at her.

Count Deveraux stood tall and erect, his face holding a stern expression. He looked at the gathering crowd with disdain; many probably still wondered what happened. Most did not yet know about his daughter's demise. The villagers happily went about their lives, ignorant of the devices those of the Craft used on the less perceptive. Today that would change. Those of the Craft could no longer be trusted to be left in peace. He walked toward the front of the platform and lifted a parchment scroll in front of him. Carefully unfolding it with both hands, he began to read.

"My friends, it grieves me to bring black news and an even blacker proclamation. My daughter, Ana, was murdered by a young woman who is of the Craft. The young woman is sentenced to be hanged before you, as an example made of criminals. Because she is of the Craft, she was taught to respect the life around her by her parents. She was taught to use her knowledge and power to help others, but they have failed. The mother will be hanged with the murderer as an example to us all. Those of the Craft wield great knowledge and power. They must be held accountable when their children transgress so wickedly. After today, those of the Craft in this region of Nereheim will be under careful scrutiny. I do not wish to be unfair in this matter, but murder has been committed, and it will not be tolerated."

Analia and Lya were led up the steps to the platform. Thena gasped as her gaze caught Analia's. The grief and quiet resignation she saw in her friend's eyes brought tears to hers. She felt Jason put his arms around her.

"Mother, are they going to hang Analia?" asked Nafaria in a whisper.

"Courage," Jason whispered. Thena gulped and blinked back her tears.

Thena could hear nothing after Jason spoke. Her mind became a whirlwind as it played various scenes from her life. The images came like a sharp knife cutting into her heart with fearless precision.

She remembered picking wildflowers with Analia when they were both children. They ran together through the meadows and played in the rivers in their village. They were sisters in a way blood sisters were not, they were closer than blood.

She remembered sharing the news of her betrothal to Jason and hearing of Analia being betrothed as well. She thought of their weddings, where each was present and shed as many tears of joy for the other. Their love for each other continued to grow, and their families grew together as a result.

Thena remembered when Analia came running through her garden faster than she ever saw her run with news that she would soon have a baby. A little girl she named Lya.

Analia had been with Thena all her life. They truly shared each other's life and the experiences that came along. She did not know how to face a future without her greatest friend.

Finally, she could take no more. Tears burst from her eyes as she continued to gaze at Analia. Her eyes held some fear but greater was a look of sadness. Analia looked as if her heart were breaking. She could not take her eyes from Thena and tears fell down her face as well.

Then, her beautiful face was hidden, stripped from Thena's sight. The executioner covered each woman with a cloth sack. After their faces were covered, he kicked the boxes out from beneath their feet. Mother and daughter dangled on the gallows. Nafaria wrenched her hand from Nathaniel's grip and buried her face in her mother's stomach. Thena sobbed as Jason held her tightly to his body. Her cries echoed his own grief and tears flowed from his eyes as well.

Nathaniel stood with his father next to him. His tears flowed like a river as he watched Analia's silent resignation to the events in which she had no control.

Analia and Thena were the two gentlest women he knew. Even his father recognized and respected their love and quiet spirits. To allow Analia to die for something her daughter did was not right. YAHWEH said himself *the soul who sins is the one who will die.*[5] Why did the village elders allow this treachery? Why was Count Deveraux allowed to exact this murder masquerading as justice? His tears of sadness turned into tears of anger as he walked home, his arm around his father.

"Nathaniel, please tell me what is on your mind," said Malcom finally. His voice was quiet, as if he were still trying to hold back tears.

"I am thinking that it is not right that Ana, Lord Raymond and Lady Analia had to die for something as evil as jealousy. It angers me that the village elders disdain our knowledge so much that they would kill someone as precious and gentle as Analia. If they can so easily justify her death, who will they murder next? Will it be Thena? Naf-" His voice cracked as a fresh wave of tears flowed from his eyes. He looked at his father. "They cannot do that to Nafaria," Nathaniel whispered. He clung to his father and buried his face in his chest. Malcom held his only child to him tightly as Nathaniel cried.

"I pray that they do not, Nathaniel. I pray that Denholm Glen will weigh what has happened and understand that every life is sacred and should be treated as such. Ana should not have died. Lya did a terrible thing, but Analia has done everything in her power to train her properly. Analia's death should never have been allowed to happen," replied Malcom bitterly. They continued their walk home in silence, as the sun crept through the afternoon sky.

Jason and his family walked back to the manor in stunned silence. Thena cried and held Nafaria as they walked.

"Mother, will they try to hurt you too?" asked Nafaria through her tears. Jason turned and looked at them as they walked. The boys also looked at her. Their tear stained faces held a worried look.

"I...I do not know," stammered Thena in a hoarse voice.

"But they know you and father are of the Craft. They know you were friends with Analia," said Philip.

"Let us worry about it tomorrow," replied Jason.

"Yes father," replied Philip. The conversation ended and the family walked the path to the manor in silence.

---

[5] Ezekiel 18:4

Lord Reinard Sallen returned from the Village Square with his daughter. Lillia had not stopped crying from the moment the executioner put the sack on Analia's head. He held her tightly on their walk home. Neither had the energy to speak; the execution left them both mute. Lillia could not speak from grief; Reinard was in shock over the event he just witnessed. What was happening in their village to make the Count turn on people he knew as good? What could be done about it? Reinard did not know himself. Perhaps it was time for a counsel of his peers.

As soon as they walked through the door, Reinard summoned four of his swiftest servants. He sent each one to a different Village Elder, asking them to meet him at his manor as soon as possible. He would not let this pass until the other elders made a decision of how to handle this in the future. The villagers; appointed by the king or not, could not be allowed to execute those of the Craft at a mere suspicion. If this incident was not contained, word would spread to other towns across the countryside. Reinard feared this part of Nereheim would result in an uprising against the king. He knew what potential power those of the Craft possessed. If they wielded their power to defend themselves, the mortal people of Nereheim would be destroyed in a bloody civil war. Those of the Craft were too noble to allow that to happen. However, even the most noble have faltered in the past.

As the afternoon passed, one by one the elders arrived. They were each seated in Reinard's study, looking at him. Finally Reinard spoke.

"I have asked you here to discuss the execution we witnessed today," said Reinard. The others continued to give him their attention.

"Count Deveraux is appointed by King Rohn to uphold the laws of Nereheim within his jurisdiction. What is there to say?" asked Lord Whitmore.

Reinard stared at the old man. He looked pointedly at the others. "We are the leadership of Denholm Glen. The people here look to us for advice and counsel. We are the ones who present to Count Deveraux, not the other way around. Did Count Deveraux seek advice from any of you about this matter?"

The others shook their heads. "He did not come to me either. He unjustly took Analia into custody when he took Lya, and Raymond was beaten to death for resisting," said Reinard.

The others looked at each other in surprise. "I did not hear this," said Lord Luxton.

"Malcom Stone told me of this. Grief drove Count Deveraux to take this matter into his own hands and act outside the laws of this country. The very laws he swore to uphold. If we allow this to continue, we will be responsible for more needless death in this village," said Reinard.

"Our authority is not greater than Count Deveraux's. Only the king can govern him," said Lord Whitmore.

"Well then, gentlemen, we need not pretend any longer. We are simply rich men with no authority of any kind in this village. We have no position to speak of," replied Reinard.

"Now wait-" Lord Luxton began but Reinard interrupted him.

"Which is it? Are we leaders in this village or not? Will we challenge the Count and demand that he come to us before he punishes anyone else unjustly?" said Reinard. He stared coldly into the faces of the other elders. One by one, their gaze dropped to the floor.

"I thought not," replied Reinard quietly. He sat still for a moment. "This was the only matter I wished to discuss. If there is nothing else, the meeting is concluded." Reinard watched as each one finally left, leaving him with weightier decisions to be made.

* * *

It was dusk as Nathaniel looked out the window of his room into the village square below. Life was suddenly different for him, much darker than it had been this morning. He thought about what Nafaria must be thinking about her heritage as one of the Craft, and having to see the consequences of that heritage on her birthday of all days. His tears flowed freely once again as he dipped his quill in ink and began to write.

After dinner, Nathaniel and Malcom sat before the fire in the great room. Both sat in silence watching the flames dance before them. Nathaniel was thinking of the letter in his pocket, wondering if he would ever need to give it to Nafaria. Would they be forced to flee Denholm Glen? Would leaving this village be far enough to escape the ignorance of the people they were meant to protect? Nathaniel watched the flames and pondered why he and Nafaria got along so well. He felt like he was made to protect her.

At that moment, Lord Reinard walked into the room, disrupting all his thoughts.

"Malcom! I am grateful you are at home," he said in a worried tone.

"Lord Reinard, to what do we owe this visit?" asked Malcom. He rose and clasped his hand to Reinard's.

"I bring warning, my friend. Count Deveraux will not be appeased with the deaths of Lya and Analia. I fear that those of the Craft will all suffer and suffer soon. I met with the other village elders late this afternoon about this matter. All were convinced that we have no authority to call Count Deveraux to account for beating Raymond and taking Analia along with Lya. It seems each one is willing to let the king's appointed man have free reign in his jurisdiction. Take Nathaniel and leave Denholm Glen before it is too late. It may not be too long before people begin to worry about the counsel of those of the Craft the way they worry about being poisoned by them. I respect you too much to see anything happen to you," said Reinard.

Malcom tried to process the warning he was given. He immediately thought of Jason and his family. "I must warn Jason," he whispered.

"It is too dangerous for you to stay in Denholm Glen. Get your things together and leave tonight, I will go warn Jason," replied Reinard.

"I have the shop to worry about, bills to pay. I cannot just leave," replied Malcom.

Lord Reinard pulled out a leather bag and handed it to Malcom. Malcom opened the bag and looked up at Lord Reinard.

"There are 75 gold pieces in the bag. Leave me the deed to the shop and I will sell the property," said Reinard.

"Lord Reinard, that is far more than the shop is worth," said Malcom. Reinard nodded his head.

"If you do not wish to return to Denholm Glen, it will be more than enough to help you leave Nereheim, or at least start again in another part of the country," said Reinard. "I fear the worst for you after what happened to Raymond. Gather your things and leave quickly."

"I cannot just leave Maia behind. She has been a very faithful servant to me since I moved here. However I cannot take her with me either. I have no idea where we will go," said Malcom.

"I understand. I will provide a place for Maia in my employ. She will be cared for and always have a position under my care," replied Reinard. Malcom nodded his head.

Malcom embraced his old friend. "Thank you for that, and thank you for your warning. I hope that times of peace will find you when this evil has run its course."

Nathaniel looked at Reinard. He pulled a folded piece of paper from his pocket. "You are going to Lord Jason now?" he asked.

Reinard looked at Nathaniel and nodded. Nathaniel handed Reinard the paper. "Please, see to it that Nafaria receives this," said Nathaniel. He quietly left the room.

"We will be gone by midnight," said Malcom as Reinard nodded to him one more time. He turned and walked out of the room, leaving Malcom to make preparations.

* * *

Jason found Thena in the bedroom after the children went to bed. She lay quietly on the bed, staring at the ceiling. He sat down next to her.

"I am sorry I did not help with the children. How is Nafaria?" asked Thena.

"She is a little shaken. I think her heritage is sinking in," said Jason.

"I do not want to teach her anymore," said Thena quietly.

"Thena, she needs to be instructed in the Craft," said Jason firmly.

"NO!" shouted Thena. She looked at her husband in shock. She felt shame wash over her. Thena never raised her voice to Jason in all the years they were married. "No," she repeated quietly.

"Thena-"

"I will not risk my daughter's life to the fate of gallows, or burning, or any other wickedness ignorant men will dream of. I cannot," interrupted Thena. Her voice choked with tears.

A knock at their door interrupted the conversation. "You may enter," said Jason.

"Sir, forgive my intrusion, but Lord Reinard is downstairs. He says it is very urgent," said the servant.

"Thank you, I will be there in a moment," said Jason. The servant left the room.

"Thena, you have a responsibility to teach your daughter the Craft," said Jason.

"Why? So that she may swing on the gallows, or be burned alive by ignorant people who have their own brand of justice? I will not risk Nafaria's life for the sake of knowledge. She will marry within the Craft and bear children as others have done in the past," replied Thena.

"You take away your daughter's future with those words," replied Jason. He got up and quickly left the room. Thena watched him go, and then began to cry.

Jason walked into the library. Lord Reinard turned his head from his gaze out the window. His dark eyes held fear and sorrow.

"Lord Reinard, to what do I owe this late call?" asked Jason. He embraced the village elder.

"I am afraid I bring you a warning, my friend," said Reinard.

"A warning?" asked Jason.

"Take your family and flee Denholm Glen. The Count is raving mad right now. He seeks revenge on those who possess knowledge. A witch-hunt will begin soon enough, with every woman and young girl of the Craft suspect. I love your family too much to see Thena's and Nafaria's fates come to the gallows," said Reinard. Tears formed in his eyes. The elder's words struck Jason with fear.

"What of the men? Surely they are just as suspect," replied Jason.

"Men of the Craft are still regarded as wise, but I fear that the time will come when mankind will live in fear of all people of the Craft. The talk in the village now is that the women are not to be trusted.

Women are fickle, ruled by their emotions. Lya proved that with her petty jealousy," replied Reinard.

"I cannot leave my property so quickly," replied Jason.

"Do you think it is possible you may return to Denholm Glen?" asked Reinard.

"This is my home. It has been part of my family for three generations. If it is possible in the future, I would prefer to," said Jason.

"Sign the deed to your property over to me. Leave tonight, I will oversee the manor until you return. I am confident that the servants in your employ are capable of managing the affairs of the manor smoothly," replied Reinard. Jason looked at Reinard. He registered the fear in his eyes and nodded his head.

"Sylvia and the others can see to it. I must speak to Malcom before I make any decision," said Jason.

"Malcom is gone. I told him I was coming to warn you and he left with Nathaniel earlier this evening. Please take my advice and leave tonight as well," replied Reinard. Jason put his hand on the elder's shoulder.

"You have done so much and risked much to warn us. I will miss this place. We have built a family here," replied Jason.

"Your family will survive as long as you leave. I have no doubt success will follow wherever you go," replied Reinard. He embraced Jason tightly and left the library.

Jason rushed into the bedroom. Thena sat quietly on the bed.

"What is wrong?" she asked. Her expression was blank, her voice dull.

"We must gather everything we need, and leave tonight. Reinard came to warn us. I will explain everything on the road. Get everyone up. Pack everything that links us to the Craft. I need to talk to Sylvia," said Jason.

"I do not understand. What does Malcom think about this?" asked Thena.

"Malcom is gone! He has left. We need to leave tonight!" exclaimed Jason. At her husband's shrill words, Thena rose and went to her dresser. She began pulling clothing together, and then stopped.

"Thena, what are you doing?" asked Jason. He watched her quiet composure. It unnerved him to see her so.

She dropped the clothing in her hand and looked at him. His last words cut her heart worse than any knife. She saw concern and panic in his eyes. She stared blankly back at him. "Did your father ever tell you my maiden name?" she asked.

Jason could not hide confusion from his face. He had a hundred things racing through his mind, but he willed himself to stay calm and listen. He sensed what Thena was about to tell him was vital.

"No. He simply said you would tell me in time, and I was not to press it," replied Jason.

Thena smiled a gentle, but sad smile in response. Lord Warrick Mauldon was the soul of discretion. There was nothing that he would divulge if he was asked not to. She wondered just how many secrets and intrigues that man carried to his grave.

"My maiden name is Coe," she replied.

Jason looked at her with wide eyes, but shook his head. "The Coe family was massacred in 1359. It was the largest scandal in Nereheim's history. I remember it because it happened a few nights after we sent my sister away," replied Jason.

"Yes. My mother, father, two brothers, and three sisters were killed that night. In the murderous frenzy of the barons, an elderly servant couple helped me escape," Thena replied.

Jason walked over to his wife and took her hand in his. All thoughts of haste were erased from his mind in a single moment. His father told him the night he was betrothed to Thena that she had a terrible secret that must stay secret until she was ready to tell it. Now he understood why. He was eight years old on the night of that tragedy. That meant Thena was six. This was a story that was terrible to tell, and worth every precious moment to hear.

He walked over to the bed with her and sat down. Thena sat down next to him. She looked into his eyes and continued.

"I do not know what my father knew about what was coming. He and my brothers spent the day bringing everyone into the house and making sure we had food and water. Why we did not run instead, I will never understand. At dusk, the other barons came for him. He refused to yield his land and everything our family worked for simply because we were of the Craft. The elderly couple took me to the root cellar before things started. We slipped away when no one was watching. We hid down there, but we could hear the massacre. The old man opened a door that led into a passageway. He told his wife to take me and follow the passageway. It opened into a cave that led into the woods. He would follow, but if he did not come to the cave mouth, we were to go. He closed the door behind us, and we never saw him again.

When the sun rose, it was completely quiet at our home. Everyone was killed and our horses and livestock were taken. The manor was burned to the ground. We could see the smoke in the distance when we emerged from the cave. We ran through the woods, but the old woman was afraid we would be spotted. We found the remains of a well and hid inside it until sunset.

That night, we made our way to Lord Briton's estate. He took us in when he recognized us without a single question. He gave us the news that everyone, including the old woman's husband had been killed. Lord and Lady Briton were not of the Craft, so they were not suspect by anyone in the area. They could not stomach what the other barons did to my family. They took on the old woman, and adopted me. We moved immediately to Illith, and I was told never to practice the Craft. That is why you had your hands full with me in the beginning of our marriage. Nafaria knows more now than I knew when we married," said Thena.

Jason pulled his wife close to him. He was at a complete loss. He understood why his father would not tell him her secret. She was so young to witness such atrocity, much less have it visited against her. His father told him to be patient with her, and help her grow.

Now, eighteen years later, Thena had grown to be a remarkable healer. Her skill in the Craft was meticulous and always for others. She could sense when a person was in despair and was a ready listener to any troubled soul. His stomach tightened when he thought of what she went through as a child.

"We will talk about this more later. For now, we must move our family," said Jason quietly. He kissed her on the cheek and rose to leave.

He turned back around and looked at her. "I love you, Thena Mauldon," he said, then turned and walked out of the room.

An hour later, the entire manor was in a bustle. The servants loaded a cart and horses with provisions. Nafaria watched every hurried motion with tired eyes. She was put into the cart with Michael. Sylvia put a basket next to her. "Freshly baked yeast rolls. Make sure you share them."

"Thank you Sylvia. I shall miss you," said Nafaria. She leaned over the cart and hugged her.

"Be safe child. Do not let this frighten you away from your craft. Use your knowledge for the good of us all," replied Sylvia.

Lord Reinard came up behind Sylvia. "Nafaria, I have something for you," he said. She looked at him curiously as he handed her a folded square of paper. "Save it for when you get where you are going," replied Reinard.

"I believe that is everything," said Thena.

"Be strong, my lady. It is only to another place you go. Our prayers go with you," replied Sylvia. She hugged Thena tightly.

"I have signed over the deed to the manor to Lord Reinard. He will oversee everything until our return," said Jason.

"Do you intend to return?" asked Sylvia.

"If it is possible, I will find a way," replied Jason. "I only wish we could take you with us."

Sylvia smiled. "Your safety is most important," she said as she hugged Jason.

Sylvia gave each of the boys a hug. Philip and Thena rode horses while Jason drove the cart. Sylvia sighed as she watched her family leave the manor.

Jason rode on in the night with his family. As he steadied his horse beside the cart that carried Michael, Nafaria, and their belongings, his mind drifted from the present to the past.

He was surrounded in darkness then as now. Firelight flickered as cloaked figures stood facing the flames. Malcom's voice echoed through Jason's mind.

"One of our own has come forth to make an oath. We will be witnesses of our young brother's pact."

Jason stepped toward Malcom. His face held a solemn look that was made even more serious in the shadows cast by the fire.

"What is your oath, Jason?" asked Malcom.

"I swear allegiance to Nereheim, to always dwell within its borders and aid mortals as they govern this land. My wife will understand that whether in good times or evil, we will stay. Whatever persecution arises, I will honor this oath until the day of my death," said Jason in a voice that all present could hear.

Malcom spoke to those in attendance. "He has chosen the glyph of Neptune as his pact seal. It is the reminder of his duty to be a servant to all people and society of Nereheim."

Malcom picked up a brand that was warming in the fire. Jason rolled up one of the sleeves of the cloak he was wearing. Malcom placed the brand on his skin. The intense pain shot through Jason's body. The memory jolted him back to the present. Thena had just pulled her horse up next to him.

She looked over to the cart and saw Michael and Nafaria asleep. Philip rode his horse on the other side of the cart. He looked tired, but he kept his hand steady. He pulled the reins and moved closer to Jason.

"Father, what of Nadia and Lord Saintclaire?" he asked.

"We will send word to them when we reach our destination," replied Jason.

"Where is that to be?" asked Thena.

"We will go to the other side of Nereheim. We will stay in our home country as long as possible. Perhaps things are a little quieter in the royal city. I wish to seek an audience with the king over this matter," said Jason.

"When we get there, I will look for a book for Nafaria. She will need it if she is to keep on in the Craft," said Thena.

Jason looked at Thena. "You have changed your mind?" he asked. Thena sighed and nodded her head.

"You are right Jason. I cannot let her live life in ignorance of the Craft. My guardians made that decision for me. When we married we made the decision together that we would teach all our children the Craft. It may be a world of men, but that may change, even in our lifetime. I want Nafaria to be ready for that. However, we have reached the extent of my knowledge. I can teach her the runes. Beyond that, you will have to take over," said Thena.

"When we settle and find a new home, I will make time for lessons with her. She will need her own Diary and to know what it is for by then," said Jason.

"I will see to it when we settle," replied Thena with a tired smile.

* * *

The next morning Alana awoke to see sunlight pouring in through the window. She climbed from her bed and moved toward the window to look out at the countryside around her house. The green fields seemed even more earthy than usual. The sky above was a brilliant blue without even a wisp of a cloud in sight. It seemed cruel that such a beautiful day dawned while she felt so horrible.

Her older sister now lay dead and buried in the midst of the apple trees her and Alana spent their early years together climbing. It was all because of petty jealousy. She still could not believe it really happened.

"It feels like it should have happened to someone else," Alana whispered. She sat back down on her bed, drained of the energy needed to think about starting another day. Catching sight of her cloak and boots in the corner of the room, she let out a sigh. "If ever there was a day to be lost in the woods it is today," she said aloud. Alana got up and opened the dresser sitting next to the bed.

It was thirty minutes later that Alana could be spotted in the meadow by the woods near her home. She almost always met Philip here around this time in the morning. There were times when Philip did not meet up with her and she hunted alone, but today she really wanted his company. She decided to visit his home and ask if he was in.

Alana made her way through the meadow and found the pathway that led to the rear entrance of the Mauldon Manor. She had no idea what she would say to anyone who would ask why she was there. She decided she would answer questions as briefly and directly as possible. That decision gave her the courage to set foot on Lord Jason's land and seek audience with his son.

She found the cook in the garden, picking vegetables. Alana greeted her when their eyes met. "Good morning, Sylvia," said Alana.

"Good morning, Viscountess," replied Sylvia. The cook seemed a little apprehensive at seeing her. Alana winced. She would never become familiar with her new title.

"Is Philip in? I was hoping to meet him in the woods," replied Alana. Sylvia shook her head and walked toward Alana.

"Viscountess, Lord Jason left with his family very suddenly in the night. They will not be returning to Denholm Glen anytime soon," said Sylvia.

Alana held her expression as steady as she could, but she felt as if the wind was knocked out of her. "They left? Why?" asked Alana.

Sylvia looked down at the ground. She could not speak, but Alana knew. "It is because of what happened to Ana," said Alana quietly. Her eyes met with Sylvia's, but the cook did not answer. "He did not even say goodbye," whispered Alana.

"He had no time. Lord Reinard came late last night and warned them to leave. The family was gone by midnight," replied Sylvia.

Alana's eyes welled with tears as she registered Sylvia's reply. She turned and ran back the way she came as fast as she could.

CHAPTER 2

THE MIDDAY SUN WAS BRIGHT and warm as two figures on horseback rode the winding country road, taking in the beauty of the open fields over rolling hills around them. One was a male with a medium build, and very tall. His dark hair was short, but his soft bangs fell into his face, partly concealing his light blue eyes. He led another smaller horse, a foal. He rode behind a young woman with a slender build and ivory skin. Her red hair fell down her back and blended well with the forest green cloak she wore. Her green eyes sparkled as she looked around her with something akin to awe.

"I absolutely love this part of the country, Ian. It is so fresh and peaceful here," she said.

"It looks just like the countryside around Illith, Nadia. To me, there is no difference," replied Ian.

"In Illith, the fields are green enough, but there are no hills. That is why father settled there. He says it is good for training horses," replied Nadia.

"Is that the reason you took time from your studies to deliver a horse?" asked Ian. "You have more important things to do."

"There will always be important things to do, Ian. Sometimes you have to choose between what is good and what is better. I wanted to see the look on little Nafaria's face when she was presented with her horse. Father made it very clear that Nafaria was to have training for a few days. I was also looking forward to spending a little time with my aunt. We live half a day's ride away from each other, yet it seems I never see her," replied Nadia.

"How many days are you planning to stay in Denholm Glen?" asked Ian.

"Three days, maybe four at the most. I need time to work with Nafaria. Father also wanted me to talk to Lord Jason about lessons for her next summer," replied Nadia. Ian made a face and sighed loudly, making Nadia laugh out loud.

"There is no worry, Ian. You need not stay if you do not want to. I know you have your own life to get back to. What is her name again?" asked Nadia.

"Julia," replied Ian. "I can stand to stay that long. I do not wish to return without my charge. I do hope for your sake, Nafaria takes to riding better than Lord Jason's second son did. What a disaster that was."

Nadia laughed again. "I quite forgot about that. Father thought that since Philip did so well, Michael would be fine. I wonder if he ever did master riding?" said Nadia.

"Besides, your father would never allow you to make this trip alone, with Rhea's disappearance," replied Ian. Nadia's smile disappeared.

"That is troubling. Rhea may not be of the Craft, but she is a very smart girl. She is not one to get lost in the woods as some of the villagers claim. I am afraid she has fallen into some trouble," said Nadia.

She turned her attention back to the countryside around her. She noted the beginning of a brook that ran along the side of the road. Woods were beginning forty yards away. "We are almost there. Lord Jason's manor is near those woods," said Nadia. She kicked the horse into a steady gallop, with Ian close behind her.

Ten minutes later, Nadia and Ian heard the clop of the horse's shoes on the cobblestone pathway leading to Lord Jason's manor. Nadia remembered the manor being busier than it was today. They stopped their horses at the rear entrance. An older woman Nadia recognized came out to meet them.

Lara Giesbers

"Sylvia! How wonderful to see you again!" exclaimed Nadia. At the sound of her cheerful tone, Sylvia's face brightened as she recognized the young woman. Sylvia threw her arms around her and hugged her.

"Miss Nadia, what are you doing here?" asked Sylvia. She seemed happy to see her, but her voice held a twinge of fear in it.

"Lord Jason bought a horse from father some months ago for Nafaria's birthday. We have been breaking and training her so that Nafaria could ride her right away. I know we are a couple days late for her birthday. Father sends his apologies," said Nadia. Sylvia looked at the horse and sighed. She knew that Nafaria would have indeed loved it.

"Nadia, Lord Jason is no longer here. Lord Reinard Sallen is overseeing the manor. Go see him quickly. He will tell you more about what has happened," replied Sylvia. She directed them into the village to where they would find Lord Reinard's manor. Nadia and Ian set off to find him.

Reinard came outside when he saw the two strange figures ride by his great room window. He stopped in front of them. A young woman hopped down from her horse, followed by a man who looked to be a little older than she was.

"Lord Reinard Sallen?" asked the woman.

"Yes, how may I be of service to you?" asked Reinard.

"I am Nadia Saintclaire. I have come to deliver a horse Lord Jason Mauldon bought from my father for Nafaria's birthday. Sylvia told me to come see you," replied Nadia.

Reinard looked at the pair carefully. "I will have my servants care for your horses while we talk inside," replied Reinard. He showed them into the great room and instructed one of his servants to take the horses to the stable. Reinard sat across from Nadia in a chair.

"I remember Jason mentioned your father once. He is Lord Bryant Saintclaire, the horse master?" asked Reinard.

"Yes, my Lord. We live in Illith," replied Nadia.

Reinard nodded his head. "He sent his oldest son Philip to your father a few summers ago to teach him to ride," said Reinard. Nadia nodded her head.

74

"It was to be Nafaria's chance to learn to handle a horse," replied Nadia. "Father hoped she would take to it a little better than Michael did."

Reinard laughed. "I do not recall hearing anything of how that went. I only remember that when Michael returned from Illith he was adamant that my daughter Lillia practice with him until he could ride," said Reinard.

"Father is very longsuffering when it comes to teaching people how to ride. In the end Michael exhausted even his patience," said Nadia with a laugh.

"Michael was a disaster akin to legend," said Ian.

"You will be happy to know that Michael did eventually learn to stay in the saddle. He knew he would have to, so he kept at it. Though he is not as skilled as Philip, he rides well enough," replied Reinard.

"I will be sure to pass the information on to my father," replied Nadia with a smile. "Lord Reinard; Lord Jason would not have left Denholm Glen without talking to my father and making arrangements for Nafaria's horse. He is not the kind of man to leave anything to chance. Has something happened?" asked Nadia.

Reinard let out his breath in a heavy sigh. "It has indeed," he replied. Nadia looked intently at him, so he continued.

"A few days ago, there was an incident in the village. A young woman of the Craft poisoned the Count Deveraux's oldest daughter, Ana. She was hanged the next day," said Reinard.

Nadia stared at Reinard with wide eyes. After a moment, she took a deep breath and spoke. "This young woman of the Craft, what was her name?" asked Nadia.

"Her name was Lya Bernard," replied Reinard. "She was the daughter of one of the merchants in this area."

Nadia nodded her head, as she blinked back tears. "I know who she is. She is my cousin. Analia Bernard is my mother's sister," said Nadia quietly. Reinard put his head in his hands and sighed. When he looked at Nadia again, he also had tears in his eyes.

"There is more. I am so sorry you have to hear it, but it is the reason Lord Jason is gone. When the Count came to question Lya, she confessed. She knew she had no other choice. He took Lya and Analia into custody and beat Raymond severely when he tried to protest his taking Analia as well. He died that evening, and Analia was hanged with Lya. It happened on midsummer's day," said Reinard.

Nadia looked at Ian and felt tears running down her face. She sat there for a full minute in silence before speaking. She carefully cleared her throat but then was still very quiet. "Why did Lord Jason leave Denholm Glen?" she asked.

"After the execution, I met with the other village elders. No one was willing to challenge Count Deveraux's authority of law in this region, as he was appointed by King Rohn himself. I urged Jason to take his family and leave until it was safe to return here. He told me he intends to return, but I fear I will never see him again," said Reinard.

Nadia folded her hands in her lap and stared at them intently. Tears continued to form and fall on her cheeks, but after a minute, she was more practical and very businesslike. "If Lord Jason intends to return, then father would have us leave Nafaria's horse with the manor. Since he paid for it, it is his property. I have no other reason to stay in Denholm Glen. We will head back to Illith," said Nadia.

"We will head back in the morning, Nadia. You need rest tonight. You are in no shape to be riding a horse late into the night," replied Ian.

Reinard nodded in agreement. "The countryside may not be as safe as it once was. I will take you back to Lord Jason's manor, and let Sylvia know you will be staying the night. She will be glad for the company," said Reinard.

"Thank you for your hospitality, Lord Reinard," said Nadia. She rose to leave, feeling a fresh wave of tears overcome her as she stepped outside.

"Nadia?" whispered Ian.

She turned and looked at him. Her eyes were wide and her lips quivered. The look of sadness there was haunting. He took a step toward her and wrapped his arms around her.

Nadia let herself completely collapse as she cried. How would she tell her mother her younger sister was dead? How could Lya do such a reckless and selfish thing? She was a year older than Nadia. What would make her do someone harm? She had no idea her aunt's problems with her cousin were so dark. She stood and cried for her aunt and uncle who were two of the kindest people she ever knew.

Ian held her and let her cry for her family. He worked for the Saintclaire family since he was a boy. He watched Nadia grow into a strong, independent young woman. She never cried, even when she hurt herself. Now she stood ready to collapse. He knew that tomorrow she would be focused and practical. Nadia would weep with her mother, and deliver news to her father. Tonight she needed him to hold her.

After a few minutes he felt her grip loosen slightly. They both turned to see Lord Reinard and two of his servants leading their horses toward them. "If you are ready, I will take you to Mauldon Manor," said Reinard.

***

Sylvia showed Nadia into Jason and Thena's bedroom. As Nadia took off her cloak and set it on the bed, Sylvia went to one of the dressers at the far end of the room and opened it.

"Did you bring extra clothes with you?" asked Sylvia. Nadia sat down on the bed.

"I brought a change of clothes, but they are still with my horse," said Nadia. Sylvia pulled out a simple night gown.

"When Thena left, she left some clothes behind, because she could not take everything. Why not sleep in this tonight?" said Sylvia. She handed the gown to Nadia.

"Thank you Sylvia," said Nadia absently. She sat on the bed, holding the piece of clothing in her hands. It was light and delicate to the touch. Nadia remembered Lady Thena preferred this kind of clothing in the summer. Her aunt did as well.

Sylvia looked at Nadia closely and with pity. She was handed awful news at a desperate time. She looked completely overwhelmed.

"Would you like me to bring you some tea before bed?" asked Sylvia. Nadia looked up at Sylvia.

"Some tea would be nice," she said quietly. Sylvia smiled and left the room.

Nadia sighed and wrapped her cloak around her. She wandered from one room to the next. They were mere shells left behind by the occupants; the furniture being the most noticeable. Yet, there were reminders to help Nadia remember which room belonged to whom. The bookshelves that were completely bare in one room told Nadia it was Michael's room. For Michael, no book on his shelf was one that could be left behind. Every word in each volume was precious to him.

Dried flowers and pictures of plants reminded Nadia of Nafaria's love and respect for all plant life. This passion was first germinated in her parents; but Nadia also knew that Nathaniel Stone cultivated her knowledge as well.

She found the last room on the floor, and walked inside. This room had large windows at the corner of the room which faced the woods beyond Lord Jason's vineyard. Nadia breathed deeply and let out a sigh. She looked around the room and finally sat on the bed. There was very little left behind to indicate this was Philip's room. Like the skilled hunter he had become; he left no trace behind him. She sat on the bed and pulled back the blanket that lay on top. She sat there with a puzzled look on her face.

"Miss Nadia?" Nadia heard a gentle female voice and looked up. Sylvia entered the room with a tray in her hand. She put it down on the table next to the bed and sat down next to Nadia. "Are you looking for something?" asked Sylvia.

"I was thinking that a certain quilt I made for Philip once would still be here," said Nadia. "He cannot surely have been able to take it with him."

Sylvia smiled at the young woman. "I am quite sure I saw the quilt you are referring to rolled up and bound to Philip's horse the night they left," replied Sylvia. "He has been mending and patching that quilt for years. When he first brought it home, Thena warned him many times of the dangers of taking it outside to play with. She finally had to teach him how to sew to keep it held together," said Sylvia with a laugh.

"The year he first came to father for riding lessons, I remember how much fun we both had. He taught me how to fish from the brook that summer. I helped him practice his riding skills. He had such a thirst for adventure. I guess now he finally has one of his own," said Nadia.

Sylvia reached over and hugged her. "Have some tea, and get some sleep. Tomorrow will come sooner than you think." Sylvia picked up a cup and filled it with tea, and handed it to Nadia.

"Thank you," replied Nadia. She let her gaze wander out the window into the night. Sylvia left her to her tea and thoughts.

After she finished her second cup of tea, Nadia pulled back the blanket and lay on Philip's bed. She let her mind drift back to her childhood.

She sat on a couch in her mother's favorite sitting room. On her lap was a forest green piece of material that she was busy sewing. The back was a patchwork of red, orange, brown and green. She was just sewing the pieces together when her mother entered the room. She walked over to her daughter and kneeled before her, inspecting her work.

"You have done well, little one. This quilt is beautiful," said her mother.

"It is nearly finished. All that is left is to embroider a figure on the back," said Nadia.

"What figure is that?" asked her mother.

"Orion, the hunter; I want to give this to Philip when he comes. Do you think he will like it?" asked Nadia.

Her mother gave her a big hug. "I think he will treasure it," replied her mother. Nadia smiled as she drifted off to sleep.

***

The morning sun was not even aware it was time to shine yet when Sebastian Cavanaugh rode across the village as quickly as he could with one destination in mind. Count Deveraux issued a proclamation that he was to post that morning. It was not often that he was called upon for duties as the village messenger, but today he was grateful to see the proclamation first. He knew of one person in particular who would be very interested in this news.

Sebastian did not get mixed into the business of others. He preferred to work hard for whoever would hire him and earn a fair wage. His father had taught him that good men who were hard working deserved the rewards of their labor. The proclamation Sebastian carried in his pocket would erase that way of thinking. He was worried, but he knew that Lord Reinard Sallen would handle this properly.

He knocked on the rear door where he knew the servants would be busy with breakfast. One of the servants opened the door and smiled. "Why Sebastian, what brings you here so early this morning? The sun is not even up yet," said the servant.

"Mordecai, I need to speak to Lord Reinard immediately," said Sebastian as he walked into the kitchen.

"I do not know if he is awake yet," said Mordecai.

"You need to wake him then! It is very important," said Sebastian sharply. The tone in his voice made the old man's eyes jump. At that moment, Lord Reinard walked into the kitchen. He took in the young man's presence and a look of concern crossed his face.

"Sebastian, you are early, my friend. Is something wrong?" asked Reinard.

"I fear there may be, my Lord. Count Deveraux has instructed me to post this proclamation for everyone in the village to see. It is a notice stating that lands belonging to those of the Craft are to be surrendered to him at once," replied Sebastian. He took the piece of paper from his pocket and handed it to Reinard. As Reinard read the notice, his brows knitted tightly together.

"So it begins," he whispered. He looked up at Sebastian. "Who does the Count suspect?"

"He has already taken the Bernard residence. He plans to go to Mauldon Manor to seize Lord Jason's property next. I do not know about Malcom Stone's property," said Sebastian.

"I bought Malcom's shop and residence before he and Nathaniel left. Jason has signed his property over to me. It is now mine. He has no right to seize it," said Reinard. He walked out of the kitchen with Sebastian following him. "What will you do, Lord Reinard?" asked Sebastian.

"I need to get to Lord Jason's manor before the Count terrorizes Sylvia. She is caretaker of the manor until Lord Jason returns," said Reinard.

"The king needs to know this is happening," said Sebastian.

"I will confront Count Deveraux first. If he will not back down from this decision, I will go to the king myself," said Reinard. He grabbed some papers from his desk and walked out of the room. He looked up at Sebastian. "Thank you for bringing this to my attention, Sebastian. This has the potential to get ugly. You may not wish to be around," said Reinard.

"Doing what is right always has the potential to become ugly," replied Sebastian. "I am coming with you." Lord Reinard nodded his head in assent and walked out to the stable.

Sebastian followed Lord Reinard to Mauldon Manor. It was still quiet when they rode up the cobblestone path. A few minutes later, Count Deveraux arrived with two other men.

"You have no business here, Count Deveraux. This is my property, leave now," said Reinard.

"Lord Jason Mauldon is known to all in this village as one of the Craft. All lands belonging to those of the Craft will be confiscated," said the Count.

Reinard took a piece of paper from the inside pocket of his cloak. "This paper is the deed to this land. Lord Jason signed over this property to me. Leave now," said Reinard. Count Deveraux stood still. Lord Reinard went on. "I also own the shop and property Malcom Stone owned and operated, Count Deveraux. I bought the shop the day he left Denholm Glen. There is nothing else for you here," said Reinard.

"You will regret this, Lord Reinard," replied the Count.

"I will never regret doing what is right, even if I die for it," replied Reinard.

"This is not over," replied the Count.

"It is over!" shouted Reinard. "You will not seize land others wiser than you have worked hard for. I will not tolerate it. Today, I will leave for Wildemere to bring this matter before King Rohn if you persist in this treachery. What do you imagine he will say if an uprising occurs in this area of his kingdom after I bring him news of your persecution of those of the Craft?" said Reinard.

The Count was silent. He glared at Reinard and Sebastian for a moment. All three men were engaged in their own battle of will. Finally, Count Deveraux conceded. "Perhaps this decision was hastily made. I mean only to protect the people of this region from those of the Craft. There is no reason for the king to know about this. However, it will only be a matter of time before such things happen," said the Count.

"Pray that you are not the beneficiary of such trouble," replied Reinard. The Count turned his horse and left the manor.

Reinard turned and walked his horse to the stable with Sebastian behind him. After putting their horses in the stable, they went into the house.

Sylvia was in the kitchen pulling a pan from the oven. The smell of yeast rolls permeated the air. She looked up and smiled when she saw them.

"Lord Reinard, you are out early," said Sylvia. "Was there some kind of trouble outside?"

"Yes, there was. Count Deveraux tried to claim Lord Jason's land this morning on a false charge," said Reinard. Sylvia's eyes grew wide.

"There is nothing to fear. Jason signed his property over to me before he left, as you know. The Count now also knows this. He will not be back," said Reinard. Sylvia gave a sigh.

"All this trouble over one reckless act. Will this nightmare ever be over?" asked Sylvia.

"I am afraid it will not be anytime soon. Is Nadia awake yet?" asked Reinard.

"Yes," said a quiet voice. Reinard and Sylvia turned to the doorway. Nadia stood there, staring at Reinard. "Is something wrong?" she asked.

"I am afraid we must get you on the road back home quickly," said Reinard.

"What has happened?" asked Nadia.

"Count Deveraux tried to issue a proclamation to seize all lands belonging to those of the Craft. I challenged him on this, and for the time being he has agreed to back down. He knows I will go to the king on behalf of those of the Craft. He is not willing to raise any suspicion. However, other Counts may decide to follow suit in this matter. You must warn Lord Saintclaire of what has happened in Denholm Glen so that he can make arrangements to protect himself if the need arises," said Reinard.

"I will leave as soon as possible," said Nadia.

"However, not without breakfast," replied Sylvia. The determined look on her face warned all three people she was quite serious.

"I will send Maia to wake Ian, so that he can eat as well," said Sylvia.

An hour later, Nadia and Ian climbed on their horses. Sylvia gave Nadia a cloth satchel made of silk. "In here are two changes of clothes and one of Lady Thena's cloaks. You may find they will come in handy," said Sylvia.

"Thank you," replied Nadia.

Sylvia then handed Ian a small canvas bag. "In there are some yeast rolls, meat and cheese to eat at midday," said Sylvia.

"Nadia, do not tarry. Your father needs to know what happened here. Though I am willing, he may need to go to the king himself if injustice occurs," said Reinard.

"I will tell him, my Lord. Thank you for your hospitality," said Nadia. She pricked her horse, and took off down the cobblestone path, with Ian riding right behind her.

***

Lord Bryant Saintclaire sat up in his bed covered in sweat. His room was dark, but the sun was beginning to show through the window. It came to rest on the slender form of his wife as she lay asleep next to him. He reached out his hand and touched her long blond hair. It fell in waves down her back and was the consistency of fine silk. Tears fell down his face as he let his fingers mingle among her beautiful tresses.

He lay back down next to her and curled up with his arms around her. As he held her, he felt tears roll down his cheeks. Something once again awoke him from his dreams. Would it allow him any more rest? Lord Bryant doubted it. This was not the first occasion his senses tingled with an awareness of things unknown at the time, only to be recognized in the fulfillment of some future event. Lord Bryant learned long ago never to ignore his senses.

As a child, his father noticed this great sensitivity very quickly as Bryant grew in the Craft. He helped Bryant understand himself and taught him how his great awareness was a gift from YAHWEH that was not to be spurned.

As he lay in bed, Bryant thought back to a sunny day many years ago. It was late morning, and his father left instruction that Bryant was to meet him in the stable. It was his tenth birthday, and he was curious about why his father would want him to be out in the stable before studies. In the Saintclaire household, studies in the Craft came first, and early in the day. Work was necessary, but wisdom was always prized as a more noble pursuit.

As Bryant reached the stable, the door opened and his father led a foal outside. The creature was beautiful, and so full of spirit. Bryant stared at it a few moments before his father cleared his throat.

"Good morning father. I was told to meet you here this morning. Will we not study first?" asked Bryant. His father smiled.

"Today, your study will begin here, with this animal. This is your horse, and you will train him. Perhaps you will become a horse master as well as one versed in the Craft, one who will find value in passing on what you learn to others who will follow behind you. It is my hope that this experience will help you grow your awareness and intuition into a useful tool. You will never be able to see the future the way some of the Craft have in the way of foresight. However, to feel change in the things around you can be vital as well, for a prudent man sees danger and takes refuge[6]. Learn to pay attention to your instincts, and to have respect for even the air you breathe. YAWHEH gives warning when danger is near. You just need to pay attention to the signs."

Lord Bryant started his new career that morning with a prize stallion that grew as he did. Through this most remarkable beast, he learned that he was no less remarkable. His father's wisdom taught him to embrace

---

[6] Proverbs 22:3

who he was, instead of labeling this sensitivity as cowardice. His father taught him that great awareness very easily led to great preparedness. Both the horse and the awareness were lessons Lord Bryant never forgot.

Now, years later, he lay in bed with his heart feeling very heavy. There was no way to know what form the treachery would take, so he would prepare for every eventuality. Today, he had a free day where he would see no visitors. There would be no riding lessons, and he would spend the day with his wife.

He was grateful for the opportunity to send his daughter with a trusted servant to deliver a horse to the household of a very dear friend. Lord Bryant instructed her to stay a few days to help train the little girl on how to ride her new filly. He smiled at the thought. He remembered the conversation early in the week between himself and Jason. The subject was the betrothal between Philip and his daughter Nadia. He was happy Jason approved of her as a mate for his oldest son. Above all, he hoped whatever calamity that was about to occur would be satisfied with him alone. He wanted his wife and daughter left out of it. However, it is not often the case when the devil comes to call. He is usually not satisfied until all within range of the fire are consumed wholly by its flames. This was the other reason why he sent Nadia away; for to be aware is to be forewarned.

He listened to that quiet stirring right now, as he gently threw back the covers and crept out of bed. Slipping a shirt over his head, he walked out of the bedroom and down the hall to the library.

The embers in the fireplace were still glowing, but only a dull red color. He was sure they would have gone out by now. He walked over to the fireplace and stirred the embers to life again. He then added two pieces of kindling and waited; letting the wood do its work. A few moments later, the fire sprang back to life, and Bryant added the largest piece of wood to the fire. The room was lit in a golden glow. Satisfied that he could see well enough in the room, Bryant walked over to the bookshelves. He looked among the volumes, and then pulled three off the shelf. He paused a moment, then took a fourth and put them on the desk in the corner of the room. He carefully wrapped the books in cloth and looked around until he found the leather pack he used to transport things on horseback. He opened his desk drawer and pulled out a large satin pouch and added it into the pack. Taking the pack, he left the room and headed for the kitchen.

Bryant looked through the cupboards and found a small piece of cured ham, some cheese and bread waiting on the stove. He put these into the pack and drew the string carefully. He then headed out the rear entrance toward the stable.

***

The sun shone through the windows and cast its yellow glow across Cassandra's face. She reached over and felt the empty spot that her husband occupied next to her. The blankets were pulled back exposing sheets cool to the touch. He had been up for quite some time.

She sat up and rubbed her eyes. Giving her arms a long stretch, she finally threw back the covers and got out of bed as well.

It was not unusual for Bryant to be up before her. Indeed, it was usually a surprise to their servants when Cassandra was up first. She had always been a late riser, even as a child. She found no magic in seeing the sun rise the way some did. The magic was waking to the sun high in the sky, showing the world to be the wondrous adventure it truly was.

Cassandra chose a simple blue dress that she slipped into, knowing it was Bryant's favorite. For the past couple days he seemed preoccupied and even a little agitated. She knew he sensed some great and terrible thing had happened, but he had not said what. It was quite possible he himself did not know. The gifts YAHWEH bestowed on those of the Craft were not always clear in their design. The strange sensitivity to the world around him that Bryant possessed was no exception. She left the bedroom behind and followed the stairs to the ground floor. She headed to the library, hoping that Bryant would be there.

Cassandra looked in the doorway, but the room was empty. She saw the fire in the hearth had died out already. She moved closer to the bookshelves. Her eye caught sight of an empty spot on the shelf. She reached out her hand and ran her fingers along the entire shelf. The diaries were missing. The only other book that was missing from the shelf was their copy of the sacred writings of the Craft that they lived by. Their whole being as a family was tied in those volumes. Did Bryant take them?

Suddenly, Cassandra heard a cacophony of noise outside. One of the servants rushed into the room.

"Lady Cassandra, there are men out here demanding you!" exclaimed the girl. A man she did not recognize appeared behind the girl. He was accompanied by two more.

"Lady Cassandra Saintclaire?" demanded the man.

"Yes," replied Cassandra, nodding her head.

"Count Vedan demands your arrest immediately. You are to come with me," replied the man.

"Why would he demand my arrest? What have I been accused of?" exclaimed Cassandra. The men stood still as statues and stared coldly.

"The Count will explain when you have your audience with him," replied the man.

Cassandra looked at the young servant girl. She was new to the household. She held a terrified look in her eyes. She turned around and looked at the empty spot on the bookshelves. Whatever was going to happen, once again Bryant *knew*. She took a deep breath to gather her courage.

"Leave the servants to their household duties. They have business that cannot be interrupted," replied Cassandra calmly. She met the man's gaze with a coolness of her own, though her heart thumped hard in her chest. Cassandra walked out of the room, the men trailing behind her.

***

Count Vedan stood in the terrace garden in the rear of his estate looking out at the fields his family owned for generations. He was proud of his heritage as a landowner. His father taught him to govern his estate well. So well, in fact, that attention was paid by the king. Vedan was given the opportunity to govern part of his country; to enforce the upright laws of Nereheim. He was given the title of Count, and he took his appointment seriously.

His heart was troubled by the news he had received the day before. Count Deveraux sent an urgent warning to him about a situation involving a young woman he had executed for poisoning his daughter. This young woman was the daughter of a woman he knew very well. Analia Bernard was a woman of great moral character, yet her daughter could not be trained to take her work in the Craft with the seriousness it deserved. Count Vedan was only mortal, but he understood the ramifications of such misuse. He knew Analia well, because he knew her older sister well. They all grew up together in Illith. He had loved Lady Cassandra Saintclaire since they were children.

Count Vedan thought of her often after his wife died. They were mostly images that popped through his mind that he thought he put to rest when he married his wife. He would see her golden hair in the rays of the sun. Her sparkling sapphire eyes would haunt his twilight. Old feelings resurfaced with such force, he could hardly sleep at night.

The Count heard footsteps behind him, but did not turn around until he heard a quiet voice ask, "Noah, why am I here?"

He stiffened and slowly turned around and faced Cassandra. He looked into her eyes, which held great calm. However still she stood, he could see nervousness in her stature. Two men stood with her. He looked at them and said, "I will speak with Lady Saintclaire alone," said the Count. The men nodded their heads and turned to go.

"No, whatever it is you wish to say, I will hear in the presence of witnesses. I have nothing to hide," said Cassandra.

The men looked at Cassandra, and then the Count. He took in her measured expression and nodded his head. "I was given a warning from Count Deveraux in Denholm Glen. His daughter was poisoned by one of the Craft. He executed her to make an example of her to the village. The Count also hanged the girl's mother for not teaching her to use her craft more nobly. I am left wondering how I should proceed with this information," said the Count.

Lady Cassandra looked at the Count carefully. "How does this concern me? You know I am of the Craft, but we have known each other since we were children. I would never do such a thing," replied Cassandra.

"The murderer was Lya Bernard. The Count also hanged Analia for not being able to teach her temperance," replied the Count quietly.

Cassandra gasped. Her eyes widened and her face became ashen. Tears welled in her eyes as she found breathing difficult.

"Analia is dead?" whispered Cassandra.

"Yes," replied the Count.

"Why are you telling me this? Do you think Nadia would do the same? Do you think that just because Analia had difficulty with Lya, that Nadia would act like her?" asked Cassandra. She looked at the Count carefully.

"The time in which we live begins to see trouble. I can assure your safety and that of your family," replied the Count. He moved closer to her and reached out to touch her long hair. She straightened to her full height once again and took a deliberate step back toward the men behind her.

"No," she replied. She looked the Count directly in the eye. "I would rather die than commit such treachery against YAHWEH and my husband," said Cassandra defiantly.

"It is one simple act to save your family," said the Count. His gaze was trained on her. He rushed toward her and grabbed her. Cassandra mustered her full strength and sent her knee into his abdomen. The Count doubled over, winded.

"I would die before seeing you have the satisfaction of violating my body!" exclaimed Cassandra. The Count's expression turned dark. He raised his voice to match hers.

"Then die you shall! You will be stoned in the Village Square!" shouted the Count.

"You cannot condemn me to die without cause! I have done nothing wrong!" shouted Cassandra. Her voice was shrill and fearful.

"I will not have innocent blood on my hands when I could have prevented it. I will not allow the people in this village to fall prey to a witch's whim!" shouted the Count in reply.

The two men grabbed Cassandra before she realized what was happening. She thrashed around, but their grip held fast. They pulled her into the house, screaming after the Count. A moment later, one of the Count's messengers stood in the doorway.

"What is it?" demanded the Count.

"We have the remains of the little girl Rhea who was missing," replied the messenger. The Count looked at him carefully.

"Remains?" he asked.

"Yes. It appears she was mauled by an animal; a wolf perhaps. We found her head and what was left of her body in the woods a mile outside Illith," replied the messenger.

"Does anyone else know this?" asked the Count.

"No, we put the remains in a sack and came straight to you," replied the messenger. A thin smile crossed the Count's lips.

"Inform her parents of the unfortunate incident. Let them know her murderer has been found and will be stoned in the Village Square at noon today," replied Count Vedan.

The messenger looked puzzled, but nodded his head and disappeared. The Count looked out and continued to survey his lands, unaware that one other heard and saw everything that happened.

Julia came back from the river with a basket of fresh berries. The cook sent her down to pick wild mulberries from the patch along the riverbank. She had just rounded the corner and saw the Count with Lady Cassandra on the terrace. She paused near the bushes and listened to the entire conversation. She ran into the house from the side entrance, and quickly dropped the berries in the kitchen. She went to her room, grabbed her few possessions and stuffed them into her leather riding satchel. She ran back outside to the stable. She understood the implications behind Count Vedan's interview with Lady Cassandra. She also understood how he would use Rhea's death to discredit the Saintclaire family. Julia knew that Count Vedan was a vindictive and dangerous man, but she had no idea that he would go so far as to destroy a noble and pure woman as Lady Cassandra. She no longer wished to be employed by such a monster. Julia needed to find Lord Saintclaire and let him know his wife was to be executed.

She made haste to the Saintclaire manor. How she wished that Ian were there, but she knew he was in Denholm Glen with Nadia. Her heart beat fast with the beat of the horse's hoofs on the countryside. The smell of the fresh grass and wildflowers aroused her senses, but she kept moving across the fields to her destination. Lord Saintclaire must be home. She knew he could stop this treachery from happening.

Julia gasped as she came in sight of the manor. Smoke was rising into the air and becoming thicker as she moved closer. She saw the servants running with jugs and pails, desperate to find water as near as possible to the flames. As she rode up, she called out to the first person she saw.

"Where is Lord Saintclaire? Is he here? I must speak to him!" shouted Julia. One of the men heard her and turned to face her.

"We cannot find Lord Saintclaire. He rose early to take Saint out for a ride," he replied.

"Is Samson here? It is important! Count Vedan plans to stone Lady Saintclaire in the Village Square at noon today!" shouted Julia. Her exclamation caught the ears of some of the others nearby. They turned to her immediately.

"Are you sure?" shouted the man in return.

"I heard the conversation myself. Find Lord Saintclaire. I will ride into the village to watch what happens," replied Julia. She turned and rode off down the pathway to the main road, disappearing into the smoke.

***

The sun was shining bright when a man of good muscular tone could be seen taking his horse for a run through the fields. His green eyes sparkled like emeralds and his face beamed as the cool morning breeze whipped his hair behind him. He urged the horse on faster and was delighted when it not only obeyed his will, but seemed to revel in it as well. Lord Bryant made a ritual of his morning run on his prized stallion, Saint. Every time he mounted his horse and rode through the countryside, he was reminded of why he chose his vocation. He loved horses for the great majesty they possessed. They were animals of beauty and grace, but could be trained to be hard workers as well. They were noble animals, able and willing to prove their loyalty to their master at a breath. Lord Saintclaire respected these qualities and devoted his life to making sure future generations learned to do the same.

Bryant slowed his horse down by degrees and enjoyed a slow and steady gallop across the flat field where he trained his horses. He used the time as he often did, to reflect on puzzles that rarely showed their solutions until he was with Saint, in the morning, with his head clear. He felt a stirring in the air, like a great storm was in the distance, ready to consume all in its path. He did not have any cause to suspect any one thing, just a shift in his spirit. A great and terrible deed had been committed, this Lord Bryant could feel. He had no idea what it could possibly mean.

Lord Bryant heard sounds of another horse coming upon him. He turned around and saw Samson riding toward him. His expression was one of concern.

"My Lord, I fear there may be trouble coming our way. I saw a group of men riding toward the manor. I thought you should know," said Samson.

"Perhaps Count Vedan sent them," replied Bryant.

"Why would he send men to us?" asked Samson.

"Count Vedan is our law enforcer, Samson. Perhaps he has news for us," replied Bryant.

"If it was just news, he would have sent one man alone," replied Samson with suspicion in his voice. Lord Bryant looked carefully at his most trusted hired man.

"Perhaps you are right, Samson," replied Bryant. He urged his horse into a gallop and took off toward his home with Samson behind him.

After a few minutes, Samson looked toward the manor. His brow furrowed. "Is that smoke?" he asked. A black column rose up from the direction of their home. Bryant creased his brows and urged Saint on faster.

As they rode up the path to the back of the house, they heard shouts and saw the servants frantic in their quest to put out a fire. He stared in horror as the front half of his house was engulfed in flame. The cook saw them and ran toward them, shouting through tears.

"My Lord, they took her!" she shouted frantically.

"Who did they take? Who did this?" shouted Bryant.

"The men, they came and set fire to the house after they took Lady Cassandra. They said she was under arrest!" shouted the cook.

"Where did they take her?" asked Bryant. His eyes held fear in them. Another man came up quickly behind her.

"Julia was here looking for you. She said they are going to stone Lady Cassandra in the Village Square at noon today," he said. Samson let out a gasp.

Lord Bryant looked at Samson. "Take Saint and go meet Ian and Nadia on the road. Take the main road into Denholm Glen. Do not let Nadia come back here. They will kill her if they can," said Bryant.

"My Lord, where are you going?" asked Samson.

"I am going to find my wife," said Bryant. He jumped on Samson's horse and took off down the path toward the main road.

***

The sun was high in the sky and shining down on the Village Square when noon came to Illith. The entire village gathered in the square and awaited the important news Count Vedan was to give. Children stood with parents, their faces grubby from their morning activities. Each little pair of hands was in the company of a larger one, holding the child firmly to their parent. Since Rhea's disappearance, anxious mothers would not let their children wander far from home.

Count Vedan stood in the doorway of his office with the door open. The little building took care of the official duties regarding the adherence to Nereheim's laws. Deeds and wills were finalized here as well as a certificate of marriage. On this day, however, it also held an alleged criminal.

The Count turned behind him and looked at Cassandra. Each of her arms was restrained by two of the Count's men. Her blond hair flowed around her shoulders, her blue eyes holding great sadness. He took a few steps until his face was only an inch from hers. He pulled her hair back from one ear and whispered, "This is your last chance. Be my lover, or be executed."

Cassandra parted her lips and whispered, "No."

He turned around and walked out of the building, leaving the door open behind him.

The crowd quieted as the Count strode toward the fountain. He looked at the water for a moment, then turned and faced the villagers.

"It is with a heavy heart that I bring this news to you today. It was brought to my attention early this morning that the missing Rhea Calloway has been found," said the Count.

The crowd sighed and whispers began to circulate through it. Parents held their children, but smiles of delight crossed their lips. The Count's face was very grave.

"Her remains were discovered in the woods near the Laurel brook headwaters. Her head was found on what can only be described as an altar with the remains of her body beneath it. A woman was caught at this altar, setting fire to the body. She is charged with the little girl's murder, and will be stoned for her crime." The Count nodded his head toward the building.

Loud cries and gasps echoed through the crowd as the men dragged a horrified Lady Cassandra toward the fountain. She now understood how the Count would have her murdered. "No! I am innocent of this charge!" cried Cassandra.

The Count raised his voice over Cassandra's cries. "This woman is of the Craft and caught in the act of a most despicable display! Will we allow her to live and butcher our children for her pleasure? Save our children; execute the witch!" cried the Count with contempt in his voice. He left Lady Cassandra standing in front of the fountain.

Suddenly, Julia rode up on her horse. She surveyed the scene before her. Lady Cassandra stood against the fountain with a sea of angry faces staring at her coldly. She heard the last words of Count Vedan's accusation. Julia looked from one angry face to another. Some faces held a shocked expression. The people she saw in the front of the crowd each held a rock in their hand. Others were searching the ground for other rocks to throw.

Many of them were men, but there were some women as well. Julia did not know why these people would assemble to do such a thing to Lady Cassandra; she never hurt a single person for as long as Julia knew her. Now she was about to be executed for crimes she did not commit, nor had reason to.

A woman stepped forward. "This is for my daughter," she whispered. She threw the rock square in Cassandra's chest. She doubled over with a loud groan. One by one, the villagers stepped forward to throw their stones.

"Stop this madness!" shouted Julia from her horse. Lady Cassandra looked up at her as others turned to look at her.

"Lady Cassandra is innocent of this charge! Do not do this awful thing!" shouted Julia.

Count Vedan quickly returned to the fountain where he left Cassandra standing. "She is not innocent of this treachery! She was found, covered in blood, igniting Rhea's body with a flame!" shouted the Count.

"That is a lie fabricated by you, Count Vedan, to discredit Lady Cassandra! She would never do such a thing!" shouted Julia.

One of Count Vedan's men stepped forward. He looked at the Count carefully. "It is not a lie! She was found only this morning, just as I reported to the Count!" he shouted.

Suddenly the people turned their eyes back to Cassandra, ignoring Julia's pleas. One by one the villagers threw their rocks. Julia gasped and turned her horse around. She needed to find help quickly.

Bryant rode toward the village as swiftly as the horse would allow. He saw another rider coming toward him. He recognized Julia, a young woman in Count Vedan's employ, slowing her horse. He slowed his horse as well. From the streaks on her face, Bryant could tell Julia had been crying.

"Lord Saintclaire, I am so glad to find you! Count Vedan has wrought a treacherous evil!" exclaimed Julia.

"Julia, what has happened?" asked Lord Bryant.

"I overheard a conversation about Lady Saintclaire's sister in Denholm Glen. She was executed because her daughter poisoned Count

Deveraux's daughter. Count Vedan threatened Lady Cassandra but she would not back down. She is being stoned in the Village Square as we speak!" said Julia.

"Stoned? Why on earth would he do such a thing?" asked Bryant.

"He said it was to protect the people of Illith from the threat of the same thing happening here. However, I heard the whole conversation. He wanted Lady Cassandra to sleep with him. Rhea's body was found by the Count's men. He has blamed her death on Lady Cassandra," replied Julia. Lord Bryant looked at Julia carefully.

"Julia, I need you to try and find Samson and Ian for me. Tell them what has happened. If Lady Cassandra and I do not return to the manor by early afternoon, they are to give the horses to the servants, and raze the manor to the ground. Samson will understand," replied Lord Bryant.

Julia's face registered shock, but she nodded her head. "Where will I find them?" asked Julia.

"They are on the road to Denholm Glen. I gave Samson instructions to make sure Nadia does not return to Illith. Find them," said Lord Bryant.

"What will you do?" asked Julia.

"I am going to my wife," replied Lord Bryant. He dug his heels into his horse and took off toward the Village Square.

***

Cassandra stared at the sky as the rocks hit her. She felt the wind go out of her lungs and she collapsed to the ground in pain. Her breath became a gasp, and her vision blurred. Her hand flew up to her head and she cowered before the fountain. She thought back to a moment in time not so long ago.

It was morning the day before. Cassandra felt a tickle on her cheeks, and the fragrance of roses filled her nostrils. Her eyes fluttered open and slowly Bryant's face came into focus. His eyes were the first thing she saw, then his warm smile. She reached up her hand to touch his face, and then gave him a smile of her own. He pressed the rose into her hand

and she lay on her back, waiting for him to kiss her. His touch was as gentle and light as the rose she held in her hand. His warmth was all she could feel. "Good morning," whispered Bryant when their lips parted.

"Any morning that begins this way is a good morning," replied Cassandra with a smile. He took her hand and kissed it. Cassandra smiled as she felt another rock hit her in the chest.

Bryant ran the horse as hard as he could to get to the village. A few minutes later, he made his way into the Village Square. He heard loud shouts and saw a circle of people around the fountain in the middle of the square. Cassandra was in front of the fountain, lying at the base. Large rocks were being thrown at her.

"Cassandra!" shouted Bryant. She looked up as she registered her name above the shouts and screams that were directed at her. Bryant jumped off the horse and pushed through the crowd until he was at her side. Her face was bruised and cut. She looked up at him with tears in her eyes.

"Bryant, you cannot be here. They will kill you too," she said weakly.

Bryant looked at her with tears streaming down his face. "This is the only place I could ever be, Cassandra. There is no life without you. I will stay here with you," said Bryant. He pulled her close and felt the stones pummel his back.

The Count watched as Lord Bryant shielded his wife from the rocks, his groans and cries of pain mingling with hers. He turned to his men and said, "Seize the Saintclaire manor. Find Nadia Saintclaire and kill her." He watched the crowd continue to pummel Lord Bryant and Lady Cassandra with rocks.

***

Nadia drove her horse at a steady gallop. Ian rode behind her and they traveled as quickly as possible. They hardly noticed the countryside that Nadia commented on the day before. Lord Reinard's concern played on her mind. Was there anything to be concerned about? The answer would reveal itself when she arrived home and told her parents the news of Lya's treachery and the family's demise.

"There is someone riding toward us," said Ian. Nadia looked out to where he pointed and saw the figure coming toward them at great speed.

"Is that Samson?" asked Nadia. She squinted her eyes to sharpen her focus.

"It looks like him. Is he riding Saint?" asked Ian.

Nadia swallowed hard. Ian was right. Samson was riding her father's prized stallion. A few minutes later, he slowed to a stop before them.

"Ian, Nadia; I am so glad to find you," said Samson with wide eyes. He looked afraid. This gave both Ian and Nadia a feeling of dread. Samson was not given to fear.

"Count Vedan and some of the men of the village came and took your mother, Nadia. Your father went after them. Before he left, he told me to take his horse and find you. You are to take Saint and do not come back to Illith. After he took off, I checked the pack your father put on Saint. You have food, some gold, and your parents' most sacred books. He means for you not to return. Go quickly Nadia, before some terrible fate happens to you!" pleaded Samson.

"Do you know if Lord and Lady Saintclaire are still alive?" asked Ian. Samson shook his head.

"I fear they are not, Ian. I will need your help with a final request Lord Bryant had," said Samson.

"I will find Lord Jason Mauldon and tell him what has happened. From there, I may continue on into North Agea. Father was a respected horse master. I will listen for news, and return only if I hear that he and mother are still alive," said Nadia.

"May your God be with you, my lady," said Samson.

"Thank you for everything, Samson," said Nadia. She hopped down from the horse she was on, and climbed onto Saint. "If YAHWEH wills it, I will see you both again soon." Nadia spurred Saint and took off back down the road toward Denholm Glen. Now, more than ever, she must find Lord Jason.

When they parted ways, Ian and Samson rode quickly toward the manor. Samson's concern was for his fellow servants, the horses and livestock. As he thought of this, he remembered a conversation he had with Lord Bryant just a few hours after Ian left with Nadia for Denholm Glen the day before.

Samson was coming back from the stream with jugs full of water for the cook. She was making stew that day, and needed all the extra water she could find. He offered to help the servants bring up water from the stream. Lord Bryant found him at the stream, and helped him fill the jugs as they talked.

"My Lord, you have more important things to do today than to help bring up water," said Samson in protest as Lord Bryant helped him fill the jugs. Lord Bryant looked at Samson carefully.

"At the moment, my greatest task is helping you and having this conversation," replied Lord Bryant. Samson filled his jug and set it down on the ground. He stood up before reaching to fill another jug. He wanted to give Lord Bryant his full attention.

"You have something on your mind, my Lord?" asked Samson.

"I do," replied Bryant. He looked at Samson carefully. "You have been in my employ since your father came to me years ago, Samson. You have known me to ask many strange questions and have you and Ian do many tasks that leave you wondering what I am thinking. Today I will give you instructions for yet another one of those tasks," said Bryant. He finished filling the jug in his hand and put it next to the others. He also straightened to his full height and looked Samson in the eye. "I feel something terrible is coming, like some kind of storm that we cannot outrun, nor maybe survive. If the time comes that Lady Cassandra and I are dead, you must raze the manor to the ground. Give each of the servants a horse and a bag of gold that I have put in a chest in the root cellar. I have made special provision for Nadia as well," said Bryant.

Samson looked at Lord Bryant in disbelief. "My Lord, what makes you think that you will be dead?" he asked.

"It is a feeling that I cannot seem to let go. It keeps me awake long into the night, and wakes me up bathed in a cold sweat in the morning. I cannot explain it; I only know that I need to be prepared. If I am murdered outright, I do not wish to see someone else steal my hard work. I wish to prepare for those in my employ the best that I can," replied Bryant.

Samson sighed heavily. "I have never known your intuition to be false, my Lord. However, this is one time that I will call upon YAHWEH myself to beg for you to be wrong," replied Samson. Lord Bryant smiled at his servant.

"I have been begging the same thing," replied Bryant quietly. He picked up another jug and proceeded to fill it in silence.

Now, as they rode at a breakneck speed, Samson began to wonder just how much Lord Bryant really knew.

Ian broke into his thoughts as he called out, "Someone is coming toward us!"

Samson looked out and saw another figure riding toward them. Ian's heart beat a little faster than before. It was Julia coming toward them. He and Samson slowed as she drew nearer to them.

Julia's face was tear-stained and she looked afraid. Ian was instantly troubled. Julia was no coward. Relief came across her features as she recognized them. "Ian, Samson, thank goodness I found you!" exclaimed Julia.

"Julia, what on earth are you doing out here?" asked Ian.

"Count Vedan has seized Lady Cassandra to stone her! Lord Bryant sent me to tell you that if he and Lady Cassandra do not return by early afternoon, you are to raze the manor," replied Julia. Samson nodded his head.

"Lord Bryant gave me that instruction a couple days ago. There is much to do," replied Samson.

"Lord Bryant left you these instructions?" asked Ian.

"Yes. It seems he knew something was going to happen," replied Samson.

"That is no remarkable thing. Lord Bryant has excellent intuition," replied Ian.

"We must act on his wishes," replied Samson.

"What were his exact wishes?" asked Ian.

"We are to give each servant a portion of gold he has set aside, and one of his horses. The servants are to leave Illith and not return. We are to raze the manor before we go," replied Samson.

Ian was troubled by these instructions. The Saintclaire manor had been his home for most of his life. He did not want to burn such a magnificent place to the ground. Samson saw his expression and looked at him intently.

"I know exactly how you feel right now. The manor has been my home as well. This was Lord Bryant's wish, we must act on it," said Samson.

"You must have some course of action in mind?" asked Ian.

Samson smiled. "I have been thinking through the instructions. We will ready the servants and prepare the manor. If the time comes, and Lord Bryant has not returned, we do as we are told. If Lord Bryant cannot be back by his appointed time, we know something has happened," replied Samson.

"We need confirmation of their deaths no matter what happens," replied Ian. He looked at Julia. "I need you to ride into the village to confirm if they were indeed killed. This news will travel fast. You should not have to ride long to hear it," said Ian.

Julia's expression was grim, but she nodded her head. "Where will I find you?" asked Julia.

"Once you know for sure what has happened, head toward the manor. If I am not there, go to Denholm Glen at once, I will meet you there. If you arrive first, ask for Lord Reinard Sallen and tell him what has happened. When I get there we will decide what we will do next," replied Ian. He took her hand firmly. "Julia, this is not the way I intended a proposal of marriage to be, but I ask you humbly to be my wife."

Julia looked into Ian's eyes and felt tears form again. She smiled and nodded her head. "I accept and will be looking forward to a long life with you," replied Julia. Ian leaned closer to her and kissed her on her forehead.

"Go," he whispered. Julia nodded and spurred her horse on. She headed back toward the village. Ian watched her disappear toward the village as he and Samson rode toward the manor.

***

Ian and Samson gathered the servants together as quickly as they could. The fire that Count Vedan's men started was now out, but smoke still rose from the damaged part of the house. The servants listened as Ian gave them the instructions. Each servant was to gather a pack of some sort with food and their belongings that could be carried on horseback. They were each to take a horse and leave Illith.

Samson disappeared into the house and into the root cellar where Lord Bryant told him he would find a cedar chest with individual silk bags in it. He found the chest and opened one of the bags. It contained a large quantity of gold coins. He counted them and noted there were enough bags for every servant in the manor. Lord Bryant had once again left nothing to chance. He sighed heavily as he dragged the chest outside.

Each of the servants was in varying degrees of readiness. Some were ready and already in the stable, saddling their horses. Samson showed Ian the chest of gold coins. "Lord Bryant has thought of everything," said Samson grimly. Ian nodded his head.

"Make sure each servant gets a bag before they leave. There is something I wish to do," said Samson. He then disappeared into the house.

The sun was high in the sky. Each servant had given both Ian and Samson a tearful goodbye and was now gone. Lord Bryant's two most trusted men looked at each other.

"I suppose it is time," said Ian. He looked at Samson. "Where will you go?" he asked.

Samson looked toward the mountain range behind the manor. "I will take my chances in the mountains. Perhaps we will see each other again," said Samson. He held out his hand to Ian.

Ian shook his hand firmly. "I will hope to see you again one day," replied Ian.

"We shall see," said Samson. He then moved toward the fire they built about an hour ago. He lit a torch and moved toward the manor, throwing it into the house through the windows. The fire took a few moments, but the interior began to smoke. He picked up another torch.

"Take a couple torches and burn the stable," said Samson. Ian looked at him and nodded. Within fifteen minutes the house and stable were ablaze. They each got on their horses and rode away from their home.

Count Vedan's men saw the blaze as they were riding toward the Saintclaire manor. When they arrived, the house and stable were completely engulfed in flame. There was a stake with a piece of parchment nailed to it. One of the men grabbed the parchment and read it carefully. He looked at his companions. "Let us go back to the Count at once with this news. There is nothing we can do here right now," he said. They turned and rode back toward the village.

The Count was busy at his desk when one of his men entered his study. He looked up from the paper he was writing on. "Why are you not at the Saintclaire manor?" asked the Count.

"The manor was empty and ablaze when we arrived. We will go back later after the fire dies down. This was left on a stake at the end of the road leading to the manor," he said as he handed the paper to the Count.

The Count felt his hands ball into fists as he read the words: *A fool and a sluggard seeks to steal what is not his own.* He threw the paper down on the desk.

"Is there any word about where Nadia Saintclaire is?" asked the Count.

"No," replied the man.

"Go, and find her. When you do, kill her and bring me back her body," replied the Count. The man quickly left the study, intent on carrying out his master's demand.

***

Nadia drove Saint at a fast pace through the afternoon. She did not stop in Denholm Glen to see Lord Reinard Sallen again. She did not know what news she would bring if she had. She only had suspicions of what may have taken place. Those suspicions wet her eyes every now and then as the countryside passed by. Her father left instruction to leave as quickly as possible. She needed to put distance between her and Illith.

She watched the sun make its path across the sky as deliberately as she made hers across Nereheim. At twilight, she began to see houses in the distance. The village of Rowall was in view. Nadia leaned forward and whispered into the horse's ear, "Good boy, Saint." She slowed to a steady gallop and rode into the village.

Nadia rode through the main road of the village, taking in the various shops and homes along the way. She saw a sign for the village's only inn further down the main road. She sighed and headed toward it, drifting on the smell of cooking meat. Her mouth began to water.

She went around to the stable and asked to leave her horse with the caretaker of the stable. Taking her pack off the horse's back, she patted him on the nose and headed inside.

The main room of the inn was still quiet. She asked the innkeeper for a room and a bowl of stew. As she ate her stew, she kept hearing pieces of conversation from the two men sitting near the fire. They each had a mug in their hands and their voices grew louder. Nadia berated herself and tried harder to tune the men out. Whatever they were talking about had nothing to do with her. She picked up another spoonful of broth and stopped with it halfway to her mouth. She distinctly heard the words "Illith" and "horse master".

Nadia looked at the innkeeper. "Excuse me sir, can you tell me what those two men are talking about?" asked Nadia in a quiet tone. She looked back toward the fire.

The innkeeper looked surprised. "Have you not heard what happened in Illith today?" asked the innkeeper.

Nadia shook her head. "I have been on the road all day sir," she replied.

"Perhaps you should ask them. They say they saw it firsthand," said the innkeeper.

Nadia looked back toward the men and smiled. "I would, but they look as though they can no longer discern fact from fairy tale," she said. The men were growing louder and starting to sway while seated in their chairs.

The innkeeper laughed, but became serious again. "I have heard two stories, and both vary greatly. The first is that a woman in Illith was stoned at noon today for the murder of a little girl who went missing. They say the little girl's remains were found at an altar out in the woods. Count Vedan gave the execution order himself.

Nadia suppressed a gasp and remained stoic for the innkeeper's tale. Anonymity would be her greatest protection until she found Lord Jason. She could not let the innkeeper know that Count Vedan was a man she was familiar with. The innkeeper seemed not to notice anything in her face, and continued on.

"The other story I heard comes from the two travelers by the fire. They say that Count Vedan had men show up at her home and take the woman in question and they set fire to the manor after they left. They were in Denholm Glen when a young couple rode into the village demanding to see Lord Reinard Sallen. They told him that the Count threatened the woman, but she did not give in to him. He fabricated a lie, and punished her by stoning. Her husband came and tried to protect her, but was stoned as well. The manor was burned to the ground, and the servants took the horses and fled for their lives," said the innkeeper.

"Horses?" whispered Nadia. The innkeeper doubtless saw question in her eyes, but Nadia was filled with dread.

"Yes, my lady. The man was a wise and talented horse master. Both he and the woman were said to be of the Craft," replied the innkeeper.

"Who were they?" asked Nadia. She felt her stomach tighten.

"Lord Bryant and Lady Cassandra Saintclaire," replied the innkeeper.

Nadia looked down at her bowl. The bottom looked fuzzy as she stared at it. Her heart quickened its pace and the room began to spin ever so slightly. She quickly rose from her seat.

"Thank you for your time," she said quietly as she headed to her room. Once inside, she threw herself on the bed and cried for her parents.

CHAPTER 3

JASON STOOD BY THE WINDOW of their room at the inn. He watched the sun shining brightly, warming everything around him. The air still felt cool, but he was confident that the day would grow warmer. He watched the various merchants opening their stores, and peddlers setting up their carts full of wares in the market square. It could have been any other market day, just like in Denholm Glen. He breathed out a sigh. This was not Denholm Glen. It was not home. He was forced to leave his home and seek help from one higher than Count Deveraux.

Jason understood the Count's grief. It was a little more than a week since Nafaria almost died from eating the elderberry jam. He was not sure how he would have taken losing his little girl. Grief can drive a man to seek vengeance, but Count Deveraux had no right to execute Analia. Jason knew the Count was suspicious of the Craft, but now he understood that no man was to be trusted. He would appeal to the king. Then he and his family would live as anonymously as they could. He could take no chances where they were concerned.

He felt warm hands caress his shoulders. Jason looked behind him to find Thena standing there. He gave her a gentle kiss.

"How did you sleep?" asked Jason.

"As well as can be expected, I suppose. Nafaria is a restless sleeper," said Thena.

"It may just be the circumstances. This is a new experience for all of us," said Jason.

"What will we do next?" asked Thena.

"I am going to see the king. He needs to know what is happening in Denholm Glen," replied Jason.

"Do you think he will see you?" asked Thena.

"I am a landowner. I must try to speak with him. Justice must be served," replied Jason.

"I am coming with you," said Thena. Jason shook his head.

"You must stay with the children," said Jason.

"If you are going to see the king, I am going with you. I do not want to wonder what happened to you if you do not return. Philip is old enough to stay and watch the others," said Thena. One look at the flash in her eyes and Jason knew she was determined. It would be easier for him to take her along.

"Very well, you may come. However, I alone will speak with the king. He may look at it as an act of defiance if you speak out of turn," said Jason.

Thena nodded her head in consent. "I will go and bring up something for the children to eat while we are gone," said Thena.

"I will wake Philip and give him instructions while we are out," said Jason. Thena turned and walked out of the room.

An hour later, Jason and Thena rode through the city to the king's castle. Jason rode his horse through the castle gate before his nerves took control and he turned back. Thena held on tightly to him. He slowed the horse when he saw a soldier walking down the colonnade. The soldier held up his hand. Jason came to a stop before him.

"State your business," said the soldier.

"I am Lord Jason Mauldon. I have an urgent matter to discuss with the king," replied Jason.

"The king does not always grant audience with the nobles. You may have wasted your time," replied the soldier.

"To see justice is never futile. I have come from Denholm Glen where Count Deveraux has taken to murdering the innocent in his quest for vengeance," said Jason.

The soldier's eyes started at Jason's accusation. "You will find the king in his throne room. If he will see you, it will be there," replied the soldier.

"Is there a place to keep my horse while we wait?" asked Jason. The soldier nodded.

"Follow me," he said.

The soldier led them to a stable just at the end of the colonnade. "The stable boy will keep your horse for you," replied the soldier.

"Thank you," replied Jason. He handed the reins to the stable boy and he and Thena walked out of the stable.

They walked into the castle and were directed down the hallway leading to the throne room. As they walked the hall, they looked at the oils of great men of the past. Each one had a steady gaze and some even a fierce expression. Thena stopped before one. "What are all these portraits?" she asked Jason.

"They are the portraits of Nereheim's past Court Advisers. They were all once great men of the Craft," replied Jason.

Thena began walking, but then stopped a few feet away, in front of the last portrait before they reached the large double doors leading into the throne room. She looked at the man with dark auburn hair and hazel eyes. His expression was concentrated, but in his eyes, Thena saw something more than the others held. Was it compassion? She did not know, but she knew that face well.

"Is this who I think it is?" asked Thena. She looked at Jason as he came up behind her. He nodded his head.

"Malcom was the last Court Adviser of Nereheim. He settled in Denholm Glen after his wife died, a few months after Nathaniel was born. He did not speak often of his time as adviser. He only said that he left because of a disagreement he and King Rohn had over the use of power. He came to Denholm Glen before we did," said Jason.

"Do you think he already came to the king?" asked Thena.

"I am not sure," replied Jason as he opened the door.

They both cautiously entered the throne room. Thena followed behind Jason and they stopped about two feet from the door. There, a pair of guards stood with their swords in hand. One of the guards spoke to them.

"What business do you have with the king?" asked the guard. Jason stared at the two figures sitting on a pair of thrones at the other end of the room.

"I come on an urgent matter. A great injustice has been done that I fear will result in an uprising," replied Jason. He glanced at the guard, but held his gaze on the king.

The king must have heard the exchange because before the guard could answer, he spoke. "You may speak," replied the king.

The guard let Jason pass, and he walked to the end of the room, with Thena behind him. He stopped about ten feet from the throne and bowed his head.

"Your majesty, I am Lord Jason Mauldon, from Denholm Glen. An unfortunate incident has occurred and Count Deveraux seeks the blood of those of the Craft," said Jason.

The queen looked at her husband. His expression showed Jason he had not yet heard what happened in that part of Nereheim.

"What has happened?" asked the king.

"The Count's older daughter, Ana, was poisoned by a young woman named Lya Bernard. She was hanged for her transgression; however, the Count went further and executed her mother as well. My wife and I knew Raymond and Analia well. They tried everything they could to teach Lya the responsibility of her craft. There was no reason for Analia to be killed. Now, Count Deveraux seeks to make an example of any of the Craft that are within his jurisdiction. I have left behind my land to come to you for help," said Jason.

"What would you have me do?" asked the king.

"Send word to Count Deveraux to stop persecuting those of the Craft before other incidents occur and you have an uprising on your hands," said Jason calmly. He kept his voice steady, but Thena could see that Jason was dissatisfied with having to answer the question.

"I know Count Deveraux well. I am sure he is only doing what will bring justice and teach a firm lesson to those who would use their knowledge against the weak and unprepared. Those of the Craft should take this incident for the warning that it is. Murder through the use of arcane knowledge will be treated just as any other murder," replied the king.

"I am not against justice being served, your majesty, however an innocent woman was executed for something beyond her control. Will you not be an advocate for justice in this matter?" asked Jason coldly.

"Those of the Craft lost an advocate in the royal court when the last court adviser fled his duty and went into exile. Count Deveraux will be free to use any form of punishment he sees fit, as long as it is in accordance with the laws of Nereheim," replied the king just as coldly. Thena's eyes grew wide as she stared at the king. She looked at Jason, and saw the same blank expression on his face as well. Each could clearly not believe what they were hearing.

"Your majesty, what has happened is not in accordance with the law," replied Jason. He spoke evenly so as to keep his temper in check.

"I will hear no more of this!" shouted the king. The queen gazed at her husband. He never raised his voice when he was in court. It was one of the reasons she respected him so.

Jason finally lowered his gaze to the floor and bowed his head. "Yes, your majesty," he replied. He turned and left the throne room with Thena behind him.

The queen spoke quietly to her husband. "Is this true?" she whispered.

"I have not heard of it until just now," replied the king.

"You have to do something. You cannot just let these people walk away," replied the queen. The king turned and looked at his wife.

"What would you have me do?" asked the king.

"Perhaps send the royal guard out to Denholm Glen and see if the story is true. It is a day's journey at least to Denholm Glen. I have heard of Jason Mauldon. His family name has owned a vineyard for three generations. This noble would not have spared his time if it were not important," replied the queen. The king remained quiet, but he was thinking through his wife's words. She quickly rose and left the throne room.

Thena took Jason's hand as they walked in silence down the hall. Without looking at her face, Jason could tell she was crying. He stopped and looked at her.

"What will we do?" she whispered. He touched her cheek, wiping the tears that rested where they fell.

"We will live in anonymity. We will put our knowledge to use and become merchants of a different sort. The vineyard will continue on for now. However, we will need a place to live. That will be our first order of business," said Jason.

At that moment, they heard footsteps and both looked up to see the queen rushing toward them. "Lord Jason, might I have a word?" she asked.

Jason dipped his head to her. "Yes, your majesty," he said in answer.

"Do you really think an uprising can occur over this incident?" asked the queen.

"It is quite possible, your majesty. Those of the Craft are taught to have great patience and to show temperance to match the skill that YAHWEH has given us. However, in the end, we are still only human. There is a limit to how much the human soul can withstand," said Jason.

"Is there nothing that can be done?" asked the queen.

Jason looked at her carefully. "Your majesty; your husband is the monarch of our country. Do you have authority that is greater than his?" asked Jason. The queen sighed, and shook her head.

"Then there is no higher appeal. I fear that Nereheim is entering into a very dark time," said Jason. He turned away from the queen and walked down the hallway with Thena in his arms.

The queen turned and walked back to the throne room. When she arrived, she found it empty. She made her way through the halls to their private chambers. There, she found her husband sitting on their bed, with a toy doll in his hands. She saw tears falling down his face as he looked at the toy. Her heart softened and she felt tears well inside her also. There was only one thing her husband was thinking of whenever he held the doll. He was thinking of its owner. His younger sister, Sasha, was a grown adult when she died, but the king always saw her as his little sister, and protected her as such. She sighed and moved toward her husband and sat on the bed next to him.

"I miss her too. There is not a day that goes by that I do not look into my rose garden and think of her. You and Malcom saw the use of power very differently. However, that does not mean one is right and the other is wrong. It also does not mean that Malcom did not love her too. Malcom's world collapsed in on itself the day Sasha died, but he was the luckiest of us all. He needed to laugh and smile and be courageous enough to go on. He had a reason to. That beautiful little boy that he and Sasha brought into the world needed all the love he could find. I only wish we could have all benefited from such a tiny little joy," said Susanna. Her face held a note of sadness as she continued.

"We will never know what may have been, thirteen years ago. We only have what is now. Your countrymen need you now to protect them," she said.

"Those of the Craft can protect themselves," the king whispered.

"Perhaps with a supernatural power or vast knowledge they may out think the rest of us. However, they can still be executed. What would Nereheim be if that were allowed to happen?" asked Susanna.

"What do you think I should do?" asked Rohn.

"I think you should listen. Once you have heard all that is said, you will know what to do next," replied Susanna. The king sighed as he thought through wife's words.

"Do you think I was wrong to let them go?" asked Rohn. The queen hesitated, and then took his hand.

"I think you know firsthand how grief brings on madness," she replied.

King Rohn squeezed his wife's hand. He looked into her eyes and kissed her. "What would I do without your steady heart and your unwavering confidence in me?" he asked. Susanna simply smiled and snuggled closer to him.

***

Jason and Thena returned to their room at the inn to find Nafaria sitting in the window, sketching. Michael sat at the desk on the other side of the room with a book open. This scene would not have surprised the parents in the least; except that one very key element was missing.

"Where is Philip?" asked Thena. Michael looked up from his book.

"He went down to the stable to check on the horses," said Michael.

"He left you up here by yourselves?" asked Thena. The perturbed look on her face made Jason smile.

"We may be young, but we can stay alone for a little while, mother. He has only been gone fifteen minutes," replied Michael. He seemed equally perturbed as well.

"I will go check on Philip," replied Jason. He quickly left the room before any objection could be made.

Philip was busy inspecting one of the horse's legs when Jason found him. He looked up with deep concern on his face.

"Your mother may have a few words for you when she sees you next. We gave clear instruction that you all were to stay in the room," said Jason.

"I suppose I deserve the correction, but I got tired of waiting. I just thought I would take a good look at the horses. I think we may have a problem," said Philip.

"What kind of problem?" asked Jason.

Philip knelt down by the horse he was inspecting. He gingerly lifted the leg and the horse whined in protest. He carefully turned the foot so that Jason could see the shoe. It looked a little crooked and he could see that some debris from the road was stuck between the foot and the shoe.

"If we do not find a farrier to fix this, the foot will become infected," said Philip.

"It does not look that bad," said Jason doubtfully.

"That is how these things start, very small. Soon, the problem grows and then it is even more costly than it would have been to simply re-shoe the horse," said Philip.

"That is what you suggest?" asked Jason.

"It is what Lord Saintclaire would do," replied Philip.

Jason smiled at his son. "I can hardly argue with that. I will let your mother know we are going in search of a farrier," said Jason.

They both went back inside and found Thena, Nafaria and Michael downstairs in the common room. Michael and Nafaria were eating a thick beefy stew.

"Philip and I will be gone awhile. We need to find a farrier. One of the horses needs to be reshod," said Jason. He looked over at the innkeeper.

"Sir, where would I find a farrier?" asked Jason.

"There is a farrier who keeps a shop on the other side of the royal city. His workshop is on the road, as you head toward Burnea," said the innkeeper.

"Is there someone closer?" asked Philip. He was concerned about walking the horse too far.

The innkeeper thought a moment. "There is a blacksmith's apprentice not more than thirty yards from here. He has taken on work as a farrier as of late. He is quite good for his age," said the innkeeper. He dropped his voice a little lower and said, "The people he works with say he has a way with horses. They say he is like the horse master from Illith," said the innkeeper.

Philip looked at Jason who raised his eyebrow. "Who is this man?" asked Jason.

"His name is Joel Blackstone," replied the innkeeper.

"Thank you," replied Jason. Philip and Jason turned and walked outside.

"Father, do you suppose this man is of the Craft?" asked Philip.

"We will know more when we meet him," replied Jason.

Jason and Philip led the horse through the market square. The loud clang of iron being beaten with a hammer in the air determined their direction. Philip went slow, watching the horse carefully. In a few minutes, they arrived at an open faced structure that looked as though it was once a stable. A large fire stood in the corner, with a young man tending it. An older man was beating a piece of iron into a farm tool. The man at the fire noticed them first.

"Good day, gentlemen. May we be of assistance to you?" said the man in greeting. He stood about as tall as Jason, with auburn hair that grazed his shoulders. A light beard was taking form on his face.

"Good day. My name is Jason Mauldon; this is my son Philip. We are looking for Joel Blackstone," said Jason.

"You have found him. How may I help you?" asked the man.

Jason turned and looked at Philip and the horse. "My son has informed me that we need to have our horse reshod. He was adamant that the horse could not walk to the farrier on the other side of the city. The innkeeper told us perhaps you could help," said Jason.

"That he can, sir. I fear I will lose my apprentice very soon to the life of a farrier, but Joel is very skilled at the job," said the blacksmith as he hammered.

"Let us take a look at the horse," said Joel. He walked over to Philip and the horse. Slowly, he put his hand out, and then touched the horse's nose.

"Here is the problem," said Philip. He lifted the horse's foot for Joel to see.

"A very good eye, you have. Had you gone on a few more days, you would have had a very nasty problem indeed," said Joel.

"We would like the horse reshod, sir. I would like to be sure there are no complications later on," said Jason. He patted the side of the horse affectionately. "This horse was given me by a very dear friend. I wish to see him have a long life."

"That is a very wise decision. We will go around behind the shop to strip the horse's shoes," said Joel. Philip and Jason followed as Joel led the horse around to the back of the blacksmith's shop.

Philip was right behind Joel as they followed him. He saw his tools lying out on a table near where Joel stopped. He grabbed one of the tools and lifted one of the horse's feet. Joel watched as Philip began to remove the shoe.

"You seem to know what you are doing," said Joel.

"I spent a few summers with Lord Saintclaire. He taught me well," replied Philip.

"The horse master from Illith?" Joel looked up at Jason. "You have very influential friends, my lord."

"We have been fortunate in the past," replied Jason.

"What brings you to the royal city? Illith is a long way from here," said Joel.

"We are from Denholm Glen. We have found it necessary to relocate," replied Jason.

"There has been news of troubling things happening in Denholm Glen," said Joel.

"I bring no trouble with me. I wish only to start again with my family," said Jason.

Joel looked at Jason carefully. His gaze held him, but there was nothing in his eyes to suggest shrewdness. He looked down at Philip and watched as he worked. Jason was a man who valued hard work; it was apparent by the work of his son. Joel nodded his head.

"The city is large enough to blend in well. Whatever you wish, you can accomplish here," replied Joel. He picked up another tool and began to clean the horse's hooves that Philip had taken the shoes from.

"At present, we need a home. Is there any property for sale in the city?" asked Jason.

"Land in the royal city is at a premium, I am afraid," said Joel. He paused from his work. "However, the Wheaton estate is vacant."

"The Wheaton estate?" asked Jason.

Joel shook his head and went back to his work. "The land was ordered closed by the king years ago," said Joel.

"Why?" asked Philip.

"No one knows exactly what happened. The story is that Lord Wheaton went insane and killed his entire family. The king's Court Adviser went to the manor to investigate, but what he saw there terrified him. He ordered that the manor be closed and advised the king to keep it so. I was just a boy when it happened," said Joel quietly. A tear formed in the corner of his eye.

"Were you close to them?" asked Jason. His tone was quiet and gentle. The delicateness he used to answer the question surprised Joel.

"Jacob Wheaton was my age. He was my best friend. I never understood what happened. Lord Wheaton was an exceptional man of integrity. I just could not understand it at the time; no one could. Even after all these years, I still cannot," replied Joel.

Jason came closer to Joel and put his arm on his shoulder. "You said the king has ordered the land closed?" asked Jason. Joel nodded.

"His Court Adviser implored him to do so. A week later, the Court Adviser resigned his position and left Wildemere. No one ever knew what became of him," replied Joel. "Now, people say that Wheaton manor is haunted. I have never believed such fairy tales. However, I have always felt there was something deeper than just insanity that took Lord Wheaton's mind." Joel shrugged his shoulders. "I guess we will never know."

Jason shook his head. "Someone always knows. Only the courageous seek answers for the wrongs of the past," said Jason. He drifted into thought as Philip and Joel worked together to shoe the horse.

Joel and Philip spent the next hour working on the horse together as Jason pondered Joel's story. After they finished, they said goodbye to Joel and headed back toward the inn.

Thena, Nafaria and Michael exited the inn, just as they walked up.

"I told the innkeeper we needed another night," said Thena. Jason nodded his head.

"Perhaps we will not need two. I need to go back to the king," replied Jason. Thena looked at Jason with surprise.

"What could you need with him? The king made his position clear today," replied Thena.

"There is land in the royal city that has fallen into disuse. Apparently there are some strange tales being told about a place called the Wheaton estate. I wish to look into the matter, but I need the king's approval to look at the land," said Jason.

"You will go alone?" asked Thena. Jason looked at Philip.

"I think it is time Philip learns the delicacies of dealing with those who hold authority over us," replied Jason. Philip looked at his father as Thena nodded her head.

"Nafaria, Michael and I will see what is in the city," replied Thena. She quickly kissed Jason on the cheek and left with Michael and Nafaria. Philip turned to Jason.

"Why do we need permission from the king to see the land? Surely the king would be willing to sell it," said Philip.

"You heard what Joel said. The former Court Adviser ordered no one to go on the land. It sounds as though the king followed that advice without question," replied Jason.

"He must have been a powerful man to rule the king with such advice," replied Philip.

"Yes; I believe he was," replied Jason quietly.

***

Thena and Nafaria stared in wonder at the many sights around them. People bustled everywhere to their destinations, oblivious to the newcomers. Nafaria's eyes lit up at the sight of the Grand Cathedral in the center of the city. The stained glass windows caught the sunshine in a brilliant kaleidoscope of color. When they reached the Market Square, a grove of apple blossom trees in the center caught her attention. She savored the wonders around her as they moved through the market.

Michael wandered behind them, his mind lost in thought. He had no doubt the king would listen to whatever case his father presented to be able to see this abandoned land. Jason's humble nature and wisdom made him a man well respected, and not easily dismissed. He was very tactful in dealing with those of greater authority than himself. He truly respected the person and the office, until respect was proven unworthy.

What kept playing in Michael's mind was what they would find when they were granted access to the place. Why would the Court Adviser make such a decision, and then leave his position? Though the position was not a lifelong office; most advisers who were appointed either outlived the king who appointed them, or died themselves. Michael suddenly realized he knew nothing about the last Court Adviser. It seemed strange to him that a man who held such an important office could disappear so entirely.

"Michael?"

Michael shook himself from his thoughts and saw his mother looking at him.

"Yes mother?" asked Michael. Thena smiled and shook her head.

"That was well played, but you do not fool me. I can tell when something is on your mind," replied Thena.

"I was just thinking about father. Perhaps I can be of some use to him when the king grants him access to see the land," said Michael thoughtfully.

"In what way?" asked Thena.

"I am not sure yet. I need to find a library," said Michael. Thena laughed.

"On such a beautiful day, only you, Michael, can think of books," said Thena.

"May I come with you?" asked Nafaria.

"If I find a library, the only thing I will be doing is picking my way through old books. It does not prove to be an exciting time," replied Michael.

"It may not prove to be exciting, but maybe I can help," replied Nafaria.

Thena stopped walking and looked across the square at one of the buildings. "Perhaps you will get your opportunity," said Thena. She pointed at the little stone building labeled "Antiquarian Manuscripts". Michael looked back at his mother.

"I will come find you in an hour. Nafaria may stay with you, but she must not get in the way or disturb anyone. Do not leave the building until I come for you," said Thena as she looked from Michael to Nafaria.

"Yes mother," they both replied. Nafaria quickly took Michael's hand and headed toward the library. Thena smiled as she watched them go.

"Why is it so important that you come with me?" asked Michael. "This really will be a boring job."

"I watch you reading and writing things down in books all the time. You know so many things, Michael. I want to learn how you do that. Why is it that you think by coming to a library you will be able to help father?" asked Nafaria.

"We need to find out anything about the royal city that we can. It is my hope that someone kept a careful chronicle of the land in this area. Perhaps what happened to Lord Wheaton will be found within the pages of a book," said Michael. Still holding Nafaria's hand, he pushed open the door and they walked into the building.

The sight before Michael made him gasp. The vestibule opened into a large room that held rows of rich mahogany wood bookshelves. Each shelf was full of books in all kinds of shapes and different color bindings. The sun shone in from the windows high above them on the second floor. Michael stood for a moment and just stared into the room. Here was a place of great knowledge. He was sure to find what he was looking for.

"Nafaria, look at this place. Just imagine what could be accomplished with such vast knowledge," whispered Michael.

Elias Wheaton saw them first. The boy and girl, standing on the threshold hand in hand. He looked up when he heard the door open, with curiosity. There were so few visitors that came to the antiquarian library at the end of the week.

His curiosity was quickly replaced with annoyance and he was about to shoo them out the door from which they entered. A library was a place of knowledge and learning. It was not a child's frivolous playground. Elias was about to say as much when he stopped. The boy stood entranced. He stared at the shelves with a sense of wonder in his eyes. This was no ordinary child who had come indoors to play. Here stood a young man, perhaps one of the Craft, who took the time to give proper respect to the pool of wisdom he found himself in. Elias smiled slightly. He felt a kindred bond with the boy already.

The little girl looked at Elias and saw him staring at them. Her eyes went wide and she tugged on the boy's arm.

Nafaria was looking at a large desk off to their right side where a man of considerable age sat looking at them. He said nothing, but stared over the tops of his wire rimmed spectacles. His straight white hair fell down to his shoulders and framed his face. He looked at them with brilliant blue eyes. Nafaria continued to stare at the old man, but Michael stood in the doorway, still looking at the massive bookshelves that reached from floor to ceiling.

"May I help you?" asked Elias. He waited patiently for Michael to acknowledge him. Nafaria looked at Michael and tugged on his arm once again.

Finally Michael looked down and Nafaria pointed at the old man at the desk. He walked over to the desk with Nafaria next to him.

"We are looking for specific information about the royal city," said Michael. He looked at the old man.

"What is it that you seek?" he asked.

"Is there anything written about a place called the Wheaton estate?" asked Michael.

The old man's face became a stone. "Is there any specific reason you ask?" he asked quietly.

"We are newcomers to Wildemere. My father is willing to see the land, if the king will allow it. We were told that the king ordered the estate closed and it has been vacant since," said Michael.

"It is true. What do you intend to do?" asked the man.

"If there is anything written about the place, perhaps it could help us understand why the king ordered it closed on the advice of the last Court Adviser," said Michael.

The old man looked at Michael carefully. The boy looked to be no more than thirteen years old; however he saw a steadiness in his eyes that most boys did not possess. He looked straight at the old man and waited for an answer. Elias took off his spectacles and rubbed his forehead. He looked carefully at them, as if seeing them for the first time. "I have not heard that name spoken aloud in over ten years," he said quietly. He looked again at Michael. "I am afraid there is no book that has been written about that strange tragedy. My name is Elias Wheaton. Joseph Wheaton was my son."

Michael looked at the man carefully. The old man stared back. He could see clearly there was no reason for him to lie about something of this nature. The sacred writings taught to trust until trust was proven not to be found. Michael took the man at his word. "Do you know what happened to him?" asked Michael. Elias Wheaton shook his head.

"When the king ordered the land sealed, I was not even allowed to retrieve anything of value. I cannot know for sure what happened without looking into his diary," replied Elias.

"You are of the Craft?" asked Michael. Elias nodded his head.

"Surely the Court Adviser would have made exception for you," replied Michael.

"The Court Adviser resigned his duty and left before I had the chance. I cannot imagine what he found that would make him leave in such haste," replied Elias.

"Who was the last Court Adviser?" asked Michael.

"His name was Malcom Stone. Few people are left anymore who can answer that question," said Elias.

Nafaria looked at Michael with a questioning glance. She could tell from the look on Michael's face that he did not wish this man to know they knew the last Court Adviser very well.

It was to Michael's credit that he did not betray his association with Malcom and Nathaniel. Nathaniel and he grew up together; he was Michael's closest friend though they no longer lived in Denholm Glen. How was it that he learned such news from a stranger?

"What was Joseph like?" asked Michael.

"He was very well studied, even from a very young age. He was at home with books and obsessed with reading. As he grew older, his interests moved toward more arcane knowledge. During the last two years of his life, he became more and more distant. His son Jacob would find me and tell me he was worried about his father. I thought it nothing more than worried tales from a little boy. How I wish I would have paid more attention then," said Elias.

"If my father is allowed on the premises, I will try to retrieve his diary for you. However, sometimes my father still regards me as a child. He may not allow me to go," said Michael. Elias smiled and shook his head.

"Do not be in a hurry to lose youthful innocence before its time. There is plenty of time for growing up. What is your name?" asked Elias.

"Michael Mauldon. This is my sister Nafaria," said Michael.

"I am Elias Wheaton. Come visit my library whenever you wish," replied Elias.

"Thank you, sir. Perhaps I will have news the next time you see me," replied Michael.

At that moment, the door opened and Thena walked into the library. "I must go," said Michael. He turned and left with Nafaria still holding his hand.

When they were outside, Thena looked at them. "Did you find what you were looking for?" she asked.

"Yes, I believe we did," replied Michael. He was still holding Nafaria's hand when he turned and headed back toward the inn, with Thena walking behind them.

***

Philip followed his father through the castle. Any other time he might have wondered at the richness of the things he saw about him: tapestries on the walls, the delicate craftsmanship of the furniture they passed. However, his mind was too concerned with the task that brought them before the king. The only question in his mind was why the king would listen so closely to the counsel of a man, without question? Who was such a man to hold sway over the king of Nereheim?

As if in answer to the question on Philip's mind, Jason stopped just outside the door to the royal throne room. Philip had noted that the hallway was filled with portraits of men. He was almost ready to ask Jason about them, when his father spoke. "I do not wish for you to be caught off guard with the king. In case he makes mention of Malcom Stone, I wish for you to know who he once was," said Jason.

Philip looked at the painting he stopped at. He saw a very majestic likeness of Malcom Stone. Why was it here?

"Father, why would there be a picture of Malcom here? Who are all these men?" asked Philip.

"They are portraits of Nereheim's royal Court Advisers. Malcom was the last," replied Jason. He turned toward the doors to the throne room and entered, forcing Philip to follow quickly, or be left behind.

This time, the king was alone, and looked just as formidable as he sat on his throne. "Lord Jason Mauldon," said the king in recognition to his visitor.

Jason bowed his head before the king. "Your majesty does me great honor in remembering my name," replied Jason.

"You left quite an impression upon the queen. She thinks perhaps I should have listened a little more closely to what you had to say," replied the king.

"I wish only to see justice served. If instances like Analia's death go unchecked, it could mean unnecessary persecution for those of the Craft," replied Jason. The king considered Jason's words more carefully than before.

"Perhaps you are right. Tell me, what advice you would give on the matter?" asked the king.

Jason thought for a moment. "I would send a party to Count Deveraux to get his accounting of the story. However, I would also talk to the village elders. Lord Reinard Sallen is one of those elders. He would give a clear and unbiased opinion of the situation," replied Jason.

The king nodded his head. "So it shall be done. I have entrusted the Counts with great power. It is time to check and see that it is used properly," replied king Rohn.

"Your majesty, this news is very welcoming, but I have come before you with a request to make," said Jason.

"What is your request?" asked Rohn.

"There is a certain piece of land that is vacant that I wish to see. If it is suitable for my family, I wish to purchase it from you," replied Jason. The king looked at Jason questioningly.

"Which piece of land?" asked Rohn.

"The Wheaton Estate," replied Jason.

"The Wheaton Estate was ordered sealed," replied Rohn.

"That is why I am here, your majesty. With your permission, I would like to investigate the estate," replied Jason.

The king was silent for a minute. "My Court Adviser implored me to order the estate closed. He said that what went on there would curse men if they knew the truth," he said quietly.

"I understand your reluctance in the matter. Malcom Stone does not utter rash words in haste. However, by following this advice, is it not possible that a curse has been left behind to those who knew Lord

Wheaton? Truth, however dark, must be revealed so that healing will begin," replied Jason.

"You know of Malcom Stone?" asked Rohn.

"He is a very dear friend. However, when he left Denholm Glen, I have no idea where he went," replied Jason. The king studied Jason carefully.

"Your thoughts are very reasonable, Lord Jason. I will allow you access to the land. I will give you the key to the estate. All I ask is that when you return it to me, you tell me what you found. Malcom refused to speak of it," replied the king.

"Yes, your majesty," replied Jason.

The king rose from his throne and walked to the back of the throne room. "If you will follow me, I will give you the key to the lock on the gate," said the king. Jason and Philip followed the king out of the door to the throne room.

***

Jason sat in a chair in the common room of the inn, waiting for Thena to return. He studied the iron key he held. It was no more than four inches in length, yet it felt heavy in his hand. With it, the weight of the world seemed to be carried. What would he find when he arrived at the estate? What darkness would be revealed that unnerved a man as steady as Malcom Stone? "Such an insignificant object to hold the answer to so many questions," said Jason quietly as he looked at the key in his palm.

Jason was roused from his thoughts as he heard his name being called. He looked in the direction of the sound and saw Thena, Michael, and Nafaria coming toward him. Jason smiled when he saw them.

"So, what did you see while you were out?" asked Jason.

"We went into the market and gathered some fresh fruit," said Thena. She noticed the key in his hand. "What is this?" she asked. She sat down on the hearth stone next to Jason.

"It is what I asked for. This key unlocks the gates of the Wheaton Estate," replied Jason.

Thena's eyes widened slightly. "The king is allowing you to look at the premises?" she asked. Jason nodded his head.

"If the place is not dangerous, we will talk about a fair transaction. His only request was that I let him know what I found," said Jason. He looked at the key again. "There was something else that was rather unusual," said Jason. Thena looked at him. He looked over at her and said, "The king remembered my name."

While his parents spoke, Michael wandered over to his father and sat in a chair next to him. "Father, may I come with you when you go to the estate?" asked Michael.

Jason looked at him carefully, and then shook his head. "I will take Philip with me. You must stay with your mother," replied Jason.

Before Michael could protest his father's decision, a voice spoke up behind them. "Father, I think it would be wise to take him with us," said Philip.

"Why is that?" asked Jason. He looked at his son, waiting for his answer.

"For years, Michael has been reading books on every arcane subject there is. Not only has he studied the sacred writings of the Craft, but he has read books on alchemy as well. We might find something important at the estate, but you and I might not understand its importance. Michael will be essential to us," replied Philip.

"I think Lord Wheaton was given over to the dark parts of the Craft, father. He became obsessed with power," replied Michael.

"What makes you say that?" asked Jason.

"I met his father, Elias Wheaton in his library. He said his grandson came to warn him that his father was acting strangely, but Elias did not think anything of it. A few days later, Lord Wheaton murdered his family," said Michael.

Jason nodded his head. "That fits with what I have heard also. Tomorrow, we will have the whole day ahead of us. Get some rest, you will need it," said Jason. He stood up from his seat.

"Where are you going father?" asked Philip.

"I want to see Joel Blackstone. We may have answers to his questions very soon," replied Jason. He rose from his seat and exited the inn.

***

Jason stopped in front of the blacksmith shop and watched a few minutes as the blacksmith inspected Joel's work. He held a dagger in his hand and turned it over; peering at it closely from many angles.

"This blade looks as magnificent as it feels, Joel. It is very sleek and delicate, yet the blade is sharp and even. The captain of the guard will be very pleased," said the blacksmith. He looked at his apprentice carefully. "It seems that no matter what metal or tool is put into your hands, your craftsmanship is fit for kings."

Joel smiled at the compliment. "There may be some truth to natural art. However, you have had great patience with me for the last ten years. You have taught me everything I know. I will never forget that," replied Joel.

Jason smiled as he regarded the blacksmith and his apprentice. Here, in the heart of the royal city, was a relationship as strong and alive as the one he was taken from. Malcom helped Jason grow in the Craft and realize his passion for the country he lived in. He now knew in his heart what he pledged so many years ago: he could never leave Nereheim. He looked down at his forearm. The pact seal that was concealed beneath his cloak was a reminder of his duty to stay, but this exchange he witnessed was a reminder as to why. He would never leave unless his soul left his body.

"Jason," said Joel as he looked up and saw him standing before them. Jason was roused from his thoughts.

"Good evening, Joel. I wonder if I could have a word with you," said Jason. Joel nodded his head.

"I shall be glad to," replied Joel. The blacksmith nodded to Jason and went about his work, leaving the two men to themselves.

"How is your horse?" asked Joel.

"The horse is very well. You did a superb job re-shoeing him," replied Jason.

"Your son did an excellent job helping me. There is a farrier in the making in him if you ask me," replied Joel.

Jason laughed. "If you could keep Philip out of the woods for more than three hours at a time, you might be right. His heart is in the woods. It would take a great change in the world or the right woman to make him stay at home," replied Jason.

"Perhaps both are coming," replied Joel.

"Perhaps," replied Jason. He continued to look at Joel. "When we spoke last, you said you wanted answers to what happened to Lord Wheaton. Are you prepared to go in search of them?" asked Jason.

"What do you mean?" asked Joel.

"I am here to offer you an opportunity to join me in finding those answers," replied Jason.

Joel raised an eyebrow. "How?" he asked.

"The king has granted me access to the Wheaton Estate. I am taking Philip and my other son Michael with me. However, I would feel more comfortable with one more adult along. Would you be willing to join us tomorrow morning?" asked Jason. "I would like to get there as soon as it is light."

Joel felt his heartbeat quicken. He was being offered a chance to clear questions that darkened his mind for so many years. He looked over at the blacksmith. "Do you mind if I go?" asked Joel.

The blacksmith shook his head. "I remember when that sad affair happened in Wildemere. I was just starting to add to my business as a blacksmith. I remember watching you and Jacob running around the market together. You were two boys who could find adventure around every corner; and your share of trouble too," replied the blacksmith with a smile. "Go find your answers."

Joel grabbed his cloak from the bench next to the fire. "I am going home for the evening. I will see you the day after tomorrow," replied Joel.

"We will have much to discuss, I am sure," replied the blacksmith.

Jason followed Joel out of the shop. "How did you persuade the king to grant you access to the land? So many have petitioned and have been denied," asked Joel.

"I guess I made an impression on him," replied Jason.

"Are you of the Craft?" asked Joel quietly.

Jason considered his answer. He found himself in the royal city because he wished to start again with his family. Should he answer Joel's question and confirm his identity as one of the Craft? He wished to be honest with this man. "Yes, I am. Does that trouble you?" asked Jason. Joel paused midstride. He never stopped to wonder if he should be worried about this stranger. He only knew he trusted him completely.

"No. I do not know what trouble has brought you to Wildemere, but I am glad to have met you," replied Joel. Jason put out his hand.

"I am glad to have met you as well," replied Jason. Joel shook his hand.

"Before we go any further, come to my home and meet my wife. Leanna may not understand if she finds that I was not at work tomorrow to help a stranger in the city and I did not tell her," said Joel. Jason laughed.

"You are a very wise man, Joel. I cannot say how many men I have seen in my lifetime that did not show such prudence and paid a great price for it," replied Jason. He followed Joel as they made their way through the market.

Joel led Jason through the market square into a row of neat, but close buildings. Each building was of either wood or stone, and at least three stories high. The lower levels consisted of shops, while the upper levels seemed to be housing. One stone building stood out in particular. It was a little smaller than the buildings that surrounded it, but it held a certain refinement. The sign "Antiquarian Manuscripts" hung neatly over the door. Jason pointed to the building.

"What is that building over there?" asked Jason. Joel followed Jason's hand. "That is a very specialized library. It is said to hold many rare and maybe even ancient writings," said Joel. "Elias Wheaton, Lord Wheaton's father, is the library's owner and curator. He has devoted his life to his collection."

"I have heard of him. Leave it to my son, Michael, to find the only library within walking distance of the inn," said Jason with a laugh.

"We turn here," said Joel. He pointed down a narrow road that left the main market area. Jason followed Joel as the street opened up and a row of cottages lined one side. He stopped at the first one and opened the door.

Inside, a young woman with light blond hair stood next to the fireplace, bent over a cooking pot. She looked up with a spoon in her hand. Her eyes brightened when she saw them.

"Welcome home!" she said with a smile. Her voice held a lighthearted note in it. She came toward them and embraced her husband warmly. Jason watched the exchange fondly.

"Leanna, this is Lord Jason Mauldon. He has recently come from Denholm Glen. He asked me to go with him tomorrow to inspect the Wheaton Estate," said Joel. Leanna looked carefully at Jason and held out her hand.

"It is nice to meet you, sir," said Leanna. She looked back at Joel. "The king has allowed this?" she asked.

"I was able to persuade him that it might be to his benefit. Though I have two capable sons who will be joining me, I asked Joel to come as well. I would feel better having another adult with me. One that happens to know the grounds as intimately as I am sure he does will be a great benefit," said Jason.

"What will your wife do while you are gone?" asked Leanna.

"I am sure she and my daughter will amuse themselves in the market while we are gone," replied Jason. Leanna smiled as she moved toward the fireplace. She picked up a spoon and stirred the contents of the pot.

"If you will introduce me to your wife, I will be happy to entertain them while you are away. If they do not mind helping me cook, we can all have a meal together when you return," said Leanna.

"That would be most welcome. Though the innkeeper is very friendly and hospitable, I am sure Thena would appreciate spending the day with a new friend," said Jason.

"Then it is settled, I will come with Joel tomorrow to meet your family," replied Leanna.

"It will be a most welcome pleasure," replied Jason. He looked at Joel. "I will be up very early tomorrow morning, so it does not matter what time you come by the inn. We will start off as early as possible."

"We will be there after sunrise," replied Joel as he shook Jason's hand. Jason turned and left the cottage.

The next morning, Joel and Leanna found Jason and his family in the common room of the inn. Nafaria had a sketchbook in hand, and was sketching a plant that was in front of her. Jason came up behind her and looked at the paper. "That is excellent work, little one," said Jason softly. Nafaria turned, and her face brightened.

"Thank you father," said Nafaria as she hugged Jason.

Jason returned her hug. He saw Joel and Leanna moving toward them. He turned to Thena. "I would like you to meet Joel and Leanna Blackstone," said Jason as he gestured to the couple moving toward them. Leanna stepped forward and put out her hand. "Perhaps you and your daughter would like to spend the day at our home?" asked Leanna. Thena smiled brightly and was touched by this young woman's warmth.

"That sounds lovely. Nafaria and I were wondering what we would do with ourselves today," replied Thena. Joel stepped toward the women.

"It is a privilege to meet you, my lady," said Joel as he also extended his hand. Thena smiled as she shook it.

"You have accorded a good reputation for yourself, Joel. I have never met anyone who was ever compared to Lord Bryant Saintclaire in anything," said Thena.

Joel looked at her with a puzzled expression. Thena went on. "The innkeeper mentioned that you do work as a farrier as well as blacksmith. He said that people consider you like 'the horse master from Illith'. That reputation is to be respected," replied Thena.

"Thank you, my lady," replied Joel.

"Are we ready father?" asked Philip. He and Michael came toward the two couples.

"Yes, we are ready. Joel, you have already met Philip. This is my other son, Michael," said Jason as he gestured toward Michael.

"Your father mentioned you have already had the opportunity to see Elias Wheaton's library," said Joel. Philip laughed.

"Michael can smell fresh or faded ink a hundred feet away," said Philip.

"It is an impressive place. I am looking forward to returning," said Michael, ignoring his brother's comment.

Jason took in the articles his sons had with them. Each wore cloaks and carried a length of rope. Philip also had a lantern in his hand.

"We will probably not need the lantern, Philip," said Jason.

"If we intend to make a thorough investigation, father, I am sure that will include the basement and cellars. It will come in handy then," replied Philip.

"Are you all quite ready for your adventure?" asked Thena. She moved toward Jason and kissed his cheek lightly. "Nafaria and I will go with Leanna. Be back by nightfall, or I shall worry," said Thena.

"I plan to be back long before nightfall," said Jason. He turned to go. Thena smiled and watched the four of them leave the inn.

"How far is the estate from here?" asked Jason.

"It is less than a mile, but it will not seem so. There will be large crowds the entire way," replied Joel.

"Then, we will walk," replied Jason.

They picked their way through the market as they went. Soon, the crowds thinned and walking became easier. Michael struggled to keep in stride with the others, but his mind raced ahead to what they might find at the manor.

The shadows grew a little longer, though the sun was still above the trees in the sky. They finally reached the locked gates of the Wheaton estate. Jason took the key from his pocket and put it into the lock. He worked it for a few moments, and then felt the lock turn as it made an audible click. The chain held in place by the lock fell into his hands. Carefully, he unwound the chain from the lock and threw it on the ground off to the side. The gate was bordered on either side by a high stone wall that stretched quite a distance in both directions. The stone looked to be quite old, but still solid.

"Does this wall border the entire estate?" asked Jason. He turned and looked at Joel, who nodded his head.

"Lord Wheaton owned land beyond the stone border as well. There is a back gate that leads into the woods beyond the stream," said Joel.

"There are woods?" asked Philip. His voice held a hopeful tone. Jason smiled as he looked at Joel.

"The woods are quite thick. Strangers have been known to lose their way in them before. It is a place of caution," said Joel. Philip smiled, clearly ignoring Joel's warning as he took a moment to ponder what he might find.

The four moved into the grounds as Jason pushed open the gate. The squeak of rusty hinges filled the air; protesting such movement after standing still for so many years. A burbling sound of water caught Michael's attention, and he moved in that direction. He saw a stone fountain, large enough to bathe in. He walked up to it and felt the water. It was cold to the touch and very clear.

Joel moved carefully toward the fountain. The stone statue was that of a wood nymph, carved with very delicate hands. Joel remembered Jacob telling him about the strange learned man his father knew who created the statue. A tear formed in the corner of his eyes as he reached out to touch the statue.

"The fountain still flows," whispered Joel. He put his hand into the cool water.

Jason looked at Joel with the pensive, caring look that Thena often said was so natural to him. He waited a moment, and then asked, "Is this fountain built on a spring?"

After a moment, Joel roused from his thoughts. "Yes. I remember asking Lord Wheaton how the fountain flowed. He said the water came up from the ground through the fountain," said Joel. Jason nodded his head.

"The king has no idea the wealth of this land. Lord Wheaton chose his property well," said Jason.

The wind moved through the trees. The rustling of the leaves reminded the four of them that the morning was getting on.

"Father, we should move into the house," said Michael. Jason nodded his head. The four moved up the path toward the house.

They walked inside, and found themselves in a vestibule outside the great room. From the tapestries that hung on the walls, and the remains of the carpeting, Jason could see this was once a majestic place. Rich mahogany furniture sat in the great room, covered with dust. All looked to be left exactly as it was when the family lived there.

"The king took Malcom at his word. He left everything and sealed the premises," said Jason quietly. "It is time to find out why."

"We need to find the library," replied Michael. He moved to go down the hallway, when Jason pulled on his arm and stopped him.

"Why do you think it necessary to start with the library?" asked Jason. Michael heard a smirk escape from his older brother, but Jason's gaze was steady, and serious.

"To find out the end result, you must go back to the beginning. That is a very basic lesson you have taught us, father. If we recover Lord Wheaton's diary, we will see what he was studying," said Michael. He looked at the floor. "I also promised Elias Wheaton I would try to recover it for him."

"Father, we need to see where the murders took place," said Philip. Jason looked from one to the other. He then looked at Joel.

"You see now why I wanted you to come along, Joel. Both my sons have raised valid arguments, though their paths lie in separate directions. However we must have a satisfactory report for the king. Michael, go with Joel and find the library. Meet us when you can. Is there a cellar in this house?" asked Jason. Joel nodded his head.

"You will find an entrance through the scullery, off the kitchen. The kitchen lies down this hallway," said Joel as he pointed in front of them. Jason and Philip set out in that direction.

Joel pointed up the stairs. "Lord Wheaton had a personal library upstairs," said Joel as he looked at Michael.

Michael followed Joel up the staircase and down the hallway. The thick rug that stretched down the entire hallway was still in excellent condition, masking their footsteps. Joel walked down the hallway looking straight ahead. He stopped in front of one of the rooms and pushed the door open. Michael looked inside the room. He saw a desk by the window, with books and papers on it. The covers on the bed were perfectly made, as if waiting for its master to turn in for the night.

There were other artifacts around the room that told Michael that perhaps this was Jacob's room. He looked at Joel, who stared into the empty room.

"Is this Jacob Wheaton's room?" asked Michael gently. Joel nodded his head.

"I cannot tell you how many hours of any given day I spent in this room with him," replied Joel in the same quiet tone. Michael looked up at Joel and laid a hand on his shoulder.

"We will find answers here before the day is over, Joel," said Michael. Joel nodded his head and continued down the corridor to the last room with Michael behind him.

Joel opened the door and they both looked inside. The room was much larger than the room they just looked into. Michael stepped into the room, his eyes fixed on the great oak bookcases that lined the far wall. They were giant monstrosities that stretched from floor to ceiling. On the top shelf of one of the bookcases, Michael saw a large book that looked to be bound in leather. He walked over to the case and stood underneath the book. Reaching up, his fingers barely reached the third shelf. The fourth shelf where the book rested was at least a foot above his head. Michael looked around the room. There was nothing that he could use as a step ladder. He grabbed the shelf and pulled himself up.

"Michael, what are you doing?" asked Joel.

"That book up there is very likely the one we are looking for. I need to get it down," said Michael. He continued to climb up the shelf.

"Michael, those bookcases are heavy. What if it falls down on you?" asked Joel. He moved closer to Michael, watching him carefully.

"Almost there," said Michael. He stretched out his hand and reached for the book.

At that moment, Michael felt the bookshelf begin to pitch forward. He grabbed the book from the shelf and threw it across the room, falling off the shelf and landing hard on the floor.

"Michael! Look out!" shouted Joel. Michael looked up and saw the shelf tilt forward and coming toward him fast. Joel reached out and quickly pulled him out of the way, as the bookshelf crashed to the floor with a loud thud. The shelf was followed by another bookshelf that lined another wall. It made an identical thud.

Michael scrambled to his feet. "Thank you Joel. You may have just saved my life," said Michael.

"Let us go find your father, now that you have what you are looking for," said Joel.

In the basement, Jason and Philip heard the hard thud the bookshelves created. "What was that?" asked Jason. He went to start back upstairs, but Philip caught his arm.

"Father, Joel is with Michael. They will be here soon. We need to keep looking through this basement. So far, we have found nothing," said Philip.

Jason ran his hands through his hair. "Perhaps we should look for a root cellar," said Jason. Philip continued to the far end of the basement, where he found a door. He opened it, and found a stone stairwell leading further down. Beyond Philip's lantern, he could see nothing in the dark.

"Father, I think I may have found something," said Philip. A moment later, Jason appeared behind him, and looked over his shoulder.

"We should follow the steps to the bottom," said Jason.

Philip carefully stepped down the staircase, illuminating the steps as he went. The steps wound in a circle as they descended. Mold growing on the stone made it difficult to keep their footing. They finally reached the bottom and found themselves standing on dry ground, instead of a stone floor. Philip looked back up the staircase.

"I counted sixty three steps," said Philip as he looked up. Jason looked forward, his eyes growing wide. When Philip saw the look on his face, he was puzzled. Jason continued to stare forward. Philip turned around and his eyes grew wide as well. He now saw what his father had been staring at.

Lying on the ground, were the bloated remains of Lord Wheaton and his family. Each of the bodies was sprawled out with the dried remains of their blood soaked into the ground around them. There was another body that was slumped against the wall. A complex sequence of figures was written on the wall above the body. "Father, what is that writing?" asked Philip, pointing to the wall.

Jason studied the wall for a moment, and then shook his head. "I do not recognize that writing. We need to see if your brother can decipher it," said Jason.

At that moment, Joel and Michael appeared at the top of the staircase. Joel was holding a makeshift torch in his hand. "Jason; did you and Philip find anything?" called Joel from the top of the staircase.

"Yes we did. Michael, I need your help down here. Be careful as you make your way down, the stairwell is slippery," said Jason. Joel and Michael started down the steps, carefully making their way to the ground floor.

"What was that loud thud we heard earlier?" asked Jason. He looked at Michael, who walked toward them, carrying a large book.

"Michael toppled the bookcases trying to reach the book he holds in his hand. He could have been crushed beneath it," said Joel. Jason could tell he was clearly agitated.

"However, I was not. Joel pulled me out of the way before the bookcase landed on me," said Michael.

"You might have been killed, Michael. Is that book so important it is worth your life?" said Joel. Michael looked at him.

"Greater men have died for less than the pursuit of knowledge," said Michael.

"Lesser men have died for greater," replied Jason. Michael did not miss the sharpness in his father's tone. He would have much to answer for later. Philip felt the uneasiness of the conversation and turned everyone's attention to the wall behind them.

"Michael, look at the markings on that wall over there. Can you read them?" asked Philip. He shined his light on the wall opposite them.

Michael walked toward the wall, carefully scrutinizing the figures.

"What are those symbols?" asked Joel.

"It is written in an ancient form of runes that alchemists still use," replied Michael.

"What does it say?" asked Jason.

"It is a confession," replied Michael.

"A confession?" asked Philip.

"Of a sort," said Michael. "It says: what does it profit a man to gain the world in forfeit of his soul?[7] For this is madness and folly under the sun."

"Lord Wheaton must have come to his senses after his black deed was accomplished," said Joel.

"Michael, is there anything else here that is dangerous enough to warrant this place be kept sealed?" asked Jason. Michael looked at the figures that were sprawled on the floor. He saw branches and flowers scattered amid them in certain areas. He walked over to the closest crop of flowers and looked at them carefully. He then shook his head.

"These belladonna flowers are long since dried. The rowan branches are also puzzling. However, I think whatever ritual Lord Wheaton tried to accomplish did not bear the result he was looking for. When he realized what he did, he must have written that message and turned his blade on himself. Perhaps a study of his diary will bring more answers," said Michael.

"I think it is safe to say we have our answer for the king," said Philip.

Joel looked at the remains on the floor. He shook his head. "This good family was destroyed; and we cannot answer what exactly for," he said.

"I think the answer lies in the message on the wall. Lord Wheaton was using the dark Craft to gain power, and he failed to do so. When he failed, he came to his senses and saw the crime he committed," said Michael.

Jason shuddered as he looked around the room. "Let us go back upstairs and return to the inn. Perhaps we will have a satisfactory answer for the king in the morning," said Jason. He started back up the stairs, the others following.

***

It was still very light outside when Jason stood at the door of their room at the inn. Michael sat at the desk in the corner. His back was to him, and he was bent over. There was no doubt in Jason's mind that

[7] Mark 8:36

Michael was pouring over Joseph Wheaton's diary looking for clues as to the tragedy they found the remains of. Though he needed to have a conversation with his son that would result in correction; Jason stood by the door watching Michael who was deep in concentration. This middle child was so different from his other children, yet he never failed to earn their respect for his diligence in study. Philip went so far as to say he was *essential* when they inspected the manor. Jason now understood that perhaps his oldest son knew his brother better than he did. He finally crossed the room, and pulled a chair next to the desk where Michael sat.

Michael looked over at his father and started. "Father, I did not hear you come in," said Michael.

"That is precisely the talk I need to have with you," said Jason. He wore his gentle smile, however Michael knew his father was here to correct him. He sat up and looked at him.

"Joel was visibly upset about how careless you were in retrieving that book. I cannot say I blame him. You put yourself at considerable risk, when you could have found another solution," said Jason.

"Yes father," replied Michael. "In my defense, I really thought the bookcase was much steadier. I did not think it would fall."

"That you tested its limits at all is what worries me," replied Jason. "We have seen this before. Such single-mindedness will destroy you one day if you are not careful. You get an idea into your head, and you do not stop to consider consequences. I need you to be wiser in the future. Do not take unnecessary chances again, please," said Jason. Michael saw a tear in the corner of his father's eye.

The single tear on his father's face affected Michael more than his father's correction. How many times in his life had he done reckless things in pursuit of a piece of knowledge he thought was necessary at the time? He would probably never know, but his father most likely did. He could not continue to add worry to his father's life by his rash decisions masked as pursuit of knowledge.

"I am sorry father. Sometimes I mistake my flippant choices as diligence in pursuit of truth. I never thought of the chances I take as dangerous," replied Michael. Jason laughed.

"Some of your decisions are about as dangerous as daring Dominic Cavanaugh to crush a Lily of the Valley with his bare hand. Your single-mindedness keeps you on task. However, you must be careful. Joel may not be around in the future to pull you out of the way of a falling bookcase," said Jason. A moment later he said, "Perhaps that is why you and Nathaniel have always got along as well as you have. Both of you have that same single-minded drive. Your interests and personalities, however, take you to separate conclusions. Not many people get along well with Nathaniel Stone," said Jason.

"I miss him," replied Michael quietly. "I always thought we would grow up together."

"I know. You may yet," replied Jason. He rose from his seat. "Have you found anything useful in that book?" asked Jason.

"There is a lot of information here I have never seen before. I am trying to remember everything I can about what we saw to come to a reasonable conclusion. I hope to have an answer for you later," said Michael.

"Be sure you get some rest tonight," said Jason, furrowing his brow.

"Yes father," replied Michael. Jason looked down at his son.

"We will be downstairs in the common room for a large part of the evening. Joel and Leanna are visiting to keep your mother company. If you need me, you may find me there," said Jason. He walked across the room.

"Yes father," replied Michael. He turned his attention back to the book. Jason turned and watched his son for a moment, then left the room.

***

The long shadows on the walls of the inn darkened as Michael continued through the mysterious book before him. The room was considerably darker than it was when his father came to speak to him. A little while after, Nafaria presented him with a bowl of stew, a chunk of bread, and a flask of water. She wrapped her arms around his neck and begged him to eat every bite. "You need nourishment to keep your mind steady," she whispered in his ear before she left.

Now the bowl was empty, the bread gone, and the flask was a third full. He looked over at a box sitting next to him. He put a candle in the candlestick sitting on the table, and reached for the box. It was a simple wooden box with a hinge holding the lid in place. He opened the lid and looked at the sulfur sticks. His mind went back to a day a couple summers before he learned to master a horse, when he and Lillia were lost in the woods together.

"Are you sure we are going the right way?" asked Lillia.

"I am sure this is the direction I saw Philip go. He brought home the sweetest blackberries from a grove not far from our manor. It has to be this way," said Michael with a confidence he no longer felt.

"Well, if it is here, we may never find it. I am getting hungry. I did not bring food in my satchel," replied Lillia.

"What do you suggest?" asked Michael sharply. He was annoyed that he could lose direction so easily. Lillia looked at him, with compassion in her eyes. She had seen Michael's sharpness before. It only showed itself when he lost his confidence. She smiled her gentle smile.

"Rabbits seem to be plentiful. We could catch one for lunch," said Lillia.

"How would we do that?" asked Michael. Lillia laughed.

"You and your brother are nothing alike," she replied.

Lillia opened her satchel and pulled out a length of string and a small knife. She went over to a tree and cut a few green branches. A few minutes after she set up a snare, Lillia was rewarded with a large rabbit. They wandered down to the creek where she cleaned the animal and put the carcass on a sturdy stick. She looked at Michael with a triumphant smile. He stared at her. "Where did you learn to do that?" asked Michael quietly.

"I watch the workers who work the fields," said Lillia. "They show me things."

"Now all we need is a fire," said Michael doubtfully.

"That is easy. Would you hold this please?" asked Lillia, handing Michael the animal on the stick. Michael furrowed his brow as he took the animal from her hand. She opened her satchel again and produced a small wooden box.

"What is that?" asked Michael.

"This represents an heirloom that has been in my family for generations. My father taught me how to make it; as well as what is inside," said Lillia.

She began picking up twigs from the ground and making a pile. Michael did as well, and soon there was a small, dense pile of twigs on the ground. She opened the box and took out a piece of flint and a thick stick that resembled a pine needle. He looked at the stick. His attention was caught on the yellow substance at one end of it.

"Is that sulfur?" asked Michael.

"Yes," replied Lillia, as she struck the stick to the flint. A small flame burst from the stick. She put it into the pile of twigs. The twigs ignited immediately. Lillia smiled. "Success on the first try is not often achieved. YAHWEH must be smiling on us," said Lillia. She took the stick from Michael and held it over the fire.

Michael sat in amazement. "How did you do that?" he asked. She looked at him and smiled.

"I will show you," she said simply.

Lillia's sweet smile from that day hung in Michael's mind along with her blue eyes. He blinked to fight tears and pulled out the piece of flint, and one of the sulfur sticks from the box. As he lit the stick and ignited the candle, a tear dropped, as he thought of the knowledge an alchemist's daughter gave him. He wiped his eyes and returned to the book by the light of the simple twisted candle in front of him.

Twilight gave way to darkness and stars popped into being as miniature pinpricks of light through a black canvas. Michael was unaware of the amazing display of stars and planets going on above him, outside the window. He sat, his eyes transfixed on the sight before him.

Joseph Wheaton's diary was as meticulous in style and layout as it was fascinating to read for the contents it held. The hand which penned such dark material was skilled and artful. Michael fell under the spell of such beautiful handwriting.

He felt as though he were reading for hours, but when he looked out the window and saw the moon begin to rise, he knew it was not as late as it seemed. The rest of the family was likely sitting in the common room of the inn. No doubt they were giving him the quiet time he needed to concentrate.

He continued to peruse the book, and noted the macabre symbols as he proceeded. As he came toward the middle of the diary, Michael felt his heart beat faster. Joseph Wheaton was drawn toward the darker aspects of the Craft, but it seemed to Michael, as he grew older, his thirst for it became relentless. The enchantments and notations he found in the middle of the book made him wary of going further. He took a deep breath and turned the page. Michael continued to scan the contents of the pages until he reached the back of the book.

At the top of the final page in the book was written 12/21. The page contained a summons and a diagram with a list of items that Michael thought he remembered seeing in the crypt of the estate. He remembered pools of wax that were found in a diamond shape on the dirt floor. An athame lay next to a body where he remembered the inscription on the wall to be. There were bunches of dried rowan branches and dried belladonna flowers.

Michael's heart continued to race as he read through the list of items written on the page and the incantation that followed. Then at the bottom of the page was written one word: OBERMAN. Michael quickly got up from his seat and headed out of the room.

Downstairs, Jason sat with Joel, Thena and Leanna and listened to Joel's life in Wildemere. His attention was haphazard as it was split between his new friend, and concern for his son. Though Michael was capable as any adult to handle the most arcane knowledge of the Craft, he was still his thirteen year old son. Jason already lamented the fact that all his children witnessed the execution of an innocent friend. Now, he was being relied upon to decipher a book that could potentially turn his heart to darkness.

As he continued to think about Michael, his attention became less. Finally, he heard Joel's sharp tone.

"Jason," he said. Jason shook himself from his thoughts.

"I believe Michael has something for us," said Joel. He pointed to Michael who was standing behind them.

Jason turned to see Michael. His eyes were wide, and though they held fear, there was also a grimness that made Jason wary.

"Father, I believe I have found something," said Michael quietly. He turned to leave, when Jason and Philip got up from their seats.

"Joel, I want to thank you for visiting with us this evening. I am afraid I must go," said Jason. Joel was about to object when Michael turned around.

"Father, Jacob Wheaton was Joel's friend. He has waited a very long time to hear a sound reasoning for what happened to him. If he wishes to hear what may have happened, he should be allowed to," said Michael. He then looked at Joel with a haunting gaze. "However, I must warn you that what you hear may sound like madness to you."

"I wish to know what happened," replied Joel quietly. Michael nodded his head and turned to go upstairs.

Leanna and Thena watched them go. "My hope is that this explanation will bring healing and peace," said Leanna. Thena nodded her head.

"My fear is that it may not," replied Thena.

Philip shut the door behind them when they were upstairs. Michael went over to the desk and picked up a piece of paper.

"When we returned, I made careful notes of everything I saw and how the crypt was laid out. I wrote down carefully where the bodies lay, and how they were displayed. The pools of wax we saw were no doubt candles that burned out, and they were positioned carefully. Remember, we saw rowan branches and belladonna flowers laid around the room in various places."

Michael put down the paper and picked up the book. He brought it to his father. Jason took the book. "This incantation is to summon the god of blood. At the top of the page was 12/21. That is the winter solstice, father, and the longest night of the year. Joseph had a notation written at the bottom about a man who had tried this summons. Have you ever heard of a man named Oberman?" asked Michael.

"Only as a legend," said Jason quietly. "It is said that Oberman traveled to Herron, and took the sacred bell to summon the spirits at his will. I have never heard if he summoned the god of blood."

"So Joseph killed his family to summon a demon?" asked Joel. His eyes held a horrified gaze. Michael nodded.

"Not just a demon. The god of blood is much more powerful; and demands blood. To show him sincerity, you must sacrifice that which is dear to you. However, just because you do, it does not guarantee he will bestow his power upon you. Lord Wheaton went through the ritual, followed all the steps, but in the end, the god of blood did not come. Therefore, he wrote his confession on the wall, and killed himself. That is what I believe happened," said Michael.

"Why would Malcom give order to seal the manor, instead of telling the king what happened?" asked Philip. "He must have come to the same conclusion you did, Michael."

"Malcom never looked through the diary," said Michael. "He may not have known."

"They say the last Court Adviser was in grief over the death of his wife. Perhaps he chose to leave," said Joel.

"Whatever Malcom's decision, it is too late to second guess it now. Tomorrow, we will go to the king, present our finding to him, and I will restate my offer to buy the land. I see no threat to our well-being there," said Jason. Michael nodded.

"Maybe it will set the king at ease to know what happened," said Michael.

The four of them sat in the room, quietly considering Lord Wheaton's fate. The longer they sat, the more apparent it became that none of them was reassured by the truth. Michael left the room.

Jason found him an hour later, sitting on the roof of the inn. He looked up at the stars. The moon cast its full glow, lighting the rooftop. Jason sat down next to his son.

"I am sorry it had to be you to sift through such darkness to help shed light on this mystery. I took some time to look through the diary. Joseph Wheaton must have been a brilliant man," said Jason.

"Yes father," replied Michael absently.

"It was never my intention for any of you to know the darkness of men's hearts. I never wanted to you to know the extent of the evil in this world. I only wanted love and peace for you. The same blessing I have known," said Jason.

Michael continued to stare into the night. "Admirable as that may be, father; evil is in this world and mine is the generation that will have to stand against it. I wish to be prepared," said Michael.

"Then continue your quest for knowledge, but with caution," replied Jason.

"Thank you, father," replied Michael. Both father and son continued to stare up at the sky.

***

The next morning, Jason led the way into the throne room. Michael, Philip and Joel followed, feeling awed by the presence of their sovereign. Michael watched as his father approached the king with confidence, but he also noticed his father was careful to show great respect as well. He stood before the king and bowed his head.

"Lord Jason; I assume from your presence, you have completed your inspection of the estate," said the king.

"Yes, your majesty," replied Jason.

"What did you find?" asked king Rohn.

Jason turned and looked at Michael. "I will leave my son, Michael, to tell you," replied Jason. Michael took a step forward and stood next to his father. He bowed his head to the king.

"Your majesty, no one will ever know what was in Joseph Wheaton's heart at the time of this great tragedy. However, we may conclude that he committed this atrocity against his family in his pursuit of great power. There is nothing left to suggest that the place is dangerous. I am quite sure, however, that once the truth is revealed; Joseph Wheaton's life and his demise will serve as a cautionary tale to both those within the Craft and without," replied Michael.

"Why would my Court Adviser, a man I so firmly respected and trusted, give me advice to seal the estate?" asked the king.

Michael shook his head. "I cannot speak for the last Court Adviser. I cannot pretend to know his motives. Perhaps he did not intend for you to follow his advice so faithfully. The estate is good land, and the people of Wildemere need to begin healing their wounded hearts," replied Michael. He thought of Joel and Elias as he said this.

The king nodded in agreement. "Very well, you have completed what you set out to do," said the king. He looked at the guards. "See to it, these men are entertained. I wish to speak to Lord Jason privately," said the king. He rose from his throne and Jason took a step to follow him. He turned and faced the others. "While I am with the king, why not go to the stable and check on the horses?" asked Jason.

"Why not?" replied Joel. They turned and followed the guards, as Jason followed after the king.

The king led Jason out on the terrace and down the steps to a beautiful rose garden. The queen sat at a table in the midst of the garden; sipping from a cup. She smiled when she saw them approach.

"Lord Jason, it is good to see you again," said the queen. Jason bowed his head to her.

"It is good to see you as well, your majesty," replied Jason.

The king turned and looked at Jason. "I am prepared to give you the Wheaton Estate for the help you have given me in this matter," replied the king.

Jason shook his head. "The sacred writings tell us to owe no man a debt except that of love.[8] I will not take such a valuable piece of land and have it cost me nothing[9]," replied Jason.

The king nodded in response. "I expected this. I will trust your judgment, Lord Jason. Pay me what you believe is a fair price. Your family will be free to move onto the property today," replied the king.

"Thank you, your majesty," replied Jason as he bowed to the king.

"Lord Jason, there is another matter I wish to discuss with you," replied the king. Jason looked at him intently, so the king continued.

---

[8] Romans 13:8
[9] 2 Samuel 24:24

"It has been some years since I have been impressed by any of the Craft. Malcom Stone left behind very large shoes to fill. You may have come from the country, but your tact and delicacy in your handling this situation with the Wheaton Estate has left me believing that perhaps you should be the next Court Adviser of Nereheim," said the king.

Jason could not hide the shock he knew must be written on his face. He could see from the king's expression that he was quite serious. He took a moment to find the words he wished to convey. He bowed his head once more.

"Your majesty, this offer of yours is quite generous. It was the very last thing I expected when I rose from sleep this morning. However, I must decline. I have moved my family here for a fresh start. You, Joel, Elias Wheaton and Joel's wife are the only people here who know we are of the Craft. I wish to begin again here, to build a safe future for my family. However; if you wish, I am not averse to giving counsel to a friend," said Jason.

King Rohn smiled and came close to Jason. He rested an arm on his shoulder. "In time, perhaps you will change your mind. For the time being, I am content to call on you as I have need. You must promise me to do the same," replied Rohn.

"Yes, your majesty, I will promise to do so," replied Jason.

***

The bell on the door of the Antiquarian Manuscripts building sounded. Elias came out of one of the passageways created by the tall shelves in the library. He was holding a book he was reading from. He saw Michael standing in the vestibule with a large book in his hand. Once again, Michael stood still, looking around the room.

Elias smiled. He stood quietly, allowing Michael his moment of wonder; however long or short it might be. Finally, Michael roused himself and noticed Elias standing off to the side by one of the tall bookcases. He nodded his head.

"I was able to find Joseph's diary," said Michael. He stepped forward and put the book he was holding on the desk in the vestibule.

Elias stood still for a moment, and then closed the book in his hands. He quickly walked over to the desk and put down his book. He ran his fingers over the cover of the diary.

"Were you able to find what happened from it?" asked Elias quietly. He looked at Michael over the top of his spectacles.

Michael nodded. "Joseph was growing in the dark aspects of the Craft as he grew older. The last entry leads me to conclude he sought to summon the god of blood," replied Michael.

"The god of blood?" gasped Elias. He quickly turned to the last entry in the book. He noted the date; 12/21, and perused the contents of the page. His eyes widened when he saw the last word on the page: OBERMAN.

"It is obvious from the result and Joseph's last words written on the crypt room of his estate that he failed," said Michael. "It is a pity he grew into the darkness of the Craft. Anyone can see from his entries that he was a brilliant man."

Elias closed his eyes to stop tears that formed from dropping to his cheek. He turned the pages backward to look through the book. "Thank you, Michael, for bringing this to me," said Elias.

He looked through the intricate incantations and the neat uniform handwriting of his son's work. He sighed and closed the book. "I have thought often of what I would do if I ever had the chance to see this book. If I could read it for myself and see what went wrong. However, that was a long time ago. Now, I am an old man and the knowledge that can be gleaned from it is of no use to me. I wish you to keep it, Michael. For perhaps the time may come when you will need to see into the heart of darkness to find the light."

Michael felt as though he were presented with the weight of the world. He took the book from Elias. "Thank you for your trust in me. Perhaps the time is coming when we shall need the darkness to find the light," said Michael. He bowed his head slightly, and left the library.

Michael wandered back through the crowded streets to the inn. He did not find his parents there, so he went to their new home, the Wheaton estate. As he walked through the gate, he found his mother and father walking around outside the house, with Nafaria sitting at the fountain. He smiled when he saw her. He knew this place would remind her of what they left behind in Denholm Glen. Perhaps it would help her adjust. He walked toward her.

"Michael, where have you been?" asked Nafaria when she saw him.

"I needed to return this book to Elias Wheaton. However, he told me to keep it. I think in the end, it was enough for him to know what happened to his family," replied Michael. "Where is Philip?" he asked.

Nafaria smiled and looked toward the gate. Michael saw the woods beyond. "He has found his new home as well," she said.

"I see you managed to find us," replied Jason.

"The innkeeper gave me your message," replied Michael. Jason looked at the book in Michael's hands.

"I thought the idea was to give that back to Elias Wheaton," said Jason.

"I thought so too, father. After looking at it, he told me to keep it. He said it might come in handy someday," replied Michael. Jason furrowed his brow, and then nodded his head.

"Perhaps he is right. I have been thinking about what you told me. I still think it is very much like playing with a forest fire, but if you think you can handle yourself with this responsibility, I see no reason for you not to keep it," said Jason. He took a step closer to his son. "You must let me know when you feel anything change as you pursue your endeavor. I do not wish to lose you the way Elias Wheaton lost his son," replied Jason. Michael came closer to his father and put his arm around him.

"I promise to talk with you about it, father. I do not wish to start down a wrong path either. I just feel that the reason I was given my abilities for study is to put them to use to protect whoever I can," replied Michael.

"A most noble cause," replied Jason. Michael stepped away from his father and headed toward the house.

"I think I will take a walk in the woods," replied Michael.

"Remember what Joel said. The woods are different, do not get yourself lost," replied Jason.

"I will not be going so far as to cause worry," replied Michael. He made his way into the house to put away his book.

* * *

The late afternoon sun shone through the trees. Michael made his way through the woods to the stream that ran there. He found a shallow spot at the water's edge and knelt beside it. The water was so clear that the smallest pebbles could be seen in the sand at the bottom.

He pulled a simple necklace of black cord from beneath his shirt. The necklace had one decoration: a black stone polished to a high sheen. It hung on the cord from the hole in the center of the stone. He recalled the day he was given this most valuable treasure.

He was in Denholm Glen, walking through the woods with Lillia. They were returning from an afternoon of gathering berries and wild mushrooms. He had shown her each of the mushrooms that they found in the woods, and how to tell the poisonous ones from the edible. She brought along her sketchbook and very steadily drew each mushroom with its name and characteristics written below it.

As they walked, she pulled out a parcel of cloth and handed it to him.

"What is this?" asked Michael.

"Something I found when my father was trading with one of the traveling merchants in the market this week. It reminded me of you," replied Lillia.

Michael opened the parcel and picked up the necklace by the black stone. "It is a simple little thing, but I thought it would help you remember me," said Lillia.

He continued to look intently at the polished stone. "It is not as simple as you might think. This stone is obsidian," replied Michael. He looked up at Lillia. "Thank you," he said.

"It is a way to say thank you for being such a good friend to me," replied Lillia.

"There is no way I could ever forget you," whispered Michael as he sat alone by the water. He kissed the stone and closed his eyes. "Let the object be seen," he said as he passed his hand over the surface of the water.

Lillia's reflection appeared on the water's surface. She was sitting under a tree in her garden. Her sketchbook was in her hands, but she was not looking at it. Tears were streaming down her face.

"Lillia," whispered Michael. He reached out his hand toward her face.

"Michael." Michael's hand fell into the water with a splash and his shoulders tensed.

"Go away, Philip," said Michael quietly.

Philip sat beside his brother. "No. You need to talk about how you feel," replied Philip.

Michael looked over at his brother. He saw the same sadness in his eyes Michael knew was in his own. He let out a sigh. "It hurts too much; I miss her so," whispered Michael.

Philip put down his bow and reached for his brother. Michael felt tears roll down his cheeks as Philip said, "I knew you must not be doing well. Though you were careful, I saw you with Lillia in the woods more often than you think."

After a few moments of quiet sobbing, Michael finally let go of his brother, and wiped his eyes. He took a deep breath and composed himself. "Father must never know. I do not wish to be a disappointment by appearing weak."

"You are no disappointment, however you may feel. This time is hard for both of us, but it will pass," replied Philip.

"I am not so sure," whispered Michael.

***

The sunlight peeked through the sheer curtains Thena hung in Philip's room. He turned over in his bed and stared at the bright white line on the floor. His breathing was soft and listless. He felt like that breath, adrift like a hollow piece of driftwood on a quiet sea.

His father had given him and Michael three days to adjust to their new home. They had the time to go and explore the country, wander into the city, or get to know their new manor. Today was the morning of the fourth day. Studies were expected to resume as before.

Philip focused on his bow, cloak and hunting boots sitting in the corner at the other end of the room. A tear formed in his eye and softly plopped onto the bed. It was followed soon after by another.

The hunting clothes brought his mind back to Alana and he wondered what she was doing at the very same moment he lay in bed. Did she miss him as much as he missed her? Did she even know that he spent his last three days in this new city, the royal city of Wildemere, thinking of her? He never even had a chance to write a letter or say goodbye in person. A few more tears began to follow.

Nafaria was the lucky one. Before Reinard left them, he handed her a note. Philip knew without even asking her that Nathaniel was its author. She skipped brightly around the manor and out in the garden or scampered through the woods as if she had not a care in the world. While he went out of his mind in his homesickness and for Alana's company, she was content.

Philip knew Michael was going through the same thing he was, only with a different girl altogether. Lord Reinard's daughter, Lillia, was as quiet and reserved as Michael was. They held everything in common; they both engrossed themselves in their studies, they both found plants and roots fascinating; they both took to the quiet of the country. There was only one thing they did not share. Lillia was not of the Craft. She could never be considered for his wife, but he never let that stop him from teaching her everything about the Craft that he could. They were careful and on friendly terms in public, but wary of showing too much affection for each other. However much they hid their feelings for each other, Philip was sure their father knew how Michael felt about Lillia. Just as he knew about Alana and Nadia before Philip admitted how he felt about each one. Jason was an excellent father. Excellent fathers knew when their sons were in love.

A soft knock on the door brought Philip back to the morning. He brushed his eyes as his father opened the door. "You are still in bed?" asked Jason.

"Yes father," replied Philip.

"We are to begin studies today," said Jason gently. Philip sat up.

"I am not ready father," said Philip. His eyes wandered to his bow. "I have other things on my mind."

"I see," said Jason. He leaned against the window sill. His eyes followed Philip's gaze to the hunting gear in the corner of the room. "Do you wish to talk about it?" asked Jason. Philip shook his head.

"No. I wish to forget. I do not want a single memory in my head of a time I can never have again," replied Philip.

Jason came near Philip and sat down on the bed next to him. "I never even had a chance to say goodbye," whispered Philip.

"I know. For that, I am truly sorry. Lord Reinard urged me to be gone by first light. There was no time," replied Jason.

"Nathaniel had time. Do you suppose he knew what would happen?" asked Philip. Jason shook his head.

"I suspect he wrote that letter the moment he and Malcom arrived home after the execution. He has always had deep concern for Nafaria," said Jason.

"She is the lucky one. To have something so precious to hold on to," replied Philip. Jason studied his oldest son. The vacant look behind puffy eyes told him that Philip was right. He was not ready for studies to begin.

"Perhaps today would be an excellent day for visiting the wild. Why not take your bow and see what kind of creatures lay in wait in the woods around Wildemere?" asked Jason.

Philip smiled slightly. "I was just thinking the same thing father," said Philip. He put his arms around Jason and hugged him tight.

"I love you my son," whispered Jason.

"I love you too father," replied Philip.

After a moment, Jason left the room, and Philip dressed for a day in the woods.

Jason wandered down the hall and gently knocked on Michael's door. There was no answer. He opened the door to find Michael sitting at his desk, with a quill in hand. An inkpot sat opened on the table off to his right. Sheets of paper surrounded him on the floor with scribbles and lines all over them. He looked as if he were attempting to draw something, and becoming more frustrated with every minute. He ran his fingers through his blond hair. He finally threw down the quill and crumpled the piece of paper that was in front of him. "I cannot do it!" he exclaimed.

"Do what?" asked Jason. Michael turned sharply to him. His eyes were wide and frantic. Whatever his second son was attempting to do, it possessed him. He looked back down at the paper in his hands.

"Nothing father," said Michael quietly. Jason smiled at his son's attempt to hide what was on his mind. Michael was as transparent as Jason was when he was consumed with something. That trait made it easy for Thena to sit patiently and know when she had to draw out a problem on his mind. He walked over to the desk and sat down on it.

"Michael, anyone can see by this mess that you are working at something. I very much doubt it is to create work for our housekeeper," said Jason gently. A slight smile crept over his face before he could suppress it.

Michael looked at his father and sighed. "I have been up all night trying to draw," said Michael.

"Why is that?" asked Jason.

"So I do not forget," whispered Michael.

"Forget what?" asked Jason.

"What our life was like before we moved here. Nafaria is the lucky one. She can draw anything with her eyes closed and her drawing looks just as real as the thing itself. I wish I could too," whispered Michael. A tear formed in his eyes before he could will it back.

Jason reached out and picked up a book from Michael's desktop. He flipped through pages, realizing it was a volume of his diary. Each page held meticulous detail about its subject, written in the most beautiful script. It had been a long time since Jason had looked at his son's books. He sat on the desk with the book in hand, almost in awe of his son's talent for writing and his beautiful penmanship.

"You cannot draw, perhaps, but your talent for capturing words to paper is more exquisite than a rare jewel. I never realized what a gift for writing you have been given. Are all your diary entries this detailed?" asked Jason.

Michael shrugged his shoulders and handed him another book. "This volume contains all the elixirs you have shown us," said Michael. Jason looked through the elixirs one at a time. Each one was written with detailed attention. Every step was carefully laid out for each elixir. Michael left nothing to chance. He laid the book back on the desk.

"You draw with words, Michael. Paint the picture by describing every detail. You will never forget then," said Jason.

Michael sat back in his chair and stared at his father. "I never thought of it that way, father. I just assumed everyone writes this way," said Michael. Jason laughed.

"No, they do not," replied Jason. He looked carefully at his son. "Why are you afraid you will forget?" asked Jason.

Michael looked at the floor. "Memories are all I have left now; and memories fade," said Michael quietly.

Jason nodded his head. "Some memories do fade. However, some memories are so vivid that they follow you through life like a bosom companion that never forsakes you. These are the memories that are so precious," said Jason.

"Do you have any memories like that father?" asked Michael. Jason heard the hopeful tone in his son's voice.

"I remember the day I met your mother for the first time. The day was sunny, and the light caught the colors in her hair. She was breathtaking," replied Jason quietly. He looked over at Michael. "I also remember when each of you was born. I am more proud of those moments than of any other accomplishment in my life."

Michael's eyes watered and he sprang out of his chair into his father's arms. Tears rolled down his cheeks as he embraced Jason. "I love you father," whispered Michael.

"I love you, my son," said Jason quietly for the second time that morning. After a moment of holding his middle child, Jason spoke. "Why not get some sleep and perhaps work on one of those memories you wish not to forget later?"

"What about our studies father?" asked Michael. There was genuine concern in his voice.

"We will begin tomorrow. Get some rest," replied Jason. He stood and left the room.

Jason closed the door to Michael's room and continued down the hall. He thought about both his sons, and how though very different, they both envied Nafaria for different things. Philip wished to forget. Michael was trying desperately to remember. They were like polar opposites in all things.

He went into the kitchen and found Thena sitting at the table with a cup of tea in hand. She was still savoring the quiet of the morning, just as she was savoring each drop of her tea. She looked up when she saw Jason approach her.

"Where are the boys?" asked Thena.

"They are not ready for studies yet. I am giving them one more day," replied Jason. "How about if we disappear together and watch the day go by from our bedroom window?" asked Jason. A mischievous smile crept across his lips. Thena sighed and shook her head.

"That is a very tempting offer. However, Nafaria is in excellent spirits this morning. She is already out in the woods. I saw her basket and cloak were missing from her room. She must be out gathering herbs and berries this morning," said Thena.

"Should she be out in the woods by herself?" asked Jason. He remembered what Joel said about the woods when they first came to inspect the land.

"She has been out every day gathering berries and herb sprigs. Yesterday I noticed a little patch of soil was turned up and worked. It was over by the fountain. I think she is planning another herb garden," said Thena.

"At least we have one child settling in well," replied Jason. Thena smiled at him. She rose from her seat and kissed him gently. She put the cup on the table and left the kitchen, leaving Jason to his own thoughts.

Nafaria walked through the woods as the sun grew brighter. The dew on the leaves was still heavy, and a light fog drifted through the trees. If the sun persisted, it would soon burn out. She stopped a moment to breathe in the fresh clean air. She closed her eyes and breathed deeply. She sighed and opened her eyes once again. She thought of Nathaniel and what he might be doing that very moment. Nafaria knew that he too was an early riser. Nathaniel Stone was not one to waste even a moment of the precious time YAHWEH granted him. Once again, a sigh escaped her lips.

"Nathaniel how I miss you," she whispered. She wandered a little farther into the woods with a basket in her hands. She missed the little herb garden she tended in Denholm Glen. Nathaniel helped her build it, and showed her how to care for it. She spent time the day before turning up a patch of ground near the fountain, her favorite thing about the new manor. Now she was scrutinizing the woods for the herbs she would fill her garden with. She stopped as she found a little patch of daisies in a cluster. She knelt down and looked at the leaves and smiled. It was wild Roman Chamomile. She grabbed a very small shovel from the basket. "Roman Chamomile will be the perfect thing to start my new garden with," said Nafaria aloud. She dug into the ground around a few of the plants and lifted them into the basket.

Thirty minutes later, Nafaria emerged from the woods with Roman Chamomile plants, lemon balm, and a berry plant she did not recognize. She would put it into the garden along with the other two if her mother could tell her what it was. She smiled as she thought about her new project.

It was late morning when Thena found Nafaria at the window seat in her bedroom. Her room was a little smaller than the one she had at the old manor in Denholm Glen, but she never needed much room. The sunlight bathed her in its warm light as it flooded through the window. Thena smiled as she approached her daughter, holding three books. "You have been very hard to find, little one. I have been looking all over for you," said Thena.

"I was out in the woods early. I found some Roman Chamomile, lemon balm, and this," said Nafaria. She handed Thena a branch with three bright red berries on it. "I know it is not elderberry, but I do not recognize it."

"It is called Hawthorn. It is a very good berry for those with a sick heart. It was not very common in Denholm Glen. You found this here?" asked Thena.

"Yes, growing in the woods," replied Nafaria.

"That is very observant of you. You will need to record this, so you do not forget it," said Thena.

"Record it?" asked Nafaria.

"Yes, write down the information that you know about it, in your diary," said Thena.

Thena put the books down in front of Nafaria. One was a plain brown leather book with the letter "T" stitched into it with black thread. The leather was old and worn. Nafaria felt the cracks in the leather as she opened the book. The pages inside were wrinkled and some had dark stains on them.

The second book Nafaria reached for was another brown leather book with no markings on the cover. She opened it and found that all the pages were blank and clean.

The third book had a black leather cover and was the thickest. When Nafaria opened it, she found writing she had never seen before. "What writing is this?" asked Nafaria.

"It is an ancient writing. They are called runes. This book is a holy book. It is from the God who gave us our power. The God the ancients referred to as YAHWEH," said Thena.

"This God gave us power?" asked Nafaria.

"Yes. Many generations ago, a descendant of your father called Marcus set himself apart to worship the God of the Hebrews. When dark times came, there were many wars. Many people were killed, and others fled. It was at this time that YAHWEH blessed Marcus and gave him the power, knowledge and wisdom to help others. YAHWEH gave this power to others as well. These people became known as those of the Craft. There were some of the Craft who turned to the black arts and worship the god of blood and murder. YAHWEH is the greatest God, the creator of everything. This book will help guide you in wisdom and knowledge as you learn about the Craft. You must read from it every day," said Thena.

"How will I learn to read it?" asked Nafaria.

'I will teach you to read it. Your father will teach you the more intricate parts of the Craft. We will continue your training in plants and I will teach you more about healing, but your knowledge there is quite advanced for one your age," said Thena.

Thena took the Wisdom book and put it in Nafaria's lap. She opened to the first page. Taking Nafaria's finger, she pointed to the symbols as she read them. "In the beginning, God created the heavens and the earth.[10] That is the basis of everything we believe. The master creator made all that you see in this world with his words. He created each plant that you know so much about. Every stone that gives us power came from him. The wisdom for every detail that you will learn to revere came from YAHWEH. You must not abuse that wisdom. The Craft is a great responsibility that he has entrusted to our family. It is very important to seek his guidance with how to use it," said Thena.

"You said some of the Craft worship another god. Which is greater?" asked Nafaria.

"YAHWEH is the greatest. He created everything. He even created the god of blood. The god of blood can only copy what YAHWEH has done. Both give power, but in the end, YAHWEH is the strongest," said Thena.

Nafaria looked at all three books. She felt herself standing at a crossroads where different paths met. She was being entrusted with greater knowledge. The feeling intimidated her. She picked up the blank book.

"This is to be my Diary? What is it used for?" asked Nafaria.

"It is your book of knowledge. You record everything you learn about the Craft in it. You will have more than one volume. Everything you learn will be written in this book. Write down all you know about each plant or herb in it. It is to be your reference, for you will not always have me or your father," said Thena.

"Yes mother," said Nafaria. A picture flashed through her mind of Analia's body swinging from the gallows. "Did Lya worship the god of blood?" asked Nafaria.

"That is a difficult question to answer, for even one of the Craft cannot decipher a person's heart. Through YAHWEH'S wisdom and

---

[10] Genesis 1:1

the Craft you can expose the intentions of the heart. To know if one is given over to evil is a hard judgment to pronounce. It is best not to judge so," said Thena.

"Then what happened to her?" asked Nafaria.

"Lya was jealous and made a wrong decision. One that cost her life and the life of her mother," said Thena.

"May I never make that mistake," said Nafaria quietly.

"Then guard your heart, for it is the wellspring of life[11]," replied Thena. She rose to leave. "It is not quite noon yet. You have plenty of time left today. I leave you to your diary to record in it what you will." Thena left the room.

***

The woods were quiet and still. The sun was up and peeking through the trees from time to time; but there was no breeze. The leaves were still green, and mostly on the trees, leaving only patches of brush to alert the animals of any other presence.

Philip moved lightly through the forest, his bow in hand and arrows over his shoulders. He spent the last hour moving from tree to bush, taking in the foliage around him. He found mugwort growing in patches throughout the forest. Seeing the familiar plant put Philip at ease. It was as if his heart knew he was still in Nereheim when he saw it. The plant seemed as prosperous in Wildemere as it was in Denholm Glen.

He heard a rustle in the leaves and turned quickly to his left. He almost expected Alana to emerge from the bushes behind him. Instead, a pair of blue jays flew off into the woods, searching for whatever they could find. He watched them fly and then the woods were quiet again. His mind drifted back in time to the beginning of happier times in the woods.

He was thirteen years old, and he stepped lightly through the woods in Denholm Glen. He listened intently for the sound of rustling leaves as he always did. He was rewarded with the sound a few moments later. He heard it again, this time much more pronounced. Looking to the

---

[11] Proverbs 4:23

direction the sound came from, Philip saw patches of brown slowly shifting in the green foliage. The rustling became louder and the pace of the brown patch slowly increased. He grabbed an arrow from his quiver and aimed the bow at the patch of brown.

Before Philip could let his arrow fly, the brown jumped out of the green foliage and stood before him. It was a girl his own age, one he knew as most others knew her. She was Alana Deveraux, the Count Deveraux's younger daughter. Her eyes widened at the sight of the arrow trained on her. Philip sighed loudly and lowered his bow. He put the arrow back in his quiver.

"It is a little early for a walk in the woods, is it not?" asked Philip sharply.

"Perhaps it is. Is it not early for you?" she asked in return. He noticed that her voice was steady.

"It is the best time to be alone in the woods, Alana. What are you doing here?" asked Philip.

"I was on my way down to the brook. I have heard there are excellent mulberry patches along the banks," replied Alana.

"Where you are referring to is back behind you," replied Philip. He pointed behind her. Then he looked at her carefully. Alana was in a dress, but it was not the elegant type that most of the other girls wore. She dressed more simply, like his little sister did. Thena taught Nafaria to dress appropriately for work as well as any other occasion. His expression softened slightly.

"Do you know where you are going?" he asked gently. "The woods here can be dangerous as they begin to look alike if you do not know them intimately."

"I am not lost!" replied Alana indignantly. Her reply was characteristic of her nature. Unlike her older sister, Alana would not allow anyone to perceive her as weak.

Philip nodded his head to her. He pointed behind her again. "Go back that way, about fifty yards. Listen for the brook, and then head to your right. You will find it soon enough," replied Philip.

He turned to walk away. Alana watched as he headed in the opposite direction. She sighed. "Philip?" she called out.

He turned and looked at her. The look on her face was almost one of shame. Her eyes moved to the ground between them. "I am lost. Can you show me the way?" asked Alana.

Philip was silent a moment, then smiled. "Let us go. Perhaps I will find something along the way," said Philip. He walked back toward Alana, and they headed into the woods together.

Now Philip looked down at the bow in his hand and threw it to the ground. He sank to his knees, put his head in his hands, and let the tears come.

"Alana, I miss you so much," whispered Philip. He could do nothing but let his emotions flow from him like a tidal wave.

At home, he buried his feelings and pretended all was well. He supposed he fooled his mother, but his father knew better. Out in the woods, however, he was free to be as overcome with grief as he wanted.

He pictured her hair and ice blue eyes, wondering how long it would take the memory to fade. For the first time in his life, Philip desperately wished he was not of the Craft.

He sat on his knees and let the tears continue. Somewhere in the back of his mind, another old conversation found its way to the present.

He sat on his father's lap after their time practicing with his bow and hunting in the woods one day. Practice paid off, and he brought home a pheasant for Sylvia to use for dinner. Jason was writing in a book while he sat with his son.

"What are you writing, father?" asked Philip. He looked over his father's shoulder at the strange book.

"I am adding an entry into our family's annals," replied Jason. Philip looked closely and found his name.

"Is it about me?" asked Philip. Jason smiled.

"Yes. I have added an entry about your skill as a hunter, and now I shall add about your success today," replied Jason.

Philip looked at the shelf off to his right. There were several books with the same binding on them. "Why does our family do this?" asked Philip.

"It is important to know where you came from. There is knowledge in history that cannot be found in a diary. Knowing what your family had done in the past helps you see what you can be capable of in the future," replied Jason.

"I wish to be as strong in the Craft as you, father," replied Philip proudly. Jason smiled again.

"It is my task to see that you are stronger. Make no mistake, one day there may come a time that you will wish you were born of common blood," replied Jason.

"Why is that?" asked Philip.

"Those of the Craft must make choices with our task in mind. We are to protect and give guidance to those around us. It is a great responsibility and with it comes the power to aid us in that task. A common man has the right to follow his heart and choose whomever he will to accompany him through his life. A man of the Craft is given that person so that YAHWEH's gift of power does not diminish from the world. Sometimes even the strongest men of the Craft die of despair and heartbreak," said Jason.

Philip sat quietly, thinking through what his father said. "I hope I never become that," he said at last.

"It is my hope that I can find you someone who will be so precious to you that you never have to be. If I fail, remember this: YAHWEH has a plan for each of us so great that we cannot always see it until it is fully revealed. What looks like the end of one thing is merely the beginning of something greater. Always keep looking for that something greater," said Jason.

Those words rang in Philip's head as he sat on the forest floor. Slowly, his breathing became even again, and his tears stopped falling. He lifted his face up into the air around him and listened to the trees. There were different birds all around, singing their songs. Once again, the rustle of the leaves alerted him to the inhabitants of the woods. A small rabbit hopped out into the clearing, a few feet from where Philip sat quietly, and smiled, waiting for his chance. Suddenly, he sprang and pounced on the rabbit, securing the feet with one hand and holding it by the neck with the other. He did not allow the creature the luxury of turning its head for fear it would bite him. He held the rabbit close to his face so it had no choice but to peer into his eyes.

"Well, little one, what shall I do with you?" asked Philip aloud. "You are too small to have any meat on your bones worth skinning for." He smiled as he thought of Nafaria and how she might like a companion at home. He quickly made his way back home with the rabbit in his hands.

Philip found Nafaria in her room. She was sitting at her desk which faced out the window overlooking the fountain. Her head was bent down, her hand scratching away with a piece of artisan's lead. Nafaria was the only person in the family who had use for the strange piece that allowed her to cover a page quickly with light wisps of lead. At a very young age, their mother discovered her talent for drawing and encouraged it.

He stood in the doorway for a moment, and then quietly entered. He walked up to the desk with the rabbit in hand. "I found you something, little one," said Philip gently.

"I am not a little child, Philip," said Nafaria as she continued to sketch. There was a hint of annoyance in her tone. Philip smiled.

"Perhaps not, but you will always be to me," replied Philip.

Nafaria finished her sketch and sat back against her chair. Philip looked and saw a flower etched into a book. "What flower is that?" asked Philip. Nafaria looked at him in surprise.

"Can you not tell?" asked Nafaria. She looked back down at the drawing. Philip continued to look at the figure on the page. He went through the list of plants he knew before he came upon the one that looked the same in his mind.

"Is that a coneflower?" asked Philip.

"Yes, it is. Mother gave me my diary this morning. I decided to start recording everything I knew about plants and herbs. I added a picture of each for reference," replied Nafaria.

Philip looked at the picture and sighed. "It is amazing how well you draw, Nafaria. Along with the Craft, you should turn your attention to painting," said Philip.

"Has anyone of the Craft ever painted?" asked Nafaria. Philip shrugged.

"There is always a first time," said Philip in reply. Nafaria looked at him for a moment.

"What do you have for me?" asked Nafaria.

Philip held up the rabbit in his hands. "I thought you might like a pet," said Philip.

Nafaria looked at the rabbit, reached out and pet its head. Then she shook her head. "Mother taught me never to become attached to an animal that could become a person's dinner. We should probably let him go," said Nafaria.

"If that is your wish," said Philip. He turned to leave the room.

"Philip?" said Nafaria. He turned back around. She turned in her seat to face him.

"Thank you for thinking of me. Instead of the rabbit, could I ask for something else?" said Nafaria.

"What would you like?" asked Philip.

"Take me into the woods with you and teach me how to use a bow and arrow. I spend a lot of time in the woods gathering herbs and plants. I should know how to defend myself if necessary," replied Nafaria.

Philip looked at her and saw eagerness in her eyes. He suddenly realized he might like the companionship of his little sister in the woods to take his mind off Alana.

"We could start tomorrow. It looks as though you have a task on your hands with your diary," said Philip with a smile.

Nafaria sprang out of her seat and gave him a big hug. "Thank you," whispered Nafaria. Philip said nothing in reply, but held her tight.

***

The sun sank lower than Nafaria realized when she looked up from her book. Her mother's book lay open before her. The shadows in her room grew longer, the light fading. Nafaria lit a candle and put it in front of her. She picked up the feather she used. Dipping it in the ink, she went back to work in her book.

It was a few minutes later when she heard a knock at the door. Nafaria looked up as Thena entered with a tray of meat, vegetables and fruit. A flask of wine and an empty cup sat next to the platter.

"Oh mother, I am sorry, I have forgotten dinner," said Nafaria.

"It is all right child. I understand your eagerness to write in your book. I did the same thing. Just remember to keep yourself disciplined. You cannot cut yourself from the world for the sake of study. A wise man once said, 'of making many books there is no end, and much study wearies the body.[12]' You must also live your life," said Thena.

"Yes mother. Would you like to see what I have recorded?" asked Nafaria.

"Of course," said Thena with a smile.

Thena set the tray next to Nafaria and leaned over to turn the pages. She saw that Nafaria began her diary with an herb dictionary. On each page, there was a very meticulously drawn picture of each plant. The name was written across the top of the page. Next on the page was a description of each plant's properties. Thena stopped at the elderberry plant. At the bottom of the page Nafaria had written one word: poisonous. Next to the word there was drawn a skull. Thena was very impressed with Nafaria's skill of drawing.

"You have more talent for art than I realized," said Thena.

"I thought it would be wise to include a picture of each plant, so I would not forget it," replied Nafaria.

"Very wise indeed," said Thena. She looked at her daughter. "I hope you will be just as meticulous in your studies with your father." Nafaria's face brightened.

"When will I begin?" asked Nafaria.

"You will begin with him tomorrow after breakfast. There is one caution about your diary," said Thena.

"What is it?" asked Nafaria.

"You must never show it to anyone. In it will contain all your knowledge both arcane and practical. All you will learn in the Craft will be written in its pages. Anyone can turn to evil. If an enemy were to find your secrets, you could be in great danger. If you entrust the book to someone before you die, that is your choice. Otherwise, one's book should be burned if the knowledge is to be kept safe. Knowledge is great responsibility. It should never be taken lightly. Only entrust

[12] Ecclesiastes 12:12

your knowledge to those who will use it as you would want them to," said Thena.

"How will I know who to trust?" asked Nafaria.

"Gain wisdom and you will learn. There is one more thing," said Thena.

"Yes mother?" asked Nafaria.

"You must never tell anyone of your aversion to elderberries. It is quite uncommon. You almost died that night. It is a secret you must take to your grave," said Thena.

"Yes mother," replied Nafaria.

"I will leave you to your books. Tomorrow, you will be with your father in the morning, and the afternoon will be spent with me," said Thena.

"When will I go to study with others?" asked Nafaria.

"I cannot be sure. I need time to teach you the ancient language," said Thena.

"I hope it will be soon. It will be nice to meet others," said Nafaria.

"I hope so, little one. Common people can be cruel in their ignorance. Be careful who you trust," said Thena.

"Yes mother," replied Nafaria.

Thena wrapped her arms around Nafaria. The smell of lavender hung on her clothes and skin like incense filling the air. Nafaria breathed deep and smothered her face in her mother's stomach.

"Good night, little one," whispered Thena. Nafaria let go of her mother and watched as she left the room.

Nafaria turned the page in her diary. Dipping the feather in the ink, she began a new page. She recorded the account of her near death experience with elderberries.

* * *

The moon shone through the window, as Jason lay asleep next to Thena. He slowly tossed and turned as his mind unfolded a great mystery before him.

He was outside his new manor. The fountain that Nafaria loved stood a few yards away. Strange men surrounded him. Some were older than him, others were younger. All were rushing him like one mad tidal wave. He resorted to using the power of the Craft, but it did not stop them. He heard Thena's cries and screams as they continued to beat him.

Then he felt a steel blade plunge into his back. He stopped moving at once as the shock of the deed settled over him.

Jason woke with a start, his body covered in sweat. His heart still raced from the dream he had.

He reached out his hand to touch Thena. When his fingers met her arm, Jason felt a shock coarse through his body. His mind filled with a picture of Thena standing in the middle of the market place in Wildemere. A sea of angry faces surrounded her. Loud shouts rang out all over. He saw one of the men who beat him, put a rope over her head and Thena's body was swinging in the air from the gallows.

Jason pulled his hand away quickly. His heart continued to race as he looked at Thena's sleeping figure. He quickly got out of bed, put on his robe, and walked out of the room.

In the morning, Thena found Jason in the library. He sat next to the fire with a book in his lap. She recognized from the color of the cover that it was a copy of his family's history. Marcus was very meticulous about writing down all that happened with the power he was given. That skill was handed down to everyone in Jason's line. He was the only man she ever knew who knew everything about his family's heritage. One of the first tasks she set herself to when they married was to learn about this line she had become a part of.

The flames from the fire danced as Jason stared at them. He was deep in thought. He jumped when she laid a hand on his shoulder. He looked up and smiled when he saw her there.

"Did she work on her book last night?" asked Jason.

"Of course she did. She started an herb dictionary with drawings of each plant along with its properties. The drawings are quite remarkable," said Thena.

"I wondered if we would have an artist in our family," said Jason.

Thena sat down in another chair near Jason. She looked into the fire. The warmth felt soothing in the chilly morning air.

"Nafaria has asked when she will go to school in the city," said Thena. Jason looked at her.

"So soon?" asked Jason.

"She was asking when we lived in Denholm Glen," replied Thena.

"I am not sure I want to send her to the city at all. I fear for her safety, Thena. More than I fear the safety of the boys," said Jason.

"You think there is danger here for Nafaria?" asked Thena. Jason nodded his head as he looked at her.

"I was visited last night by a gift that runs in my family. I saw my own death. According to my family's annals, the vision comes unexpectedly when one is granted the gift of foresight. My grandmother, Isabella, must have just died. This is why I had the vision. She must have willed her power to me, as has been the family's tradition," said Jason.

"What does this mean?" asked Thena. She was visibly troubled by Jason's news.

"It is a gift from YAHWEH to help us serve others. We can also use what I learn from the vision to protect the family. My mind has already been troubled since we left Denholm Glen. The persecution that drove us from our home will follow us, and I fear it will grow worse. I want Philip, Michael, but especially Nafaria to have very little to do with the city," said Jason gravely.

"What are you saying? You would hold them prisoners in their own home?" asked Thena. A troubled look crossed her face. The tone of her voice matched that look.

"No. They need to live their lives. Limit time in the city and they should only go with one of us," said Jason.

"Nafaria will not like that," said Thena.

"I know," said Jason. "There is something else we need to discuss," said Jason. Thena looked at him.

"Because of this vision, I fear I may not have much time. We must make certain to stay as anonymous as we can," said Jason.

"That is a tall order. The king has recognized your diplomacy and he will call on you when he needs to. Joel already knows about us," replied Thena. Jason nodded his head.

"Yes I know. However, Joel understands discretion. He will be no worry to us," said Jason.

"Do you believe we can trust him?" asked Thena.

"I do," said Jason.

"Then we must simply live our lives and see what happens," replied Thena.

She rose from her chair and moved over to Jason. She knelt down beside his chair and took his hand in hers. "I love you and trust you with all that I have. You will protect us," she said as she kissed his hand.

Jason lifted her chin so that he could see her face. He loved to gaze into her eyes. His heart melted as he leaned forward and kissed her lips.

"Let us retire for now. I would like to do something else in Wildemere besides worry about the future," said Jason. He smiled mischievously.

Thena smiled and rose to her feet. She quickly moved through the library to the entrance. She looked over her shoulder, smiled and started running as Jason jumped from his seat and took off after her. The sounds of their giggling and laughter echoed through the halls as they ran to the bedroom.

Later that morning, Nafaria ate breakfast and went out into the garden. She saw her father sitting at the fountain. He looked up as he heard her approach and smiled brightly.

"Good morning, Nafaria," said Jason.

"Good morning father," replied Nafaria. She hugged him and then sat down next to him at the fountain.

"I trust your mother is teaching you about the use of wisdom. I will not waste valuable time on that. I will show you a simple use of your power. This incantation is very useful to see things that are far off," said Jason.

Nafaria looked into the shallow pool. The sun's reflection danced along the sides of the fountain.

"What do you wish to see?" asked Jason.

"I wish to see Sylvia. I miss her very much," said Nafaria.

"I do as well. Let us see what can be seen," said Jason.

He took out a gold chain with a heart charm on it. "This belonged to Sylvia. Your mother found it when she unpacked some things. To see her, you only need to use an object she owned. Take the chain," said Jason.

Nafaria took the necklace in her hand. It was very light and delicate. "Close your eyes and picture Sylvia," said Jason.

Nafaria closed her eyes. She pictured the cook busy in the kitchen. "Now say the words: 'let the object be seen' and pass your hand over the pool," said Jason.

"Let the object be seen," said Nafaria. She opened her eyes and passed her hand over the pool.

In an instant, the pool filled with Sylvia's face. She was working in the kitchen of the manor. Nafaria could see her hands kneading dough, as she had done so many times when they lived there. Her face held a sad expression, and tears poured from her eyes. Jason looked into the pool and saw the picture as well.

"Why is she sad?" asked Nafaria.

"It is hard to say. Perhaps the witch hunt that Lord Reinard feared has come to pass," said Jason. He passed his hand through the water. The image disappeared as the water rippled. "You can also use this same incantation to see other places. You do not use an object as you do to see one person. You picture the land you wish to see and do the same thing. Your power needs to grow a bit, but as you practice you will do it easily."

Jason closed his eyes. "Let the object be seen," said Jason. Nafaria watched as an image of a place she did not recognize came into view. It looked to be a town square. There was a gallows set up with small bodies hanging from them. Nafaria looked at Jason, a horrified look on her face.

"Father, were those children?" gasped Nafaria as she looked into the pool.

Jason's eyes filled with tears. He passed his hand through the water. Again, the image faded. "Maybe this is why Sylvia was sad," replied Jason quietly.

Nafaria fought back tears. The midnight journey made sense to her now, where it didn't before. Lord Reinard saved their lives with his warning. Had he kept his tongue still, it could have been her on the gallows.

"Now you have learned your first incantation. To protect yourself from being seen by another in that way, use your crystal," said Jason.

Nafaria looked down at her chain. She drew out the crystal that her parents gave her for her birthday.

"Hold the crystal over your heart and say 'YAHWEH, conceal me from prying eyes'," said Jason.

Nafaria closed her eyes. She pulled the crystal over her heart and whispered, "YAHWEH, conceal me from prying eyes," said Nafaria.

"That is very good. Keep your crystal on at all times. It is for your safety," said Jason. "Now, let us take some time to record the instructions in your diary. We will continue on something else after that is finished. After lunch, you will spend the afternoon with your mother," said Jason as he rose from the edge of the fountain. He looked over at the patch of soil that Nafaria had made her garden out of. He walked closer to it and recognized the Roman Chamomile instantly.

"Did you find these plants in the woods?" asked Jason.

"Yes father. I have left space to add in other plants as I find them. I hope to find some good sage plants as well as mint," replied Nafaria.

"Perhaps you should look for lavender as well," replied Jason. "You have done a good work here, Nafaria," replied Jason. Nafaria smiled brightly.

"Thank you father," replied Nafaria. "It reminds me of Nathaniel. I miss him."

Jason smiled at his daughter and looked back at the garden. He thought carefully and smiled. "I think you have just found our new vocation," said Jason. He turned and headed into the manor.

Nafaria lingered at the pool, staring into the water. She thought heavily about all she had seen and done. Once again the dangers of being of the Craft played on her mind.

She looked up into the sunlight. Its warmth gently caressed her face. How she would love to spend the afternoon picking wildflowers and running through the streams near this new home.

She thought of her responsibility to the Craft and wondered what it would be like to not live with such a legacy hanging over her like a gray cloud. The bodies hanging on those gallows were people like her. Fear and ignorance bought their deaths. Would she allow only those who used the Craft for an evil agenda to wield the power? She opened her eyes. She looked at the flowers in the garden. *I will not allow that*, Nafaria whispered. She got up from the fountain and walked back into the manor.

***

Later that afternoon, Jason stood once again at the little garden Nafaria made, thinking intently. She managed to find all the herbs for her garden from the woods. He could easily expand on the concept and use the manor for the sole purpose of growing herbs. Everyone in the household used the herbs Nafaria gathered. He could sell fresh herbs in the market, and both he and Thena could concentrate on running an apothecary just as Malcom did in Denholm Glen. It was not wine, but it was another fruit from the earth. YAHWEH had provided, and Nafaria had shown them the way. "A little child shall lead them[13]," whispered Jason as he lost himself in thought.

A few minutes later, he was roused from his mental planning by a sense of someone very close. He looked up to see Philip standing next to him, holding a large pheasant in one hand.

"You have had success?" asked Jason. Philip smiled slightly.

"It is only a pheasant. I would not call it a feast, father," replied Philip.

They were interrupted by the sound of horse's hooves. Both looked up to see Joel riding up to them. Jason smiled instantly.

"Joel, it is a surprise and honor to see you," said Jason brightly.

"So it is also for me," replied Joel. He hopped down from his horse.

---

[13] Isaiah 11:6

"What brings you here today?" asked Jason.

"I bring news," replied Joel grimly. When Jason did not respond, Joel continued.

"When we first met, Thena mentioned 'the horse master from Illith'. I have heard a most wild tale, but I fear it is true. Do you know Lord Bryant Saintclaire personally?" asked Joel.

"I know him very well. Illith is only a half-day's ride from Denholm Glen. Thena's friend, Analia, is Cassandra Saintclaire's sister. Two women were never closer than Thena and Analia. Cassandra could be a sister to her. A few days before we left Denholm Glen, Lord Bryant came to me with a proposal to betroth his daughter, Nadia, to Philip. I need to get back to Lord Saintclaire to tell him where we have disappeared to," replied Jason. Joel looked unsteadily from Philip to Jason.

"The news I have is that Lord Bryant and Lady Cassandra were stoned in the Village Square in Illith. His manor was burned to the ground, and his servants fled. You are of the Craft. It is thought that Lord Bryant was also. Please be very careful my friend," said Joel.

Jason barely heard Joel's final words. Philip stared at Jason with wide eyes. He was too stunned to speak. They looked up at Joel expressionless. A single tear floated down Jason's cheek, followed by another. He finally collapsed in Joel's arms and cried as Joel silently held him. Philip dropped his pheasant and bow and put his arms around his father.

After a few moments, Jason finally composed himself. Wiping the tears from his eyes, he asked, "What of Nadia Saintclaire?"

Joel shook his head. "I have heard no mention," he said. "Those of the Craft are now feared in Nereheim. Why do you stay?" asked Joel.

"Because I am in love with my homeland as much as I am in love with my wife. Nereheim is endless beauty for me. I wish to use the power YAHWEH has entrusted me with to serve its people. I keep thinking that this persecution will pass, and someday men will return to their senses. It will be better for us all if that day would come soon," said Jason.

"It would. In the meanwhile, I will guard your secret for as long as I am alive," replied Joel. Jason put his arm on his shoulder and smiled.

"Thank you for telling me this news. The rest of the family will need to know. This is a black day for all of us," said Jason.

Joel put his hand on Jason's shoulder. "The news is grave, indeed. However, I thank your God for bringing you to Wildemere. You have eased many burdens with your presence," said Joel.

"It is good to have a friend at such times," said Jason. He turned toward the manor as Joel mounted his horse and rode off.

Jason and Philip entered the house and found Thena with Nafaria in the library. Nafaria was busy studying runes while Michael sat quietly in another corner reading a book.

"I have something you all need to hear," replied Jason.

Jason moved over to Thena. Philip stood behind his father. Thena could see he was holding back tears.

"Joel was just here. He came to warn me to be cautious here in Wildemere. He is afraid for us. Apparently what has happened in Denholm Glen has repeated itself in Illith. Lord and Lady Saintclaire are dead," said Jason.

The look of shock and horror on each of his family's faces made Jason crumble inside.

"What happened?" asked Michael after a moment. He was the first to try to speak.

"Joel said only that they were stoned in the Village Square. He could not tell me why," said Jason.

"Where is Nadia?" asked Thena.

"He could not tell me," said Jason. He looked at each member of his family carefully. "We must all take great care here. There are only a few people in Wildemere who know we are of the Craft. Tell no one our secret. All study will be conducted at home. For Philip, that barely matters, but Nafaria and Michael, you will study from home."

Michael sat in his chair and held his pensive look. Nafaria looked as though she wanted to cry. However, both children stayed silent. Jason continued.

"I have also decided on what our vocation shall be. We do not have time to build another vineyard, and I am sure that the vineyard we left behind is still providing for us as the servants are tending it.

After looking over Nafaria's herb garden, I think we will concentrate on growing herbs here on our land, and we will operate an apothecary in the city. This will give us a chance to serve others, as well as provide for ourselves and our servants here. Each one of you will be of great use in this endeavor."

"Father, will it be wise to operate something of this sort? Will people not guess that we are of the Craft?" asked Michael.

"Not if we are careful. I am certain this can be accomplished in a city like Wildemere and still keep our anonymity," said Jason.

Michael closed his book and rose from his seat. "If there is nothing else, father, I wish to be alone," said Michael.

"There is nothing else," replied Jason. Michael quickly left the room, his eyes misting with tears as he left. Philip rose and left the room as well.

Thena looked at Nafaria. "I think that we should conclude study for today," she said quietly. Nafaria nodded her head and closed her book as well. She came over to her mother and hugged her tightly as tears came to her eyes.

"Mother, why would they kill Lord Bryant and Lady Cassandra?" asked Nafaria.

"I do not know. Perhaps we shall know more if we find Nadia," said Thena quietly. Jason left the two of them alone in the library.

***

Michael sat outside looking up at the sky. It was clear and bright with puffy white clouds that made excellent pictures in the blue sky. It took almost an hour, but Michael was not surprised when Jason sat down next to him on the little hill behind their home. Though the brook was not visible, they could both hear its wild gurgle winding through the countryside.

"You chose a very dramatic exit to come look at the clouds," said Jason gently.

"I am sorry father," replied Michael.

"There is nothing to be sorry for. I merely wondered if there was something you wished to talk about," replied Jason.

"When you told us what happened to Lord and Lady Saintclaire, I could only think of one thing. I have been thinking about it for the past hour," said Michael. Another tear rolled down his face.

"What is that?" asked Jason.

"The time, two summers ago, when I spent a week with Lord Saintclaire. You sent me to him so that I could learn to ride a horse," said Michael.

Jason smiled. "I remember that summer. I thought it would be quite an adventure for you, just as it was for Philip. You were so upset when you came home. I noticed two things right away about you," said Jason.

"What were they?" asked Michael.

"You became more studious, if that was even possible; and you were determined to ride a horse," said Jason. Michael smiled.

"Lord Saintclaire was such an accomplished horse master, father. He had such great patience, and no matter how I tried, I could not master his most elementary lesson. The last day I was with him he threw his hands in the air and said, 'You will be a great and learned man one day, Michael, but one who will walk to his destination. There is nothing in you that will allow you to ride a horse,'" said Michael. "All I wanted was to be able to stay in the saddle in front of him. I could not even do that. Now he is dead, and he never knew how much his lessons meant to me. He never knew I learned to ride!" sobbed Michael.

Jason leaned over and pulled his son into his arms. He held him for a few moments and let him cry. "I often wondered what happened that week you were gone. Lord Saintclaire never said," replied Jason.

"He never told you?" asked Michael. Jason shook his head.

"Lord Saintclaire always kept his lessons private. If you were willing to tell me what happened, he would talk about it. If not, there was no need for him to say anything. He believed in total discretion," replied Jason.

"I wish he knew his time with me was not in vain," said Michael quietly.

"I think he always knew. Since he was of the Craft, he also believed that imparting whatever wisdom he had to offer whether in teaching a person to ride a horse, or showing them some profound truth was never a wasted effort. Look what it produced in you. Such seeds of tenacity are never sown lightly, Michael. In the end, you have accomplished a task that was very difficult for you. You will appreciate your skill for riding even more than those who come by it naturally," said Jason.

Michael squeezed his arms together and hugged his father tighter. "I hope one day I am able to give my son such words of encouragement," said Michael.

"Love hopes all things[14], Michael. I am confident that when you are a father, you will be able to give your son just the right words at the right time, because you will love your son just as much as I love you. That much has never changed, except to grow deeper. I am so very proud of you," replied Jason.

"I am so very proud of you, father," whispered Michael.

Father and son sat on the hill in silence and continued to look up at the sky. Neither said a word, for each wanted to enjoy the moment they had together. That moment when finally words fail; and silence is of greater worth than gold.

* * *

That night, the pale moonlight trickled through the bedroom window, filtered even more by the sheer curtains hanging across it. Jason lay in bed, but his sleep grew restless. His heart fluttered like the beating of so many butterfly wings in the meadow during late summer. His pulse quickened, sweat formed tiny pearls across his forehead. A very vivid picture in his subconscious was the villain in his dreams.

A gallows was standing in a village square. It was a place he knew very well. The square was Denholm Glen, the home he fled. The crowd around the gallows was large, but subdued. Shock and sadness were the key emotions on every face that watched the spectacle. Every eye from the oldest present to the youngest was puffed, red, and dripping with

---

[14] 1 Corinthians 13:7

tears. Jason felt his stomach tighten as he watched his dream unfold. His attention was now drawn to the figure swinging from the rope.

It was a young girl, not much older than Nafaria herself. The figure was lean, but not frail. It spoke of an upbringing of gentleness and quiet activity. Long blond hair flowed in curls around the shoulders. There was no covering on the child's head, so Jason could see the porcelain skin and pink cheeks perfectly. Her eyes were wide open, bright sapphire orbs stared into the sky. Jason screamed as he sat up in his bed shaking. "Lillia!" he shouted again.

"Jason!" shouted Thena. She sat up and was shaking him. "What is wrong?" she shouted.

Jason opened his eyes but tears streamed from them. He clenched Thena, and held on to her, shaking and sobbing. Thena held him and whispered in his ear. For as long as they were married, Jason never had a bad dream. She was frightened at his state. "Sshh, let it go. It was just a bad dream," soothed Thena. Jason shook his head.

"No, it was more. I have no doubt now that I have inherited my grandmother's gift. I can see what will happen in the future. I have already seen my death. I told you about that. Now I have seen the death of another. I must try to stop it from happening," said Jason. He threw back the covers and got out of bed.

"Where are you going?" asked Thena.

"I am going to see the king. I fear that nothing less than his authority will stay this madness," replied Jason. He dressed and grabbed his cloak.

"Jason, it is nearly dawn. Whatever it is, it can wait until later this morning," said Thena.

"No, it cannot! Thena I must try!" shouted Jason. Thena rose from the bed.

"Who, Jason, who did you see that is worth so much trouble?" demanded Thena.

"Lillia Sallen," replied Jason. He turned and rushed out of the room.

***

The castle was still very dark inside, though the sky outside was brightening to a light gray. King Rohn was awakened to the news that he had a distraught visitor waiting in his throne room. The king rushed through the corridors of the castle, at a complete loss as to who his visitor could be. Only a man who feared no earthly being could be bold enough to wake a king before first light of day.

Rohn thought of his wife lying in bed beside him. She gently coaxed him into seeing his visitor and implored him to use grace and wisdom in his dealings. "Though you are king, there are times when you must be servant as well. Wait on your subject with patience and care. For the time may come when you need his fealty." She said this before she drifted back off to sleep. Rohn thought of those words as he made his way hurriedly to his throne room.

He thought that perhaps king Lian had sent a messenger from North Agea. Queen Clara was his wife's younger sister. Both were as close as a heartbeat growing up. When Clara met Lian, she fell in love with him completely. However, neither she nor Susanna counted on how hard it would be to live in separate countries, even when the countries were as close as Nereheim and North Agea. The countries had called themselves "sister kingdoms", each seeing themselves as part of the other. Rohn and Lian enjoyed amiable relations, some on account of their ability to rule together wisely. However mostly it was because Rohn and Lian were married to two women who were sisters. Rohn had learned added delicacy over the years.

Rohn thought of these things as the guard opened the door and he entered his throne room. The last person he expected to see was Lord Jason Mauldon hurrying toward him wild eyed and in panic. He immediately sank to the floor on his knees. The king was taken aback. Lord Jason never once fell to his knees before him.

"King Rohn, I beg you to forgive my intrusion this night. I come to you with a very urgent request," said Jason with his head bowed. His voice quivered. It was nothing of the steady commanding tone that Rohn had come to recognize and respect of the young noble.

"You may rise Lord Jason," said the king quietly.

When he stood, the king could see that Jason was indeed distraught. His eyes held the queer terrified look of a man out of his wits with fear. "My king, have you sent out a guard to Denholm Glen yet?" asked Jason.

"Two days ago, after we spoke, I heard strange reports of an unjustified execution in the village of Illith. I sent 12 men from the royal guard to look into the matter. I also instructed them to stop in Denholm Glen on the way, as you suggested," replied the king. He looked carefully at Jason. "What has happened?"

"King Rohn, you already know I am of the Craft. For reasons I cannot explain to you, I have been granted a short glimpse of the future. I saw the hanging of a little girl I know well. She is the same age as my son Michael," said Jason.

"You knew this girl?" asked the king. Jason nodded his head.

"She is Lord Reinard Sallen's daughter," replied Jason.

"The guard has instruction to speak to Lord Sallen when they stop in Denholm Glen. This was instruction left on your recommendation," replied the king.

"Thank you, your majesty. I only hope it will save Lillia's life," replied Jason. The king put his hand on Jason's shoulder. He looked the young lord directly in the eye. The king's cold steel eyes met Jason's bright blue. The steady gaze of the king had a calming effect on Jason.

"Go now, and rest. We will find the solution to this question together," replied the king.

"Thank you, your majesty," said Jason. He turned and left the throne room, his shoulders sagging with the weight of his knowledge resting squarely on them.

***

Lillia made her way through the village early in the morning as she always did. Education was principle to her father and she learned very early in life that he took her lessons more seriously than she did. Lillia supposed one day she would be the same way when she had children of her own. However, that prospect was as far from her as the moon.

She passed by the apothecary shop that was now closed. All the jars that Malcom Stone kept in his windows were still there, but her father knew nothing of the wares and would not open the shop to just anyone. A young couple from Illith approached him and offered to buy the shop, but her father was wary. Though the couple was knowledgeable; they were not of the Craft. He did not wish Malcom's work to fall into disarray out of ignorance.

Lillia paused a moment at the windows. So many times she would get a glimpse of Michael with Nathaniel through those windows. Now there was nothing but sunlight and shelves filled with containers, and no one to use the ingredients they contained. Tears formed in her eyes as she thought of Michael in another place far from her.

The Count Deveraux was to blame for this. He drove Jason and Malcom away along with their families. He murdered needlessly. Would there ever be any absolution for his crimes? She walked on down the main road toward the library and their place of education.

Lillia's thoughts were wandering toward where Michael might be and what he could be doing that very morning. She did not see the men who were waiting for the girls to arrive.

"Lillia, you must come with me," said a rough but quiet voice. She looked up and saw the soft green eyes of Lord Luxton.

"I am on my way to my studies," replied Lillia simply. She did not understand her detainment.

"I know, child. However, Count Deveraux has asked to see each girl this morning, before their studies," said Lord Luxton. His calm voice did not hide the worried look in his eyes.

"Why?" asked Lillia.

"I am sure he will explain all to you. It is a very simple matter that once indulged, will go away quickly," replied Lord Luxton. He put out his hand for her. She took it and let him lead her to the back of the library.

Count Deveraux sat at a table that was set up in the corner of the room. He glanced at her with a stern look. He motioned toward the pack in her hand.

"Please put your sack on the table," said the Count. Lillia looked at him quizzically.

"Count Deveraux, these are only my books for school," said Lillia. She obediently put the sack on the table.

The Count opened the sack and emptied the contents on the table. Lord Luxton saw the same three books all the girls carried. There was also a piece of fruit, some cheese, and a flask. He also saw another book he did not recognize. Count Deveraux saw it also, and picked it up.

"What is this?" asked the Count.

"It is only my sketchbook, Count Deveraux," replied Lillia.

He looked through the book. As he did so, his expression hardened. "What are these drawings?" demanded the Count. He handed the book to Lord Luxton who looked at the book carefully, his eyes widening in fear.

"They are drawings of plants and herbs found in the woods around the village," replied Lillia. Her expression showed she did not understand why the Count would be upset by this.

The Count turned to Lord Luxton. "Take her to the prison," said the Count.

"Count Deveraux, you cannot be serious," said Lord Luxton. "Lord Reinard is not of the Craft!" he exclaimed.

"It is only a book of herbs! Please give it back!" shouted Lillia. She reached for the book, but the Count held her back.

"Belladonna is an herb," replied the Count with contempt. He shoved her toward Lord Luxton who caught her in his arms.

"Child, come with me. We will clear this matter soon," said Lord Luxton. Lillia felt tears well up in her eyes.

"Please, may I have my book?" pleaded Lillia.

"Only a witch begs for her incantations. The book stays with me," replied the Count.

"Lillia, please come," said Lord Luxton softly.

Tears poured down Lillia's cheeks as she glanced one more time at the last gift Michael left for her; his knowledge. She suddenly burst in tears as Lord Luxton led her away.

An hour later, Count Deveraux and six other men rode up the cobblestone path to Lord Reinard's home. One of the servants opened the door and they poured through the doorway.

Lord Reinard came up the hallway toward the Count as the other men began to move through the house.

"Count Deveraux, what is the meaning of this?" demanded Lord Reinard.

"I am searching for evidence of anyone in this village who is of the Craft. All women and young girls who are suspect will be executed before they can claim any innocent lives. I will not allow anyone else to suffer as I have suffered," said the Count.

"Why do you search here? We are not of the Craft," said Reinard.

"Your daughter had a book of herbs in her possession. Why else would she draw plants and herbs if she were not a witch?" demanded the Count.

"She has been drawing plants and flowers ever since she could hold a lump of coal!" shouted Lord Reinard.

"There are details of each page about the picture. It is a witch's book!" shouted the Count in return.

Lord Reinard looked at the Count with a stern expression. Before he could speak, one of his men came into the room with a large book. "Count Deveraux, we found this book in the library," he said.

Count Deveraux took the book and opened it. Each page contained strange drawings and other markings he did not recognize or understand.

"What witchery is this?" demanded the Count.

"It is a book of alchemy. It has been my family practice for generations. We are alchemists. We are not of the Craft!" shouted Lord Reinard.

Count Deveraux shut the book. "You are a dangerous man, Lord Sallen. You do not deny that your family holds arcane wisdom akin to sorcery and your daughter possesses a book of herbs and plants. Your daughter will be executed tomorrow morning as a lesson to all that we will not tolerate arcane knowledge of any kind!" shouted the Count.

"You cannot do this!" shouted Lord Reinard. "I will appeal to the king!"

"Any pardon from the king will not save your daughter. Be grateful I allow you to keep your land," said the Count. He dropped the book he was holding on the floor and walked out with his men.

Lord Reinard slumped to the floor and cried out in fear and agony for his daughter.

***

Alana rushed into her father's library. It was a private place, and very foreboding. This was where he conducted his business for the king. Alana imagined very grave concerns were discussed here and equally grave decisions were made. She was never allowed in this room. Indeed, when her father desired to speak to her about anything, he always summoned her to some other place. Never had she once set foot in this room. Never had she had a desire to. However, today she came into the room with courage and purpose to match her quick stride.

Alana's presence in the room surprised the Count greatly, but in no means made him nervous or upset. He looked at her with a gaze of expectation. She saw that he was not unnerved by her presence, so she stated her business.

"Father, there is talk all over the village. Tell me it is not true. Have you imprisoned Lillia Sallen and condemned her to execution by hanging tomorrow morning?" demanded Alana. Her tone started even, and became tighter with every word she spoke. The Count continued to gaze at her.

"It is true," he said simply.

"For what reason?" demanded Alana. Her face was white with shock. She was prepared for the answer, but when it finally reached her ears from her father's lips; she found she could not believe it.

"She possesses arcane knowledge. Lord Reinard Sallen also possesses knowledge akin to witchcraft. She is a witch," replied the Count.

"What arcane knowledge? Lord Reinard Sallen is an alchemist. His family has studied science for generations. Lillia is not of the Craft!" replied Alana. The Count picked up a sketchbook that was sitting on his desk. Alana recognized it immediately. How many times over the years had she seen Lillia drawing in that very book?

"This book was in her possession. She admitted freely that it was her own and the drawings in it were done by her. Why else would she have it?" demanded the Count.

"Lillia Sallen is an artist. She has been drawing pictures of flowers and plants for years!" shouted Alana. She grabbed the book from her father and opened it. On each page was a beautifully drawn plant or herb and near the bottom of some there were descriptions of the plant. She read one page, and then turned to the next.

"This is Lillia's sketchbook. She has been drawing in this book since she was eight years old. I have seen her in the meadow, or in the woods with it. This is knowledge that, while very useful, is still only basic. Anyone in Denholm Glen might know this," said Alana.

"How would you know this?" demanded the Count.

"I know this very information! I know the properties and functions of every herb, flower, and plant in Denholm Glen. Do you condemn me to die?" demanded Alana.

The Count's face registered shock for a moment, but his stony expression quickly returned. "Where did you learn such information?" asked the Count.

"I have spent the last three years of my life in the woods with Philip Mauldon. He taught me how to shoot a bow, how to hunt, how to fish, and everything about every root, berry, herb, and plant in those woods and in the village. Michael Mauldon must have taught Lillia the same thing. She is not of the Craft. She was just simply willing to learn," said Alana.

"You do not know if she is of the Craft-" the Count thundered, but Alana cut him off.

"Philip told me the names of everyone in the village that was of the Craft. You have executed one, murdered two others, and drove the other seven away. No one else in Denholm Glen is of the Craft!" shouted Alana in return. She looked at her father. His expression was hard and unyielding. Her voice softened. "Executing an innocent young girl for the wrongs of someone justly executed already will not bring Ana back to us. I know you grieve the loss of your favorite, but I am still here. Father please; let this vendetta go and let me grieve with you," pleaded Alana.

The Count's expression darkened. "I will never yield until I have rid Denholm Glen of the threat of those with higher knowledge," said the Count bitterly.

Alana closed the book and laid it on his desk. "Then you give me no choice," replied Alana. She turned and walked out of the room, a quiet determination laying the foundation of a plan in her mind.

***

Lord Reinard moved into the prison area of the building the Count used as his office. He did not merely walk, for a man of his stature and mood does not simply walk from one place to the next. Each step taken is one of clarity, dignity, and purpose. His presence was strong and felt by all who were there to witness such an event. On this black day, Lord Reinard moved into the room his daughter was kept with purpose.

Lillia looked in his direction and her face brightened. Her blue eyes sparkled as she rushed toward the bars of the cage she was kept in. "Father!" she exclaimed as she wrapped her delicate fingers around the bars.

Lord Reinard felt his pulse quicken as he looked at the cell. He put his hands on hers, and looked down at the floor. Lillia could see he was repressing anger.

"Why is my daughter in a cell?" he demanded. He did not need to look at the guard to know he was nervous about the task he was given. The guard answered the question with a steady voice that belied his confidence.

"The Count Deveraux was specific, Lord Reinard. She was to be locked and guarded," said the guard.

Reinard let out a sigh and wrapped his hands around her face. She looked so much like her mother.

"Father, I am so sorry. My sketchbook; it was everything Michael ever taught me. He noticed me sketching plants one day when we were younger, and he told me the characteristics of all the plants in my book. I never thought this would ever happen!" cried Lillia. Fresh tears burst from her eyes. Reinard pulled himself as close to her as he could and planted a kiss on her forehead.

"My dear child, you are not to blame. Everyone knows we are not of the Craft. This doing is through no fault of yours," replied Reinard.

"Then, why am I here father? Why does the Count believe me to be a threat to people in the village?" asked Lillia.

"Grief makes madness in even the most just of men. The Count believes that because I am an alchemist, the knowledge you hold in your sketchbook will give you the same knowledge and power Lya possessed. He will not see reason. Our family heritage has condemned you," said Lord Reinard quietly.

"Father, is there nothing that can be done?" whispered Lillia. Lord Reinard shook his head.

"I will not leave you alone to go petition the king. I would not make it to him in time. I have decided to stay right here, and be with you until the end," said Reinard. Tears formed in his eyes. One of the guards came up behind them.

"Lord Reinard, I am afraid you must go. Your time of visitation is at an end," said the guard carefully.

Lord Reinard tightened his grip on his daughter's hands. He looked up at the ceiling and said, "The Count has unjustly accused my daughter and sentenced her to an unlawful execution. The least he can do is to allow me to spend the last night of my daughter's life by her side!" he shouted.

The guard bowed his head and quickly retreated to the corner from which he came.

"Is there nothing you can do?" whispered Lillia again. Lord Reinard felt hot tears on his cheeks.

"The only thing I know to do is pray to a God I am told is listening. I have been doing that all morning," whispered Reinard in return. He pulled Lillia as close as the bars of the cell would allow and wept bitterly.

***

Sebastian found Alana in the stable with her horse. The horse's chestnut hair closely resembled Alana's coloring. He stood in the doorway a moment, watching her carefully brush out the horse's mane. The animal stood quietly, looking as though she were thoroughly enjoying the attention her mistress was giving.

Alana's eyes flitted to the door, and she saw Sebastian standing there. He gave a nod and came toward her.

"I was told you wanted to talk to me, Viscountess," he said. He walked closer until he stood within three feet of her. He looked at her, patiently waiting for her to state her business.

Besides Philip, Sebastian Cavanaugh was the only other man Alana knew that unnerved her. He was quiet, considerate, and worked hard. She could never understand how he seemed to move unnoticed through Denholm Glen, patiently adding the bidding of others to his daily tasks. He was nearly three years older than Alana, and she never saw him with anyone. He seemed content with his father's land and whatever the villagers needed done that they could not do for themselves.

"Viscountess?" The sound of his voice brought Alana out of her reverie. She quickly averted her attention to her saddle as she spoke.

"Please do not call me that. I am in no frame of mind to be thankful for my father's position in this region," said Alana.

"Whatever you wish, Alana. My mother said you wanted to talk to me about something," said Sebastian. Alana nodded her head.

"I have no doubt you have heard of Lillia Sallen's fate?" asked Alana. Sebastian nodded his head.

"I was asked this morning to assist in the hanging," replied Sebastian. "If the truth be told, I want no part of it."

"Only the vilest of men would want a part in hanging an innocent girl. I have a plan to save Lillia, but I need your help," said Alana.

"What do you need?" asked Sebastian. He looked at Alana carefully.

"Can you ensure Lillia will only hang for a moment, and not have her neck break, or strangle instantly?" asked Alana.

"The noose could be tied so it will not tighten. There would be no danger from her breaking her neck. She would dangle indefinitely," replied Sebastian.

"That is all the time I need. I intend to shoot her free with an arrow. From there, Lord Reinard will need to get to her quickly and take her away. He needs to get to the king and tell him what is happening here. If too many things like this are allowed to happen, the king needs to know that an uprising could occur," replied Alana.

"You will become a fugitive, Alana. Your father will not stand for you, of all people, impeding his justice," replied Sebastian.

"His justice would see innocent people die, Sebastian. It already has! I will not stand by and watch Lillia Sallen be murdered for something she had no part in!" exclaimed Alana. After a moment, she calmed down. "I cannot see that happen. I am willing to do what is right, if no one else will. Do you wish to help me?" pleaded Alana.

Sebastian looked at Alana carefully. He had seen her for years in the woods, the meadow, or even in the river and playing in the creek beds. She was younger than he was, and he thought her a little girl, always running outdoors to play. Somewhere in the last few years, she became a woman, strong in her conviction, and her willingness to carry out what she believed in. How did he not notice this before? She was willing to do the right thing, where fear impaired everyone else. He found himself wanting to do more than merely assist her.

"Where will you go?" asked Sebastian quietly.

"I do not know. Perhaps I will see the rest of Nereheim before going into North Agea," said Alana. "Who knows? Maybe I shall go to the Anenderes and see faces in the water, or search for the ruined city of Herron."

"You will need an escort. I will go see Lord Reinard and tell him what you are planning. Let me think this through a little more. We need more help, if we are to make this happen," said Sebastian.

"I cannot ask you to go with me. You will be a fugitive as well. You do not deserve that," replied Alana.

"Lillia does not deserve death. Ana did not deserve death. You do not deserve to be alone in this, Alana. I will go with you," said Sebastian firmly.

When Alana understood Sebastian would not yield, she nodded her head. "Gather your things after you speak with Lord Reinard. I need to see the gallows and where I can get a good shot," said Alana.

"Today will be a busy day, after all," said Sebastian.

He left the stable and moved quickly to his horse. He did not notice the Countess standing some yards from the stable, moving toward the manor with resolution of her own.

***

Ian stood in front of the apothecary shop looking thoughtfully at the windows. The building was a two-story structure, leaving him no doubt that living quarters were established on the second level. The building itself was in excellent shape. Malcom Stone was known to be very meticulous in nature. Ian had no doubt that with Julia's assistance; they could run the shop confidently. He smiled as he continued to look at the building. This would be the opportunity he and Julia needed to start again.

Julia came from around the back of the building. Her eyes were bright. "Ian, the back garden is still completely intact. There are no labels on the rows, but I know some of the plants by sight, the rest I am sure we can figure out. The back yard needs to be tended, but the herbs that are growing could probably be harvested and used right away." She put her arms around him as they stood in front of the building.

"This could be a whole new beginning for us," replied Ian with confidence.

Julia looked at him thoughtfully. "Ian, do we really want to live here in this village?" asked Julia. He looked down at her and saw a slight apprehension in her eyes.

"I was hoping to stay in this region of Nereheim. I have no wish to leave the country or move closer to Wildemere. The land is still wild enough here that hard work will earn a day's wage. Why do you ask?" said Ian.

"Do you remember Lord Reinard's daughter, Lillia?" asked Julia. She looked down at the ground as she asked the question. Ian gently lifted her chin so her eyes met his.

"Yes," replied Ian.

"I have heard whisperings that she is sentenced to be hanged tomorrow morning for witchcraft," replied Julia.

"She is just a child," replied Ian. His brow furrowed. Julia nodded.

Before either could speak, the sound of horse's hooves grew behind them. They both turned to see Sebastian Cavanaugh riding up to them.

"Greetings, Sebastian. How is your day going?" asked Ian. Sebastian Cavanaugh was one of the first people Ian and Julia met when they first rode into Denholm Glen a few days before.

"It would be better served if Count Deveraux were not raving mad," replied Sebastian.

"Julia just told me that Lillia Sallen has been sentenced to execution," replied Ian.

"She is unjustly accused and sentenced without witnesses of any kind. She has done nothing wrong. Her only crime is in possessing a sketchbook that has certain information she was most likely given by another," replied Sebastian grimly.

"Is there anything that can be done?" asked Julia.

"That is why I am looking for you. There is no one in this village that I can trust with what the Viscountess and I have in mind," replied Sebastian.

"The Viscountess and you have a plan?" asked Ian. Sebastian nodded.

"It is a most desperate plan, but if it works, it would catch Count Deveraux off his guard, and afford Lord Reinard and Lillia a chance to escape Denholm Glen and go to the king," replied Sebastian.

"Why do you need our help?" asked Ian.

"I need extra help insuring that Lillia is taken off the platform after she is hanged," replied Sebastian. Ian looked carefully at Sebastian, and then nodded gravely.

"You intend to shoot her down the moment she hangs," replied Ian.

"Yes. I am to make sure the noose is tied so that she can still breathe. Alana will shoot an arrow from a distance and cut the rope. Once the rope is cut, I will drop Lillia off the stage, and I need someone to catch her and get her out of the platform area before the Count can stop us. Lord Reinard will undoubtedly need an escort to Wildemere to let the king know what is happening in Denholm Glen. Since you both know every detail of what happened in Illith, it would be good for you to accompany Lord Reinard to see the king," said Sebastian.

"What will happen to Alana and yourself?" asked Julia.

"We will no doubt become fugitives and will leave Denholm Glen. Alana has decided she wishes to travel Nereheim, and perhaps go into North Agea," replied Sebastian.

Julia shook her head. "This trouble all began with Lya Bernard did it not?" asked Julia.

Sebastian nodded. "How did you know?" he asked.

"Count Vedan threatened Lady Cassandra and mentioned her niece by name. He thought he could get Lady Cassandra to commit adultery against her husband to save her own life. He was wrong," replied Julia.

"Count Deveraux cannot be allowed to continue in Vedan's footsteps," said Ian. "We will go to the king with Lord Reinard."

"I will see Lord Reinard and let him know to be ready tomorrow morning. I will meet you later to finalize our plan," said Sebastian.

"We will be at the inn," replied Ian.

The shadows grew longer outside in the late afternoon when the Countess slipped into the barn where Alana kept her horse. It waited for her mistress, quietly in the corner. She crept closer to the horse and rubbed her nose. She remembered when Alana was young and received the horse for her thirteenth birthday. She was so excited; she did not wait for a saddle to be put on before leading the horse outside into the air. The Countess smiled at the memory. They were happier times, when Ana was still young enough to be considered a girl, and Alana was playing in shadows, learning how to live in the wild.

The Countess quickly opened one of the saddle bags Alana had slung over the horse. In it, she placed a package of dried plums, a sack of gold coins, two gold bars from her husband's stores, and a book. She had no doubt of her daughter's skill with a bow. She knew if anyone could save Lillia, Alana could. When Alana succeeded, Lillia would certainly want her sketchbook. On top of the sketchbook, the Countess placed a letter sealed with wax, for Alana to read at another time. She quickly slipped out of the barn, feeling that she could give her daughter no better way to face the world.

***

The next morning, Lillia stood on the platform with the rope hanging down before her. She looked out at the gathered villagers who all wore tear-stained faces. The gloom matched the cloudy day that was before them. She looked up for a moment at the gathering clouds. For one moment, she allowed herself not to think of her fate. "Looks like rain is coming," she whispered. The look in her eyes was as vacant as her tone.

She looked down at her father who watched her carefully. He wore the same face as the others, but with one subtle difference. He looked expectant. What was going to happen besides the obvious?

The Count came up to the platform and spoke words of justice and duty. They were vain ramblings in the ears of all who heard, but Lillia herself knew them to be hollow. Condemned or not, in her heart, Lillia knew she was innocent.

She felt strong arms on her shoulders. She looked up into the gentle blue eyes of Sebastian Cavanaugh. He leaned close to her and whispered, "Whatever happens, take courage, Lillia." She looked back at him again and felt the warmth of his eyes. She walked up to the rope with steady resolve and stepped up on the box below it.

At the bottom of the platform, Lord Reinard watched his daughter walk to her death. The calmness she possessed while doing such a thing almost unnerved him. She had no idea what was to happen next; none of them knew if this would truly work. Reinard put the life of his only child into the hands of a sixteen year old girl with a bow and arrow. His heart raced.

Thirty yards away stood a grove of trees that began the outskirts of the village. An arrow protruded from the trees, guided by a steady hand. Alana took a deep breath as she lined up the arrow to her target. Many doubts tried to crowd Alana's mind as she waited for the moment to strike. Would she be able to slice the rope? Would Lord Reinard get away with Lillia? Would Sebastian be caught in his attempt to help Lillia? What of the Kellers? They were a new couple who came to Denholm Glen to report atrocities that Count Vedan had done. Would they suffer any consequences for their part in this most desperate plan?

Alana pushed away the thoughts with a deep breath. Philip always told her, when she could not focus, always focus on breathing. She felt her mind clear, as she held the bow steady.

Sebastian put the rope around Lillia's neck. He felt tears threatening to cloud his vision as he did so. He wanted to believe that the things that happened only a few weeks ago were just a dream that he would wake from. Any moment, he would sit up in his bed, his body dripping with sweat, gasping for breath. He would look around; see sunshine pouring through his window and he would know that the world was still right.

However, Sebastian knew this was not a dream. He glanced into the darkening sky and whispered, "YAHWEH, do not let this girl die." He stepped back from Lillia and kicked the box from under her.

Alana let the arrow fly as soon as she saw Sebastian kick the box. She grabbed another arrow and quickly aimed it, and waited to see the arrow do its work.

Lillia felt herself fall freely, when the box was kicked out from under her. The rope held her in the air, but she did not feel it close around her throat as she thought she might. Then she felt a tug on the rope and it began to weaken. A moment later, she felt another tug, and she was dropping to the platform, with the rope still around her neck.

Sebastian lunged forward, and picked Lillia up off the platform. The crowd gave gasps and shouts as he threw her over the side. Ian caught her and rushed with Lord Reinard to the side and away from the crowd before anyone could respond.

Sebastian heard the angry shouts of the Count as he witnessed his execution going awry. He pulled a note out of his pocket, unsheathed his knife from his side, and stuck the paper to the platform with it. He then jumped off the back of the platform and ran as fast as he could.

He heard horse hooves coming up behind him and saw Ian slowing to a stop. As Sebastian climbed the horse to sit behind Ian, the Count's shouts and the cries of the people were drowned out by a large number of horses entering the village from the opposite direction. Ian and Sebastian turned around to see the Royal Guard surrounding the platform. "We better get out of here," said Ian.

"Where is Lord Reinard?" asked Sebastian.

"He is already on his way to meet Julia," replied Ian.

Alana rode hard toward the point she agreed to meet the others at. She could already see Julia, waiting in expectation. She pulled up and stopped next to her. Julia had Sebastian's horse with her.

"Did it work?" asked Julia hopefully.

"We shall soon see," replied Alana.

A few minutes later, they heard the sound of horses. Both women were relieved to see Lord Reinard and Lillia riding toward them. A few moments later, they could see Sebastian and Ian as well. Julia kicked her horse and rode toward them. "Ian! I was so worried!" exclaimed Julia.

"Everything went according to plan, but we must keep moving. The Count may suspect we are on our way to see the king and try to beat us to Wildemere," said Ian.

"Agreed," replied Lord Reinard. "It has been a long time since I rode hard, but I would suggest we ride through the night."

Sebastian hopped down from Ian's horse and climbed on his own.

"We will ride as far as Rowall. From there, we will make our own way. Alana wishes to study abroad," replied Sebastian with a smile.

Lord Reinard moved closer to Alana as they began down the road to Rowall.

"Alana, I can never repay the service you have done for me this day. Know that you will always be welcome in my household in Denholm Glen," said Lord Reinard.

Alana nodded her head. "I was taught by one wiser than I to never tire of doing what is right. May YAHWEH always be with us as we strive to this end," she replied. The group continued to move quickly and in silence under the gray sky.

***

Lord Luxton watched Count Deveraux as he rushed up the steps to the top of the platform. He bent down and picked up one of the arrows that were lying on the platform. He reached over and ripped the paper from the knife Sebastian left behind. The Count read the paper, and then screamed as he threw it on the platform. He raced down the stairs again and shouted for his guards. When he was gone, Lord Luxton picked up the paper off the platform. On it was written, "*I will never tire of doing what is right,*[15]" and signed Viscountess Alana Deveraux. Lord Luxton bowed his head and silently praised her for her courage, continuing to hold onto the paper.

He looked over the platform and saw Sebastian on the back of another horse. The air was suddenly filled with the thunder of horse's hooves. He turned and saw a great number of the Royal Guard surrounding the villagers with their swords drawn. "In the name of King Rohn Catalane of Nereheim, I order you to stay this madness!" shouted the Captain of the Guard. He blew his horn three times, and repeated his command. At the blast of the horn, all the villagers froze and became quiet. Lord Luxton quietly walked down the platform steps and up to the captain.

"What is your name sir?" asked the captain.

"I am Lord Luxton," he replied.

"Can you tell me exactly what is going on here?" asked the captain.

"Count Deveraux ordered a young girl by the name of Lillia Sallen to be executed under false charges. She was saved by a few of the villagers; one of them being the Count's daughter. I am sure they are all safely on their way far from here," replied Lord Luxton. He handed the Captain the paper in his hand. The Captain of the Guard took the paper and read it.

"Where is the Count Deveraux?" asked the Captain. Lord Luxton looked around and saw him standing amidst the villagers.

"Count Deveraux, you cannot hide. Step forward," said Lord Luxton.

---

[15] 2 Thessalonians 3:13

The Count stepped toward the captain. "Count Deveraux, you are ordered to come with me to Wildemere to answer to the king for your decisions over the past week," said the Captain.

"The King has summoned me? I have done nothing wrong!" shouted the Count.

"Then you have nothing to fear," replied the Captain. He shouted for one of his subordinates. "Put the Count on a horse and make sure he is flanked on all sides by the swiftest riders. We will not stop until we reach Wildemere," said the captain.

Once the riders were settled, the Royal Guard rode out of town as swiftly as they rode in, leaving questions and speculations in their wake.

CHAPTER 4

NAFARIA WALKED IN THE WOODS near her new home. They had been living in this new manor that once belonged to Joseph Wheaton a week, and she still felt out of touch with it. The halls in this new place were darker, gloomier. Even the smells seemed heavy and foreboding. Outside, in the woods, the smell of the foliage was clear and crisp. She loved the woods. Here, she was at peace.

She spent the morning with Philip learning how to hold and shoot a bow. It was much harder than she thought it would be. However, Philip seemed pleased with her accomplishment, and was never cross with her. He was an excellent teacher. He told her that daily practice at home would help her grow in this skill.

It was now midafternoon, and she walked the woods alone. She carried her basket with her, but her mind was elsewhere. She remembered a time when she went out gathering herb plants for a garden. It was a beautiful spring day, and it was spent with Nathaniel Stone.

She was just eight years old then, but Nathaniel always made time to play with her. Time with him was fun for Nafaria; but it was a time of learning as well. Nathaniel coached Nafaria regularly on various plants and their uses. He was always kind and patient, but he was a diligent tutor as well. He did not let her finish until he was sure she understood a principle he was trying to teach her.

Nafaria smiled at her memories of her friend and continued through the woods. She kept her eyes to the ground and was rewarded with a mandrake plant. She bent down and took her shovel from the basket. As she dug in the earth around the plant she could almost hear his voice. *Be careful, little one. You must make sure to dig up enough soil around the plant to take its roots as well. Without its roots it will not survive.* She heard the words as the wind whispered through the trees. She put the plant in her basket. It was next to a couple lavender plants and a lady's mantle plant she found earlier. She felt tears drop onto her cheeks as she sat on the ground.

While she sat and cried she wondered why Lya had been so foolish in the first place. Lya and her family were dead, and she was driven from her home. Her father was fond of saying that one opportunity lost is another gained; but to Nafaria, all was lost. "Nathaniel, I miss you so much," whispered Nafaria. Her tears continued to roll down her cheeks.

A moment later, she heard the rustle of leaves and twigs breaking. She looked up to see Michael move toward her. He knelt down beside her. He saw the basket of plants, and could tell she was crying. "Michael, what are you doing here?" asked Nafaria defensively. She tried to quickly wipe the tears from her eyes. Michael smiled gently.

"I was just out in the woods, gathering berries upstream. I thought I saw something in the clearing, and when I got closer, I realized it was you. Is everything alright?" he asked.

Nafaria took one look at her brother and shook her head. She knew it was useless to tell a lie. Michael would know better. He sat down next to her, and she moved closer to him. He wrapped his arms around her and let her cry.

"I miss Nathaniel so much. He was my only friend," whispered Nafaria.

Michael smiled. "I know. I remember there were times when I was jealous of your friendship. In the last year, I realized that it was foolish to be jealous of a close bond between you two. I never saw Nathaniel fonder of any girl than he was of you. He may be gone now, but you can be sure he will return for you. However, if I know my friend, it will be at a time when you least expect it. So be sure you do not let your knowledge of plants and herbs falter," said Michael. Nafaria smiled.

"Mother will make sure that does not happen," she replied.

Michael looked up at the sky. The sun was still bright, but beginning its descent. "We should probably go," said Michael. He stood up and pulled Nafaria to her feet.

"You go ahead. I want to keep looking for some wild rosemary," said Nafaria.

Michael looked at her with concern. "Do not be too long. Father does not want any of us in the woods after dusk," said Michael.

"I will be home before then. I need to plant what I have already found," replied Nafaria. She turned and continued through the woods. Michael watched her a moment, then headed in the opposite direction.

Nafaria wandered further into the forest, searching for wild rosemary. She did not know if it would be as common as in Denholm Glen, but she hoped to find it in the woods. Wild rosemary could cost quite a bit if it needed to be bought. Nafaria heard the rushing sound of water off to her right. Feeling thirsty, she went in that direction.

When she found the brook, she let out a gasp. A young girl, about her size, was lying face down on the ground. One hand dangled in the water. She rushed up to the figure on the ground. Instantly, a green snake popped out of the water and lunged at Nafaria.

"You devil!" shouted Nafaria. Grabbing the dagger she carried with her from her basket, she shouted, "You shall not kill again!" She lopped the snake's head off in one quick motion. She then surveyed the reptile thoughtfully. The skills she learned while following Philip in the woods were paying off.

Nafaria turned the girl over. Searching her body, she found the bite on the girl's forearm. She put her mouth to the wound and began to suck it. She grimaced as she felt the venom in her mouth. She turned away and spat. After repeating this, Nafaria could finally taste a different, sweeter taste. She washed the wound with water from the brook, and cupped the water in her hands. She threw it on the girl's face to revive her. After a couple splashes, the girl's eyes fluttered open.

"What happened?" the girl asked weakly.

"You were bitten by a snake. I happened to be gathering herbs and came upon you," said Nafaria.

"I was getting some water from the brook, when the snake bit me," said the girl.

"The snake is dead now. My name is Nafaria," said Nafaria.

"I am Ephratha," the girl responded. She sat up, and then she put her hand on her stomach and winced. "My stomach hurts."

"Did you have anything to eat while you were in the woods?" asked Nafaria.

Ephratha looked at the ground. She held up a branch with a cluster of purple berries on them. Nafaria saw the green heart shaped leaves. Her eyes widened and she threw the berries back down on the ground.

"You ate moonseed berries?" asked Nafaria. A worried look crossed her face.

"I thought they were wild grapes," said Ephratha.

"How many did you eat?" asked Nafaria.

"I had a few branches. That's when I got thirsty, and looked for some water," said Ephratha.

Nafaria looked at her basket. After rummaging a few moments, she pulled out a green plant. "Here, eat this. It is called peppermint. It will help ease your stomach. When you get home, have some peppermint tea. The moonseed will wear off by tomorrow," said Nafaria.

"How do you know this?" asked Ephratha as she chewed the peppermint leaves.

Nafaria hesitated. Her father's warnings about the family's anonymity were running through her mind. She remembered Analia's hanging. Ephratha was just a girl, perhaps her own age. Would she betray her? Nafaria looked at Ephratha as she munched the peppermint. Her eyes held thoughtfulness. Why would she be alone in the woods? Nafaria thought she could trust her. She decided to risk it and reveal herself.

"My family is of the Craft," replied Nafaria.

"You?" said Ephratha quietly. There was fear in her voice when she spoke.

Nafaria looked at the girl with sadness in her eyes. Would she never have the opportunity to use the Craft without the fear of common people hanging over her? Nafaria began to understand why those of the Craft chose to live in anonymity.

"Yes, I am of the Craft. I have also saved your life," replied Nafaria.

Ephratha looked at Nafaria. They were nearly the same size. Where she had blond hair, Nafaria had hair as dark as midnight. Her eyes held warmth as well as sadness. There was also knowledge in her gaze. While Ephratha learned about history and meaningless etiquette, Nafaria learned something more useful. She knew those of the Craft were to be feared because their knowledge could hurt people. Yet, she would not be alive if it was not for this young girl. She wondered how many others like Nafaria there were.

"Thank you. I have never met anyone of the Craft," said Ephratha.

"You must not tell anyone we have met. My family could be in great danger if our secret was known," said Nafaria.

"I will tell no one. Will I see you again?" asked Ephratha.

"We can meet in the woods. I think it will be fine as long as no one knows," said Nafaria.

"There have been hangings and burnings in Wildemere. People fear those of the Craft," said Ephratha.

"People fear what they do not understand. Men use the wisdom of the Craft, and call on wizards to guide them. They regard women as rash and governed by their emotions," said Nafaria quietly. She thought of Analia's body swinging from the gallows. The price paid for her daughter's rashness.

Nafaria looked at Ephratha's forearm. She picked up her basket and pulled out a piece of a long green plant. "Let me see the arm where the snake bit you," said Nafaria.

Ephratha held out her arm. Nafaria rubbed the plant over the bite mark. "This is aloe. It will help heal the mark on your arm. Tomorrow when you wake up, break off this end piece, and rub the plant on your bite mark again," said Nafaria.

"Thank you. You have been very kind," said Ephratha.

"May I ask you a question?" asked Nafaria.

"Yes," replied Ephratha.

"How old are you?" asked Nafaria.

"I am ten years old," replied Ephratha. Nafaria smiled.

"So am I," said Nafaria.

"We are the same age!" exclaimed Ephratha.

Nafaria looked up at the sky. The forest shadows were growing longer. "I need to get back home. Are you all right to walk?" asked Nafaria.

"I should be fine. Can we meet again tomorrow?" asked Ephratha.

"I think so. I can show you the meadow where I gather hawthorn and coneflowers," said Nafaria.

Ephratha hugged Nafaria. It was a simple gesture, one that Nafaria did a thousand times or more. This, however, was different. This young girl was a stranger to her. Yet she was not afraid.

"Until tomorrow," whispered Ephratha.

"Until tomorrow," said Nafaria. The girls parted and went their own way.

Dusk settled as Ephratha found her way through the city of Wildemere. The "w" pattern that made up Cassiopeia would become very noticeable soon. The night was clear. Perhaps after dinner, she would spend the evening in the garden locating the pictures in the sky her father showed her as she was growing up.

Lord Robert Stowe was a noble in Wildemere and held a fascination with the night sky. He studied whatever he could find on the subject. He told her the corsairs and others who sailed the wild waters used the stars to guide their journeys and reach their destinations. He taught Ephratha the stars to guide her if she was ever lost. "The ways of men change, but the stars stay the same," her father would say. This knowledge always gave Ephratha comfort when alone at night.

As she walked up the path to her manor, she looked up again. The sky was darker yet, and Cassiopeia was now shining brightly. She would bear her mother's anxiety and worry about her late hour. If she told her parents about the snake, she would never be allowed out in the woods again.

The lamps burned brightly in the windows as she walked through the arched door at the side of the manor. Servants were bustling about, preparing for the evening meal. As she entered the sitting room from the side entrance, she heard Marta, one of the house servants.

"Ephratha, your father and mother have been worried about you!" exclaimed Marta.

"I am sorry. I was in the woods," replied Ephratha.

"Your mother will likely be in the kitchen," replied Marta. She turned and left the sitting room.

Marta found Ephratha's mother in the kitchen. "My lady, Ephratha has returned," said Marta.

"Thank you Marta. Where is she?" asked Lydia.

"She is in the sitting room," replied Marta. Lydia left the kitchen at once.

"Child, wherever have you been?" she exclaimed in a relieved tone. Her father heard his wife and entered the sitting room.

"We were just ready to send out servants to look for you. What kept you?" asked Robert.

"I am sorry, father. I lingered in the forest longer than I realized," said Ephratha. Her father smiled at her.

"I think we have had this talk before, my princess. When the sun starts to make its descent, you need to be out of the forest and into the city. There are those that would not hesitate to violate a child. If you cannot abide by this rule, I shall have to forbid you from leaving the city," said Robert.

"Yes father," replied Ephratha.

Lydia put an arm around her daughter. She looked down and saw that Ephratha clutched something in her hand. "What do you have in your hand?" she asked.

Ephratha opened it to reveal the aloe leaf Nafaria gave her.

"What is this?" asked her mother. Ephratha was silent for a moment.

"An old woman in the marketplace gave it to me. It is for the cut on my arm," said Ephratha. She showed her mother the snakebite. Lydia peered at it closely. "She told me to put it on my arm every day until it was gone."

Ephratha looked down at the floor. It was the first time she consciously lied to her parents.

"I see. Dinner is ready. It is time to eat," Lydia replied with a nod.

Ephratha enjoyed the meal in silence as she listened to her mother and father talk of the happenings in Wildemere. Usually this was something she would tune out, but she heard her father mention the word "Craft". Ephratha listened intently. As her father spoke, she felt the food in her mouth lose its flavor. The tasty stew that was filled with sage and thyme tasted like old water that collected dust.

"A woman of the Craft cannot be trusted, Lydia, no matter how wise she may seem. We cannot allow one into the affairs of our household. We must find another as a tutor for Ephratha," said Robert.

"There is no one else. Most women in the city are more ignorant than Ephratha. Only the very wealthy have more education to give, but I would not have our daughter go near them. In another year or two she will be past the schoolmaster's expertise. Nora is kind and gentle natured; and we must find someone soon," said Lydia.

"We will find someone else," said Robert. The firmness in his voice told Lydia that discussion on the matter was finished. Ephratha addressed her mother after a moment.

"Who are you talking about?" asked Ephratha.

"We have been looking for someone who can tutor you, so that your schooling will progress. A young woman came to me this morning while I was in the market. She heard that I was looking for a tutor for you. She has a broad range of knowledge, though her passion seems to be herbs and their uses," said Lydia.

"What happened in Denholm Glen and Illith and other places will surely happen here if we allow those of the Craft in our midst. It is already widely known that the tragedy with Lord Wheaton that happened so many years ago revolved around his misuse of the Craft. What if this woman was to turn on us and poison Ephratha out of revenge? Those with that kind of knowledge cannot be trusted," said Robert.

"It is also possible that one of the Craft possesses healing skills as well, is it not?" asked Ephratha.

"Yes, it is quite possible, Ephratha," replied Lydia when her father did not readily answer the question.

"I wish to learn this knowledge of plants and herbs. The schoolmasters do not teach these things," replied Ephratha. Her tone of voice held a finality that neither Lydia nor Robert ever heard from her before.

"I do not wish to borrow trouble for our family by accepting the aid of one of the Craft into our midst," said Robert. His voice continued its firmness.

"But father, for everything evil, there is also good in this world. Is it not possible that there are good women of the Craft? We do not fear wizards this way," said Ephratha.

"Wizards give wise counsel," replied Robert.

"How do you know for sure? Was not Lord Wheaton considered a wizard?" asked Ephratha.

"I will not put any person who lives under my roof in mortal peril. I will not be ruined for the pursuit of arcane knowledge," said Robert. The sharpness of his tone told everyone that discussion on the matter was over. The rest of the meal was finished in silence.

Ephratha spent the evening in the garden staring at the stars. She continued to think about her father's words as she looked for her favorite pictures in the sky. She found Orion quickly. The three stars that formed the belt were very easy to spot. She found Taurus and Gemini soon after.

She feared for Nafaria and her family. Ephratha always looked at her father as wise and generous to any man who would need his aid. Now she saw that bigotry was alive in her father just as it is in all men. As Nafaria told her, men fear what they do not understand. That night, under the stars, Ephratha made a pact with herself to judge no man or woman before she had a chance to know them personally.

***

Nadia rode swiftly through the countryside on the outskirts of the royal city. From the widening of the country roads, and the larger groups of people she passed, she knew she was getting closer to the city. How she hoped Lord Jason was there among the people. She had been traveling for the past two days, but in the last four hours, she was forced to push Saint to the extent of his abilities to outrun four men whom she recognized, and that recognized her. Nadia no longer had any doubts. Count Vedan had dispatched some of his faithful and most ruthless servants to deal with her.

She leaned down to whisper in the horse's ear. Saint breathed heavily and sped up a little more. The woods were becoming thicker by the moment. Nadia veered off the main road she was on and disappeared into the trees.

"She is heading into the woods!" shouted one of the men.

"Follow her!" replied another and the four men headed into the woods.

The way was slower, as Saint had to jump dense underbrush and various bushes, but Nadia was confident in his abilities. She knew the other men were not skilled riders. She would lose them quickly. Saint broke through the woods into a meadow, where she found two of them waiting for her. The others came up behind her and one knocked her off her horse. Saint took off into the woods.

"Your faithful steed has left you, my lady," snarled one of the men. Nadia picked herself up off the ground and tried to catch her breath. She pulled a dagger from her cloak and held it out in front of her.

Philip decided to end his day in the woods. His father kept him and Michael busy with studies during the mornings, and would ask for a few more hours of his time at night. Sometimes it became very tedious studying so much. He would rather spend his days with Nafaria in the woods. The quietness was a soothing balm to him at times.

He was not like Michael, who would throw himself into study upon more study until the sky grew dark and another day passed. "Michael will be a great wizard someday," said Philip aloud as he walked along. There was, of course, the chance he would go mad from his vast reading.

Philip followed the path behind his home toward the brook. This was the fastest way into the woods that were still part of his family's land. He tried to respect other people's land in the beginning, but he soon found the barons did not mind the trespass. They found Philip interesting with his hunting skills. They offered to help him turn his skill into a profitable business, but he always turned down any offers of that sort. The woods were special to him; he wished them to remain so.

He stopped at the brook and looked into the clear water. It was only a week since they left Denholm Glen, but Philip still thought of Alana. The memories were not as painful as before, but he wished them gone altogether. Time spent with Nafaria; teaching her to shoot a bow, teaching her to tread quietly through the woods to hunt, those times helped him build a deeper relationship with his sister. He did not believe YAHWEH would allow persecution of those of the Craft simply to bring him closer to his sister, but Philip was grateful for that result at least.

As he kept going, he also thought of Nadia. He banished her from his mind when he returned home from Illith when he was thirteen. He did not wish to let painful thoughts eat him alive from the heart out. Lord Bryant's revelation brought a whole new spectrum of things to consider. However, now he was dead, his respected trade was completely gone, and no one seemed to know anything of Nadia. Philip knew Lord Bryant enough to understand that he would never let anything come in the way of his daughter. Second only to Cassandra in his heart, Lord Bryant loved Nadia with everything he had in this world. He felt honored to have been chosen as a mate for Nadia. As he thought about the possibility, he felt more humbled that she would accept him. He looked up into the trees again. Only YAHWEH knew where she was now. Philip hoped they would find her before Lord Bryant's trouble became her own.

His eyes wandered to a patch of yellow flowers surrounded by wide light green leaves. He learned about Lady's Mantle from Nafaria. The first few days in the woods with her, she chattered on about every plant and flower she saw. Philip found that time spent in the woods with Nafaria were also times of refreshing his knowledge of the plants and herbs as well. He did not realize how many different plants were here in the outskirts of the royal city. Nafaria was so happy at the arrangement of learning from Philip. She never knew how much she taught him in return.

He continued on through the woods when he spotted movement in the trees ahead. He moved toward the movement which now had noise attached to it. A majestic black stallion bursting through the trees was the last thing Philip expected to see. He quickly lowered his bow and grabbed the reins as the animal passed by him. The horse pulled slightly, and continued to make noise, but Philip spoke softly, "Sshhh, everything is fine. You are in no danger." Philip threw his bow over his shoulder and put his other hand on the horse's snout. He gently turned the animal to face him. His eyes widened as he looked into the deep amber eyes of the stallion. Philip *knew* this animal. It was Lord Bryant's prized stallion. What was Saint doing here alone? As he stroked the horse, it calmed down by degrees. "How might you have come to be in my woods?" asked Philip as he looked intently at the animal.

Suddenly, a loud high pitched scream sounded through the wood. "Nadia?" Philip wondered aloud. He jumped on the horse and turned into the wood searching out the scream.

He urged the horse up to speed as he made through the woods. He was not sure he recognized the voice, but it must have belonged to Nadia. It was the only explanation for Saint being here. He continued to ride swiftly, hoping to get to the voice quickly. He burst through the trees and into the meadow where he found a scene worse than he imagined.

A young woman was on the ground with two men holding her down. She thrashed wildly on the ground trying to buck off the third that kneeled over her with a knife raised above his head. Still another stood by some horses. He could see the long red tresses of the girl's hair before he saw her face clearly. Philip stood up on the horse, grabbing his bow. He readied an arrow and took aim; knocking the knife out of the man's hand with the arrow.

The man with the knife looked up in astonishment to see a young man riding toward them with a bow in his hand. Philip quickly halted the horse, jumped down and readied an arrow on the bow string.

The man looked warily at Philip, but soon regained his composure. He raised his empty hands. "This is nothing that concerns you, boy. Let us alone," said the stranger.

Philip kept the bow trained on the stranger with a steady hand. He stood a head taller than Philip, once he was off his knees. "You are trespassing on land that does not belong to you. Leave now," said Philip sharply.

"We are of no consequence to you. Let us alone," snarled one of the men on the ground in reply. He kept his eyes trained on the young woman whose eyes were wide with fear.

"You will leave now, and the girl stays behind. Make no mistake, I am an excellent shot," replied Philip.

The stranger standing before Philip laughed. "You may be able to shoot deer, boy, but there is no way you will shoot a man to murder him," he said smugly.

Philip aimed at the hat on the stranger's head and let his arrow fly. The hat was instantly shot off his head, and continued some twenty feet beyond them, stuck among the wildflowers along the floor of the meadow.

"Do not leave me to make judgments of morality while my blood boils. You may find I make a misstep," replied Philip angrily.

The shock registered on the man's face told Philip he won the fight. The stranger turned to his companions who were still holding the girl down. "Leave the girl. She is not worth the trouble," said the stranger. He turned and walked away from Philip and grabbed at one of the men holding the girl down.

Philip let another arrow fly in their direction. It landed a few feet beyond them. "Go quickly. My hunting was disturbed," said Philip sharply. The men picked up their pace to a run and quickly disappeared across the meadow.

Once they were gone, Philip walked over and sank to his knees next to the girl. She was still lying on the ground, but slowly willing herself to rise. He helped her sit up. After a moment, he helped her to her feet. They stood looking carefully at each other.

She was tall and slender, but by no means frail. Her cloak was a forest green that went beautifully with her red hair. Bright green eyes were wide, but no longer shone fear. Philip found he could not take his eyes off her. They stood there for at least a minute; taking each other in, before finally embracing each other.

"Philip! I am so grateful to find you. I have been looking for your father ever since I left Illith," said Nadia. She continued to cling to him.

Philip wrapped his arms tighter around her. He just stood there another moment in silence, thankful she was alive.

"Who were those men?" asked Philip. Nadia looked at him.

"They were sent by Count Vedan to kill me. I am certain the Count wishes to claim my father's property. I have heard talk in a couple areas of the Counts seizing lands from owners that are known to be of the Craft under false pretenses. The false pretense that Vedan used to kill my mother is that she killed a missing little girl from our village," said Nadia. She looked carefully at Philip as she spoke. "That was quite a display of horsemanship you put on. Father would have been proud." She looked at the horse as she pet it. "Even Saint agrees," said Nadia as she pet the horse.

"Nadia, what are you doing in Wildemere?" asked Philip.

Nadia's expression took on a worried look. "I have been looking for your father for days. I must speak with him right away. When Ian and I dropped off the filly for Nafaria, we heard about what happened. We were on our way back home when Samson met us on the road and told me my father urged me to find your father. I have unfortunate news of my parents," said Nadia with a sigh.

"We know of your parents. A friend brought news to us one day when he heard in the marketplace about what happened," replied Philip. He helped her back on the horse and climbed up behind her. Taking the reins in his hand, he directed Saint back the way he came.

The men were crouched on the edge of the clearing and watched them go. "What do we do now?" asked one.

"We wait for a more opportune moment," replied the leader. They headed deeper into the woods.

Philip and Nadia rode Saint back through the woods to the manor. Nadia took in the fresh blossoms in the wild trees that grew. She also noted patches of familiar plants and berries as they rode toward the large house she saw just over a wide brook. Philip urged Saint over a small, but well-constructed footbridge that connected one side of the brook with the other. It was easily twenty feet in length.

"I would spot your handiwork anywhere, Philip. You have been busy," said Nadia as they crossed the bridge. She was looking down at the planking. Each was perfectly uniform, without a blemish on any of the wood.

"Michael and father helped, but the design ideas are mine," said Philip. He tried not to sound too proud. They continued up the foot path to the barn where Philip left Saint. After water and some food were found, they continued toward the house.

"So, what exactly is your family doing now?" asked Nadia. "I noticed bunches of many kinds of herbs and plants throughout the woods, and Nafaria seems to have started another herb garden." She noticed the garden as they moved toward the house.

"Father wishes to start an apothecary in the city. He believes that the city is large enough to support the business without attracting attention to the fact we are of the Craft. I think it is a risk, but I believe in father. He has never been wrong," replied Philip.

They entered the house through the kitchen area, and headed down the hallway toward the library. Jason sat at his desk with one of his books open before him. He looked up when he saw Philip and Nadia enter. Instantly his eyes widened and he jumped from his seat.

"Nadia! I am so glad to see you!" exclaimed Jason. He rushed toward her and engulfed her in a strong embrace. She wrapped her arms around him.

"I am very glad to finally find you, Lord Jason. I have been looking for you and your family for days," replied Nadia.

"I was intending to send your father a letter as soon as we were settled. We needed to leave Denholm Glen in haste," replied Jason.

"Lord Sallen told me. Sylvia sent Ian and me to him as soon as we arrived at the manor to speak with him. He told us of Uncle Raymond and aunt Analia's deaths. He told us how Lya caused Count Deveraux to react as he did. Unfortunately, her actions, also gave Count Vedan a motive to kill my parents," said Nadia.

"We heard what happened, but perhaps there is more that you can share?" asked Philip quietly. Nadia looked up at him and nodded her head. She walked over to one of the chairs in the corner of the room and sat down. Philip sat down on a bench next to her. He gently took her hand in his.

Nadia looked down at their hands and felt tears come quickly to her eyes. She was afraid, relieved, tired, and wanted rest. She knew she was finally within a safe haven.

"Ian and I were heading to Denholm Glen with the filly for Nafaria. Father had said that he told you it would not be ready in time for her birthday. We were two days late. When we arrived at the manor, Sylvia told us that you had gone, and that we needed to speak to Lord Reinard Sallen immediately. Lord Reinard told us of Lya's treachery, and how he urged Malcom Stone and you to leave Denholm Glen quickly. The next morning, Count Deveraux tried to seize the manor for reasons of treachery. He did not succeed, because Lord Reinard produced the deed that proved you signed over the land to him. He was now the rightful owner.

Ian and I headed back to Illith early the next morning, and Samson met us on the way. He was riding Saint. He told me my father instructed him to meet me on the road and send me away from Illith. I knew better than to go back to Denholm Glen, so I continued on toward the royal city. I had no idea how I would find you. Count Vedan's men must have followed me," said Nadia.

"There is a possibility they are still in the area. You must be careful not to go into the city alone," replied Philip.

Jason sat quietly as he thought about the news Nadia gave. "Lord Reinard was adamant that I sign the deed to our property over to him. He even went so far as to buy Malcom Stone's property before he left Denholm Glen with Nathaniel. He seemed to have an intuition about this matter that drove him to action," replied Jason.

"The Count did not succeed in taking the land. He knows that Lord Reinard is the owner of the vineyard and that Sylvia has been left in charge of it. He also knows that he has no right to Malcom's property," replied Nadia.

"Father, did Count Deveraux use Lya's execution as a means to gain land that was not his?" asked Philip. He was shocked at the idea. He never really cared for Count Deveraux that much, but he respected the man for his judiciary talents. Count Deveraux kept peace in his area for the past ten years without incident.

"I believe Count Deveraux has gone mad in his grief for his daughter. I do not think he originally decided to take the property of those of the Craft. He was just seizing the property to make sure it did not fall into disrepair. However, there are other men who would take advantage of a situation like this," replied Jason.

"Count Vedan is one of those men. My father has never trusted him, and it had more to do with his character than it did with the affection he held for my mother. Count Vedan would seize property not his as his reward for doing justice in his county. The only trouble is, the justice would be done after the treachery he caused," said Nadia with disdain.

"Noah Vedan has always had the reputation of being a shrewd man. Even as a child he was very conniving and calculating," replied Jason.

"You knew Count Vedan, father?" asked Philip. Jason smiled.

"I did not always live in Denholm Glen, Philip. I became acquainted with your mother by following my father's trade through villages like Illith," replied Jason.

"Joel also said that your father's manor was burned and the servants fled," said Philip.

"I have heard that as I traveled, but I cannot account for it," replied Nadia.

"I am sure more facts will be brought to light soon," said Jason. "For now, how about if we find Thena and let her know that we have a guest." Nadia smiled, relief flooding over her face.

"I would like that very much," replied Nadia. She rose from the chair and followed Jason out of the library. As they walked down the hall, Philip whispered to Jason.

"Father, is this killing spreading all over Nereheim now?" asked Philip.

"I am afraid it might be, Philip," said Jason.

"Will anything happen to us?" asked Philip.

"So far, only Joel and the king know about us. We should be safe," replied Jason. Nadia heard their whispers and stopped in the hallway.

"If I had not been delivering Nafaria's horse, I would have been dragged out into the Village Square with mother. I would have been stoned as well," said Nadia with a shudder. She turned and looked at Jason.

"You may still be in danger here, Lord Jason. Are you truly planning to stay?" asked Nadia.

"I do not wish to leave," said Jason.

"I only hope we do not suffer the same fate as father and mother," replied Nadia.

At that moment, Nafaria and Thena entered the house from the side entrance. Nafaria's face lit up instantly. "Nadia!" exclaimed Nafaria. She rushed up to her and threw her arms around her.

"Nafaria, you have grown, I think," said Nadia as she hugged her. Thena came up to them and put her arms around Nadia.

"We have been so worried for you," said Thena. "I am so very sorry about your parents."

Nadia hugged Thena tightly. She felt tears cloud her vision once more. "Thank you," she whispered. Thena held her a moment longer.

"We must go find a place for you to sleep," said Thena. Without another word, she led Nadia up the stairs.

* * *

Philip walked through the market the next morning with Nadia. She was entranced with the bustle of people buying and selling so many things. Never had she seen so many people out gathering what they needed for the day. Philip had a week and he still had not accustomed himself to the great throng of people that hustled about from one place to the next. He was not in a panic; but he wished to be in the woods where things were much quieter.

Nadia glanced over at him and smiled. "I never would have thought you would be at home in the market, Philip," said Nadia. Philip shook his head.

"The truth of the matter is that I prefer the forest," replied Philip.

"I prefer the open fields with the horses," replied Nadia with a smile.

"That would be nice too," replied Philip with a sigh. He looked from one vendor to the next. "Why does mother need agrimony anyway? I have not seen it anywhere," replied Philip. Nadia laughed.

"That is why it is considered a rare herb," replied Nadia. She grew thoughtful.

"Philip, may I ask you a question?" asked Nadia.

He turned to look at her. She took a breath. "Did you enjoy your summers with father?" asked Nadia.

"Very much," replied Philip quietly.

"Then why did you never return?" asked Nadia. Philip smiled weakly.

"Since we left Denholm Glen, I have spent time thinking about that," said Philip. He looked at her again. She looked back, intently. She was completely focused on his word.

"The summer when I was thirteen, I was mistaken for a work hand, and I guess I felt I was not taken seriously; by you or anyone else. Now that your father is gone, I regret the decision not to return and work through my feelings of pride. The sacred writings tell us that pride goes before destruction[16]. Perhaps my fall is not as far as some, but it has cost me precious time with your father, Samson and Ian," replied Philip.

"I heard you spent much time with Alana Deveraux," said Nadia.

"I found Alana lost in the woods when I returned from your father's the next morning while I was out hunting. We spent time in the woods ever since. She is very much like you; gentle, humble, and willing to learn most anything. She has become quite a skilled shot with a bow, and can live in the woods easily for weeks if she chose to. She has a very adventurous spirit that she hides well from her father," replied Philip. Nadia looked down at her feet. Philip lifted her chin to look her in the eye.

"She is not you," replied Philip. Nadia felt her breath catch at his touch. He stood so close to her, she felt as if they were the only two people in the market.

---

[16] Proverbs 16:18

She turned her head and saw Nafaria next to an old woman smelling roses from her cart. There was another little girl about the same size as she was standing near the cart with another woman. The two girls smiled at each other. She watched as Nafaria closed her eyes and drank the scent in through her nose, rising on her toes to bury her face further into the blossoms. Nadia thought that Nafaria was truly lucky to be in the market of a new place, stripped of her home, and still able to find enjoyment in such a simple pleasure. She was so fixed on the sight; she did not realize Philip was pulled away from her. He thrashed about as two men held him in place. A voice snarling in her ear woke her from her reverie.

"So the great protector is subdued. Who will protect you now?" said the voice quietly. Nadia focused on the face next to her and saw it was one of Count Vedan's men who followed her across Nereheim. She should have known they would not give up so easily. He clamped a hand over her mouth to muffle her cries, and then pushed her to the ground.

"Witch! This woman is the witch who killed my wife!" he shouted as loudly as he could. Nadia sat up on the ground, horrified as people turned to look at her. Nafaria looked over at the scene and gasped. Thena also noticed Nadia sitting on the ground. Now that he had the attention of the market, he continued on. "This woman killed my wife with poison! I demand justice!"

He grabbed Nadia and pulled her to her feet. The other two men that Nadia recognized had joined him. One pulled out a rope and began trussing her with it. The other raised his hand to strike her.

Before he brought it down on her face, it was caught in midair. As he shook his hand free, he turned and faced Jason. Michael was right beside him. He moved forward to help Nadia against the other two men. Nafaria caught her breath as the men faced each other. The man held uncontrolled rage in his eyes. Jason's eyes held a steady repose.

"You will not be allowed to take this woman," said Jason firmly.

"The woman is a witch!" shouted the man. The accusation continued to draw the attention of the market. The air grew quiet.

"You have no proof this woman is of the Craft," said Jason in a firm loud voice. He pulled the man closer to him and said quietly, "How dare you attack a noble woman! You crawl back to Vedan and tell him Nadia Saintclaire is under the protection of Lord Jason Mauldon. If he wishes to pursue me, he shall answer to the king himself. Now go!" Jason snarled as he pushed the man to the ground. Nafaria gasped as she looked at the men, then at her father. She had never seen him in fury. Nafaria caught Ephratha's wide-eyed gaze as she turned to leave.

***

The afternoon sun cast a yellow glow on the meadow. The grass took on a golden hue, mixed with its rich green. The flowers and tall grass swayed in the gentle breeze that blew from time to time.

Nafaria brought Ephratha to her favorite place. There they sat among the coneflowers fashioning the flowers into wreaths. Ephratha picked another flower. As she worked it into the wreath, Nafaria asked, "What is it like to go to school in the city?"

"Have you never been?" asked Ephratha in surprise. Nafaria shook her head.

"No. My main task is to learn the herbs, stones and how to read and write in runes. However, I always wanted the chance," said Nafaria.

"It is probably like any other teaching. I sit in a class with other girls and boys my age. We learn to read and write, and some history. We learn etiquette and what they call 'social grace' in our homes. You probably know more than our schoolmasters," said Ephratha. Nafaria smiled.

"My mother says the same thing. She is very particular about my schooling. I think it is because my father takes on my brothers' teaching. However, he also teaches me," said Nafaria.

"Are you close to your father?" asked Ephratha.

"Yes, very close. We spend time together every day," said Nafaria.

"That is the way it is with my father and I as well. He teaches me the stars. I love my father, but I fear him," said Ephratha.

"Fear him?" asked Nafaria. Ephratha rested her hands for a moment.

"The other night at dinner, my parents were talking about a person to tutor me. She was a young woman who mother said was one of the Craft. Father would not hear of mother's proposal to have her tutor me.

He mentioned a place called Denholm Glen, and would not consider this girl, for the position. It is the first time that I remember my father ever being ruled by prejudice," said Ephratha.

Nafaria sat quietly and worked with her wreath. She nearly dropped her project at the mention of her old home.

"Have you always lived here in Wildemere?" asked Ephratha.

"No," said Nafaria quietly.

"Father says that those of the Craft have brought their own fates upon themselves. That their rashness has brought on this fear," said Ephratha.

"He is correct. Rashness has decided the fate of a few. However, paranoia and fear of the unknown have been the true murderers of the masses," said Nafaria.

"How can you be sure?" asked Ephratha.

"I lived in Denholm Glen. I was born there. I know very well the incident of rashness your father speaks of. It is responsible not only for the death of the guilty one, but also of one who was innocent. Her only crime was giving birth to the murderess," replied Nafaria. Ephratha looked intently at Nafaria.

"Will you tell me what happened?" asked Ephratha quietly. Nafaria met her gaze. After a moment, she spoke.

"There was a murder in Denholm Glen. The Count Deveraux's daughter, Ana, was poisoned. The one who poisoned her was a young woman named Lya Bernard. She was the daughter of Raymond and Analia. Analia was my mother's best friend and confidant. She was a gentle woman with a quiet spirit. She possessed much knowledge. However, she failed to make Lya understand how to use her power for the good of others. Lya chose to use it for her own personal end, and she was discovered. It was decided that the mother would share the daughter's fate, as she was responsible for teaching her temperance. They were executed on the gallows as an example for the village. It happened on my tenth birthday. We left Denholm Glen that night and settled here.

My father has chosen not to become too involved in the matters of Wildemere. He wishes to help, but not to be conspicuous. He is just another merchant who owns land here. He has chosen anonymity to protect my family," said Nafaria.

Ephratha felt her eyes well with tears. She reached out her hand and took Nafaria's in hers. It looked the same as hers. It was gentle and delicate. In her eyes, Ephratha saw more grief than she could ever know in this life of hers.

"I hear it has grown worse in Denholm Glen," said Ephratha.

"I know. I have seen it. Now even children younger than we swing on the gallows," replied Nafaria as she nodded her head.

"How can that be? Who would be so cruel?" asked Ephratha.

"The Sacred Writings say that perfect love drives out all fear[17]. Those who have let fear rule their lives have become murderers," said Nafaria.

"How have you seen it?" asked Ephratha. Nafaria looked down at their hands.

"If I show you, promise me, you will tell no one," said Nafaria.

"I promise," said Ephratha nodding her head.

Nafaria got up from the ground, and pulled Ephratha to her feet. "Come with me. I will show you through something my father taught me," said Nafaria. The girls each put their wreaths on their heads and held hands as Nafaria led them into the forest.

They stopped at a shallow pool a few yards into the forest. Nafaria knelt down on the ground. Ephratha knelt down next to her. The pool was clear and the bottom held many colored stones. Ephratha saw greens, reds, blues, and browns scattered across the bottom.

Nafaria closed her eyes. She took a deep breath and passed her hand over the water. "Let the object be seen," said Nafaria.

Ephratha continued to gaze into the pool. The multi stone floor of the pool disappeared and in its place was a picture. A village square was depicted. Ephratha gasped. Smoke rose in the background. There were bodies on the gallows, just as Nafaria said. Tears came from Ephratha's eyes. She saw how small the bodies on the gallows were. She stared at the picture as the tears fell down her cheeks.

"How can man be so cruel to each other?" whispered Ephratha.

---

[17] 1 John 4:18

Nafaria looked over at her friend. She saw the grief in her eyes. She wondered if Ephratha had ever seen anything like this. Nafaria reached out her arm and put it around her. She passed her hand through the surface of the pool. The image faded.

"I have chosen to show you the power of the Craft. My life is in your hands. I beg you to keep my secret," said Nafaria.

"I promise I will. No one will find out from me about you or your family. I could not bear to see you come to the same fate," replied Ephratha. Tears started to form in her eyes.

"Is something wrong?" asked Nafaria.

"I was thinking about what happened in the marketplace earlier today. What your father did was very courageous. If he wishes to remain in secret here, why did he stand up and draw attention to himself that way?" asked Ephratha.

"Father says that if something is wrong in the world, those who have the ability to do something about it, have the responsibility to do so. That is what gives him the courage to stand and do what he knows is right," said Nafaria.

"He is a very courageous man. I imagine you are quite proud to be his daughter," said Ephratha.

"I am. I would never do anything to harm him or my mother," replied Nafaria. Ephratha's eyes filled with tears. Nafaria put a hand to her cheek and brushed them aside.

"Why are you crying?" asked Nafaria.

"I am sorry that you and your family must go through so much pain because people do not understand you. You have so much to teach us," cried Ephratha. Nafaria felt tears well in her eyes at Ephratha's words.

"You have a good heart. You have great respect for things you do not understand. This is the key to all knowledge. We will always be friends," said Nafaria.

Nafaria put her arms around her friend. She held Ephratha tight. The two girls stood in the woods and cried on each other's shoulders.

* * *

Three horses bearing four riders rode swiftly through the royal castle gate. They stopped at the stable and dismounted. A soldier came quickly down the vast colonnade that ended a few yards from the stable. He seemed perturbed until he spied one of the riders. His face lit up instantly.

"Uncle Reinard!" shouted the soldier as he moved closer to the older man. Upon hearing his name, the man turned in the direction of the voice who called it. The soldier embraced him heartily.

"Colin, it is good to see you," replied Reinard as he embraced his nephew.

"What brings you to Wildemere and with Lillia no less!" exclaimed Colin. As he hugged her, he picked her up and twirled her around.

"We have come on urgent business. I must speak to the king immediately, concerning what has happened in Illith and Denholm Glen," replied Reinard, his tone turning serious.

"Denholm Glen? Why, the captain has taken a company of soldiers to investigate some strange happenings out there. I was on an errand for the queen in North Agea, or I would have gone as well. What happened?" asked Colin.

"Let us go to the king, and I will explain all," replied Reinard.

Colin led the group to the throne room. Lillia was wide-eyed as she surveyed the splendor of the room. Though her father was a land owner, they lived much less complicated lives than most nobles. She was not used to seeing such extravagant furnishings or tapestries on the walls. The king sat next to his queen who seemed to Lillia to be the most beautiful woman in the world. She was snapped from her reverie when she heard her father's voice. She looked over to see him on one knee before the king.

"You may rise, Lord Reinard. Is this your daughter who is with you?" asked the king.

Lord Reinard rose and faced the king with a puzzled look. "Yes, your majesty," he replied.

The king smiled and with what seemed to Reinard with relief. He looked at Colin. "Summon Lord Jason Mauldon. He is to come at once," said the king. Colin bowed his head and left the room. Lord Reinard looked at the king with a puzzled look on his face.

"Lord Jason has arrived in Wildemere under troubling circumstances. He urged me to send a guard to Denholm Glen regarding Count Deveraux's actions concerning the death of his daughter. Two days ago, he came to me very early in the morning, distraught with news that this girl, Lillia, was in danger," said the king.

Ian looked at Lord Reinard. Lord Reinard glanced at Ian and Julia and looked again at the king. "My daughter was sentenced to be executed for being one of the Craft. However, my family is not of the Craft," said Reinard.

The king nodded. "I have heard of your family name, Lord Reinard Sallen. We keep excellent annals in the royal library. Your family has a reputation for vast knowledge as alchemists. You revere great wisdom. However, you study science; there is nothing of the Craft in your blood," replied the king.

"Yes, your majesty. Tragic though it may be, this has been nothing more than a case of grief gone mad. I do not condone Count Deveraux's actions, but I do pity the man," replied Lord Reinard.

The king turned his attention to Ian and Julia. "Are you also from Denholm Glen?" asked the king. Ian bowed his head.

"No, your majesty. We are from Illith, where Count Vedan has murdered Lord and Lady Saintclaire," said Ian.

The king's shock registered clearly on his face. "The horse master? Why would he do such a thing?" demanded the king. Ian looked at Julia who then turned to the king and bowed.

"Count Vedan unjustly accused Lady Saintclaire of using her knowledge of the Craft to murder a child from our village who went missing. He hoped to turn Lady Saintclaire from her husband so that he could have her for himself. When she was condemned in the Village Square, Lord Saintclaire came to her side and was stoned with her," said Julia.

The queen let out a gasp and turned her horrified gaze to her husband. He looked back at her and she could see lines of worry furrow his brows. "Lord Jason was correct. He feared that incidents of this kind would arise in the western parts of Nereheim. We have sent a guard, but we will continue to investigate this matter and bring Count Vedan to justice. For now, Lord Reinard, please accept my hospitality as guests in my castle."

Lord Reinard was surprised at the offer. He bowed again. "That is truly a most gracious offer, my king. I would be honored to accept while we are here," replied Lord Reinard.

* * *

Colin rode swiftly through the city and up the cobblestone path to what he still considered the Wheaton estate. He knew Lord Jason Mauldon had made the place thoroughly his own, but the Wheaton tragedy was the stuff of legends. Legends hold their ground as strong as deep-rooted trees. They do not simply vanish because someone new occupies the space. For this reason, Colin shuddered as he viewed the house.

Jason was standing outside. He was with his daughter looking at something she was showing him with great interest. They both looked up to see him riding toward them.

"Lord Jason, King Rohn summons you to the castle immediately. Lord Reinard Sallen has just arrived," said Colin.

Jason's eyes grew wide as he turned to his daughter. "Nafaria, find Michael and Philip quickly. I need them with me," said Jason. Nafaria rushed away, eager to obey her father's wish.

"What has happened?" asked Jason.

"I do not know. I only know that Lord Reinard, Lillia, and two others from Denholm Glen are here," said Colin.

Philip, Nadia and Michael followed Nafaria out of the house. "I have been summoned to the king. Lord Reinard is here, and I fear the news cannot be good. I want you to accompany me. Nadia, perhaps you should as well," said Jason. They made their way quickly to the stable, and followed Colin to the castle.

* * *

Lillia stood next to her father in the throne room. She was quiet, but her eyes took in every part of her surroundings. Though it was a tragedy that brought them here, she could not help being mystified by the presence of the king and queen. He was stoic; resonating an air of intimidation. She was not only regal, but the twinkle in her eye as she winked at Lillia belied a sense of mischief or good nature. Lillia gave her a faint smile in return.

A moment later, Jason walked into the throne room with Philip, Nadia, and oh, she dared not hope, but Michael was also with them! She gasped as her eyes watered and filled with tears.

"Lillia!" shouted Michael as he rushed over to her.

She saw him come toward her, and she moved toward him as well. She wrapped her arms around him as he held her in a strong embrace. He breathed deeply.

"You always smell like lavender," he whispered. She smiled as she hugged him. "How have you been?" he asked.

"It has been an exciting few days for me," replied Lillia. As they parted, Michael noted the book in her hands. He took it and held it closer to him.

"You still have your sketch book," said Michael.

"Yes, there is no way I would ever part with it," replied Lillia with a smile.

Jason looked at Lord Reinard who looked at him and shrugged. He seemed to realize that if Jason did not know of their infatuation, he was well-informed now.

"Lord Jason, I wished for you to be reacquainted with your friend. This is why I have called you. The little girl is safe, and Count Deveraux will answer for his actions. Lord Reinard seems to think that Count Deveraux acted out of grief for his daughter. What do you say?" asked the king.

Jason looked at the others in the room. From the king's question, he gathered that his vision had happened and Count Deveraux was involved. Yet Lillia stood before them in perfect health. He bowed his head to the king.

"Your majesty; it is not for me to know what has recently happened in Denholm Glen. From your question, I can guess that Count Deveraux has committed an atrocious act. However, Count Deveraux has always been a fair and impartial voice in his area. Nereheim's laws have been upheld fairly under his jurisdiction. I agree with Lord Reinard. I believe he should be allowed to continue as Count but warned to be more prudent in the future," said Jason.

Jason saw a young man and woman look at each other carefully. He recognized Ian Keller right away. One was not a good friend of Bryant Saintclaire and not be able to recognize Ian.

"What of Count Vedan? He has murdered Lord and Lady Saintclaire for no more than pure lust and greed," said Ian. He was trying to be respectful, but anger was boiling within him.

Again, the king looked to Jason. Jason bowed his head as he walked over to Ian and put his hand on his shoulder.

"Ian, I am very sorry for what has happened. Lord Bryant was one of my closest friends. I know the lengths to which Count Vedan will aspire to," said Jason. He then looked at the king.

"For years, Count Vedan has played many political games that have made him rich. I respect his shrewdness, but his audacity cannot be overlooked. He believed himself above the laws he swore to uphold. Count Vedan should be removed of his duties, and imprisoned for his crimes," said Jason.

"Do you recommend execution?" asked the king.

"I cannot recommend an action that ends the life of another, whatever his crimes may have been. I will leave that decision to you," replied Jason with a bow.

The king looked at Colin. "I will not wait for your captain to return. Take twelve men with you and escort Count Vedan back to Wildemere. I will pronounce my judgment when you arrive," said the king. Colin bowed and quickly left the throne room.

"Your majesty, there is one more matter I wish to address," said Lord Reinard.

"Yes?" asked the king.

"Lillia's escape was due in large part to Alana Deveraux and Sebastian Cavanaugh. They made it possible to free Lillia from the gallows at the last possible second. Right now, they are traveling abroad, under the assumption that they are fugitives of the law," said Reinard.

"What do you wish?" asked the king.

"Send out a proclamation pardoning Alana and Sebastian for their part in saving Lillia's life. While they are on the road, perhaps they will hear the news and know that it will be possible to return to Denholm Glen whenever they wish," replied Lord Reinard.

The king nodded his head. "I will issue the proclamation right away. When you return to Denholm Glen, I wish you to take a written copy to post in the Village Square so that all will know they have been pardoned," said the king.

"It will be my pleasure, your majesty," replied Lord Reinard. The king then addressed Jason.

"Lord Jason, I am sure you have many questions for your friends. I have nothing else I wish to ask of you," said the king.

"Thank you, your majesty," replied Jason.

As they left the throne room, Reinard said, "Whether you sought the position or not; it seems that Nereheim has a new Court Adviser."

* * *

Philip was sitting at the window in his room. The moon made its ascent into the night sky. A single candle glowed brightly next to his bed. He was thinking about Nadia. It was like having a gift presented to him to have her here with him again. He did not realize how much he missed her adventurous spirit. She also had a gentleness that reminded him so much of his mother.

"You are still awake." Philip looked over to see his father standing in the doorway.

"I like to watch the moon rise. I usually go to sleep after that," said Philip.

"I was not aware of that. Nafaria and Michael always went straight to sleep," replied Jason.

"We all have our strange ways. Nafaria can always be found in her herb garden or in the woods. If you can find Michael without a book, that is rare. As for myself, I hunt and watch the moon rise," replied Philip.

Jason sat down across from Philip on the window ledge. He looked into his oldest son's face. He did see great wisdom for one of only sixteen years of age. His features were strong and sharp. Philip matured much in the past week. He felt pride as he looked at the life he helped to create, but sadness as well.

"Is something wrong father?" asked Philip. After a few moments, Jason spoke.

"Things in Nereheim are changing, Philip. Events are about to unfold that I fear greatly. You need to take Nadia and leave Nereheim. There may come a time when your brother and sister may need you. Go start a new life in North Agea. I think you will be safe there," said Jason.

"We have faced danger before, father. Why do you worry now?" asked Philip.

"Do you know that YAHWEH has given me the gift of foresight?" asked Jason.

"Yes, father. You have mentioned it before. You can see the future," replied Philip. Jason nodded. His face looked grim in the light of the candle.

"I have seen my death and the death of your mother. I have told no one else this. I intend to send you and Michael away," said Jason. Philip looked stunned.

"What of mother and Nafaria?" asked Philip. He was blinking back tears that formed with Jason's news.

"Your mother will never leave me, even with certain death. Nafaria's future I cannot see. I feel there is something great that she will do, but my sight will not allow me to see what it is. If I can find Malcom, I will betroth her to Nathaniel. Otherwise, she may have to be witness to what will happen. The three of you must further the family line. YAHWEH's wisdom cannot be allowed to leave the world," said Jason. He put his hand on Philip's shoulder. "I have always held great pride and confidence in you. I love you, my son." Jason's eyes filled with tears as he pulled Philip close to him and held him tight. Philip wrapped his arms around his father and let his tears flow.

"When do you wish us to leave?" asked Philip.

"When a wedding ceremony is completed, of course," said Jason. "I do not wish to miss everything in your life!" Philip wrapped his arms around his father.

"I love you so much father! Is there no other way?" pleaded Philip as he felt tears form in his eyes. Jason smiled and held his son. "I do not know if there is a better way. I only know I want you and Nadia to be safe," whispered Jason. They parted and Jason disappeared through the doorway. Tears fell down Philip's cheeks as he continued to ponder his father's words.

Jason came into the bedroom and found Thena lying between the blankets on the bed. She watched him as he walked over to the bed and sat down.

"Where have you been?" asked Thena.

"I needed to speak to Philip. He and Nadia will be married here in the royal city, and then they will leave for North Agea," said Jason. Thena's eyes widened.

"Is that necessary? Surely we will be safe here in Wildemere," said Thena.

"I do not wish to take that chance," replied Jason.

"I trust your judgment," replied Thena with a sigh. "It will be hard to let them go."

Jason smiled back at her. He leaned over and put his hand to her cheek. Her skin was as soft and smooth as the first time he touched her, so many years ago. He kissed her lips as his hands found their way to her head and buried themselves into her hair. As he kissed her, he was aware of her scent, the sweetness of her breath. He took in every sensation as he kissed her face and neck. His tears flowed from his eyes and he whispered, "I love you Thena. I will always love only you. Even after death and we go to YAHWEH, I will love only you."

Thena looked into Jason's face and was puzzled by his emotion. His eyes seemed to hold great sadness, as he continued to touch her and take in every part of her. "Is something wrong?" asked Thena.

"No. I just needed to tell you again," said Jason.

"We need to sleep. Come to bed with me," replied Thena. Jason smiled. He leaned over to the bedside table and blew out the candle sitting on it.

***

Jason walked up the colonnade toward the royal castle. His stride was steady, and very light. A smile stretched across his face as he glanced up, into the clear blue sky. If the rest of the day was as beautiful as the morning, it was truly going to be magnificent.

Queen Susanna saw him first, as she walked out onto the terrace. His confident stride told her at once who it was. "Lord Jason!" she called out as she waved her hand. He stopped and on seeing her, bowed slightly in her direction.

"May I have a word with your majesty?" asked Jason approaching the terrace.

"Why do you wish to speak to me?" asked the queen.

"I wonder if I might ask a favor. Philip and Nadia are going to exchange vows today. They were betrothed before Lord Saintclaire's death. We are going to have a ceremony for them today before they head to North Agea," said Jason.

"They are going to North Agea? Is it for a visit, or to stay?" asked the queen.

"They will stay," replied Jason.

"They are both so young," replied the queen absently. She then came out of her thoughts. "What is it you wish of me?" she asked.

"Nadia's favorite flowers are roses. I understand if it is too much to ask, but I wanted to make her a bouquet from some of the roses in your garden," said Jason.

Queen Susanna smiled brightly, a mischievous glint in her eye. "I shall do more than that. I insist that you have the ceremony here, in the rose garden. You may pick however many roses you wish for her bouquet," replied Susanna.

Jason's eyes widened. "That is a most generous offer, your majesty. I only intended a small gathering. We do not have many friends among us in Wildemere," replied Jason.

"Then the arrangements will be less complicated. I shall take care of everything here. When will you arrive?" she asked.

"We will arrive a little before noon. Philip and Nadia wish to cross the Anenderes while it is still light," said Jason.

"Take whatever flowers you need. You and the men arrive early, and I shall send the royal carriage for Nadia and the women before noon," replied the queen. Jason bowed.

"I thank you once again for this most honored surprise," said Jason.

"It is my pleasure, Lord Jason," replied the queen. She watched him move toward the garden before turning to go back into the castle.

Nafaria sat next to Nadia as the queen's carriage carried Nadia, Thena, Leanna, and herself to the castle. She never thought she would ever be so lucky to meet the king and queen of Nereheim. She was anxious to see Queen Susanna's rose garden. Leanna told them that the queen had it constructed as her place of quiet reflection. Roses happened to be her favorite flower. Nafaria looked out the window, excitement building in her as she spied the castle. Nadia smiled and rested a hand on her arm.

"My, you are restless, little one," said Nadia.

"This is easily the most enchanting day of my life," beamed Nafaria. Nadia laughed.

"One might think it was your wedding day!" she exclaimed.

"I am a long way from being married," replied Nafaria in a defiant tone.

"One never truly knows what the future holds. Nathaniel may come for you sooner than you think," said Nadia with a wink. Nafaria blushed and became silent.

The carriage pulled through the gate and stopped at the end of the Colonnade. Jason opened the door and took Nadia by the hand.

"Everyone is waiting in the rose garden, Miss Saintclaire," said Jason with a wink. He leaned in and whispered, "That will be the last time I will be able to address you as such." Nadia smiled and followed Jason to the rose garden; her arm on his.

Nafaria felt a gasp escape her lips at the same time as Nadia. The roses were stunning with every color imaginable. Amid the flowers and on tables scattered through the garden, were crystal objects of every shape and size. The sun glinted off them and created a dazzling display.

Queen Susanna walked toward Nadia carrying a beautiful bouquet of fresh cut roses. They were a pink color, so delicate, and Nafaria could see no thorns on them. She thought they were the most perfect and beautiful flowers in the world.

"Lady Saintclaire, please accept these as your wedding bouquet," said the queen.

Nadia bowed her head. "It is my honor and my pleasure, your majesty. Thank you for your hospitality and generosity," said Nadia.

Nadia took the flowers, and Jason took her hand. She drew in a breath as she walked toward Philip.

"Do not be afraid," whispered Jason. Nadia smiled.

"I have been waiting for this my entire life. Yet I am still afraid," replied Nadia with a smile.

Nafaria watched the scene around her, as Philip and Nadia pledged themselves to each other. Michael stood by Lillia, and every now and then they stole a glance at each other. The king and queen presided over the affair to give it the authority it deserved. Joel and Leanna stood next to Jason and Thena, holding hands. The Kellers, the couple that came with Lord Reinard to Wildemere looked on at the couple with great adoration. As she looked at the queen again, she thought she saw her give a wink. Nafaria took in the roses and the crystal that surrounded them. "There would be no better place in the world in which to be married," she whispered as Philip and Nadia exchanged their kiss at the end of the ceremony.

* * *

Nadia and Philip galloped across the countryside on the main road heading to the port city of Burnea. Nadia had no fear of anyone following her. She had a new husband, the man of her dreams, riding by her side. Lord Jason sent a clear message to Count Vedan by way of his henchmen. Nadia was no longer within reach.

They had ridden a couple hours when she felt a cool breeze on her face. She looked to her right and saw the edge of the great Anenderes River; the border to Nereheim and North Agea. The cool breeze was a welcome change from the hot sun. Ahead, she could see the outskirts of Burnea begin to sprawl along the countryside. Philip slowed his horse. She slowed down next to him. They trotted along like this for a few moments.

"We reached Burnea quicker than I imagined. How about if we wait until morning to cross the river?" asked Philip. Nadia smiled.

"I was thinking the same thing. We can get an early start in the morning. Perhaps watch the sun rise from the river," replied Nadia.

"That sounds lovely. I have never been to Burnea," replied Philip.

"Neither have I. We should have one last adventure in Nereheim before we leave it forever," replied Nadia. She nudged Saint out of his trot and took off down the road.

"Hey, at least wait for me!" yelled Philip as he took off after her. He loved the freedom he felt right at this moment. It may not have been what he expected, but then YAHWEH always seemed to deliver the unexpected.

Later that evening, Philip stood at the window of the inn overlooking the mighty Anenderes River. The sun was setting and twilight was coming on in the port city of Burnea. He watched the crowds of people along the river begin to diminish as the sky darkened.

The Anenderes River was the stuff of legends. It was, in fact, so vast, that one could not see across it to the neighboring country of North Agea. Philip thought it should have been a sea or an ocean, but Jason had told him that the currents driving the river were what made it a river. It was vast, to be sure, but a river nonetheless to the inhabitants of the sister countries.

So many tales were told by villagers far and wide all over Nereheim and North Agea. Philip knew they were probably all true. No one was ever bold enough to make up a tale about what they saw in the depths of the Anenderes River. The truth of what one saw could be terrifying enough.

Philip felt Nadia's soft touch on his shoulders. He turned and put his arm around her as, together; they stood and watched the river below.

"What do you suppose we will become in North Agea?" asked Nadia.

"That is what I have stood here pondering. I suppose we could run an apothecary like Malcom or father," replied Philip. Nadia laughed.

"Neither of us have the disposition to be merchants. I would be longing for the horses, and you would be running off to the woods at every opportunity," replied Nadia.

"I guess we will have to wait and see. Perhaps a vocation will present itself," said Philip. He pulled his hand through her soft red hair.

"I know this is not what you hoped your future would be," he said quietly. Nadia smiled.

"It is who I hoped my future would be with," replied Nadia softly. She moved closer and kissed him.

Philip sighed as he felt her lips gently brush against his. He pulled her closer and kissed her again. Her body shuddered as he touched her neck.

"It is who I hoped my future would be with also," he whispered.

* * *

The next morning, Philip stood at the front of the large ferry boat waiting for it to push off to North Agea. He looked into the water, letting the waves hypnotize him a little.

He never really had the same fascination for water that his sister Nafaria had. He viewed the bubbling streams as an annoyance while hunting. Now, he stood ready to sail across the largest body of water he had ever seen. The thought was a little intimidating.

Nadia stood next to him with the reins to Saint in one hand and the reins to Strider in the other hand. Philip's chestnut colored horse was almost as large as Saint, and almost as willful. She was pleased to know that Philip trained his horse well. Strider and Saint stood stock still, looking out at the water. They did not whine or stomp their feet the way the other horses did. They were very composed.

"The animals seem restless," said Nadia.

"It is because we are at the Anenderes River. Father told me once that most animals become agitated when crossing the Anenderes. We are lucky that Saint and Strider are so well trained. They will keep their composure," replied Philip.

The boat finally pushed off and began its journey across the water. A mist began to settle around them. Nadia looked at Philip. "The mist will sometimes occur in the mornings," replied Philip reassuringly. Nadia smiled, but gripped the reins of the horses tighter.

"I do not doubt the stories are true, but I wonder if we will see faces in the water?" asked Nadia. Philip shrugged his shoulders and looked out across the water.

At that moment, a horse near the bow reared up and tried to get loose from its master. It neighed louder and continued its violent behavior. The man holding the horse was joined by another, but they could not contain the animal. Finally another man, in a long black cloak, came closer and addressed the men.

"What is the matter?" he asked.

"The animal senses the stirrings in the river, Count Lucerne," replied the older of the two men.

Philip quietly walked up to the men and stood before the horse. He reached out his hand to touch its mane. The horse came down on all fours again and Philip whispered soothing words in its ear. A few moments later, the animal was as docile as his own horse.

Count Lucerne looked at Philip carefully. "How did you do that?" he asked. Philip smiled as he continued to stroke the horse's mane.

"I simply spoke a few soothing words to calm him down," replied Philip.

"You have a great way with horses," replied Count Lucerne.

"I learned from the best. Lord Saintclaire taught me everything I know," replied Philip quietly. Nadia made her way to the front of the boat with the horses. The Count introduced himself.

"I am Count Lucerne of North Agea," said the Count.

"I am Philip Mauldon. This is my wife, Nadia," replied Philip.

The Count looked at the young couple carefully. "You do not seem to have many possessions with you," said the Count.

"We are hoping to start a new life in North Agea," replied Nadia. The Count brightened.

"Do you both have much experience with horses?" asked the Count. Nadia smiled.

"My father was Lord Bryant Saintclaire," she replied.

The Count stared at the young couple. "Would you be willing to tend and train horses for me?" asked the Count.

Philip and Nadia looked at each other and smiled. "Yes sir, I think we would like that very much," replied Philip.

* * *

The Count and his group of attendants talked easily with Philip and Nadia as they rode toward his manor. Philip and Nadia discussed the details of what Count Lucerne was offering as they went.

"Nadia, your father was the finest horse master who ever lived. His instincts are unmatched by anyone. Indeed, far too few people in this world see a horse as more than a creature of either beauty or utility. When you see that these creatures are the very essence of nobility among the animals YAHWEH created, you begin your journey toward the excellence Lord Bryant exhibited. You must respect these animals, for they command respect," said the Count.

"That is well said, my lord. I am quite certain my father would agree," replied Nadia.

"For this reason, I would have you both work as horse masters for me. I am quite certain that your training and temperament with the animals will make you successful," replied Count Lucerne. After a moment he added, "Besides, you both seem far more suited for the outdoors and adventure than you are for quiet reflection in the library."

Both Nadia and Philip smiled as they glanced at each other. Philip said, "That would be my brother, Michael. The only time he is ever in the woods is when he wishes to observe something in nature that he has learned from a book."

"Or when he is observing alchemy at close range," replied Nadia with a wink.

The Count gave a hearty laugh. "That sounds like my wife," he replied.

They continued on in this way, Philip asking questions about their duties as the Count laid out his ideas to continue breeding and training horses the way Nadia's father did.

Soon, the Count's property came within view. As they rode the pathway toward the manor, a striking woman appeared in the doorway and ran out to meet them. Her face held a large smile and a look of relief.

"Thank the creator you arrived home safely. We have heard reports of terrible happenings in Nereheim," she said.

"I am afraid the reports are true," replied the Count as he hopped down from his horse. Philip and Nadia dismounted as well. The Count pulled her toward him. "However, I am perfectly safe and we had great success in our trading. I also have a plan to expand our horse trade." He smiled and turned to Philip and Nadia.

"Philip, I would like you to meet Contessa Mauldon Lucerne; my wife and your aunt," said the Count.

Philip's eyes grew wide as he looked at Contessa. She also looked at Philip with the same wide eyed expression.

"I have read of you in our family annals. Father keeps excellent records of the family. He says the Mauldon family has been doing so for generations. You were sent away when you were just three years old to live in North Agea. I should have realized when you introduced yourself to us, my lord," said Philip.

"I barely remember my brother. I mostly remember images of him. He had such a sweet, but often sad, smile. I never knew why," replied Contessa.

"Contessa joined our family in 1359 when the persecution against those of the Craft took place in Nereheim. I was six years old at the time. Her father came to an arrangement with my father over her care. She came to live with us and we grew up together," said the Count. "Sadly, those times may be returning."

"This is why my father sent me and Nadia to North Agea. The men who murdered Lord and Lady Saintclaire pursued her and he felt that we would be safer here," replied Philip.

Contessa's eyes grew large. "Lord Saintclaire, the horse master is dead?" asked Contessa.

"Yes my lady. The whole intrigue went back to a selfish whim of Count Vedan. He loved my mother when they were children," said Nadia.

"Let us come inside and continue our discussion. Philip and Nadia have agreed to be our horse masters," said the Count.

"We will help out wherever needed, my lord. I do hope our skill can match your confidence in us. We do not know if we will be able to be as successful as Lord Bryant was. For as you said, there is no one else ever who was like him," said Philip.

They walked into the manor. As they continued down the hallway, Philip paused to look in one of the rooms. He slowly walked in, his eyes focused forward.

There was a large board hanging from a wall on the far side of the room. It was covered with glyphs and symbols. The same symbols were very familiar to him. Michael often wrote these symbols wherever he had free space when he was studying alchemy. He glanced around and saw there was a writing desk covered with parchments. Another table nearer the board had a stack of books on it; a few were opened to various writings. Philip smiled as he looked around.

"This scene is very familiar to me," he said quietly. Nadia smiled as she looked around the room.

"Contessa lives her life in constant study. As a child, she was fascinated with all things shiny," replied the Count with a laugh. "It later grew into a study of precious metals and alchemy."

Contessa smiled back. "YAHWEH has given us a whole world to explore. What a shame it would be to disregard the details for the larger pictures they create," she replied.

"You have another nephew who would whole heartedly agree with you," replied Philip with a smile.

"Perhaps in addition to your duties with the horses, you could help me as the children grow older with their studies. I am sure they would benefit from your perspective," said Contessa.

"It would be a pleasure," replied Nadia. "Where are they now?"

"They should still be in the nursery napping. They are twins, age two," replied Contessa.

"Oh, how wonderful!" replied Nadia.

"It is settled then. Philip and Nadia welcome to our home," said the Count with a smile.

* * *

Count Deveraux was brought before the king and queen in chains. There was a very somber air about him and was silent. He understood which sins he committed to bring him to this place. However, as he went back through the annals of his mind, he could not recall why he chose the path of vengeance. Malcom Stone himself reminded him that it was a foolish venture. Why had he not listened? He would make no appeal. As he stood in the magnificence of his king, he would accept whatever fate was his to bear.

He kneeled before the king and queen as quietly as the clinking chains would allow him.

"Rise, Count Deveraux," said the king. There was no emotion behind the command. Count Deveraux stood again, but did not look his sovereign in the eye. "Today is a day of judgment. I have been told of the events that have happened in Denholm Glen. I would first like to say that I offer you my condolences for your daughter Ana's death. The death of a child must be a terrible loss to bear," said the king. The queen shifted her gaze to her husband. She did not expect to hear such words from him. The king continued. "However, you have a position of authority that I myself gave to you. This authority was abused and resulted in the wrongful death of Raymond and Analia Bernard and very nearly the death of Lillia Sallen. These are facts that cannot be overlooked.

Witnesses have come forward to assure me that your authority as Count in the area of Denholm Glen and its regions bordering Illith has been very fair and productive. They termed these abuses as 'grief gone mad.' I was urged very strongly to show mercy and allow you to return to Denholm Glen as Count so that you may continue to govern diligently. I am willing to show you mercy, however, the business of the village of Denholm Glen will fall to the village elders, with you supporting their decisions with your authority. This provision is a cautionary measure against future happenings of this kind. You will govern the outlying areas and the village of Illith. If you are willing to learn from this incident, I am willing to allow you to continue to serve me by keeping justice in the western lands. Let this lesson be a cautionary tale that you tell to the people you serve that this will not happen again. I also hope you remember that while tragedy has taken one daughter from you, there is still a blessing in your other daughter. I have issued a full pardon to her so that she will know she is still a citizen of Nereheim," said the king.

Count Deveraux held his eyes closed through the entire pronouncement. Tears found their way through when he realized he was free to go. Could it be? Was he absolved from all the harm he caused? Who were the witnesses that came forward on his behalf? Why was he to govern the village of Illith and the rest of the West?

"Your majesty, this pronouncement is certainly more than I could ever ask or imagine. Am I to continue to dwell in Denholm Glen?" asked the Count.

"No. I wish you to be more centrally located in your new region. I am convinced that the elders in Denholm Glen are capable of handling affairs in their village. They will seek you out as needed for advice. You will move your family to the village of Illith upon your return," replied the king.

"What of Count Vedan?" asked Count Deveraux.

"His time is at an end. I can no longer trust his judgment with my people. You will move into his house. His property is now yours. The

Saintclaire lands belong to Nadia Saintclaire Mauldon. Part of your duty as Count in this region is to replenish the land and care for it in her absence," replied the king.

Count Deveraux bowed his head. "I shall go at once, your majesty." He turned and left the throne room with the guards.

"That was an incredible thing you did," replied the queen.

"I was given sound advice from those closest to the situation. I decided to take it," the king replied with a sigh. "Lord Jason has said that mercy is a greater act of responsibility than condemnation. Time will show how this decision has fared," said the king. He looked his queen in the eye. "However, the next pronouncement will not be so light."

* * *

Count Vedan was escorted into the throne room. He moved swiftly and with the air of someone who has had their life completely upended. He was met by an underling of the Royal Guard and escorted across Nereheim to Wildemere. His duties were interrupted. He could not imagine what would have caused such a summons. He stopped before the king and queen and bowed slightly.

"Your majesty, to what do I owe this summons?" asked the Count.

"I will have you bow properly before royalty," replied the king sternly. The queen shifted her gaze to the king. Gone was the look of compassion and mercy she saw the day before. She saw a fire in his eyes that made her nervous. She watched as Count Vedan sank to one knee and bowed his head.

"Your majesty," he said quietly.

"You may rise, Count Vedan," replied the king. Count Vedan stood and looked at the king expectantly. He could see by the king's face that this meeting was serious.

"We wait for the witness I have summoned," said the king. At that moment, Lord Jason entered the throne room. He glanced at Count Vedan and stopped. His eyes were fixed on the Count. A few moments later, he looked at the king and bowed his head.

"Your majesty, I was told to come at once," said Jason. He stood still, not advancing toward the king, but closer to the Count.

"I have asked you here to be witness to the judgment which I will pronounce. It is a grave matter, and I wish one of wisdom and reason to hear what I have to say," replied the king.

"Thank you for your consideration, your majesty," replied Jason. The king nodded his head and looked at Count Vedan.

"Certain events have happened in the village of Illith that I cannot allow to go unnoticed or unpunished. Witnesses have come forward to state that you executed by stoning Lord and Lady Saintclaire," said the king. Count Vedan interrupted him.

"Lady Saintclaire murdered a village child. We found remains on an altar-" Count Vedan started, but the king interrupted him.

"How long will you cling to this lie? Lady Saintclaire has shown herself to be the model of virtue in Illith and abroad. You yourself must know she is not capable of such a despicable act!" roared the king. Both Jason and the queen stared at the king. Neither had seen such a display of rage from him before.

"Witnesses have come forward to tell the truth about the 'remains' you found of a girl named Rhea Calloway. You were moved by lust to ensnare Lady Saintclaire, and you failed! So you chose to have the village execute her by stoning. In the process Lord Saintclaire, because of his love for his wife, was stoned as well! You then pursued Nadia Saintclaire to kill her also. Tell me, is this not so?" shouted the king.

Count Vedan was silent. He knew to answer at all would be to invoke punishment. The king continued.

"The Saintclaire estate is still burning from being set ablaze by its master. I have heard reports from other villages assuring me this is so. Answer me!" shouted the king.

Count Vedan continued to be silent. Who were the witnesses that came forward? How could anyone have known? At that moment a shadow crossed his mind. A lone figure rode into the village and shouted that the people "stop this madness". She rode off before she could be stopped: Julia. The Count closed his eyes as he sighed. "It is so," replied the Count quietly.

Jason looked at the Count in disbelief. He did not doubt the words that Ian and Julia spoke about that fateful day. However, it was still shocking for him to hear the admission come from Count Vedan's lips. He shook his head as pity filled his eyes.

"Noah, what have you done?" whispered Jason.

"Count Vedan, you have been stripped of your title and your lands and your authority are forfeit to another. You will be executed by hanging tomorrow at sunrise," replied the king.

Jason looked now to the king. "Your majesty, is it not prudent to show mercy in this situation? Surely a more lenient sentence can be granted. We cannot be allowed to act as executioners," said Jason.

"I believe the sacred writings are filled with examples of how YAHWEH used men to bring about punishments as he saw fit. Count Vedan has acted in arrogance. He felt he could take what he wanted and not feel consequence for his actions. He will be executed as an example to all that would do the same in the future. He plotted and murdered because he could. He must pay the price for such arrogance," replied the king.

Jason closed his eyes for a moment and blinked back tears. He looked at Count Vedan. "I am sorry, Noah," he whispered as the Count was taken away.

Part 2

CHAPTER 5

❧

T HE MORNING SUN SHONE BRIGHTLY as Leanna merrily led Thena
into the little room next to the kitchen.

"We finally decided on a color, and I have everything set," said
Leanna. Her smiles were infectious.

"How could you have everything? Why, you are only a few weeks
along!" said Thena with a laugh.

As she walked down the hallway, Thena thought back to the day
she knew she was carrying Philip inside her. Her excitement and energy
fueled Jason's until it was impossible to tell which parent to be was the
most excited. She smiled at the thought.

"What are you smiling at?" asked Leanna.

"I was just remembering how excited I was when I was pregnant
with Philip," replied Thena.

"We decided on a simple blue color for the room," said Leanna as
she opened the door.

The small room was well lit with the sunlight that spilled in from
the window that showed the bustle of the main street. A cradle was in a
corner opposite the window. A blue velvet blanket draped over the side.
The light curtains that hung in front of the window had a silvery blue
tint to them. They reminded Thena of what she thought fairies' wings
would look like.

Other blue cloths and blankets sat atop a table near the cradle. As she looked around the room, she smiled, until she saw a large vase of dried flowers sitting on a small table in another corner. Her smile vanished as she walked toward the corner. She reached out and carefully touched the dried blossoms.

"Is something wrong?" asked Leanna.

"This flower is monkshood. It makes a lovely decoration, but you need to be careful. Move the vase when the child begins to crawl. This flower is very bad for the heart," replied Thena.

"I will remove it right away. Thank you for telling me," replied Leanna. She walked over to the vase and picked it up.

Thena nodded and her smile returned. "I am sure you will have a fine child, Leanna. I am very happy for you and Joel."

Leanna walked over to Thena and put her arms around her. "I am so glad we are friends," whispered Leanna. Thena smiled at her remark.

At that moment, Leanna felt a sharp pain in her abdomen. She dropped the vase as she bent over and cried out. The vase broke into various pieces on the floor. Thena grabbed Leanna and gently sank to the floor with her. She cradled Leanna in her lap.

"Take deep breaths, Leanna. It will ease the pain," said Thena. Leanna breathed slowly and deeply. A few moments later, she felt relaxed again.

"Thank you," gasped Leanna.

"Has that happened often?" asked Thena. Her voice held an alarmed tone.

"It has happened a few times. I keep hoping it will go away as the baby grows," said Leanna.

"It may. I want you to lie down and rest. I need to get to the shop and let Nafaria gather herbs. Stop by later. I will have lemon balm and roman chamomile for you. You can take both mixed with hot water and honey," said Thena.

"All right, but please, say nothing to Joel. I do not wish him to worry if it turns out that there is nothing wrong," said Leanna.

"I will say nothing. Now, you rest," said Thena as she helped Leanna to her feet.

Thena left the house, thinking deeply. She worried for her friend, but perhaps there was nothing truly wrong. She tried to let it go as she walked through the city toward the shop, but the thought of a bad omen played on her mind.

* * *

The sun was high in the sky which was a spectacular shade of blue. A young man drove a small carriage of sorts with his horse and was accompanied by a young woman on horseback along the country road from Burnea to Wildemere. They had a third horse which the woman held the reins to. The horses as well as the couple seemed to be thoroughly enjoying their leisurely pace. Philip Mauldon looked at his wife. "We have had excellent weather for this trip," he said. "Are you sure you did not conjure this fairness before we left?" he asked. Nadia laughed.

"I may be of the Craft, but I did not inherit my father's gift of intuition. Besides, if either of us would have a proclivity to play with forces out of our control, your family has more arcane knowledge at its disposal," said Nadia.

"I fear you have mistaken me for my brother. Arcane knowledge was always Michael's domain," replied Philip drily.

"I cannot wait to see them again. When we left, Michael dispelled a great tragedy and Nafaria was enchanted with everything around her. I wonder what they have become?" said Nadia. Philip laughed aloud.

"Michael has most likely become a curator at Elias Wheaton's antiquarian library. Nafaria probably still disappears to the woods to look for herbs to plant in her garden the way she always has," replied Philip. Nadia smiled as they rode on, anxious to see their family once again. A happy bout of laughter caught her attention and she looked into the carriage. In it were a small boy and girl, about the same age, struggling to move around.

"No, no, you two must stay in one place a little while longer," said Nadia as she peered into the carriage. The little boy looked up and smiled at her.

"He looks so much like your brother," said Nadia.

"That is because Michael resembles mother," said Philip. "Rowena favors your mother."

Nadia smiled at the mention of her mother. Her father and mother both were victims of the treachery caused by Count Vedan, and were killed by stoning in the village of Illith. She did not dwell on such thoughts for long, but Rowena did indeed remind Nadia of her mother.

After an hour, Philip saw the familiar cobblestone pathway that led to his father's home in Wildemere. It was four years since his father sent him away with a bride, an inheritance, and his blessing. His only command Philip and Nadia obeyed and along the way were taken in by a man of great stature in North Agea. Count Lucerne was very influential and was called to Arioth quite often to be a part of the king's council. On one occasion he took Philip with him. It was here that he was reunited with old family friends; Malcom Stone and his son Nathaniel.

Nathaniel had grown in stature, and his wisdom was sharp as any man's twice his age. He was sure Michael would still best him in a battle of wits, but Nathaniel had shown himself no one to be trifled with. He could not wait to give his father the letter which burned in his pocket that Malcom had written for Jason. Along with this letter, was another letter for Nafaria written by Nathaniel. He wondered if Nafaria was already betrothed.

"At least we found Malcom," he said quietly. Nadia smiled, and then both heard their names shouted. They looked over near the fountain to see a tall young woman with flashing eyes and a wide smile. She washed her hands in the fountain and hurried toward the couple. Philip jumped down from his horse.

"I simply cannot believe you are here!" she shouted as she wrapped her arms around Philip. Philip gave her a great bear hug.

"How could I forget your sixteenth birthday, little one?" asked Philip with a laugh. She pulled away from him.

"I am not little anymore!" exclaimed Nafaria defiantly.

Philip pulled her close and hugged her again. "You will always be little to me," he replied.

After a moment Nafaria whispered, "How I have missed you, Philip."

"I have missed you too. Along with your new nephew and niece, Nadia and I have brought you a present. I am fairly certain you never received the horse you were intended to have when you were younger. Am I correct?" asked Philip.

"Yes," replied Nafaria. Philip took the reins from Nadia. He gave them to Nafaria and she noticed the third horse for the first time. It was a beautiful chestnut mare with golden eyes. The animal looked at Nafaria for a long time, and then put its muzzle in her hand.

"Meet Shasta. She is completely trained and very gentle. She and Saint often take rides together," said Philip.

Nafaria's eyes grew wide. "She is for me?" she said faintly. "She is beautiful."

"You do know how to ride a horse do you not?" asked Philip. Nafaria laughed.

"Yes, Michael has helped me learn," she said. Philip and Nadia burst out laughing.

"He is very skilled now," said Nafaria defensively. She looked at the carriage, and saw two little heads peeking over the side. She squealed with delight. "Are these Roland and Rowena?" she asked. Nafaria quickly held her arms out, and Rowena happily bounded into them. Nafaria smiled and touched her cheek. "She so favors Lady Cassandra."

"She does; just as this little one favors mother," said Philip as he lifted Roland out of the carriage. Nadia came closer to Nafaria as she passed Rowena to her.

"A beautiful girl can only help to have a beautiful horse," said Nadia. She came toward Nafaria and wrapped an arm around her as she carried Rowena. She examined her carefully after a long hug. "You have turned into a remarkable looking woman. Nathaniel will be very impressed," said Nadia.

"You have seen him?" asked Nafaria. A blush of color brightened her cheeks. Philip smiled and pulled a letter from his pocket. "When Nathaniel heard I was coming home to see you, he wanted me to give you this." He handed Nafaria the letter. She took it, and walked the horse toward the stable, not saying a word.

Philip knew they were forgotten, but not for long. Soon their names were called again, and this time, the voice was male. He looked toward the house to see his father coming to greet them. He squeezed his son tightly then Nadia. "I wanted to give you a moment with Nafaria before I came outside. The horse is absolutely beautiful. Lord Bryant would be proud," said Jason.

"I have missed her more than I thought. As I grew up, she was always my little shadow. I feel as though I have spent the last four years without a part of me," said Philip. Jason smiled and laid a hand on his shoulder.

"Perhaps in the future, you will not wait so long for a visit," replied Jason.

"Count Lucerne keeps us very busy, so I make no promises," said Philip with a smile. "However, meet your grandson, Roland." A smile burst onto Jason's face once again as he lifted Roland into his arms.

"He is quite big," said Jason. "You are right; he has your mother's eyes." Roland squirmed in his grandfather's arms.

"I think this little one wants to play," said Jason as he let him to the ground.

"Roland always wants to play. He is a very busy little boy. He is constantly running outside after me in the mornings as I tend the horses," said Philip. At this Jason gave a hearty laugh.

"Did you really think he could be any different? He is, after all, his father's son," said Jason. He grabbed his son and hugged him tightly.

"It is wonderful to have you here," said Jason. He looked at Philip carefully. "I have something important I need to discuss with you," he said. Nadia looked at them.

"I will put the horses in the stable and give them some water. Please take Rowena with you. I will take Roland," she said. She walked toward the stable with the horses and Roland trailing behind her. Jason and Philip walked toward the front of the manor where Philip could see lilac bushes growing.

"The lilacs are new," said Philip.

"They were Nafaria's idea," replied Jason.

"Philip, you know that as the oldest, you are entitled to my diary and the family annals that I keep," said Jason.

"Yes father," replied Philip. A feeling of apprehension crept over him.

"I have decided to pass them to Michael. He is very meticulous and would keep the annals well. I also think he would divine more use from the diary than you would," said Jason. Philip smiled with relief. This was the one family responsibility he was dreading. He knew he was not suited to take care of such precious documents.

"Michael is the best choice you could make, father. At least I know where to go when I need them," replied Philip.

"I am glad you approve of my choice. However, had you decided you would rather take them, I would have allowed it," replied Jason.

"No father, Michael is the wiser choice," said Philip again.

"There is something I wish you to know. It is written in the annals, but I have never spoken of it until now. You may be the oldest; but you are not my first born son," said Jason.

"What do you mean father?" asked Philip.

"Two years before you were born, your mother gave birth to my first son. He was stillborn. It was a devastating time for both of us as we were so young when we first married. Your mother was melancholy for months, until she found she was pregnant with you," said Jason. "I buried the child on our property in Denholm Glen. Just on the border of the vineyard before the meadow starts there is a small marker with a symbol of a fish on it. Joshua was born in the month of March."

"Is that why you never sold the vineyard?" asked Philip.

"I never sold the vineyard because I grew up there. I helped father tend that land my whole life. It is a part of me I could never let go of," said Jason with a smile.

"Thank you for telling me father," said Philip.

"I always wanted to tell you this to prepare you in case the same thing ever happened to you. It is important to never lose hope. In the end YAHWEH delivers," replied Jason.

"Yes father," said Philip quietly.

Jason put his arms around Philip and hugged him once again. "Your mother will be home from the apothecary shop soon. She will be very excited to meet her two little guests." Philip looked at his father and reached into his pocket.

"In the meanwhile; I have a letter from an old friend," he said.

Jason took the letter and his heart skipped a beat. He recognized the careful script of Malcom's signature. He looked at Philip. "You found Malcom?" he asked.

"He has set up shop in Arioth, and advises the king from time to time," replied Philip. Jason smiled brightly.

"Why does that not surprise me," said Jason quietly.

"Father, I have found someone else as well. Count Lucerne is married to your sister Contessa," said Philip. Jason nodded his head.

"Yes, I know. I never talked about her, as I wished to keep her life anonymous for her protection. How is she?" he asked.

"She is very well and very much like Michael. She spends her time in books, studying alchemy," said Philip.

"I am very pleased that she is well. It is amazing how YAHWEH brings us together in various times in our lives," said Jason. The two headed toward the house, but Thena came running up the cobblestone path. Her eyes were wide and she threw her arms around her son, engulfing him in a big hug.

"Philip! You are earlier than I expected! It is so wonderful to see you," said Thena brightly. She looked down and saw the little girl next to him. "Is this Rowena?" she squealed. The child looked up at her, and then put out her arms toward Thena.

"Mother, I have missed you just as much as I missed Nafaria," replied Philip as he held her close. He breathed in the lavender scent he was used to smelling on her. "Nadia has Roland out in the stable." Thena took Rowena in her arms and cuddled her close. The child smiled brightly.

"She looks so much like Cassandra," said Thena wistfully.

Nadia walked up to them holding Roland's hand. "I was putting the horses in the stable while Lord Jason and Philip talked. This is your grandson Roland," Thena then gave Nadia a hug as well.

"Our new grandchildren are not all their news," said Jason with a smile. He showed her the letter Philip handed him. Thena looked carefully at the script.

"Is that a letter from Malcom Stone?" asked Thena.

"Yes. I am very interested in the contents," replied Jason.

"I am as well. Nathaniel asked me to give Nafaria a letter from him," replied Philip.

"Let us go inside and open this together. My curiosity is getting the better of me," said Jason. The four of them entered the house together.

Philip followed his parents into the great room. He could see the lilac bushes outside the large windows. "Where is Michael?" asked Philip.

"He is most likely with Elias Wheaton. He left early this morning for the library. He said something about an old text he wanted to look up," said Thena.

Nadia and Philip both burst out laughing. "What else could Michael possibly be doing?" asked Nadia with a smile.

Jason opened the letter and began to read it out loud.

> *Jason,*
>
> *I pray that this letter will find you alive and well, my friend. I have been in North Agea these past years, and never a day goes by without thinking of you and your family. I wish to come personally and speak with you about a decision that will be mutually advantageous to making our families stronger in the Craft, and also make my heart grow warm. If you will consider betrothal of Nafaria to Nathaniel, please send word with Philip and we will come to see you. It greatly warms my heart to think of the possibility. May YAHWEH keep you safe, my friend.*
>
> *Malcom*

"He told me once that he wished me to betroth Nafaria to Nathaniel. That was when we still lived in Denholm Glen," said Jason.

Just then, Nafaria walked into the room. She held a piece of paper in her hand. Her face was blank, as if she was in shock. Jason looked at her intently. "Nafaria is there something wrong?" he asked. She handed him the paper in her hand.

"Nathaniel wrote me a letter. He asked me to marry him," said Nafaria. She looked at her father again.

"Malcom has asked me to betroth you to Nathaniel. He wants me to send word back with Philip. What shall we tell him?" asked Jason.

"Nathaniel remembers me?" asked Nafaria quietly. Her eyes filled with tears. Philip came up to her and put his arms around her.

"His first question when he saw me was about you. He never stopped thinking of you," said Philip. Nafaria looked at Jason again.

"May I tell him yes father?" asked Nafaria.

"You most certainly may, and you have all my blessing, little one," replied Jason. He came close to Nafaria and put his arms around her as well.

"Nadia and I will go to Arioth as soon as we return to North Agea. It is on the way to Count Lucerne's estate. He will not mind a couple extra days," said Philip. "We will return to North Agea early the day after tomorrow."

* * *

The next morning Nafaria stepped from the woods with Shasta by her side. Ephratha turned around quickly when she heard a branch break. She was relieved when she saw her friend step into view.

"You startled me," said Ephratha.

"I am sorry. I wanted to make sure no one saw us together," replied Nafaria.

"Yes, of course. I also made sure I was not followed," replied Ephratha. She looked at the horse by Nafaria's side.

"Is this your horse?" asked Ephratha.

"Yes, my brother brought it from North Agea with him for my birthday. He is a few days early," replied Nafaria.

"She is beautiful," replied Ephratha as she reached out to touch the horse's mane.

Nafaria stepped closer to her friend and gave her a hug. "Happy birthday, Ephratha," she whispered as they embraced. When they parted, Nafaria pulled out a wrapped package.

"What is this?" asked Ephratha as she took the package.

"Just something I made for you. I thought you might like it," replied Nafaria.

Ephratha opened the paper. Inside a small satchel lay on the paper in her hand. It was made of white silk and a light purple lace was used as a decoration bordering the corners. On the pillow itself the letter "E" was embroidered with care. It was an elegant piece of work. Ephratha put the satchel to her nose and smiled.

"Lavender, my favorite," said Ephratha.

"I could think of nothing else that I could make," replied Nafaria. Ephratha's eyes widened.

"You made this?" she asked.

"Yes," replied Nafaria.

"It is beautiful. I shall keep it forever," said Ephratha.

"I hoped you would like it," said Nafaria.

Ephratha smiled at her friend. She looked around the woods. "It is hard to believe that it was six years ago when we first met. We were just ten at the time."

"Yes, so much has changed between us. I have news," replied Nafaria. Ephratha looked at her.

"What is your news?" asked Ephratha.

"My childhood friend Nathaniel Stone has sent me a letter through Philip. He asked me to marry him!" exclaimed Nafaria.

"That is wonderful news!" exclaimed Ephratha. "Does that mean you will leave Nereheim?"

"I believe so. He and his father live in Arioth, in North Agea," said Nafaria.

Ephratha looked at Nafaria. Tears formed in the corners of her eyes.

"What is wrong?" asked Nafaria.

Ephratha could not speak at first. She enjoyed her times with Nafaria. Now, she would be leaving Wildemere to marry her childhood friend. Soon, Ephratha would also be married. How could she bear to not have her best friend?

"Ephratha, please tell me what is wrong," said Nafaria. She was confused by her friend's silence. Ephratha sighed.

"I am happy for you, of course. I just wish you would not be leaving Nereheim. I will miss you," said Ephratha. "I am going to court. My parents told me last night that I was invited to a royal ball. It is a party for all eligible young women to meet with the prince. Since I am a nobleman's daughter, I am expected to make an appearance."

"Why, that is wonderful! You will make a grand princess," replied Nafaria. She beamed with delight at Ephratha. Ephratha smiled.

"What would I do without your unwavering confidence in me? I can only hope to catch a young noble's eye. The competition will be fierce for the hand of the prince," said Ephratha.

"We shall see to it that you are noticed. You have natural beauty that others would envy. We will see what can be done to enhance that beauty," said Nafaria.

"I wish you could come to court with me. I know some of the girls that would be there. They could stand to be put in place by your wisdom," said Ephratha.

"You shall have to do it instead. When is the ball?" asked Nafaria.

"Two days from now. On midsummer's eve," replied Ephratha.

"That is the night before my birthday! Any good fortune you have at the ball will be my birthday gift," said Nafaria.

"You seem assured of my success. Is that not a little premature?" asked Ephratha with a laugh.

"The first step to achieving a goal is to envision that you have it. That is what my father says. Now, what I want you to do is drink more milk than you normally do. Eat fresh fruit as well. Apples, grapes and melons are good as they are very juicy and sweet," said Nafaria.

She stopped speaking and rummaged through her herb basket. Before she met Ephratha, she spent the morning gathering herbs.

"Take this. It is Roman Chamomile. Before bed, drink this with hot water and honey. It will soothe you and help you sleep," said Nafaria. She went back to her basket and pulled out another type of sprig.

"This is mint. It will make your breath fresh. Chew this before you arrive at the ball. Then keep another sprig close by for throughout the night. Your breath will always be fresh, and make you all the more desirable," said Nafaria.

"If I keep myself busy remembering your instructions, I may get through this event," said Ephratha.

"You will do fine, and soon we will both be married," said Nafaria.

The wind blew through the trees. It was cool and refreshing as the lowering sun cast its warmth on the forest. Nafaria noticed the shadows first.

"Well, I guess it is time to say goodbye. Make sure you bathe in lavender before the ball. Let the scent set you apart from the others," said Nafaria.

"Thank you. I shall heed your good advice," said Ephratha. Nafaria smiled and touched Ephratha's hands.

"Which is which?" she asked.

"Roman Chamomile," replied Ephratha holding up her right hand. "Mint," she said again, holding out her left hand.

"Good. I will not look for you until after the ball. Stay at home and rest. Have fun while you are there," said Nafaria. Ephratha wrapped her arms around Nafaria and held her tight.

"I am very happy for you. We shall have to write each other when you leave," said Ephratha.

"I promise to write you once I am married and settled in North Agea," replied Nafaria. The two parted, heading home in separate directions. Nafaria's mind filled with visions of her friend's grand appearance at the ball.

* * *

That night, Jason sat up in his bed gasping and covered in a cold sweat. The vision of his death continued to grow stronger the past two years. He knew for certain that his end would come in his own home. He put his head in his hands. The time had come to send his second son away. He got out of bed and quickly left the room.

Jason was in the library, his book of wisdom on his lap. A tear rolled down his cheek as he sat in thought. He closed his eyes and prayed aloud.

"YAHWEH, I beg you, show me your design. Has the age of the Craft passed? All I have seen is my demise. Will a phoenix rise from the ashes? Or will your gifts pass from man?" Jason was quiet a long time. The only sound that was made was the gentle breeze that swept in through the window.

Then, his mind was filled with the image of a young woman holding a stone in her hand. The gem was about an inch long and a deep red color. It had markings etched into it, but Jason could not see clearly what they were. The only marking he recognized was his family's insignia, the triquetra. It was the symbol for all of the Craft who followed YAHWEH. The girl chanted an incantation in an ancient tongue and then took an athame and cut her finger. She never even winced at the pain. Taking a leather cord, she smeared blood from her cut along the cord as she continued her incantation. When she finished, the girl looked up at him. He gasped, as he recognized Nafaria's eyes.

That moment Jason woke with a start. He knew his line would go through great peril, but in the end a child of Nafaria's would decide a great fate.

"Thank you for showing me what will be, YAHWEH. Give me the strength to let your will be done. Upon my death, I will my power of foresight to my son Michael," whispered Jason.

* * *

It was later that morning when Jason found Michael in his room. He sat at the table by his window. On the table, a large book lay open. Jason took a moment to watch as his son feverishly wrote in another book. No doubt he had found something else of use for his diary.

This middle child, the second son, was the quietest and least restless of his three children. Michael often preferred the solitude of the library to sunshine and the garden that enchanted Nafaria. He never felt the weight of the older son's responsibilities, even after Philip left for North Agea. He continued to go his own way and study as he wished.

Michael stiffened for a moment, as if he were finally aware he was being watched. When he turned around he saw Jason in the doorway.

"Father, I did not know you were there," he said. Michael closed both books and turned around to face him.

"I have put this off for a long while, but the time has finally come to talk with you about something important," said Jason. The look on his father's face puzzled Michael.

"What is it, father?" asked Michael.

"Before Philip left with Nadia for North Agea, I had a vision of my death. That vision has grown stronger. I need to send you away, for your safety. I wish for you to take the family annals, and this," Jason said as he produced a large, thick book. Michael took the heavy book and rested it on the table.

"What is it, father?" asked Michael as he opened the cover. Before his father answered, Michael's breath caught.

"It is my diary of the Craft. There are things in here that I have never shown you or Philip. There are other volumes. You will take them all when you leave," said Jason.

"Father, as Philip is the oldest, these should go to him," said Michael. For the first time, Jason saw the fear of responsibility in his son's eyes.

"I know. However, I have always believed you to be the one who would derive the most use from them. You are the one who has always thirsted for knowledge. That is why I have saved them for you. You are very meticulous; you will document the family annals with great care. That is why I have saved those for you as well," said Jason.

"Thank you father," Michael whispered.

"You are welcome. My only wish is that you use them well. There are incantations here that will help you in great need," said Jason.

"Where will I go?" asked Michael. He looked up at his father. The idea of leaving his home was strange to him.

"That is for you to decide. Where do you think you would like to go?" asked Jason. After a moment, Michael spoke.

"I would like to return to Denholm Glen, to our old manor. Even if I were recognized, I doubt there would be trouble. Besides, I long for another taste of Sylvia's yeast rolls," said Michael with a wistful smile.

"Well, that is something I certainly never thought of. What do you hope to accomplish there?" asked Jason. Michael tapped his father's diary.

"Grow in the deepest studies of the Craft and in alchemy. That is a discipline that has always fascinated me," replied Michael.

"I have no doubt that you will become an adept in Denholm Glen," replied Jason.

He came closer to his son and embraced him. Michael felt security and warmth in his father's embrace.

"I need you to be ready to leave at the end of the week," said Jason after a moment.

"Yes father," said Michael.

"I will write a letter for you to give to Lord Reinard. I am sure that you can move in immediately," replied Jason.

"It would be nice to see the meadow again," said Michael. He stood up from his chair and looked around the room.

"What of Nafaria? Will she stay here?" asked Michael.

"Malcom and Nathaniel will arrive in a few days for Nafaria. We plan to have a quiet ceremony before they leave," replied Jason.

"What will you tell her of your vision?" asked Michael.

"I will tell her nothing. I know that the time is coming; this is why I need you to leave quickly. You, Philip and Nafaria will carry on in the Craft," replied Jason.

"Father, there is something that I have always wanted an answer for," said Michael.

"What is it?" asked Jason.

"That mark on your forearm, is that a pact seal?" asked Michael.

Jason looked at his son carefully. "Why do you ask?"

"I have read about them. They are not common. Sometimes when one of the Craft pledges allegiance to a person or place, they will make an oath before a few witnesses and be branded with a mark to seal the pact," said Michael.

Jason lifted the sleeve of his shirt to reveal the mark. "This is the glyph of Neptune. It is said that those born under Neptune are blessed with the capacity to rise above themselves to serve the people and society around them. I chose this glyph to remind me of YAHWEH'S greatest rule, to be a servant to all."

"That is why we did not leave Nereheim," said Michael quietly. Understanding now dawned in his eyes about their flight from Denholm Glen so many years ago.

"Yes. In truth, I always thought the persecution would end without much bloodshed. When Nadia came to us with news of Lord Bryant's and Lady Cassandra's deaths, I knew this was not the case. So I sent Philip to North Agea. Now it is important to send you away too. That is why you need to go as quickly as you can," replied Jason.

"What made you decide to make the pact?" asked Michael.

"I love this country. I have lived here my whole life. I have never once thought about what lay beyond its borders. I have traveled at length across the whole country. I even made a trip to the bank of the mighty Anenderes River. Just to see if the legend is true, of course. You do know the legend?" asked Jason.

"I know of the legend of the faces of the dead who move on the waters. Did you see any?" asked Michael.

"I saw one, my great grandmother," replied Jason.

"Did she whisper anything to you?" asked Michael.

"Yes. She whispered, 'All things to all men'[18]. I have tried never to forget that," replied Jason.

Michael moved closer to his father. He wrapped his arms around him and hugged him tightly. His parents were always such a constant in his life. Now he knew he would leave them behind forever.

"Father, give me the courage to be just like you," Michael whispered as he hugged Jason.

---

[18] 1 Corinthians 9:22

"You already have it in you," replied Jason as he squeezed his son harder. After a moment, he parted from his son and rose to leave the room. When he reached the doorway, he turned and looked at Michael. "It is not forbidden to marry outside the Craft, Michael, just unprecedented," said Jason. Michael looked up at him, his face blank and his eyes wide. He felt his heart begin to pound so hard he thought it would come through his chest. Jason smiled at his son and left the room.

"Thank you father," whispered Michael.

* * *

Dearest little Nafaria,

Many things have passed through my mind this night. Watching Analia die, I fear we are all in great danger. We are told that those of the Craft are bound by YAHWEH to protect mortal man. Who will protect us from the ones we are sworn to care for?

You will always be a little light that brightens me when I am alone or afraid. If we ever become separated, know that I will come and find you.

You are such a special girl, filled with wonder for all things around you. Let that joy continue in your heart, as you grow older. We shall see each other again, though I do not know when. Let YAHWEH'S love sustain you until we see each other again.

Nathaniel

Nafaria looked at the precise and beautiful writing on the paper. It was written when he was thirteen, but even then Nathaniel had always been so meticulous. He was just like Michael, who was always so much more mature than his years. She wondered where he was at this moment. A smile crossed her lips when she looked at another piece of paper she held in her hand. It was the more recent letter that Philip brought her. She could hardly believe she was to marry her childhood friend.

The sun dazzled the familiar surroundings of the manor. Nafaria sat by the fountain looking up into the trees behind her home. She saw a nest high in the branches. A bluebird flew back and forth from time to time, no doubt bringing food to hungry chicks.

She breathed in the cool morning air. It was fresh, clean, and full of promise. The fingertips of her right hand dragged lazily through the water in the fountain. She sat there, perfectly content on this glorious morning.

She remembered Ephratha and thought about her preparing to meet the prince at the evening ball. She was on her way to the apothecary just this morning, and all the eligible young women were talking of it. She wondered what it would be like to be in such company. She hoped Ephratha would have a grand time.

Things seemed so different now. She just said goodbye to Michael only an hour before. He seemed very intent on leaving at first light. She thought back on that conversation.

"Leaving to where?" she asked.

"To find my adventure, I guess. I decided I would go back to Denholm Glen," he replied.

"Is that wise?" she asked.

"Wise or not, that is where my heart has always been. I will face danger to have what I most want. Tell Nathaniel to be a good husband or I will come looking for him. Always have faith, little sister." he replied before taking off down the pathway.

Faith. It came down to having that gentle confidence that YAHWEH would protect those who were his. Nafaria was not very troubled about the safety of her brother. She was more troubled with the possibility of missing him.

Like her father, Michael took the Craft seriously. He knew where his path lay. Now she finally had that same quiet confidence: faith.

* * *

The sun began its descent as Ephratha followed her parents into the king's castle. She looked around the bright hall that led to the

267

grand ballroom where the festivities took place. Large chandeliers hung down from a cathedral ceiling so tall it rivaled the great cathedral in Wildemere. The velvet rugs that covered the floor masked her steps as she walked the great hall alone.

Ephratha smiled at people as she passed by, a little nervous with anticipation of what the evening would hold. The music set her mind at ease as she entered the ballroom.

The whole room was lit with bright lights set in crystal lamps so that the room sparkled. Each young man was dressed in a richly made tunic or uniform of military style. Every young woman wore a bright dress that flowed to the floor where they stood. Bright pink, yellow, red, blue or green colors melded together to form an endless collage of satin, chiffon, and silk.

Ephratha followed her parents toward a young man surrounded by a small circle of young women. He was handsomely dressed in a red velvet tunic. It was a color very fitting for royalty. His perfect smile was radiant and his eyes sparkled as he laughed with them about something that seemed to be amusing to all of them. She listened to their conversation for a moment, and then her face filled with a look of dismay. He seemed to be jovially making jokes about each young lady he was speaking with, but they did not notice at all. They laughed right along with him as if he told the most marvelous jokes.

"If only they understood his quips to be at their own expense. I wonder what they would think of him if they knew," Ephratha thought to herself. A slight smile crossed her lips. She quietly slipped away from her parents and away from the prince.

Ephratha's actions were lost in the hustle of the evening to all but one. A pair of green eyes watched her. They belonged to a young man who smiled at that moment. He followed her through the ballroom, always keeping just a couple yards distance between them. Her actions intrigued him. He never met a young woman who would pass up an opportunity to meet with royalty. He wondered what else she might do.

It was not public knowledge that there were in fact *two* princes at the ball. Prince Jared Saint Marc arrived the day before to spend time with his aunt Susanna and perhaps find himself a suitable wife. He knew all the women of noble birth in North Agea, but they lacked any real conviction or self-respect. He wanted a wife who would respect him as a man, not just fear his authority.

After seeing the way his cousin quickly and effortlessly debased courtiers without one of them gasping in indignation, Jared almost made up his mind that women were all the same. The only women who seemed to have a sense of self-respect were those of the Craft. He did not understand the recent murders and the bloodlust that seemed only satisfied through the killing of the wise ones. He knew his uncle Rohn would handle the problem and teach his Counts the lessons they needed to learn. However, Jared hoped such trouble did not come to North Agea.

He watched the young blond woman as she floated through the ballroom. She smiled graciously to all and silently made her way to the terrace.

Ephratha strolled outside and looked up at the sky. She breathed the cool air. She looked for the five bright stars that formed a "w" in the night sky. The constellation of Cassiopeia on her throne twinkled brightly when she finally spotted them. Though Cassiopeia was vain, Ephratha thought she could use some of the celestial queen's confidence at the moment. Though she was a noble's daughter, she felt as though she did not belong at the ball. The prince's manner not only shocked her, but it appalled her as well. She hoped that any husband she would be bound to might have more respect for her than the common dog. Did such a man exist?

At the moment she could not bring herself to go back into the ballroom. If the other noble men were as pretentious and snobbish as the prince was, she did not want to be near them. She wondered what Nafaria would do. Ephratha closed her eyes and took a deep breath. "Give me strength, great queen," she whispered.

"The night air is quite refreshing." Ephratha's thoughts were interrupted by a young male voice she did not recognize. She snapped open her eyes and looked over at him.

"Is it not?" he asked with a smile.

He stood only two feet from her. His vivid green eyes, Ephratha noticed first. So green, they were like shining emeralds. His hair was a brown color, but not so dark as to contrast with his pale skin and light features. His pronounced cheekbone and jaw gave him a look of strength. His smile was not only gentle and kind, but dignified. *He* looked like royalty. She finally became aware that she was staring at him. Ephratha averted her gaze to the ground.

"Yes, it is," she finally replied to his somewhat rhetorical question.

"How is it that you are out here alone during such a grand event?" he asked. Ephratha looked at him.

"I found the company disagreeable," she replied simply. He smiled again.

"Yes, I would apologize for the impression my cousin left on you, but he needs to learn certain lessons of maturity on his own," he replied.

Ephratha laughed. This young man had such gentleness about him. Yet she felt he had confidence in himself to not resort to snobbery. His good-natured attitude put her at ease.

"What is your name?" he asked.

"I am Ephratha Stowe," she said.

"I am pleased to make your acquaintance. My name is Jared Saint Marc," he replied.

Jared looked back up at the stars again. "I noticed you were looking at the sky before. Was there something in particular that caught your fancy?" he asked.

"I was looking for pictures in the sky. I happened to spot Cassiopeia when you found me," replied Ephratha.

"Ah, the vain queen. Royal women would do better if they were more like Princess Andromeda," replied Jared. He smiled his gentle smile again. She laughed at his comment.

"You mentioned the prince was your cousin?" asked Ephratha.

"Yes, my mother is the queen's sister. I am from North Agea where my father is king," replied Jared. Ephratha's eyes widened.

"You are a prince as well?" she asked as she looked at him. She suddenly wondered if her conduct was befitting royalty. Jared seemed to sense what she was thinking. He took her hand.

"I have told no one who I am. Please treat me as you would any other noble," said Jared.

"Most noble men I know do not deserve the respect due you," said Ephratha. There was certain disdain in her voice.

"In that case, treat me better," replied Jared. They both laughed at his comment.

"Do you stargaze often?" he asked her.

"My father taught me the stars and their stories when I was a little girl. He taught them to me so I could find my way if I was ever lost," replied Ephratha.

"That is very wise. I have found the study of the stars fascinating as well," replied Jared. He moved close to Ephratha. Her scent was mingled with lavender.

"The lavender is a very exquisite scent for you," said Jared quietly. She smiled as her face reddened.

"Do you see the Corona Borealis?" she asked quickly to change the subject. He smiled again, sensing her embarrassment at his remark. He looked up at the sky again.

"It is that "u" shape next to Hercules," replied Jared, pointing. She followed his pointed finger. He looked at her again. "Is that mint?" he asked.

A sharp female scream ripped through the night, cutting their conversation short. Instantly Ephratha ran down the steps that entered into the courtyard. A stone path wound through the garden. Jared ran after her.

"Ephratha, wait!" he shouted as he ran.

The scream erupted again, and Ephratha came upon three young men who forced a young woman to the ground. She looked up at them with fear in her eyes. Ephratha looked at the girl and her eyes widened.

"Rina!" shouted Ephratha, as she ran up to the girl and put herself between her and the three men.

"What on earth do you think you are doing?" demanded Ephratha.

"In the name of King Rohn Catalane, I insist that you stop this madness at once!" shouted Jared when he caught up to them.

"Who are you to demand anything in the name of the king?" the tallest of the three men said with a sneer.

"I am Jared Saint Marc, Prince of North Agea. King Rohn is my uncle," replied Jared.

"The king does not care for the welfare of those of the Craft," the young man replied. The other two looked uneasily at Jared.

"That does not give you the right to force your will on another, as if they were a common dog. The king's opinion of the welfare of those of the Craft has changed in recent years. Guard your actions, lest you find yourself on the wrong side of that opinion. Wiser men have been hanged for less," replied Jared coldly. He stared at each one of them. "The night is still young, gentlemen. Go enjoy the ball before this incident is brought to the attention of the royal guard," said Jared. The tallest of the three looked at Jared, then to his friends.

"Perhaps the good prince is right. Let us go back to the ball," he replied.

The three young men left, leaving Jared, Ephratha, and the young girl, Rina, alone. After they left, Jared turned to Ephratha.

"Are you quite all right?" he asked as he looked carefully into her eyes. His concern for her nearly took Ephratha's breath away. It was a moment before she could speak.

"Yes, I am fine. I think we should see Rina home," replied Ephratha.

"I will see to it she is accompanied home by one of the royal guard," replied Jared.

"Thank you," replied Ephratha. She turned and looked at Rina. The girl was shaking, as Ephratha took her in her arms.

"There is nothing to fear now, you will be safe on your way home," she said. The three walked back up to the ball.

Jared led them down the colonnade toward the stable. He found one of the sentries and asked if there was anyone who could accompany Rina home. "She has had an unfortunate incident that has left her unable to leave alone," said Jared as he talked to the sentry.

"There are always one or two men of the guard in the stable area. Follow the colonnade to the stable and you will be able to speak to them, your highness," said the sentry.

Jared thanked the sentry and the three walked down the colonnade. After finding a guard to take Rina home, he led Ephratha back up the colonnade toward the ball.

Ephratha looked at Jared. "Thank you," she whispered and burst into tears. Jared pulled her close to him and held her while she wept.

"That was incredibly brave of you," said Jared.

"I do not understand why we common people feel as though we have the right to persecute those wiser than we," sobbed Ephratha. "Why do we continue to mistreat those of the Craft?" she asked herself out loud.

"I have often asked the question of my aunt and uncle as well. My uncle has changed his ambivalence toward those of the Craft, but still these incidents do occur. I do not understand it," replied Jared.

Ephratha looked into Jared's eyes. They sparkled in the moonlight. Tears formed in the corners of his eyes as he looked deeply into hers.

"Such things do not happen in North Agea," replied Jared quietly. He helped her to her feet. "I have not yet witnessed a noble woman in this country that cared for those of the Craft. Tell me why you would risk your safety for one?" asked Jared.

Ephratha looked at Jared intently. His eyes told her she could trust him with her secret. She decided to risk the promise she made Nafaria so long ago.

"You must promise me you will not repeat what I tell you. A very noble family will come to ruin if you do," said Ephratha quietly. The sobriety in Ephratha's voice told Jared she was quite serious.

"I take what you tell me to the grave," replied Jared.

"A great friend of mine is a daughter of one of the Craft. His name is Lord Jason Mauldon. When he first came to Wildemere, he helped dispel a terrible rumor about another of the Craft named Joseph Wheaton. It is also rumored that King Catalane himself calls on Lord Jason whenever he needs prudent advice. I first met Nafaria when we were both ten years old at the side of a brook. A poisonous snake bit me after I ate some poisonous berries. She saved my life. Tomorrow is her birthday, and I have no idea what to give her. She is both beautiful and wise. I can only hope that one day I shall be as strong as her shadow," said Ephratha.

Jared sat down next to her on the stone bench she was sitting on. He took her hand and looked into her eyes.

"You are stronger than anyone's shadow," said Jared. He put her hand to his lips. Her body quivered at the soft touch of his lips. "Any king would be proud to have you as his wife." He stood up and gently urged her to do the same.

"Will you have breakfast with me tomorrow?" My parents are coming to collect me. In a few days I will return to North Agea. I would like them to meet you. I would also like you to bring your parents," said Jared. Ephratha could hardly believe what she heard.

"Why, yes, that would be quite nice," she said with a smile.

"Good. I will come in the morning with a servant. How is the ninth hour?" asked Jared.

"Fine," replied Ephratha.

"Then let us return to the festivities at hand. I shall like a dance with the finest young lady at the ball," said Jared as he smiled at Ephratha. She returned his smile, and together, they returned to the ball.

* * *

The sun was bright by the time Jared left with one of the king's servants to get Ephratha and her parents. King Rohn did not know Robert personally, but Queen Susanna informed him that she knew Lydia by reputation. She was a very kind and generous woman, always willing to help the poor. She hired the people in her household based on their merit, not on their family name. As a result their manor was one of the most efficient in Wildemere. Jared was pleased to know that Ephratha had a wise mother.

As he pulled into the pathway that led to the manor, Jared saw Ephratha sitting on a bench near a patch of flowers. Her eyes were closed and a peaceful smile rested on her face. Her smooth pink skin was complemented perfectly with the pale blue dress that clung to her light figure. She was delicate and pure. Yes, she would make a perfect queen someday.

He smiled when she looked over in his direction and her face lit up at the sight of him. The carriage pulled to a stop before her, and he jumped down from the driver's seat.

"Good morning," said Jared. He placed a kiss on her forehead. She smiled back at him.

"Why were you riding by the driver, instead of inside?" asked Ephratha.

"Here in Nereheim, I am able to. It is not common knowledge that I am a prince. I like to drive the horses every so often," said Jared.

"So, do you have this type of experience in all that you do?" asked Ephratha.

"Perhaps one day, you shall be able to tell me," replied Jared. He gave her a cryptic smile that made Ephratha wonder what he could mean.

Breakfast at the castle was the most glorious meal Ephratha ever enjoyed. Each delicacy served her was beyond compare, but Jared could not take his eyes from her. He purposely sat across from her and watched every move she made with great intensity. Every time she picked up a berry or a piece of melon, he was acutely aware of her choice. He seemed to memorize how many knife strokes she used to butter a roll.

She found herself watching him just as intently. She knew what type of cheese he preferred. The wine he chose was a deep red color, rather than the king's white. He chose apples instead of melons and chose only chicken or fish. He joyfully ate the berry muffins.

After the meal, he left with both her father and his. Queen Clara came to her and said, "I am very pleased to make your acquaintance, Ephratha. Jared has talked of nothing but you ever since we arrived." Ephratha blushed.

"I hope he has not overstated my importance," replied Ephratha.

"I hope you have not understated it in your mind," replied the queen with a wink.

After breakfast, Jared led Ephratha through the long corridors of the castle. He paused every so often so that Ephratha could take in the tapestries, or linger over a particular painting. When they came to a room filled with glass and crystal objects, Jared stopped a moment before going inside.

"This room is special to me. It is Queen Susanna's blown glass and crystal collection. The light from the fire glints in many different ways, and even various colors can be seen at times. The whole room sparkles as if it consisted of a million stars twinkling together in a confined space," said Jared in a voice so low and gentle, Ephratha could have mistaken it for a whisper. Jared finally moved into the room to give her opportunity for a closer inspection.

She watched him move from one object to the next; always pausing to give attention to each item that caught his eye. She smiled at this. Ephratha was unaccustomed to a man, much less a future king, being captivated so entirely by intricately placed pieces of glass and crystal.

"Your mother seems very sweet," said Ephratha as she examined one of the glass objects in front of her. Jared looked over at her from across the small room.

"She is. Though she finds herself queen, mother is actually ill-suited for the role. She has unmatched intelligence, however she never lost the naiveté she was born with. She is bright, but not cunning. Were it not for the protective spirit of an older sister, I am sure mother would have been completely lost at court. She does not do well with intrigue, though she has often become its chief subject," said Jared.

"You said that Queen Susanna was your aunt," said Ephratha. Jared nodded his head.

"My father once told me about the day he first met both my aunt and my mother. They were both taking tea in their father's flower garden. Competition among suitors was strong in those days; even for two princes such as Rohn and my father. Most men had their minds set on Susanna, for she was not only beautiful, but quick witted, and liked the challenge of a day's labor. However, when father first saw mother, he said he was reminded of something he once read in the sacred writings. 'A husband was to honor his wife and regard her as the weaker partner[19]'," said Jared. At this, Ephratha wrinkled her nose.

---

[19] 1 Peter 3:7

"He thought of her as weak?" asked Ephratha. Jared looked at her carefully. He could see she thought this comment ungracious.

"Not exactly," replied Jared. A slight smile crossed his lips. He picked up a tiny orb of blown glass, carefully, so as not to destroy it. He opened his hand and laid the object in the hollow for her to see.

"This tiny object is very delicate, but beautiful. If you are not careful with it, you will destroy it. Father saw mother's gentle spirit shine through that day. It rang through her laughter, and penetrated his heart. Much like I will take great care not to break the delicate object in my hand; father vowed to protect that goodness from the rest of the world for as long as he lived. He cherishes mother with everything in his heart, body and soul. One day I hope to do the same for the woman I marry," said Jared quietly.

Ephratha watched as Jared carefully replaced the orb back on the stand he took it from. She knew at that moment, she would be in love with Jared forever. He gently took her hand and led her out of the crystal room into the hallway.

They walked outside onto the terrace and into a quiet space surrounded by various kinds of roses. Queen Susanna sat at a table in the middle of the garden. She smiled when she saw them approaching.

"Jared, your mother went to look for you. Your father would like to speak with you," said Susanna. She gave Ephratha a smile. "Ephratha, please join me for a cup of tea while Jared finds his parents."

Ephratha nearly jumped when the queen said her name. "Yes, your majesty," she stammered quietly. She sat down at the table with the queen.

Jared carefully pushed in her chair, and bent down to whisper in her ear. "Do not let the queen frighten you. It is still morning; she has all day to get into mischief."

Ephratha laughed and looked at the queen. Susanna smiled playfully back at her. "The only way to start the day is with a hot cup of tea," she said. She picked up a cup and poured liquid into it and handed it to Ephratha.

"Thank you, your majesty," Ephratha replied, taking the cup.

"Now, while Jared is busy, this will give us the opportunity to get to know each other," said the queen with a smile.

It was almost noon when Jared found Ephratha out on the terrace off the grand ballroom. He might have guessed he would find her out where they first met. She was sniffing a rose from a bush that grew up over the stone railing. Her eyes were closed, and she drank in the rose's scent. She looked over at him when she heard his footsteps. He smiled as he walked toward her. She saw that he held a velvet bundle in his hands.

"Lunch will be served soon," said Jared.

"Oh, thank you for coming to find me. I lost track of the time," said Ephratha.

"So, how was your tea with the queen?" asked Jared.

"It was very nice. Queen Susanna is not like any royal I have ever heard of," said Ephratha. Jared laughed.

"Queen Susanna has never fallen into the conventions of royalty. She is her own person, and uses her wit and poise to subdue those around her. King Rohn is a formidable personality. It is no wonder she fell for him. Susanna loves challenges. Rohn's personality provided not only an enigmatic puzzle for her to work out, but a challenge to live by," replied Jared. He handed Ephratha the bundle in his hands.

"This is for you, to give to your friend for her birthday," said Jared.

He handed Ephratha the velvet bundle. She let out a gasp as she opened it. She pulled out an exquisite knife about six inches long and made of polished silver. On the handle was carved a figure of interlocking circles to form a triangular pattern. It was so intricately detailed that it held Ephratha's gaze.

"It is a hunting dagger. You mentioned you met your friend in the woods," said Jared.

"What is this figure?" asked Ephratha. She pointed to the figure on the handle.

"It is called triquetra. It symbolizes the three deities of YAHWEH. The way the symbol is interwoven symbolizes the equality of YAHWEH," replied Jared.

"How do you know this?" asked Ephratha.

"Those of the Craft are respected in North Agea. They come and go as they please and they talk freely of their ways. One can learn much if one only listens," replied Jared.

"It is stunning. I am sure Nafaria will love it. Thank you," said Ephratha. Jared smiled and took her hand.

"I could do no less for the woman who saved the woman I have fallen in love with," he said softly. Her eyes jumped at his statement. "Now, for the second thing; I am not returning to North Agea with my parents. I have asked to stay for a while longer so that we might get to know one another better."

"Really?" asked Ephratha. Her smile broadened at the news.

"Yes, I will probably return to North Agea in a month. So, for now, you can show me everything you know about Wildemere," said Jared with a smile.

"Well, where would you like to start?" asked Ephratha.

"Right here," he replied. He leaned toward her and gently kissed her lips. Ephratha felt her toes tingle at his soft touch.

"I need to go see Nafaria today. Perhaps we can meet tomorrow?" asked Ephratha, quickly filling the quietness.

"Of course; I hope I shall be able to gain your trust enough to meet her before I leave," replied Jared.

"We shall see," she replied with a smile. She rose from her seat and walked into the ballroom with Jared close behind her.

* * *

It was early afternoon, Nafaria guessed, as she sat in her window. The bright sun exposed every dark shadow of the manor. A warm breeze blew. She felt the air caress her cheeks and pull through her hair like tiny fingers. A peaceful smile crossed her face. The scent of the flowers from the garden rode the breeze and filled her nose with their fresh scent.

As she enjoyed the air, she wondered how things went for Ephratha at the ball. Did she meet the prince? Was he a witless snob, or did he have a sense of honor and wisdom? She could not wait to talk to Ephratha and listen to her glamorous adventure of the night before.

She decided to go into the woods to gather herbs and hopefully see her friend.

She made her way along the garden path out toward the meadow behind the manor. Nafaria had long ago found a nice trail that led her to the woods. Now the trail was even more worn over with the time she spent moving from the garden to the meadow to the woods, collecting the herbs the family used.

The trees blocked the sunshine from the paths along the brook that she normally followed. She smiled as she looked ahead a few feet to find the blackberry bushes were full of berries. As she eagerly picked them, she heard branches snap on the ground. Nafaria turned around and watched her friend approach.

"Ephratha! How was the ball?" asked Nafaria.

"It was enchanting. I did meet a prince, but not the prince of Nereheim. He was awful," replied Ephratha.

"Tell me what happened," said Nafaria. She sat down on a stump of tree that lay in the woods.

"I arrived in the ballroom, and he was making fun of all the courtiers around him. No one seemed to notice. I did not even approach him. I was a little intimidated, so I went outside for a brief moment, and I was followed," said Ephratha with a sly smile.

"By who?" asked Nafaria. She returned Ephratha's smile.

"The prince of North Agea! Oh, he is wonderful, Nafaria. He has great respect for those of the Craft. He has told me some interesting things that he has learned from them in his own country," said Ephratha.

"North Agea is where Philip lives. He and Nadia are horse trainers for Count Lucerne. He also mentioned they tutor his children from time to time. They are stopping in Arioth to give Nathaniel my decision," said Nafaria.

"You may be leaving soon as well?" asked Ephratha.

"I am not sure yet. However, if all goes well, we will be reunited in North Agea, and able to be close friends," replied Nafaria.

"I look forward to that day," Ephratha said as she took out the velvet satchel Jared gave her.

"What on earth is this?" asked Nafaria.

"Jared gave me this to give you as a birthday present. He seemed to think you would really like it," replied Ephratha. Nafaria smiled as she opened the velvet and took out the dagger.

"This looks like a hunting dagger with our family's seal engraved in the handle. This is an exquisite gift," replied Nafaria beaming. She put down the knife and hugged her friend. "Tell Jared that I thank him dearly."

"He would like to meet you. From your gift, you can guess that I told him you were of the Craft. I am sorry, Nafaria, but I think we can trust him," replied Ephratha. Nafaria looked at her friend with understanding in her eyes.

"You are a great judge of character, Ephratha. I am sure he will keep my secret. Tell him I will use this gift and pass it on to my children. It will always be in my family line," replied Nafaria.

"Jared has chosen to stay in Nereheim for the next month. I do not wish to read anything into it, but he told me he wishes for the two of us to become closer," said Ephratha.

"I am sure it is only a matter of time before a wedding is announced," replied Nafaria with a smile. Ephratha blushed at her words.

"I am right?" guessed Nafaria.

"He kissed me before lunch today," replied Ephratha. Nafaria giggled.

"I am happy for you, Ephratha. Once I am with Nathaniel, all will be right again," replied Nafaria wistfully.

"I am sure that will happen very quickly," replied Ephratha with a smile.

The two girls sat and giggled and talked as the sun continued its path across the afternoon sky.

* * *

The next morning was gray and cloudy as Leanna stood at the worktable of her small kitchen. The room had very little space to spare, but Joel made the space that was available very efficient for her. He took great care to build her sturdy cabinets and a worktable to prepare the many foods they ate, entertained with, and gave to those in need.

She stood before this table kneading bread dough in her hands with a firm and uniform touch. She looked up and saw gray skies. It looked to be a gray day, even perhaps a bit of rain. She would need her cloak when she went to market today.

A sharp pain shot through her, and Leanna gasped as her hands went instantly to her belly. They cradled the slight bulge that was peeking out of her lean frame. It was finally showing that she was with child. She breathed deeply the way Thena always told her to when the pains hit.

Leanna began to worry when the pain finally subsided. It was now three months to the day when she found she was pregnant, and the pain still had not gone away. She would speak to Thena later in the day to ask her if there was anything else she could do for her baby.

She finished kneading the dough, and then put it into the bowl sitting on the table. She took a wet cloth from a pot sitting over the fire with a pair of iron tongs. She waited for it to cool and then wrung it out over the kettle. She placed the cloth over the bowl and sighed. She would have to tell Joel of her complication after all.

She took a ladle and dipped it into the hot water and then poured the water into a mug. She reached for a stone jar by the window. Taking off the cover, Leanna took sprigs of Roman Chamomile from the jar and put it into the water. She added a spoon full of honey and stirred the hot drink. Leanna put it to her lips and felt the hot liquid soothe her throat. She smiled slightly.

She put on her cloak and picked up a piece of coal. She wrote out a note for Joel, in case she did not find him outside on her way to the market square.

The market was crowded this morning. More people than Leanna ever remembered seeing threaded through the little shops and crowded around merchant carts, bartering for their wares. She made her way toward a familiar face.

"Good morning Lydia," said Leanna as she approached the woman standing next to a baker's cart. The woman turned at the sound of her name.

"Leanna, how good to see you," said Lydia.

"Where is Ephratha?" asked Leanna.

"She is still entertaining her friend Jared. They left early this morning," said Lydia with a smile.

"I have seen them together. He seems to be quite a gentleman. Wherever did she meet him?" asked Leanna.

"They met at the royal ball on midsummer's eve. Now it is rare to see one without the other," said Lydia.

"There will be a wedding soon," said Leanna with a smile.

"Nothing would please me more. Jared is a very honorable young man," smiled Lydia.

"Well, I guess I must get on with what I came into the market for. I need to go to Thena's apothecary shop and speak with her," said Leanna.

"Perhaps we will see each other later," said Lydia.

"Perhaps," smiled Leanna. She gave the older woman a hug and went about her shopping tasks.

It was an hour later, and the sky was lighter. However, the sun did not wish to be seen. It stayed hidden behind clouds and the day was locked in gloom. Leanna collected what she needed and wanted for dinner that evening. She found good firm fruits. She even found a street vendor who sold a pastry filled with crushed nuts and honey that Joel loved. She was looking for one of the old women that sold herbs when she caught sight of Ephratha and the young man she was with. They made such a handsome couple. He stood tall and confident, but never perceived that he was better than those he spoke to. He seemed to her to have an air of royalty in the way he carried himself, but was kind. He was not at all like the son of the king who lived in Wildemere. That son was more arrogant than anyone she could ever meet. She hoped the king lived long for his heir would never be able to rule as competently.

While Leanna continued about her business, she was becoming aware of a loud commotion near the stables of an inn by the Market Square. A spooked horse broke from its master and ran wild in the market place.

Jared grabbed Ephratha and pulled her to the stone wall of one of the shops. The horse thundered by them, crashing through carts, and trampling those in its path.

Leanna heard the commotion, but before she could look to see what was happening, she clutched her belly and doubled over in pain. She cried out and gasped for air.

Ephratha watched from her place by the shop wall. The horse was running mad and right at Leanna.

"Leanna, run!" shouted Ephratha. Jared followed her gaze and watched as the horse reared up on its hind legs and came down on a young woman who seemed to be in pain.

Leanna heard her name. She looked up just as the horse came down upon her, its hooves trampling her body as it ran wild in the market. Leanna lay unconscious in the square.

Jared reached her limp form first. Ephratha was at his side in an instant. Tears ran down her cheeks. Jared picked Leanna up.

"She is still alive. Do you know where she lives?" asked Jared.

"Yes," she said quietly.

They hurried through the market place; Ephratha leading as Jared struggled to carry Leanna. Lydia saw them, and hurried up to her daughter.

"Ephratha, what has happened?" asked Lydia.

"Leanna was trampled by a spooked horse. We must get her home," said Ephratha. Lydia's eyes widened.

"I will go get Thena," said Lydia. She turned and hurried through the market.

Jared and Ephratha burst through the door of Joel's house. He rushed into the living room to find Ephratha with Jared carrying Leanna in his arms. She was unconscious and lay limp.

"What happened?" demanded Joel as he motioned Jared down the hall and into their bedroom.

"A runaway horse trampled her in the market. She did not see it coming," replied Jared.

"Mother went to get Thena," said Ephratha.

"You brought Leanna all this way? Thank you," Joel said to Jared as he sat down next to his wife. He touched her cheek. His cool fingers against her skin revived her. Leanna's eyes fluttered open.

"Joel?" she whispered.

"I am here. Lie still Leanna, Lydia went to get Thena," said Joel as he caressed her forehead.

"Joel, the baby; I have had such pain," gasped Leanna.

"Stay still," said Joel. Jared held Ephratha as she sobbed.

Lydia burst through the open door of the bedroom. Jared watched a woman with long golden hair follow her and kneel by the bed. Next a man with blond hair walked in and tapped Joel on the arm.

"Jason, thank you for coming," said Joel as he looked up at his friend. So these were the parents of the girl Ephratha had told Jared so much about. They were indeed a pair with much wisdom. He could see the look in their eyes.

"Come, let us help Thena. She will need space to move," said Jason. Joel got up quietly and followed Jason out of the room, looking back at his wife who lay on the bed. Lydia tapped Ephratha on the shoulder.

"We must give Thena room to work," said Lydia. Thena had begun to undress Leanna.

"Lydia, please stay and help me. Ephratha, will you bring us some clean water and linens?" asked Thena.

"Yes Thena," replied Ephratha. She walked out of the room with Jared following after her. Thena looked at Lydia.

"We must get her out of these clothes and clean her up. We need to see where she is hurt," said Thena.

Ephratha brought Thena water and clean linens as Lydia and Thena took off Leanna's clothes and began to clean her. Thena's eyes widened when she saw a patch of blood on the bed between Leanna's legs.

"What does it mean?" asked Lydia.

"It means Leanna's baby may not have survived," said Thena quietly. Thena felt Leanna's forehead. It was shiny and wet with perspiration. "We must get her cool again, or she may not survive the night."

Slowly the night crept, as the wax of the candles next to the bed formed pools at their bases. Thena tried in vain to stop Leanna from bleeding, as Lydia cleaned her and continued to bathe her forehead in cool water. The moon shone through the window as large as life.

Thena continued to sob as she wrung out the linens and rinsed them in the bucket of water that Ephratha would periodically change for her.

YAHWEH, please do not let this young one die so soon. Let her live… she silently prayed.

Leanna lay on the bed, moving her head from one side to another. "Joel, I need Joel," she said weakly.

"Go get Joel," said Thena. Lydia got up and left the room. Thena covered Leanna with a clean sheet. "Joel will be here soon. How do you feel?" She asked Leanna.

"I need some water," Leanna gasped. Thena took a cup from the table by the bed and held it to her lips. She tilted the cup and let the water run into her mouth. Joel appeared at the door, and walked into the room. Tears were in his eyes as he sat on the bed next to his wife.

"Joel," Leanna gasped.

"Shh, do not speak. Try to rest," said Joel as he caressed her face.

Tears streamed down Thena's face as she felt a light touch on her shoulder. She looked up and saw the cool blue eyes of her husband. Jason saw the grief in Thena's eyes. She rose and led him out of the room.

"She is bleeding heavily, Jason. I cannot stop it. I have done everything I could but it will not stop!" Thena's whisper was wracked with sobs.

"We have to tell Joel. He needs to know," said Jason grimly.

They entered the room again. Lydia dabbed Leanna's head with the damp cloth. Jason tapped Joel on the shoulder. "A moment please, Joel," whispered Jason. Joel saw grief in Jason's eyes.

"Of course," said Joel. He left the room with Jason.

"Thena has done everything she can, but Leanna is still bleeding too greatly. She will probably die this night. I am sorry," said Jason. Tears fell from his eyes.

Joel clutched his arms. "Please, I beg you. Is there nothing that can be done to save her? You have such great knowledge and power. Can you not save her?" gasped Joel.

"There is nothing. She was hurt too badly by the horse. Leanna is Thena's greatest friend. I know she has tried everything in her power to save her," said Jason.

Joel dropped his arms and turned away from Jason. "What good is having knowledge and power at your hands if you cannot save those you care about? Do we mean nothing to this God of yours?" asked Joel bitterly. Jason shook his head.

"YAHWEH is not always clear in the details of his design. We are told that all things work for his good[20]. If this is indeed his will, you need to accept it. For none of us can know his reasoning. His ways are higher than ours[21]," said Jason.

"If the will of this God of yours is to let my wife die, I do not wish to have any part of it," replied Joel as he turned to walk back into the bedroom.

Joel's tears fell freely down his face as he sat next to his wife and took her hand again.

"Joel, it looks as if I am going. Know that I have always loved only you," gasped Leanna.

"Leanna, you have always been and always will be the bright star that shines in my heart," whispered Joel. Leanna smiled weakly and gasped once more. Her body went limp and her breathing stopped.

"Leanna!" shouted Joel. He fell on his wife and clutched her to him, his sobs growing louder.

Jason moved toward Joel as Thena sank to the floor sobbing.

"GO! All of you! There is nothing that you can do for her now. Leave me to bury my wife in peace."

"Joel I-" Thena began but he cut her off.

"You had your chance. I trusted you, and now she is dead! Leave my house now!" shouted Joel.

Lydia came over to Thena and helped her from the floor. "Come Thena. There is nothing more left to do," she said gently. Silently, the three left the room.

Ephratha and Jared sat in the living room waiting. Her eyes filled with tears as she looked at the three. "Mother?" she whispered.

"It is over, Ephratha. We must go," said Lydia.

[20] Romans 8:28
[21] Isaiah 55:8

Jared took Ephratha by the arm and led her out of the house as Joel's cries continued to echo through the halls. The group exited the house and walked down the street in silence.

"YAHWEH has given me all this knowledge and yet I could not save my only friend. Jason, what good is this knowledge we possess if we cannot save the ones we love?" asked Thena.

Jason stopped. "We cannot look at the world in such a way, Thena. We are instruments of YAHWEH, his vessels. We are not gods to decide who will live and who will die. That is a decision for YAHWEH alone. I do not understand why he had to take Leanna, but I trust his decision. You must as well. Never forget the creator is in control of the created."

Jason looked at the others with them. He became painfully aware that he had given himself away. Now others were aware of the secret they bore. Jared understood the concern he saw in the man's eyes.

"We will say nothing of this. The wise ones are needed but not respected as they should be in Nereheim. I pray that will change in the future," said Jared.

"Thank you," replied Jason. He put his arm around Thena and walked silently with her.

Jared watched as the tired and grief-stricken couple walked on alone. Lydia watched them go as well. "Ephratha, you must promise never to repeat what you heard this night. No one in Wildemere must know the secret they bear. You cannot tell your father. He would never understand."

"You do not fear those of the Craft?" asked Jared.

"I do not fear the kindhearted and those who use their knowledge for the good of others. Thena has always done this. Jason has always been a voice of wisdom and logic in the meetings of the merchants of this city. How is it said? That wisdom is proved right by her actions[22]. They won my respect years ago when Jason took Nadia Saintclaire and sent her away in safety. I will never doubt their intentions," said Lydia. Jared smiled and looked at the woman with great respect. He now knew where Ephratha gained her respect for things unknown.

---

[22] Matthew 11:19

"Indeed, wisdom is proved right by her children[23]," replied Jared quietly.

* * *

The sky darkened and clouds gathered the next morning as Joel sat silently by Leanna's grave. He stared at the single granite stone with the symbol of a cross cut into it. The gray sky overhead gave the place a hue of ash. He thought of his wife's sweet smile. Her skin was a milky white that was pure and cleaner than snow. His world would never be the same without her, or the child she carried that was to be theirs. Bitter tears filled his eyes as he sat at her grave.

His thoughts turned to the ones who were responsible. They had knowledge and power. Yet, for all their wisdom, they did not save her. They said there was nothing they could do. Joel spat bitterly as he recalled Jason's words. *YAHWEH is not always clear in the details of his design. We are told that all things work for his good. If this is indeed his will, you need to accept it. For none of us can know his reasoning. His ways are higher than ours.* "So easy for one to spout lofty ideals that mortal man cannot fathom in the face of another man's tragedy. Let this tragedy come to your house, Jason. We will see how you accept your YAHWEH's will then," whispered Joel.

He took the knife in his palm and cut the opposite palm. He winced at the pain. Drops of blood spilled on the ground. Joel let his blood fall on his wife's grave. "With your death, my fate was sealed. I will avenge you, my love," vowed Joel. He rose to his feet and walked back toward his house, plotting Jason's demise.

* * *

Thena found Nafaria in her room. She sat at a small table with a single candle burning on it. She held a piece of charcoal in her hand. With it, she was sketching a plant that sat on the table next to the candle. It had three pointed leaves on each branch. As Thena silently

---

[23] Luke 7:35

approached her daughter, she saw on the page, not only a perfect replica of the branch and leaves, but Nafaria had added some flowers as well. Small white blossoms crowded the leaves.

"What is this?" asked Thena. Nafaria stopped her work and looked at her mother.

"I was just wondering what the ivy plant would look like if it actually had blossoms on it," replied Nafaria.

"You doubt YAHWEH's design?" asked Thena.

"I just question it from time to time. In the sacred writings we are told to 'test everything[24]'. I am only doing that," replied Nafaria.

"It is very beautiful. You have such a gift for creating, Nafaria. I think that is why you are so drawn to nature. You have always been able to see what your brothers could not; the beauty of YAHWEH's created things," said Thena.

Nafaria looked up at her mother. Her soft features were worn with lines of worry. Her eyes were filled with sadness.

"Mother, please tell me what is wrong," said Nafaria. Thena sighed.

"I cannot. I want to take this time to entrust you with a tome that may help you when you are older," said Thena.

She handed Nafaria a large book. Its leather was worn, and the pages were wrinkled. Nafaria remembered seeing this book before. She turned the pages carefully. Near the end she stopped at an entry. It was a tisane used to counteract the effects of elderberry. She recognized it from an entry in her own Craft diary.

"This is your diary? Mother, I cannot-"

"Take it," replied Thena, cutting off her daughter's protestation.

"What is happening, mother?" asked Nafaria. She looked intently into her mother's face and waited for an answer. Thena sighed. She knew her daughter would wait indefinitely for the answer to her question.

"Your father's gift of foresight has shown us our end, Nafaria. You will go on a different path. You will give birth to a very powerful child. Teach her the Craft; keep her power anonymous as we have kept yours. Use this book to continue your journey in YAHWEH's power. Do not

---

[24] 1 Thessalonians 5:21

forget the sacred writings. Continue to use your gift and knowledge to help all you meet. Since I cannot be with you in the future, I can only arm you with knowledge," replied Thena.

"Oh mother," Nafaria's voice choked on tears that formed in her eyes. She pulled her mother close to her, clutching her tightly as she wept.

* * *

Nafaria entered the library. She noticed the bookshelves were a little emptier. The dust showed places where books had sat. The fire burned brightly, in the fireplace, but her father was not there. She sighed as she walked toward the window and looked out. The fountain in the garden where her father taught her so much was visible in the night. The moon would rise soon.

"Looking for me?" Nafaria heard a voice behind her. She slowly turned and faced her father.

"Mother gave me her diary. Father, please tell me the truth: are you going to die?" asked Nafaria. Tears welled in her eyes as she asked the question.

Jason looked at his daughter. She had grown into a beautiful young woman, and he did not notice until just now. Her thick dark hair covered her shoulders and framed her delicate face. Her eyes were wide and innocent, yet filled with knowledge and wisdom. She was childlike, but no longer a child.

"I have lived with this knowledge since we moved to Wildemere. That is why Philip was sent to North Agea, and why Michael has gone back to Denholm Glen," said Jason.

"But why did we stay here? Why did you not move us to North Agea? There is still time, why do we stay?" asked Nafaria.

"Nereheim is my home; I will die here if necessary. I have sent Philip and Michael on so that you will have allies when it is over," said Jason.

"Allies?" asked Nafaria.

"Nafaria, you must listen to me carefully. I do not know when my death will come, but I feel it is coming soon. If Malcom does not come soon, you will witness my death. I hoped that would not be necessary.

You must remember above all else, not to avenge my death. The sacred writings of YAHWEH tell us he will avenge. Swear to me you will not seek vengeance yourself, Nafaria," said Jason. The stern look in her father's eyes told her he was quite serious. She took a deep breath and closed her eyes.

"I swear to you, father. I will not seek vengeance for you, even if I see your murderers with my own eyes," replied Nafaria.

Jason walked over to his daughter and placed his hands on her shoulders. "Good. Your role in this life is greater than you realize. You must survive. The fate of kings will rest in you."

Nafaria looked into her father's eyes. She saw such confidence there. How could he be so certain?

"How can you know for sure, father? I am only one, and the youngest. How will I ever make a difference?" asked Nafaria.

"Do not underestimate YAHWEH's design. You are the youngest, but you are by no means handicapped. You are of the Craft and you have learned well. You will pass your knowledge to your children. Trust only those of the Craft. YAHWEH will guide you to a safe haven," said Jason.

"Father, I do not want to lose you," said Nafaria. Tears spilled from her eyes down her cheeks. Jason wiped away the tears on her right side with his hand.

"I do not wish to be lost, child. But this is the part YAHWEH has given me to play. Remember the love your mother and I have for you. Always remember that we have been so proud of you. A more precious jewel YAHWEH could never have given me," said Jason, as he pulled Nafaria close to him and hugged her tightly.

"I love you so much father!" cried Nafaria as she clutched his robe.

"I know, my child. I have always known," replied Jason as he held Nafaria. "Perhaps we could do one thing together?" he asked.

"What father?" asked Nafaria.

"Watch the moon rise out in the garden together," replied Jason. Nafaria looked up at her father and smiled.

"I would love that," replied Nafaria. Jason smiled as he and Nafaria left the library.

* * *

The next morning, Jason awoke. The sun was shining through the window. Thena still lay asleep next to him. He walked over to the window and looked down on the little garden. All life seemed still. He could hear a lone bird's cry in the air. It was a strange sound, so solitary. He quickly dressed and left the room.

He found Nafaria in the dining area, sipping a cup of tea. She looked up as he approached.

"You are up early, little one," said Jason.

"Father, I am hardly a child. Somewhere between our departures from Denholm Glen to Michael's leaving us, I have grown up," replied Nafaria.

"It is a father's right to think of his only daughter as his little one. No matter where life takes you, or how you grow, that is what you shall remain to me," said Jason with a smile. He came closer to her and wrapped his arms around her, hugging her tight.

"I need you to find me some woodland ginger when you are out in the woods today," said Jason. Nafaria gave her father a puzzled look.

"It is the wrong season for woodland ginger, father. It will be scarce, if I can find it at all. I may have to go to market to get it," replied Nafaria. Jason shook his head.

"Stay away from the market today. Look in the woods and the meadows extra carefully. Maybe you will surprise me," said Jason.

"Yes father. We need more sage and lemon grass as well," replied Nafaria. Jason looked at her.

"What do you use lemon grass for?" asked Jason. Nafaria held out her teacup.

"It goes wonderfully in chamomile tea," she said smiling.

"Take your time out in the woods today," said Jason. With those words, he turned and left Nafaria to her tea.

It was later when Thena found Jason at the fountain. The sun was higher now, and its brightness made even the smallest blemishes visible. He sat at the fountain, absently trailing his finger in the water. He looked up as he watched her approach.

"I thought we might enjoy the sunshine today with a picnic in the meadow," said Thena. She stood in front of him and put her arms around him. She kissed him with a gentle firmness that always made Jason's heart quicken. He pulled her closer to him, the water from his hand running down her shoulders as they kissed.

"With an offer like that, how could any man refuse?" he asked dreamily. He looked into her eyes as she smiled her mischievous, playful smile.

"I will get everything ready," said Thena. She quickly pecked him again on the cheek and started back inside.

"I love you Thena, my goddess," he called to her. She turned her head, smiled and continued inside.

When Jason was alone again, he heard the sharp cry of a bird. A raven, blacker than any Jason ever saw, lighted on a tree above. The bird looked intently at him. It sat silent in the tree, unwilling to move. Jason bowed his head.

"So it begins," he whispered. He bent down and picked up two rocks from the fountain the size of his palm.

At that moment, the sound of horses' hooves filled the air. A dozen men rode up the main entrance to the manor. Jason walked forward to greet them.

"Good morning, gentlemen. May I ask why I have been honored by this visit?" asked Jason.

No one answered, but the men jumped from their horses and rushed toward him. In a moment, Jason was surrounded and the men lunged toward him. He fought them back, using the stones in his hands to bludgeon one man in the head. He crumpled to the ground, unconscious. Jason closed his eyes and whispered *send your light from heaven to save me.* Instantly, a bolt of lightning flashed from the sky and struck another man. No one else dared to go near him.

Thena heard the noise and rushed outside. She gasped in horror as she saw the men of the city attempting to attack her husband.

"What is the meaning of this madness?" demanded Jason. He picked one man up from the ground and shook him hard. "Where is he?"

"Jason, behind you!" shouted Thena. Her eyes widened as a knife went into her husband's back. Jason gasped in pain and shock.

"Right behind you, friend," Joel said softly into Jason's ear. He thrust the knife further into his back and twisted it.

"This pain is nothing compared to what I live with. Leanna is dead. Thena will die too," Joel hissed as he pulled the knife out of his back. Jason slumped to the ground and lay there gasping.

"Grab the woman. Search the house for the daughter, and kill anyone else you find," shouted Joel.

"No! Leave her out of this! She is innocent!" shouted Thena. Joel moved toward Thena and slapped her across the face.

"No one is innocent! When we find her, she will die too," shouted Joel menacingly. The men quickly mounted the horses, then pulled cowls over their heads, and placed masks over their faces. Joel wrapped a length of rope around Thena's neck and threw her over his horse, leaving her gasping for air. They rode off as Jason lay on the walkway. He continued to writhe and gasp while he heard the screams of his house servants being murdered.

Nafaria heard loud cries from the path as she walked back to the manor. She quickly entered the garden from the back gate that led out toward the woods. She panted heavily and her chest ached. She ran out into the main entrance to the manor, where she let out a cry. She rushed over to her father, her eyes filling with tears.

"Oh father!" cried Nafaria as she gently cradled Jason's head in her lap. His eyes flickered when he heard her voice.

"Go," he whispered.

"Not yet," she said gently. She heard the shouts and cries of those inside her home. Jason whispered again.

"Go to Arioth. Find Malcom and Nathaniel," he gasped and was silent. Nafaria cried out and held her father as she sobbed.

Her cries attracted the killers inside. She saw them rushing out through the entrance.

"There she is!" one of them shouted as they ran toward her. Nafaria closed her eyes.

"Spirit of YAHWEH, hear my cry, let me walk unseen to the naked eye," she whispered.

All at once she vanished. The men looked at each other bewildered.

"Where did she go?" another asked. They all turned and looked in every direction. Nafaria quickly rose and moved into the garden to wait for them to leave.

* * *

Andrew Catalane walked along the narrow streets toward the market square looking for Jared and Ephratha. He was a little annoyed with his cousin for leaving without him, but not surprised. He and Jared never really got along, and for some reason Jared's new fiancée did not care for him either. He knew Lord Robert's daughter Ephratha, but he could not understand why she disdained him so.

"Perhaps they truly belong together," said Andrew aloud as he walked along. He was disappointed by this. Jared was attending the ball meant for him to find a bride, and found a beautiful young woman. He had not been as lucky. He turned a corner and headed for the tree grotto where the apothecary was located. Perhaps the jasmine elixir Lady Thena promised to make him was ready.

Jared wandered around Wildemere's marketplace by Ephratha's side. Her soft hand was clutched in his. She chattered on excitedly about the Market Square and the Cathedral they spent an hour looking through. Ephratha confided her dream of someday being married in the chapel.

"When the sun hits the glass dome at the right time of the day, it lights up the entire chapel in beautiful color," Ephratha said as she walked next to Jared.

Jared walked next to Ephratha, amused by her chatter. She smiled and laughed as she continued to find new things to show him. She was such delightful company; he wondered how she escaped betrothal before he met her. He had enjoyed his stay in Wildemere with her as daily company.

He stopped in the center of the market square. It occurred to him that they walked in a circle, and now he stopped and looked at the center of the circle. A grove of apple trees stood clustered together. A cobblestone path cut through the center, and a bench was placed on either side of the path. A young couple, not much older than Jared and Ephratha, sat on one of the benches enjoying the shade of the trees.

"What is this place?" asked Jared.

"No one knows for sure. It is just a group of trees that had never been cut. I remember an old legend once that my history teacher told me. He said that when Wildemere was founded, the workers began to cut the trees. When the first tree fell, the workers heard a great wailing in the grove. It was so loud and haunting that the workers were all frightened. They said the grove was haunted, and they left Wildemere. No one ever tried to cut the trees in this area after that," said Ephratha. She sighed as she looked at the grove. "It has always held a peaceful place in my heart," she replied after a few moments. Then she said, "Nafaria likes this place as well. I think she is very much at home with nature."

"That does not surprise me. When do I get to meet her?" asked Jared with a smile.

"I should think very soon. You have already met her parents," Ephratha replied with a sigh.

Their conversation was interrupted with sounds of shouts in the marketplace. Jared took Ephratha and led her off to the side of the tree grove as a group of men wearing masks rode up on horses. One of them dragged a woman behind him.

"Thena!" Ephratha gasped as she recognized the woman's face. Thena looked at Ephratha when she heard her name. There was great sadness in her eyes. Jared looked in horror as she struggled to a standing position. Her face was as beautiful as he remembered, though tear stained. Gasping for breath, her chest heaved as it desperately tried to fill its lungs with air. Even now as she stood before the gathering crowd of spectators, Thena carried an air of dignity. Jared bowed his head slightly in her direction.

Ephratha watched as Joel jumped down from his horse. In a loud voice he exclaimed, "This woman has lived among us as a witch in hiding." He waited for the shock to ripple through the crowd. He continued on.

"The witch is responsible for the death of my wife. She may also be responsible for other catastrophes as well. She will be put to death so that no one else will die." Ephratha rushed toward them with Jared close behind her.

"You monster! You know Thena never harmed Leanna. They were friends!" shouted Ephratha. Joel locked eyes with the young woman and walked over to her. Jared stood squarely between them, his gaze also matching Joel's.

"You would do well to stay out of this matter," spat Joel vehemently.

"Give the woman the trial she deserves," said Jared in a cool tone.

"There is no trial for a witch. The law of Nereheim states that witches are to be put to death. Death to the witch!" Joel shouted aloud for everyone to hear.

"Which law is that? All men or women accused of murder are to have a fair hearing before the king. You are taking vengeance for no good reason!" shouted Jared. Joel came closer to Jared and shoved him to the ground. He pulled out a dagger and held it to his throat.

"You would do well to remain quiet," spat Joel.

One of the masked men grabbed Thena and dragged her to the closest tree in the grove. A rope dangled down from one of the apple blossom branches. A noose was slipped around Thena's neck. Ephratha gasped as she realized that Joel truly intended to go through with the murder. She pushed toward Thena, addressing the crowd that gathered.

"You cannot allow this! She has lived among us for years. We all saw her every week in the marketplace. Her husband has provided wise counsel for the merchants and even the King himself. Do not let this happen!"

"Kill the witch!" a voice, shouted from the crowd. Minutes later the air was filled with the chant. Jared came up to Ephratha and held her back as he watched those in the crowd hoist Thena's body off the ground. The apple blossoms blew in the breeze and fell like snow all around. Ephratha's face streamed with tears as she screamed Thena's name over and over. Jared was finding it hard to contain her. His eyes filled with tears, watching in horror as Thena's feet were suddenly still, and her body swayed in the air. Joel and his men brought lit torches and set her body on fire. Ephratha finally collapsed to the ground, and buried her face in his arms.

Joel then moved toward the apothecary and threw a large barrel through the window. The glass shattered with a loud crash and shards flew everywhere. He then lit a torch and threw it into the shop.

"We will rid Nereheim of those of the Craft!" shouted Joel.

As Jared sat on the ground holding Ephratha, he looked up into the trees. Through his tears, he saw a pure white dove sitting on one of the branches. The bird looked down at him. He heard a soft female voice whisper: *find Nafaria*. He watched as the dove flew off into the sun.

Jared quickly reached out to the ground around him. He drew the symbol of the triquetra in the ground. Then he picked up a handful of dust. Blowing it in the wind, he whispered, "Go in peace, Thena."

"What are you doing?" asked Ephratha. Her tears had slowed enough to notice he drew a symbol in the ground.

"It is part of an ancient ritual to honor the passing of those of the Craft. Come, we must find Nafaria," replied Jared. He rose quickly and helped Ephratha to her feet. They quickly left the crowd to Thena's burning.

Andrew heard shouts coming from the apple grove and came around the corner to a riot going on in the streets. Flames were coming from the apothecary the Mauldon family owned. Other shop owners locked their buildings and fled. He saw people trying to force their way into the antiquarian library that Elias Wheaton owned.

"What is this madness?" he shouted as he looked around. People ran everywhere, and horses became wild. He heard a female cry and looked over to his right to see a young woman lying on the ground.

Andrew ran toward her and found that she fainted. He picked her up and looked around for a place of shelter. He spied the spire of the cathedral and quickly headed in that direction.

Jared and Ephratha made their way quickly back to her home. The crowd in the market square erupted into a frenzy as they ran. They stopped in the stable and readied Ephratha's horse and mounted it. As swiftly as Ephratha's stallion could carry them, Jared urged the horse on. He felt Ephratha's tears on his shoulder. With broken speech she guided him to where she heard Jason's manor stood.

Smoke rose over the trees and spilled into the pathway they rode, creating an eerie fog. It stung Jared's eyes as they rode up the path to the manor.

Jared halted the horse and quickly jumped down. As he helped Ephratha down, he saw the whole manor was now ablaze. Twenty feet away from where they stood, a great fire burned separate from the house.

"What is it?" asked Ephratha.

"A funeral pyre," replied Jared. "When one of the Craft dies, their body is burned."

At that moment, Jared saw an exquisite young woman come from another path near the manor. Her hair was full and dark as midnight. She held the reins of a horse in her hand. When she saw him; her eyes widened in terror. She began to whisper quickly when Ephratha rushed forth into her arms.

"Nafaria, thank God you are still alive!" she exclaimed through her tears.

"What has happened here?" asked Jared. Nafaria turned her head toward him.

"Is this the man you spoke of?" asked Nafaria to Ephratha.

"Yes, he gave me the hunting dagger to give you," replied Ephratha. Nafaria turned her gaze to Jared again.

"Thank you, I can trust you," said Nafaria as she put her hand in Jared's. She looked solemnly to the pyre.

"My father was betrayed by the only man he confided our secret to. He lost his wife and unborn child, and blamed my mother because she was there the night she died," said Nafaria.

"I remember. I was there that night as well. This Joel was the murderer?" asked Jared.

"Yes," replied Nafaria.

"We must leave this place. He will soon come looking for you to finish what he started," said Jared.

"I know. I am ready and will be passing across the river by nightfall," replied Nafaria.

"You cannot go alone. You need an escort," replied Jared.

"You think me incapable of traveling alone?" asked Nafaria. Jared looked at the pyre. Its fire was waning as it consumed its fuel.

"I have heard uncle Rohn describe your father as very wise in the Craft. However, even he was not powerful enough to stand alone," replied Jared. Nafaria regarded him carefully.

"It is true. Even the sacred texts say that two together have a greater return[25]," replied Nafaria.

Jared turned to Ephratha. "We must tell Uncle Rohn and Aunt Susanna what has happened," said Jared.

* * *

Andrew gently lay the young woman down on one of the cushioned benches at the front of the cathedral. He went back to lock the door, when the bishop came out to greet him.

"Your royal highness, it is a pleasure to see you," said the bishop.

"Your excellency, there is a riot outside. I dare not go out until it has passed. This young woman fainted in the market square. May we stay until everything is calm?" asked Andrew.

"You may. I heard the riot, but I have no idea why it is happening," replied the bishop.

"I have no answer for that. I was walking toward the apothecary when I came upon it," said Andrew.

The young woman stirred and opened her eyes. She blinked and slowly sat up. Andrew felt his heart melt at the sight of her. She had soft brown hair and even softer blue eyes. She looked fair and pure like

---

[25] Ecclesiastes 4:9

a rose, but had a look of wisdom in her expression. He was instantly reminded of his mother. He sat down next to her.

"Are you all right?" asked Andrew. She looked at him for a moment then slowly nodded her head.

"Yes," she replied. She looked around and noticed the stained glass of the cathedral.

"How did I get here? I was in the market square," she said.

"You fainted, I think. There is a riot going on in the market square. Please stay here with me until it is passed," said Andrew.

"Lady Thena," the girl whispered. Andrew frowned.

"What?" he asked.

"I saw them hang Lady Thena Mauldon and then set her body on fire," she said quietly.

"That is what started this whole thing?" asked Andrew. His heart was pounding wildly.

"I believe so. I was going toward the antiquarian library, when I heard wild shouts, and saw Joel Blackstone ride up with some masked men on horseback. He kept shouting about Lady Thena killing Leanna. However, they were such good friends. Lady Thena would never hurt anyone; especially not Leanna," she said. Andrew nodded his head.

"Joel Blackstone is grieving and has gone mad. He most likely has killed Lord Jason as well. Father needs to know about this, but we cannot risk leaving the cathedral right now," said Andrew. For the first time in his life, he felt completely helpless. The girl seemed to sense this and motioned for him to sit next to her. He sat down and she reached for his hand.

"Whatever has happened, we cannot change it now. We may as well enjoy the time we have until this madness has passed. My name is Nina Westen," she said. Andrew smiled.

"My name is Andrew Catalane," replied Andrew. Nina laughed.

"Do you not mean, 'his royal highness, Andrew Catalane'?" she asked. Andrew returned her laugh.

"I did not wish to be found out just yet, if I could help it," replied Andrew.

"I am afraid royalty cannot hide for long in Wildemere," replied Nina.

"No, I suppose not," said Andrew. He looked at her thoughtfully.

"I do not believe we have ever met. Were you at the ball on midsummer's eve?" asked Andrew. Nina shook her head.

"I am afraid not. I was sick that evening and could not be there. I was hoping to make it, as I have never been to an event so grand," replied Nina.

"Perhaps we shall throw another, so that you can be there," said Andrew with a smile. Nina returned his smile as they sat together waiting for the storm outside to pass.

* * *

Jared, Ephratha, and Nafaria quickly rode to the castle. When they entered the throne room, they found the king and queen anxious. The queen was pacing the floor. A look of relief swept over her face when she saw them.

"Jared, thank goodness you are safe!" she exclaimed as she rushed over to them.

"Is Andrew with you?" asked the king.

"No. We were in the market square, but we never saw him," replied Jared.

"He was headed toward the apothecary a little while ago," said Susanna.

"The apothecary is destroyed. Lady Thena and Lord Jason were murdered," said Ephratha. She blinked to hold back her tears.

The queen looked at her husband in disbelief. "Who would do such a thing?" she asked.

"Joel Blackstone. He blames them for the death of his wife," replied Jared. "He and a band of other men instigated a riot, that I am sure is all over Wildemere by now."

At that moment, Andrew rushed into the room holding Nina's hand. "Mother, father, you will not believe what has happened!" exclaimed Andrew. Susanna came over to her son and threw her arms around him.

"Thank goodness you are safe!" she cried. After she let go of her son, she looked at Nina thoughtfully. "Who is this?" she asked.

"Mother, this is Nina Westen. I found her in the market square," said Andrew.

"It is a pleasure, your majesty. Andrew is being modest. He actually saved my life," replied Nina. Susanna looked at her son once again.

"I need to go back to North Agea, today, Aunt Susanna. I am taking Ephratha and Nafaria with me. Can you send word to Lord Robert Stowe that Ephratha is safe and on her way to North Agea?" said Jared.

"Of course," replied the queen.

"You will not go without an escort. I will send most of the royal guard into the city, but two riders will accompany you to the Anenderes," said the king.

"Thank you, uncle Rohn," said Jared. He turned to Ephratha. "It is not the proposal I had worked on in my mind, but if you will have me as a husband, I wish you to be my wife," said Jared. Ephratha stared at him a moment before she finally realized she needed to say something.

"I would be honored," replied Ephratha as she smiled broadly. Jared caught her in his arms and spun her around.

"You will send us word as to when the wedding is to take place," said Susanna as she smiled.

"Of course, Aunt Susanna, I would not dream of being married without your presence. Besides, mother would be beside herself if you were not there for the big day," replied Jared as he smiled back at Ephratha.

"Now that we know there is to be a wedding soon, I shall turn my attention to the royal guard and have them secure the city. I will also issue a proclamation stating Joel's treachery and offering a reward for his capture. When he is brought to me, justice will be served for Lord Jason's death and of his wife and household," said king Rohn.

Nafaria kept silent at the king's words, but she knew in her heart her father would never want Joel executed, even though he was responsible for killing her parents. His last words to her had been not to take vengeance on anyone, even if she saw the killers herself. She knew the king was working on issues of grief for himself. King Rohn and her father began to enjoy a friendship that was cut short. She also knew that Rohn did not trust lightly those of the Craft. This latest tragedy would cut deep indeed.

* * *

It was late the next morning when two lone figures were seen walking their horses down the roadside. The air was still and all around silent. Not a bird flew in the sky, or even whistled. There was a thick haze that blanketed the whole area.

"Father, what is this haze? It reminds me of fog, but it is dry."

The oldest sniffed the air. "Smoke," he replied. "Something has been burning in the night."

"Philip said we would reach the manor before we came to the city. He said to look for a cobblestone path that will lead through iron gates," said the oldest.

They continued on and found the cobblestone walkway. The gates stood wide open, so they led the horses up the path toward the manor. The younger looked carefully at the fountain that stood beside the house. He remembered a fountain from another time and place. Then his attention was called to the great smoldering pile next to it.

"Father, what is that?" he asked.

"A pyre," replied the older man grimly. He looked at the great building next to it. Smoke continued to escape through windows and doors that were long ago burned or blown out.

"Something terrible has happened here," said the younger man.

"We must leave this place. Maybe there is one in town who knows what has happened," replied the older man. He looked at his son, who wore a look of grief. Tears began to trickle down his face.

"Father," was all he could whisper.

"Come Nathaniel. Let us find more answers before we form conclusions. Perhaps no one was home," said Malcom. He spoke the words, but he did not believe them, even as they left his mouth. He knew they were most likely home, waiting for them to visit. They turned and rode up the pathway back to the road.

The town was bustling with everyday activity. The market was very busy, but in great disarray. Shops were destroyed, and piles of burned wood lie everywhere. Women rushed from one place to another, gathering their food for the meals of the day. Nathaniel and Malcom walked with their horses. They circled the market place. After a moment while they walked, Malcom noticed the wood in the center of the Town Square. He could tell it was an apple blossom grove, but most of the trees looked badly burned. A lone woman stood before one of the most badly burned trees, with a basket in her hand. She stared at the charred branches, standing perfectly still.

Malcom walked his horse up to her quietly, so as not to startle her. She looked in his direction as he came closer.

"Good morning, my lady," said Malcom.

"Good morning, sir," she replied.

She stood tall and straight, looking him in the eyes. Her large green eyes seemed to shimmer. Tears were formed in the corners, threatening to fall at any moment. Her hair was a beautiful auburn color and flowed down her back. It matched perfectly with her cream colored skin. She was quite beautiful.

"What has happened here, my lady?" asked Malcom in a gentle voice.

"There has been a great injustice, sir. A woman who was both beautiful and wise was hanged and burned here. She never harmed anyone as far as I knew her, and was generous to anyone in need. Her husband has been killed as well," replied the woman.

Malcom closed his eyes at the news. He blinked back tears. "Why do you think she was killed?" he asked in a husky voice. He could barely speak.

"Wicked men murdered out of vengeance, nothing more," she replied with disdain ringing clearly in her voice.

"She must have been a great friend for you to stand here like this," said Malcom.

"I am afraid she may never have known how much I loved and respected her. I pray that her daughter escaped-"

"Her daughter?" interrupted Nathaniel.

"Yes, she had a daughter, the same age as my own. She has gone to North Agea, along with her fiancée. The mayhem that erupted yesterday was unparalleled in the history of this place. Many people were killed or injured in the riot that followed," replied the woman with tears in her eyes.

Malcom looked at his son who began to cry as well. They were both thinking the same thing. They had been too late to find Jason and convince him to abandon his calling and come to North Agea. Thena was murdered in the public square. Was Nafaria lost as well?

Malcom felt a nudge at his arm. "Sir, you look as though you have been traveling all night. Please, come and enjoy the hospitality of my home," said the woman.

"Your kindness is great, my lady, but I can no longer stay in such an evil place. I will not break bread in a place where the wicked prey on the righteous," said Malcom. He nodded toward the woman and climbed on his horse. Nathaniel did the same and they rode away quickly, leaving the woman to stare at the charred apple blossom tree.

CHAPTER 6

$\maltese$

MICHAEL WOKE WITH A START. His body was damp with sweat. He panted as he gasped for breath. The shirt he wore hung like a damp cloth on his body. Slowly he sat up in the bed he lay in. The sun shone brightly through the window to his left.

Outside he heard the bustle of business and pleasure in the little village of Rowall. He was about a day's ride from Denholm Glen.

He put both feet to the floor. His arms felt weak as he sat looking down. Tears fell, a few at first, then a flood. His chest heaved as he thought of his father and mother. He saw his father die by the only man in Wildemere he trusted. He heard his mother's cry. The end his father foresaw was now a course of history. The greatness of Jason Mauldon would now only exist in the annals of his family. Michael rose from the bed in the room at the inn and walked over to the small table at the other end of the room and sat in the chair next to the table. He opened a book lying on the table and began to write of his father's demise, and the passing of premonition that was now his gift.

After his meticulous recording, Michael quickly gathered his things and packed his horse for the journey to Denholm Glen. He thought of the midnight flight so long ago which put him on the road to Wildemere. His father saved their lives so long ago. Now he, his brother and his sister were all that was left of his father's line. What was to become of him? He owed it to his scattered family to devote himself to the Craft and further his knowledge. He had no reason for any fear, but in his heart, Michael feared his family would have to face an even greater evil than the betrayal of Joel Blackstone.

The sun was setting as Michael rode his horse into Denholm Glen. He longed to see his old home, but he knew there was another he should seek first. He rode to the manor of Lord Reinard Sallen.

Michael stood in the great hall. As a child, he had been here many times. The oils that clung to the walls depicted great men in Nereheim's past. Men who all had one thing in common, but it was not royalty. Lord Reinard kept paintings of most of the great court advisers who reported to the king in Nereheim's history. Michael asked his father once why he never aspired to the greatness that other men of the Craft seemed to dream of. He smiled as he remembered his father's answer. "Great glory and comfort destroys more men than it makes. I desired a quiet life and opportunity to raise a great house. So far I have succeeded. Time will tell now."

Michael's gaze remained on the painting in front of him as he heard footsteps behind him. He turned to see a man with silver hair and bright green eyes walking toward him. His eyes brightened when he saw Michael standing in the hall. The man advanced quickly before him and embraced him.

"You favor your mother still, but you have your father's steady gaze," said Reinard. "Tell me, what brings you back to Denholm Glen, Michael?"

"My father has sent me away, my lord. The only place I could think of to come was home," replied Michael.

"How is Jason?" asked Reinard.

"I am afraid he is dead, my lord. I had a premonition last night. I saw his death, he has passed his gift to me," said Michael. Lord Reinard closed his eyes and bowed his head at the news. When his eyes opened again, the lashes were wet with tears.

"I am very sad to hear such news. Only Malcom Stone was greater than your father," replied Reinard.

"Thank you, my lord," said Michael. Lord Reinard regarded Michael carefully, and then smiled.

"So, you have come home to Denholm Glen. You will take back the vineyard I presume?" asked Lord Reinard.

Michael nodded his head. "Yes. However, the daily operations I will leave in the capable hands of the servants and managers that my father entrusted them to. We have received regular reports over the years about the business and how everything fares. I have come back to Denholm Glen specifically in hope that I may study Alchemy and further my knowledge of the Craft so that I can help my family. I have a fear my sister is in for an evil future."

"How do you know this?" asked Reinard.

"My father said once before he sent me away that she will decide the fate of kings," replied Michael.

"Lord Jason has never been wrong. What do you need from me?" asked Reinard.

"I would like to study the art of Alchemy under your guidance," said Michael.

"Surely you do not wish to wile away your time making gold out of stone?" asked Reinard.

"I credit your study with more respect than that. If your family line has devoted so much time to study it, there must be good use for the art," said Michael with a smile.

"Indeed there is, and I will show you the use in time. You will find the manor very busy, but open. A few years ago I found it necessary to post a guard on the property to keep it safe and intact," replied Reinard. He pulled Michael to him and embraced him again. "Welcome back to Denholm Glen."

"Thank you, my lord. I will go tonight. I am very eager to settle in at home," replied Michael.

Lord Reinard called for one of his servants while they stood in the hallway. "I will send a servant with you for your safety. He will vouch for you so the guard will let you pass and those in the manor who may not remember you will accept your presence there. When would you like to begin your studies?" asked Reinard.

"Three days from tomorrow. Where is Sylvia?" asked Michael.

Lord Reinard looked sadly at him. "She died in her sleep six months ago. I placed her in the village burial ground."

"Thank you, my lord," said Michael. As he turned to leave he said with a sigh, "I had hoped for one more of her yeast rolls."

* * *

Michael wandered the dimly lit halls of the manor with Lord Reinard's servant who volunteered to stay the night with him. Though the manor was darkening with the coming on of twilight, much was happening in the kitchen and other areas of the house. The servants all chattered about his arrival.

"It seems so strange to be back here again," said Michael. "I was a child when we left."

"Lord Reinard left specific instruction that all was to stay as it was left. I think he always believed at least one of you would return," said the servant.

"Lord Reinard has always been faithful to Malcom and my father. If only Joel would have been more like him," said Michael. The servant laid his hand on Michael's shoulder.

"Come, all your things have been brought inside. Retire tonight and rest. Enjoy Denholm Glen once more," he said.

"One more thing," said Michael.

"Yes?" asked the servant.

"If you are to spend the evening under my roof, I think I should know your name," said Michael with a smile. The servant smiled in return.

"My name is Peter. Those of the Craft are certainly an interesting breed," said Peter.

"How so?" asked Michael.

"They always want to know a person's name. Even if that person is nothing more than a common peasant," replied Peter.

"No one is common in the eyes of YAHWEH. We are taught that everyone is precious to him," replied Michael.

"It is a shame more nobles do not know this wisdom," replied Peter. He bowed slightly and left Michael to his thoughts.

* * *

The sun shone brightly the next morning as Michael walked amongst the graves in the village burial ground. He stopped at a grave marker near the edge of the grounds.

He knelt down and faced the stone with Sylvia's name on it. He laid a single white rose on the grave in front of him. Tears trickled down his face.

"You have been so faithful to my family, Sylvia. We never would have made it without you. May you always rest in peace," Michael bowed his head out of respect for the dead.

He wandered through the streets of the village. He saw the blacksmith shop and the farriers busy with horses. He drifted along on the scent of the warm baked bread of the bakery. He followed the scent until it led him past a grove of trees. Under the trees, a young woman sat with long blond hair that fell past her shoulders in soft curls. Her skin was a creamy ivory color with just enough pink in the cheeks to give her a girlish charm. Her head was bowed into a book and she appeared to be sketching.

Michael stopped on the pathway he walked and continued to stare at her. After a moment, he came to his senses. Seeing an old woman with a cart of flowers, he quickly moved toward her and purchased a single white lily. He quietly approached the young woman and put the flower within her eyesight.

"For the woman who has everything," said Michael quietly.

The woman stopped her sketching and looked at the flower. She carefully took it.   "There is only one man who would care to learn of my favorite flower. He was a boy when last I saw him," said the woman quietly. She looked up into Michael's eyes. Her blue eyes widened as a smile crossed her face. She nearly jumped into his arms.

"Michael? Is it really you? Father said you had returned," she said. Her eyes sparkled as she smiled.

"Yes, it is me, Lillia. I did not realize how much I missed you until just now," said Michael. He held her tightly. "I am sure you are betrothed to a count's son by now?"

Lillia smiled as she buried her face into his chest. "My father would not so lightly betroth his only daughter. For that I am grateful. The men here crave power, and do not have the temperance to handle it. I think father regrets that though we are a noble family, we are still only mortal. He only respects those of the Craft, and of course, none would have me. So, here I wait. But all is not lost. I am content to wait for a good husband," said Lillia.

"Not even one of the Craft could hope for so great a treasure," said Michael as he kissed her forehead. He gently pushed her from him. "I think I should go."

Lillia looked into his eyes and smiled. "Go, I shall find you again," she said.

Michael let her hand drop from his and with a smile, left Lillia to her sketches.

* * *

After he wandered about the village; Michael sat by the fountain of his manor. He looked up into the trees and drew a deep breath. He wondered about Nafaria. Was she safe? Was she in danger? He had nothing of hers to use to see her through incantation. He sighed as he caught sight of a patch of coneflowers growing in the sunlight. He walked over to the patch and picked one. He closed his eyes and thought of his sister.

At that moment, he heard the sound of hooves on the pathway coming toward him. Peter rode up to him.

"Peter, what brings you here this fine day?" asked Michael.

"Lord Reinard wishes you to join him for dinner at his manor," replied Peter.

"Please tell Lord Reinard I am honored for the invitation. What time shall I arrive?" asked Michael.

"Arrive at dusk. He will be very glad of the company," replied Peter. With his message delivered, he pulled the reins of the horse and turned back the way he came.

* * *

Darkness crept over Lord Reinard's manor, but Michael measured time spent by the meat on the hen carcasses dwindling. The yeast rolls were ever present on the table. He had eaten at least a dozen. Everything was wonderful. Throughout the evening, his gaze drifted to Lillia who sat at the opposite end of the table. She wore a flowing light blue dress that fell to her feet. Her soft curls fell over her shoulders. The way she looked reminded Michael so much of his mother. He remembered her best when she dressed in light flowing dresses that moved with her figure. Lillia was now a grown woman, and she lit up the room more fully than the fire burning in the hearth.

Lord Reinard noticed the flickering exchange of glances between his guest and his daughter. He said nothing as he well remembered their special friendship. Even as a child, Michael was advanced in his study of plants and herbs. He taught Lillia everything he knew. This had stayed with her, and her love and knowledge of plants and nature continued to increase.

The night Jason fled with his family was like death for Lillia. She cried for days afterward. Now that they were together again, Lord Reinard saw that something else had awakened between them.

The candles on the table were a little lower than when they were first lit. The food was cleared away, and Lillia excused herself from their company for the evening.

"Thank you for your hospitality, my lord. The dinner was absolutely delicious. I dare say Sylvia could not have cooked a better meal," said Michael.

"I should hope so. After your family left, I hired one of the cooks that helped her in the kitchen. It was out of charity, but it turned out to be the smartest thing I could have done," replied Reinard. He looked fondly at his young guest. "It has been a pleasure to have you here tonight. Evil times have come and gone from Denholm Glen. I can only hope that more will not follow in their wake."

"We have seen from afar, the times of which you speak. I will never be able to thank you enough for the late warning you gave that night so long ago. Because of it, my mother lived longer. I only hope my sister has the chance to live out whatever destiny my father saw before he died," said Michael.

"I wonder what destiny was so important to Jason," replied Reinard.

"I have had time to review the last few entries of my father's diary and the family annals. He spoke of a dream he had of a young woman who had Nafaria's eyes. He seemed to think that Nafaria will decide the fate of kings," said Michael.

"Then we must pray that she is safe," replied Reinard. Michael nodded, and then asked a question on an entirely different matter.

"If I may ask, have you any intention to betroth Lillia at this time?" asked Michael. He looked Reinard in the eye and did not lift his gaze.

Lord Reinard was struck with how very much he looked like Jason at that moment. He always thought Michael favored Thena, but years have a way of adding steadiness to a man's gaze. He hesitated a moment before answering.

"No, I do not at the moment. The young men here are buffoons. I do not wish to lose her to one. She has expressed no interest either. Your presence has brightened her heart considerably," said Reinard.

"Mine as well," said Michael quietly. Then with a louder, more confident voice he added, "I wish you to consider something that is rather unprecedented. It will be of benefit to me. Perhaps it will be for you as well."

Lord Reinard looked at Michael intently. "What is it?" he asked.

"Let me take Lillia as my wife," replied Michael.

"I would love nothing more, but we are a mortal family. We have no ties to any who are of the Craft," said Reinard.

"I understand that. I realize that with this proposed union, my family's power will eventually diminish from my side. Philip has married Nadia Saintclaire, so the Craft will continue in their family. The knowledge my family has acquired will be passed on, of course. I

315

am a stranger to this place. It would be safer for me to take a wife of a family here in Denholm Glen. No one would care that one of the Craft walks among them if they felt like they had something in common," said Michael. He paused and took a moment to look at the fire that burned in the hearth. The embers were growing redder. Perhaps Peter would soon be in to put more wood on it to keep it going. "I have always loved Lillia. I turned to books and study when we moved to Wildemere to take my mind from thoughts of her. Of course it did not always work, but I passed my time well enough. Since I am of age, I wish to make my own decision. If she will have me for a husband, and you will have me for a son, it will make my joy complete to make her my wife."

Reinard bowed his head slightly. "If this is your decision, and you will not yield it, I will be honored to have you as my son."

"Thank you, my lord. Please, do not mention this to Lillia. I would like to ask her tomorrow," said Michael.

"Make it early. I may not be able to conceal my excitement for long," replied Reinard.

"It will be early. I do not wish to lose my nerve," replied Michael with a smile.

Reinard rose from his seat and walked over to Michael. He put a hand on his shoulder and said, "Go home and get some sleep. We will begin your study of Alchemy after the wedding."

"I shall be grateful for that," said Michael. He rose from his chair and embraced Reinard. Soon afterward, he left the manor, lost in his thoughts.

* * *

The next morning Michael walked the pathway leading to Lord Reinard's manor. He found Lillia, sitting with her sketchbook, considering the small shrub she sat next to. It was green, with frail but full branches. Mugwort was common in all of Nereheim, Michael found. In his travels from Wildemere, he found the shrub on many roadsides.

She looked up from the bush and smiled when she saw him. She broke off a piece of the shrub, and handed it out to him. "For the traveler who has everything," said Lillia.

Michael took the shrub from her hand. "Thank you for your protection, my lady," he said.

Her eyes were even more radiant than yesterday. The thin lavender dress she wore perfectly complemented her blond curls. It was a light airy color, one that showed her true nature. Lillia was absolute perfection. Michael began to wonder if he was up to the challenge of asking her to marry him. He wondered if his father felt the same doubt on his wedding day.

"I was hoping to see you today," said Lillia. She closed her sketchbook and rose to standing.

Michael put his arms around her and gently squeezed her. He smelled lavender on her skin and breathed deeply. After a moment, he parted from her. "Come, let us talk."

They walked the path toward her home. "What do you wish to talk about?" asked Lillia.

Michael looked into her eyes. The bright blue color he saw staring back at him was watching him intently. "I wish you to be my wife," said Michael in a voice barely above a whisper.

Lillia's eyes jumped as he said the words. She put a hand to her mouth. She swallowed once and replied, "You cannot marry a mortal. It is forbidden."

"It is unprecedented, to be sure, and perhaps unthinkable; but it is not forbidden. The power my family was entrusted with will begin to fade, but the knowledge will always be a part of my family's heritage," said Michael. He looked into her eyes and gently placed a hand to her cheek. "I cannot bear the thought of marrying another woman, Lillia. I have loved you since we were children. I will love you even as we are both committed to the ground in death. You are all I ever wanted," said Michael.

Lillia clutched the hand on her face. Tears streamed down her cheeks as she whispered, "If that is your decision, then I am most honored to be your wife."

Michael pulled her into his arms and held her tightly. Tears streamed down his face as he whispered, "A happier man there never was."

* * *

The next morning, Michael found Lillia in the sunroom that was part of Lord Reinard's manor. Lillia showed it to him the first night he visited. It was her refuge against the powers that took Michael away from her. He watched her for a few moments alone. He could see nervousness in her beautiful features. Her eyes were bright, but still reflecting a twinge of fear. What there was to be afraid of, Michael may never understand. She was pinching leaves off one of the plants before her; a hawthorn plant. Perhaps she was as nervous as he was at this moment in their lives. In a few hours, they would be husband and wife. Forever joined, just as he always knew they should be. Would those of the Craft forgive him his treachery? Perhaps not, but many if not all, would understand his choice. Great power comes to those who wield it with heavy responsibility; such is a high and noble calling. In the end, love is what makes those things worthwhile. He looked down at the worn leather book in his hands. Taking a deep breath, he stepped out of the shadow of the doorway toward her.

Lillia looked up at the sound of footsteps. Michael walked toward her with a book in his hands. She smiled, her eyes lighting up at the sight of him. She pictured him just this way her whole adolescence when his family fled Denholm Glen. He always had the same thoughtful expression over handsome features; and always with a book in hand. He smiled as he walked toward her.

"I would have thought you would be getting yourself ready for today, not your plants," said Michael.

"I have a while yet," replied Lillia. She looked around the sunroom. "This place calms me. What about you?" she asked. Michael looked down at the book in his hands.

"I wanted to give you this, before the ceremony," said Michael. He handed the book to her.

Lillia took the book and opened it. The first page held one word, her name, in Michael's beautiful and very careful script. She turned the page. Her breath caught at the date on the top of the page. It was dated one week after Michael and his family left Denholm Glen.

"It was my father's idea. I was upset one day because I could not draw your face. He told me to write what I did not want to forget. I always dreamed, but never dared to hope to give this to you on our wedding day. I love you, Lillia. I always have. There could be no other life for me," said Michael softly.

Lillia's eyes filled with tears as she threw her arms around Michael. "I did not dare to hope that I would one day call myself your wife," she sobbed. Michael's arms tightened around her.

"Then meet me in the meadow at noon," whispered Michael.

"I will be there," said Lillia. She looked at him and smiled. "Now, go get ready."

She let go of Michael and watched as he left the sunroom. She sat down on the stone bench that was off to the side of the room, opened the book to the first page and began to read.

* * *

With the sun high in the sky, Michael and Lillia stood in the meadow where they both had many fond memories. It was the place Michael would go with his sister to help gather herbs for various things the family needed. It was a calm place, quiet and peaceful. It was a place that spoke of a happier time in his life, when his family was alive and whole. Amid coneflowers and lady's mantle, Michael faced Lillia. She was absolute perfection, and on this day, he felt no nervous passion. The sacred writings say that perfect love drives away all fear[26]. Their love was nothing short of perfect. He felt complete with Lillia. He wondered if his father had to die so that he could have this perfect love. Was this what YAHWEH had in mind all along?

Lord Reinard smiled as he watched the exchange of vows between his daughter and new son in law. It was indeed a proud moment for his

---

[26] 1 John 4:18

house. The truest bond is not one of kinship knowledge, but of enduring love. Michael and Lillia shared this love, for that Reinard was grateful. She would always be happy, as long as she was by his side.

They each slipped a band of gold on the other's fingers. Michael then kissed Lillia as they stood there under the shining sun.

CHAPTER 7

Jared, Ephratha, and Nafaria continued to ride north. They were but a few miles from the Burnea ferry that would take them across the Anenderes River into North Agea. Burnea was a large city on Nereheim's side of the river built through years of trading between Nereheim and North Agea. It was an established trade route that many merchants chose. No doubt Philip and Nadia took the same route just a few years before.

It was amazing to Nafaria how much could change in so little time. In less than ten years since she was born, Nereheim had thrown itself into the turmoil of spilling innocent blood, for the sake of only a few that were the true monsters. That innocent blood was meant to protect man from evil. Instead, it was being regarded as the true evil. The question burned in Nafaria's mind: was Nereheim bettering itself with the blood of so many being wasted?

The countryside began to give way to houses and soon shops came into view. The dirt highway became cobblestone and many people thronged the streets. Nafaria could smell fresh baked bread.

"Oh, the smell of bread," she said aloud. A smile crossed her face.

"How can you smell that above the rest of the city?" asked Ephratha.

"It is a learned passion. Sometimes I think I should become a baker's wife," replied Nafaria.

"We can stop at a bakery and buy a couple loaves before we board the ferry. It is still a bit of a ride to the castle once we cross the river," said Jared. Nafaria smiled at him.

"That would be lovely. You could almost be a god among men," said Nafaria.

"I decline the post. I do not wish for that kind of responsibility," replied Jared with a smile.

"You are wise enough to be one of the Craft," said Nafaria.

"I think I will settle for a kingdom one day," replied Jared. He turned his attention down the lane. "The baker is just up ahead. Let us get some bread and make way to the ferry."

The sun set on the horizon as the three boarded the ferry. The stars began to peek through the purple sky while they watched the boat pull away from the shore of Nereheim.

"I leave my home for what lay ahead," said Ephratha quietly. Her eyes misted slightly. Jared embraced her and kissed her neck.

"Your kingdom is ahead, my lady," replied Jared.

Ephratha found a seat near the ship's bow and sat down. Nafaria seemed very distant; as if also contemplating this flight they were sharing. After an awkward silence, Ephratha spoke again. "This river seems quite wide. I can barely make out Nereheim's outline, and I do not even see North Agea yet." Jared nodded his head in agreement.

"The mighty Anenderes is indeed a large river. It could almost be a sea. There is a legend that I have been told since I was a boy about it. The legend is this:

It is said the dead have highways all their own
Which they walk, silent and alone
In the North Land they roam free
As moonlit fantasies to you and me
Here they dance in our flights
Taken in the stillness of the night.
There is a barrier that no man crosses
The mighty Anenderes River which rages and tosses
Winding on forever, it was meant to keep

The souls of those who wail and weep
A thick heavy mist falls all around
To ensure the spirits are not found
To leave them as a mystery
A tale to be told to you and me.
If you should have nerve to travel
And said nerves will not unravel
With the sound of Specters tolling
Then perhaps this is your calling:
In the town of Herron, the Legends tell
Of a beautifully crafted silver bell
That the spirits of the North have fashioned
For those who strike may hear their passion
If the one who strikes the bell, is pure in heart and soul
The spirits come to minister, the world's secrets told
But if one's soul is impure
The spirits come so swift and sure
To carry them to the North land
Where they are left to wander until driven mad.
For the Anenderes is the end
What one has wrought, no other can mend
Once one has found his way across
The mighty waves which billow and toss
There is no coming back again
To this world, our mortal land.
Another fable of which the village elders speak
If your bravado dares to seek
If you stroll along the river
Your blood may freeze and send you shivers
For what you could find looking back at you
Are faces of the dead, both wise and fool
Look to see if their lips move
They may yet be of some use to you
For the spirits have been known to whisper
Short messages of wisdom to us creatures

323

It is your choice, their words to heed
Or turn away, if you need
Wisdom comes from no stranger place
It can also leave without a trace.
So make your choice, if you dare
Turn away from words both wise and fair
Or take your place where egos fell
Walk down the quay and strike the bell
Or suffer spiritual torment and pain
Never to have the chance again.
Many as I look around the room
May be ready to leave soon
To find the river and strike the bell
And be enchanted by the spell
To go where only the truly brave have gone
To listen to the spirits' songs
But when you've been enchanted by the spell
With one hand raised to strike the bell
With the power to set your anxieties free
I wonder, what will your choice be?

"What a strange tale to be told," replied Ephratha. "Does the bell truly exist?" she asked.

"I do not know. I have never set out in search of the bell. I have been too concerned with learning to mind a kingdom," replied Jared.

"You are certainly different from your cousin. He seems to be uninterested in such trivialities as justice and responsibility," replied Ephratha. The disdain in her voice did not escape Jared.

"To govern wisely, one must be an avid student," said Jared.

At this moment, he looked over to Nafaria. She had been sitting next to Ephratha looking out at the river. She was very still as she looked out over the water.

"Is all well, Nafaria?" asked Jared.

"I was just thinking that if my father would have made this trip, my family would still be whole," said Nafaria. She then burst into tears.

Ephratha pulled Nafaria to her and held her as she cried.

"I miss my father so much. There was much he still could have taught me. Why is rashness not judged among men and masked with such words as vengeance?" cried Nafaria.

"Even vengeance is not ours to claim. The sacred writings tell us this plainly[27]," said Jared.

"You must teach me these ways when we are married. I feel there is so much for me to learn," said Ephratha.

"You will learn, and teach our children," said Jared. To Nafaria he said, "I have come too late to Nereheim. I should have liked the honor of knowing a man such as your father, this Jason Mauldon," said Jared.

"A greater man, there never was," replied Nafaria softly. She turned her gaze back to the water as tears still rolled down her cheek.

* * *

The ferry docked on the shore of North Agea. Nafaria and Jared led the horses off the boat. Jared helped Ephratha on his horse as Nafaria climbed on hers.

"We shall reach Arioth by midday," said Jared. "Mother will be most happy to see you again." He winked at Ephratha as he climbed up behind her.

"It will be a pleasure to see her again as well," replied Ephratha.

The sun rose through the morning and shone over the lush green fields of North Agea. Nafaria thought the countryside very much like that of Nereheim. The only thing separating the two lands was the Anenderes. Ephratha actually mentioned this to Jared.

"Do you ever worry about invasion from the Anenderes?" asked Ephratha.

"It is always possible, for all things are. However, tradition has always held against it. Relatives as long as anyone can remember have ruled the two kingdoms. The prince of Nereheim is my cousin. I may not enjoy his company; however I will not war against him. He is my kin," said Jared.

---

[27] Deuteronomy 32:35

"You may be inclined to peace, but that does not stop your cousin from invading," said Nafaria.

"In theory, that is true. However, my self-indulgent, self-centered cousin believes the world to be revolving around him. Planning an attack of any sort would be a task too tedious for him," replied Jared with a smile.

"You do not hold a high opinion of your cousin," replied Nafaria.

"He has not earned it," said Jared. Ephratha noticed the sharpness of his voice. It was clear to her that he did not like his cousin.

Jared grew quieter and more distant as they drew closer to Arioth. Ephratha left him to his thoughts and enjoyed the countryside view.

They rode through the castle gate while the sun was still high in the sky. They dismounted their horses and left them to the servants who met them.

"Jonathan, have the things on that horse brought into the castle guest wing," said Jared, nodding to the horse next to his.

"Very well your highness. Please see her majesty immediately. She has been very worried about you. There have been riots in Nereheim," replied Jonathan.

"Yes there have been. I shall see her at once," replied Jared. Jonathan bowed and led the horses away to the stable.

"Do not worry, Nafaria. Jonathan is very skilled with horses," said Jared.

"I do not worry for my horse. You have long ago earned my trust," replied Nafaria.

They entered the throne room and walked toward the thrones where both king and queen sat. The royal scribes were seated at their writing table taking a dictation for the king. The queen stood when she saw her son coming toward them. She rushed toward him and wrapped her arms around him.

"Jared, thank the Lord you are safe," said the queen. She looked at the girls. "I see you have brought Ephratha with you." She gave her a hug as well. "And who is this?" asked the queen looking at Nafaria.

Nafaria bowed her head slightly to the queen, but she really had no idea how to act in the presence of royalty. She thought that she could have used a few of Ephratha's lessons in social grace at that moment.

"Mother, this is Nafaria, daughter of a man named Jason Mauldon. He is of the line of Marcus, a very long legacy of men of the Craft.

"I know of Jason Mauldon. He owned a vineyard in Denholm Glen, but then moved to Wildemere and opened an apothecary. Is he the same man?" asked the king. He had come to his son while the queen was speaking.

"Yes your majesty. We all took on the apothecary business in one way or another. The vineyard, as far as I know, continues to operate successfully. We still receive a shipment of wine each year and profits from sales," said Nafaria.

"We have been so worried for you since we heard the news of the riot in Wildemere," said the queen.

"What happened over there?" asked the king.

"I do not know, father. Nafaria's parents were murdered. Her mother, Thena, was hanged and burned, right in the middle of the marketplace. Jason was murdered on his own land," said Jared. His eyes began to swell with tears. "They were of the Craft, father. They were killed out of vengeance, nothing more." Ephratha held Jared in her arms as he wept. Ephratha spoke to the queen.

"They were betrayed and murdered by a man named Joel Blackstone. His wife, Leanna, was pregnant with their first child. We were in the market wandering around when a horse broke from its master and ran wild in the street. Leanna was trampled. Jared carried her back to her house. My mother saw what happened and went with us. She went to find Thena. She and Jason came quickly and Thena worked all through the night to try and save her. In the end, there was nothing she could do. She was so distraught. Leanna was her best friend. They were always together," said Ephratha.

"I remember Rohn telling me of Jason Mauldon. He was a very wise man, and very prudent in all his advice. It is such a tragedy this happened," said the king.

"Father, Nafaria needs protection. She cannot go back to Nereheim," said Jared.

"You shall be welcome in this house for as long as it takes you to become established in North Agea," replied the king.

"Thank you, your majesty. I shall find a way to earn my keep, but I do need to find my brother and his wife. I also need to find Malcom Stone and Nathaniel," said Nafaria.

"Your brother is the horse master for Count Lucerne. We will send a messenger for him and Nadia to come to Arioth right away," replied Jared. "Meanwhile, we have a wedding to arrange. Ephratha has agreed to marry me."

"That is wonderful news, though I must say, I expected to hear it long before now," replied the queen with a chuckle. Ephratha smiled at the queen.

"Would it be possible to send a letter to my mother? I know she will be greatly worried until she hears from me," said Ephratha.

"We will send it as soon as it is written. Come with me and refresh yourselves before dinner," replied the queen. She led the girls out of the room.

Jared was left alone with his father. He looked at the king intently.

"All the way home, I could only think of one thing," said Jared.

"What would that be?" asked the king.

"That I am very lucky to be a citizen of North Agea. I have learned so much from the wise ones who share their ways with those who listen. I am very grateful that you have taught me to be open to the world around me. I am so proud to be your son," said Jared.

The king's eyes filled with tears as he pulled Jared into his arms. "My son, you have made me proud to be a father," he whispered.

* * *

Dearest Mother,
I hope this letter will allay any fear for me that you have. I am safe, and will not be returning to Nereheim. I

am writing this note to you to beg you to come as quickly as you can to North Agea, to the king's castle at Arioth.

Jared has asked me to marry him and I have accepted. I do not wish to take my vow to him until you and father can be present.

I will explain all as soon as you come. Please bring my star book, I am sure you know of which I speak.

Come quickly,

Ephratha

Ephratha burned a piece of wax with the flame of the candle sitting on the table where she wrote. She dabbed the wax on the paper and sealed it with the insignia Jared gave her.

"That is a very quickly written note," said Nafaria.

"I wanted it to be brief. I wish to tell my parents everything when they come," said Ephratha.

At that moment, Jared walked into the chamber. "Forgive the intrusion, but I wanted to let you know that I will be sending a messenger to Count Lucerne for your brother. I will also send a messenger to the apothecary to summon Malcom and Nathaniel Stone," said Jared. Nafaria's eyes lit up.

"I will finally meet this Nathaniel Stone. He must be quite remarkable," said Ephratha.

"He is very brilliant for his age. He has a very wide understanding of plants and herbs, and is quite skilled in other knowledge as well," replied Jared.

"When we were young, we spent much time together in the woods gathering herbs and planting and tending my herb garden. He would never let a day pass without quizzing me on the plants in Denholm Glen," replied Nafaria. A slight shadow crossed her face. "I cannot wait to see him."

"He speaks very often of you," said Jared.

"He does?" she asked. Jared nodded his head.

"He always said that he was awaiting his opportunity when it came to marriage. It was almost as if he had the perfect girl in mind all along.

It turns out that he did," replied Jared with a smile. Nafaria smiled as well.

"I have finished my letter," said Ephratha. She gave it to Jared.

"This will be sent out by nightfall," said Jared.

"Thank you," replied Ephratha.

"I shall see you both at dinner," replied Jared. He bowed, and left the room with the roll of paper in his hand.

As he walked the long corridor back to the main staircase of the castle, he smiled brightly when he looked up and saw a young man about his own age and one a few years older walking briskly toward him.

"Coleman! Raphael! Never have I been so glad to see you, my friends!" exclaimed Jared. He gave each of the men a hearty embrace.

"Yes, you go off to Nereheim for a royal ball, and you actually come back with an intended wife!" said Raphael.

"When do we get to meet her?" asked Coleman.

"You will see her at dinner. She and her friend are upstairs resting," said Jared.

"A friend?" asked Coleman. His expression brightened instantly. Jared laughed and clapped his hand on Coleman's back.

"I am sorry my friend. Nafaria is just about as beautiful as any young woman can be, but she is of the Craft, and she is betrothed," replied Jared.

"Betrothed to whom?" asked Coleman skeptically. He was the youngest captain King Lian had in his guard. A truly handsome man with rugged features, most women naturally gravitated toward him.

"This is the part you will not enjoy," replied Jared. "She is betrothed to Nathaniel Stone." Coleman made a sour face. Of all of Jared's friends, he liked Nathaniel the least. It was not about a display of haughtiness or pride, which some men of the Craft displayed at a young age. Nathaniel was above such behavior. Coleman simply did not trust him.

"Perhaps her judgment is lacking," said Coleman.

"So, about your intended bride, how did you meet?" asked Raphael. He felt it wise to change the subject.

'We met at the royal ball my uncle threw for all the courtiers in Nereheim. Ephratha was invited, but my cousin's manner was not agreeable to her," replied Jared with a smile.

"She must have a strong will to resist the enticement of royalty," said Coleman.

"My cousin is such a buffoon, he never even noticed her. I found her outside the ballroom, gazing at the stars," said Jared.

"So what is the name of this young woman who has stolen your heart?" asked Raphael.

"Her name is Ephratha Stowe," replied Jared. As he said her name, he felt a chill ripple down his back. He was truly enchanted by her.

The three continued down the staircase and out the rear entrance where Jared knew he would find his father's couriers. He found his two most trusted couriers sitting under the apple tree near the stables.

"What luck!" Jared thought as he moved toward the men. They stood as Jared approached them.

"Your highness," said the taller of the two said as they both bowed.

"Solomon, it is truly good to see you. I have a most worthy task. You must ride out to Count Lucerne and find the horse master, Philip Mauldon. Tell him his sister Nafaria is here and he is to come at once to Arioth. He must also bring Nadia with him if she can make the trip,"

"Is there to be given any explanation?" asked Solomon.

"Only that the girl is safe and at Arioth. He must come at once for important news regarding his family," replied Jared. "Also, will you stop at the apothecary and tell Malcom and Nathaniel Stone they are to come at once to the castle?"

"Yes, your highness," replied Solomon.

"Shall I go as well, your highness?" asked the other man.

"No James, I have a letter that needs to go to the house of Lord Robert Stowe in Wildemere. He and his wife must come quickly," replied Jared. He handed James the scroll that was sealed with wax.

"Gentlemen, both these tasks are of special importance to me. Please go quickly," said Jared.

"Yes your highness," they replied. They each took leave and walked toward the stable. Jared watched them for a moment before turning back to his friends.

"She must be special indeed to entrust your two greatest messengers to task," said Coleman.

"Never again will I ever meet another like her," replied Jared softly. The three young men turned and walked back to the castle.

* * *

The servants were still putting the last of the food on the table when Jared, Coleman and Raphael walked into the room. Jared's eyes lit up as he saw the turkeys that sat at either end of the table.

"Truly a meal of kings," said Jared.

"Yes it is," said a deep voice behind them. Jared turned to see his father approach them. Coleman and Raphael bowed to him. "Apparently, one of the young ladies has a fondness for turkey and wild rice."

"Father, as always you are a most gracious host. I have sent Ephratha's letter to Wildemere, and sent word to Philip Mauldon and Nathaniel Stone. It is my hope that we will have news very quickly," said Jared.

"In the meanwhile, we have a wedding to plan," replied the king.

"That is my intention," said Jared. "Have you had a chance to speak with Ephratha?"

"I have. She and her friend are very delightful. Your mother is greatly enamored with both. I must say that I am very surprised that Ephratha has such a strong friendship with a one of the Craft. Nereheim has done nothing but butcher them," said the king.

"I thought so as well, but Ephratha owes much to Nafaria. She said when they were children, Nafaria saved her life," replied Jared.

"Such a tie is truly one that is as strong as iron. It will never be broken," said the king.

At that moment, the queen entered the dining hall with Ephratha and Nafaria following behind her. Coleman felt his heart stop when he looked at Nafaria.

"Ephratha, Nafaria, I would like you to meet my two greatest friends," said Jared. He gestured to Coleman and Raphael. "This to my left is Coleman, captain of the royal guard. A finer marksman, you will never find, in North Agea or Nereheim. This man to my right is Raphael. A finer craftsman there never will be. He has a special talent for the Crafting of special hunting and ceremonial knives.

"Did he craft the hunting dagger you gave me?" asked Nafaria.

"Yes," said Jared.

"It truly is a marvelous specimen. Thank you," replied Nafaria as she looked at Raphael. Raphael smiled and bowed slightly toward her.

The meal was lively and jovial. Ephratha learned much about her fiancée and his practical jokes. Nafaria learned from the king of the freedom those who were of the Craft held in North Agea. Time and again she glanced up to find Coleman staring at her. She smiled slightly. He seemed so lighthearted and happy. If he were of the Craft, Nathaniel might have competition for her.

Nafaria sighed quietly. She knew that whatever good fortune had smiled on her, she was bound in her heart to find Malcom. He would know what to do next. First she must find Philip. He deserved to know of the death of their parents.

"Is everything all right?" Nafaria heard a voice gently speaking to her. She looked up to see Coleman staring at her. He held a look of concern on his face.

"I am fine. I was just thinking of my brother Philip. There is so much to tell him," said Nafaria.

"How long has it been since you last saw him?" asked Coleman.

"A little over a week ago, he and Nadia came to visit us in Wildemere. They brought me the horse I rode here on as a birthday gift. That seems so long ago. Much has happened that has changed us all," replied Nafaria.

"Jared mentioned it was not safe for you in Nereheim. He did not say anything more," replied Coleman. Nafaria looked at him intently.

"My parents were murdered, and I know the man who did it. Jared and Ephratha saw my mother killed," said Nafaria. Her eyes misted as she remembered how Jared and Ephratha told her about Thena's death.

"I am sorry to hear that so much trouble has come to you, but I am not sorry you are here," said Coleman. He kept his gaze fixed completely on her. She smiled gently at him.

"You are very kind. I can see why you and Jared are good friends. You have the same spirit and respect for others," said Nafaria. She was silent after that.

After a few minutes, Jared looked down the table. He saw Coleman and Nafaria staring at each other intently. Ephratha had finished eating and was talking to Raphael.

"Coleman, are you up to giving Ephratha and Nafaria a demonstration of your skill?"

Coleman looked over at his friend. "If that is what you wish. I do not mind showing off a bit," replied Coleman with a smile.

"Then let us go out to the courtyard and watch the sun set," replied Jared as he got up from the table. He turned to his father and said, "Thank you for showing my friends such grand hospitality."

Jared's father rose and came over to his son and clapped him on the shoulder. "Your friends are always welcome in my halls," he replied. "Go, enjoy youth."

The others rose, and thanked the king and followed Jared out of the dining hall.

"I have never seen him so happy," said the queen.

"Why should he not be happy? He has found great treasure in Nereheim," said the king.

Coleman grabbed his bow from the corner in the main hall where he always kept it. He followed Jared out to the courtyard where he and Jared practiced for hours. They became good friends over the years, while Jared's skill with the bow began to match his own natural talent.

Jared had a target set up at the end of the courtyard. It was about twenty yards away.

"Oh come on, Jared. That is hardly a worthy shot," said Coleman as he rolled his eyes.

"Do you prefer a different target?" asked Jared with a smile. Coleman looked up into the tree above the target. He spotted golden apples ripe on the branches.

"As a matter of fact, I do." He drew an arrow and put it on the bow. He took aim and a moment later the arrow came down with a thud. Raphael ran and retrieved the arrow. He came back holding it. On it was a large golden apple.

"Not a bad shot," said Raphael.

"Anyone else care for a try?" asked Coleman. He held out his bow. Nafaria stepped forward and took it.

"I shall try, but I will aim for the target," she said with a smile.

She put the arrow on the bow and took aim. A moment later, it took to the air and landed in the center of the target. Raphael whistled.

"Where did you learn that?" asked Coleman.

"My father taught my brother Philip, and Philip taught me," said Nafaria. "It was more for sport, than it was for hunting for me. I wanted to be with Philip, so I begged him to show me."

"He did a good job teaching. You would be a good marksman," said Jared.

The sun was very low in the sky and the first stars began to twinkle. Ephratha found a bench and sat down. Jared sat down next to her. She smiled at him.

"This is the longest amount of time I have ever spent with her. She knows so much, but is so innocent. It is almost as if all the extraordinary things she knows mean nothing to her," said Ephratha.

"I am sure that her knowledge means everything to her. When you grow up immersed in something, you see it as commonplace, not extraordinary. It only becomes extraordinary when you have to do something with that knowledge," said Jared.

"You are entirely too wise to be a mere man," replied Ephratha with a smile.

"I am not of the Craft, but if I was, I would break their most cardinal rule to marry you," he replied. A questioning glance came across Ephratha's face.

"What rule is that?" asked Ephratha.

"Those of the Craft marry within the Craft," replied Jared. Ephratha looked over at Coleman and Nafaria.

"Is that why your friend is so intent on her?" asked Ephratha.

"Nathaniel could only think of Nafaria for as long as I have known him. He came to North Agea when he was thirteen. Nafaria has not mentioned her brother Michael, but they were very good friends," replied Jared.

"I wonder why she has not mentioned him?" asked Ephratha.

"Most likely, there is so much going on, that she has her mind on Philip right now, because he is closer by. I have the feeling the news that she bears, Michael already knows," said Jared.

"How can that be? If he was at the manor when Lord Jason was murdered, would Joel not have killed him as well?" asked Ephratha.

"He would, but who knows if he was at the manor? Those of the Craft have very arcane ways, and Michael Mauldon was said to know much in those ways. Nathaniel said he spent almost every hour of his life in books," replied Jared.

"Nafaria comes from a mysterious family indeed," replied Ephratha.

* * *

The artisan room of Count Lucerne's castle was a lively one indeed. At the window one child sat with a sketchbook in his hand. He was busy capturing the apple tree outside on the paper before him.

Another sat at an easel working on an intricate painting of a floral arrangement before her. She swirled the colors together with the confidence of the greatest of artists.

Two little ones, a boy and girl played on the floor with toy blocks that were painted a variety of colors. Art period was their favorite time of day, for they played quietly while the older children worked on their fine art skills.

Philip moved from one to another while he watched the children work. He and Nadia took turns throughout the day tutoring Count Lucerne's children and tending to the horses.

"Sela, that is very good. The colors you have used are vibrant indeed."

"Thank you Philip. Nadia helped me understand how to pick colors," said Sela.

"You have listened well," replied Philip as he moved to the window again.

"Peter, your sketch of the tree is perfect," said Philip. He looked closer at the picture Peter drew. It was a sketch of what could be seen of the tree outside the window. Philip stood entranced by the sketch. The tree reminded him of an object his young sister might have sketched.

"Philip, are you all right?" asked Peter. Philip looked down to see Peter staring up at him.

"Yes, I am. I was just thinking of my sister. She loves nature. She drew sketches of plants all the time. Sometimes she would draw a plant, and imagine it a different way. She was very fond of nature," said Philip quietly.

The sky outside began to cloud as Solomon rode with a couple horsemen to Count Lucerne's castle. He rode quickly and was able to reach Count Lucerne's estate before sunset. His horse slowed to a stop as he rode into the courtyard and Solomon jumped down.

"Is there a message from the king?" asked the servant who came out to meet him.

"Prince Jared has a message for Philip Mauldon," said Solomon.

"Yes sir, follow me," replied the servant.

Solomon followed the servant through the main hall of the castle. He looked at the tapestries that hung on the walls as they passed. The servant led him into a large room where there were four children, and a young man. A moment later, the Count himself walked into the room accompanied by a young woman.

"The prince of North Agea has a message for you sir," said the servant to Philip.

"What is the message?" asked Philip. Solomon handed him the parchment in his hand. Philip broke open the seal and unrolled the paper. His brow instantly creased, and his eyes misted.

"What is it?" asked Nadia.

"My sister is in North Agea, awaiting our arrival at Arioth. She has news of the family, but I already know what it could be," said Philip. He sighed heavily.

Nadia looked at him intently. "We need to go to her," she said.

Philip nodded his head and looked at Count Lucerne. "We will need a few days leave, my Lord," said Philip.

"It is well, Philip. You and Nadia hardly took a break when you went to Nereheim to visit your family. Take your time and enjoy your visit with your sister," said the Count.

Philip turned to Nadia. "Get the children ready, we must be quick."

"I will have bags packed for us in ten minutes," replied Nadia. She went over to the two playing on the floor and beckoned them to come with her.

Philip and Nadia sat in the front of a small cart that held their son and daughter. The sun was sinking lower in the sky, and clouds continued to gather overhead. He remembered a time from his childhood when his little brother and sister rode in a cart much the same as he now drove. His sister was older now and here in North Agea. He feared what that might mean.

* * *

Lydia read the brief note that the king's courier from North Agea had delivered to her.

A sigh fell from her lips.

"You say that Prince Jared himself asked you to deliver this note?" she asked.

"Yes, my Lady. He was quite earnest that it be delivered as quickly as possible," replied James.

"Did you see Ephratha with him?" she asked.

"Yes, I met her. She is very charming," said James. Lydia's eyes welled with tears as her heart filled with relief. She then remembered something and looked at James.

"Was there another girl with her?" asked Lydia.

"Yes, her name was Nafaria. Prince Jared said they were friends," replied James.

"Thanks be to God," whispered Lydia as she sighed again with relief. She looked at James. "Please give us one hour and we will be ready to go with you," said Lydia.

Lydia left James in the main entrance and went in search of her husband. She started down the hall and found him in his study.

"We were sent a message from Ephratha. She is with Prince Jared in North Agea," said Lydia.

"She is alive?" Robert asked with wide eyes. He put down the book he was reading.

"Yes," replied Lydia, holding out the letter James had delivered. Robert took it and read it through. Tears formed in his eyes that he shut to stop from falling.

"We must be ready to leave soon," said Robert quietly.

"I will pack a trunk for each of us," said Lydia. She quickly left the room.

Lydia went to Ephratha's room first. She took her three favorite dresses and a cloak from her closet. She packed the star book and a journal Ephratha kept at her desk. She also packed her favorite china doll and closed the trunk. She quickly packed Robert his trunk, and then packed one for herself. She carefully lined the bottom with her best cloak. Then she took a smaller leather box from the closet. It was heavy, and Lydia struggled to put it into the trunk carefully. She then put her clothes over the box and smiled as she filled her trunk with the things she needed for the trip.

* * *

Night settled over the countryside and still Solomon urged them on toward Arioth. Philip kept his horse steady and looked out over the rolling hills. He could vaguely see the outline against the sky. With no moon present, there was very little light to see by. Philip trusted his escort, and they continued on down the dusty road toward Arioth.

"Something is on your mind sir?" Philip roused from his countryside gaze to see Solomon riding next to him.

"I just wonder what it could mean, Nafaria in North Agea. My father was very protective of her. To my knowledge she has never left Wildemere since we moved there. If she is here, something terrible must have happened," replied Philip.

"Whether good news or ill, does it matter? You will have the chance to be reunited with your family. Even if under the worst circumstances, you can thank the God you serve that she is safe," said Solomon. Philip looked over at Solomon.

"Yes, I suppose that is true," replied Philip.

"Do not borrow trouble for yourself. How is it written? Each day has enough trouble of its own[28]," replied Solomon.

"It is written as such. I am grateful to live in a land where the sacred writings are so well known and often quoted by everyone," replied Philip with a smile.

"They are truly wise sayings. Though I am just a common man, I have tried to live my life by them. I feel that I am much happier than those who do not," replied Solomon.

"I have no doubt," said Philip. "How much longer before we reach Arioth?"

"It is about a half day's ride from here. I am fortunate that Count Lucerne lives close by," said Solomon. Philip smiled as they rode on.

They stopped at a small village to rest and water the horses. He sat in the main room of a very well kept inn. A short respite felt good to Philip but he was still longing to get to Nafaria and receive her news.

He was deep in thought when he noticed a mug was held in front of his face. Nadia stood in front of him with a mug of ginger beer. Philip took the mug and drank deeply. The tingling sensation of the ginger made him smile.

"I thought you could use a drink," said Nadia.

"Thank you. Father was right you know. He told me you would be a good match for me. Every year we have been married has proven that to me," said Philip.

Nadia smiled. Her hair fell around her shoulders in full curls. Her eyes sparkled the way his mother's sparkled when she looked at his father. Philip felt truly lucky to have the same kind of love from his wife that his parents enjoyed.

---

[28] Matthew 6:34

"Your father is a great man. I am so proud to see you grow into the kind of man I remember him to be," replied Nadia.

"Where are the children?" asked Philip.

"Solomon is loading the horse and cart. He wanted to make sure you had one more drink before we started off," said Nadia.

"He is a good man. I do not wonder why he is in the king's employ," said Philip. Nadia nodded, and then smiled. She laid her hand on Philip's.

"Though the news she brings may not be good, I am very much looking forward to seeing your sister. She will be so excited to see Nathaniel. She must have some interesting tales to tell. Not the least of which is how she became associated with the Prince of North Agea. That is a story I cannot wait to hear," said Nadia. She smiled mischievously and finished her drink. "Come, let us finish our journey and find the tidings at the end of it." Nadia stood and held out her hand to Philip. After a final drink from his mug, Philip took her hand and followed her outside.

The moon was full in the sky as the small group rode through the great castle walls. Servants milled about from one place to the next as they were about their tasks. Solomon spotted a young man walking toward them. He carried a bushel basket filled with fresh apples. "Joshua, put down those apples and take the horses. All the things in this cart must go to the guest wing of the castle," said Solomon.

"I will see to it. I am glad to see you have completed your task so soon, Solomon. The prince has been anxious for news," replied Joshua.

"News he shall have," replied Solomon to Joshua. Then he turned to Philip. "Come; let us find the prince and your sister."

Philip followed Solomon through the castle and into a vast hall. "This is called the great hall of the kings. Here you will find portraits of all the kings of North Agea. Through the door at the end is the throne room," said Solomon.

Philip looked around the brightly-lit hall as they passed through it. Rich portraits of noble men clung to the walls. The details in the paintings were so intricate that Philip felt as though the paintings could come to life. The ceiling was painted with lavish pictures of long ago adventures. Before he knew it, they were walking through the doorway into the throne room. He saw robed figures standing at the far end before their thrones.

"Your majesties, I present Philip Mauldon, and his wife Nadia," said Solomon.

King Lian nodded toward them. "We have met them, Solomon. Congratulations on completing your task so soon. Jared has been anxious for them to be here," said the king.

Philip bowed as reverently as he could, and Nadia politely curtsied. He really had no idea how to act before royalty. The sacred writings said a man was just a man, nothing more. He never learned proper etiquette for court.

"Your majesty, where is my sister?" I am most anxious to hear her news," replied Philip.

"Philip!" Philip turned toward the direction he heard his name coming from. He saw Nafaria rushing toward him. Her face was beaming. He held her close in his arms and squeezed her tightly.

"I have so missed you, little one," he said softly in her ear.

"And I have missed you as well," replied Nafaria. Nadia came up to them with a boy and a girl clinging to her skirts.

"Nadia, how wonderful to see you as well!" exclaimed Nafaria. She hugged Nadia warmly and then bent down toward the children.

"Hello Roland and Rowena," she exclaimed as she held out her hands toward them. They each took one of her hands in theirs. "They are absolutely precious."

"Nafaria how is it that you are here in North Agea, and in the king's castle at that?" asked Philip.

"Before I tell you, I would like you to meet a very good friend of mine." As she spoke, Ephratha and Jared came up to them.

"This is Ephratha. We have been friends since we were ten years old. No one knew, of course, we kept our friendship a secret. I think you already know Prince Jared," said Nafaria.

Philip looked closely at Ephratha. "I know who you are. You are the daughter of Lord Robert Stowe."

"Yes I am," replied Ephratha in a matter of fact tone. Nafaria drew in a breath before she spoke.

"Philip, father and mother are dead. Joel sought revenge against them and he killed them," said Nafaria. Her eyes began to mist with tears.

Philip felt his head spin with the news. Their father was dead? By the only man in Wildemere he trusted with the family secret? He felt his heart beating fast and his breath tried to match it.

"Joel killed mother and father? Why? Joel was father's best friend!" exclaimed Philip.

"Leanna was trampled by a runaway horse in the market. She was pregnant at the time. Mother did everything she could for her but she could not save her. Joel blamed mother and father and killed them. He would have killed me too, but Ephratha and Jared helped me escape," said Nafaria.

Nadia felt tears roll down her eyes at Nafaria's news. Jason, the man who saved her life and even honored her enough to have Philip marry her, was now dead. She pulled Rowena and Roland close to her as she wept.

"What of Michael?" whispered Philip.

"Father had the gift of foresight. He sent Michael away before it happened. He took father's diary and the family annals with him. He went back to Denholm Glen," replied Nafaria.

Philip smiled weakly at this. Though they were all young, Philip knew very well the crush Michael had on his childhood playmate, Lillia. It was possible Michael had decided to marry her. To forsake the rule that those of the Craft must marry within the Craft to preserve YAHWEH's gift. Michael would be happy enough to live out his life in quiet study with the love of his childhood. Philip hoped he was doing just that. He turned to Jared.

"Thank you, your highness, for saving my sister. There is nothing I could possibly offer you that would show gratitude enough for such an act," said Philip.

"I am honored to know such a noble woman. She will always be welcome here at Arioth," said Jared.

Philip did not hear Jared. He fell to his knees and buried his face in his hands and cried for his parents.

* * *

Robert and Lydia arrived the day after Philip and Nadia. Nafaria watched Ephratha squeal with delight and run into her mother's arms. She smiled as she watched them embrace. After a moment, Lydia noticed Nafaria and came over to her. She pulled Nafaria close. "I am so sorry about what happened to your parents. There is nothing that will ever justify their deaths," said Lydia with sadness in her voice.

"Thank you, Lydia," said Nafaria quietly.

Lydia put her hands gently to Nafaria's face and looked at her closely. Nafaria could see tears falling from her eyes. "You look to be such a perfect mixture of the two. You have your mother's soft features, but that quick eye and steady gaze are from your father," said Lydia.

Nafaria smiled. Out of the corner of her eye she noticed movement and saw a man approaching them. As she noticed the man's face, she felt her blood freeze. Her eyes grew wide. "I know you," she said quietly as she pointed to the man.

Lydia looked from Nafaria to her husband with a questioning glance. She had no idea that Robert had ever met her. Philip stood next to Nafaria.

"How do you know him?" he asked.

Nafaria felt the room begin to spin. She gasped for breath and shut her eyes. The image of her home with flames coming from inside came quickly. She heard the screams once more of all the servants that were cruelly executed only because they worked for her father. She was still gasping for breath when she opened her eyes. Tears flowed down her cheeks.

"He was one of the men with Joel the day father was killed. I returned from the meadow too late to see the deed, but I saw father lying on the ground. I heard Joel give the command to execute anyone else alive and to look for me," said Nafaria quietly.

Philip stared at Robert. His eyes blazed with anger. He moved toward Robert, but Nafaria caught him by the arm and pulled him back.

"No Philip. Father warned me that we are not to take vengeance for his death. We do not have the right. Only YAHWEH does," said Nafaria. Philip's face turned red and his eyes filled with tears.

Ephratha stared in shock at her father. She knew that he had strong feelings about associating with those of the Craft. Those feelings were the reason why she never even confided in her mother her friendship with Nafaria. However, she could not believe that he could be party to such an atrocious act as murder for those beliefs. He had taught her better than that.

"Father, is this true?" she asked quietly.

Robert stared coldly at Nafaria and Philip. He did not answer.

"Answer your daughter, Lord Robert. She deserves to hear the truth from your mouth alone," said Philip. There was no mistaking the disdain in his voice.

Instead of answering her question, Robert asked one of his own.

"How long have you been in the company of this woman? How many times have I told you those of the Craft are dangerous people? They kill whenever it suits them, you cannot trust them!" shouted Robert at Ephratha.

Ephratha listened to his accusation and took a deep breath. She squeezed the hand that Jared was holding tightly. "Yes father, some do. Some prey on the weak, and some become jealous of others and use their knowledge only for themselves. There are others who are not like that. They look out for people. They help strangers whenever possible, and ask for nothing in return. They stand up to the crowds around them and demand that justice be done at every turn.

I have known Nafaria for six years. We met one day when I was lost in the woods. You remember that day father, do you not? You forbade me to be out after dark ever again that night. She found me by a brook after I had eaten poisonous berries and was bitten by a very poisonous snake. She revived me, and healed me. She saved my life, father," said Ephratha.

"I remember that night. We were wild with worry trying to figure out where you were, when you wandered into the manor after dark," interrupted Lydia. She looked at Nafaria as Ephratha continued to speak.

"You, father, have killed a family that does nothing but help other people. Lord Jason helped Nadia leave Nereheim so that she would be safe. He knew it would only be a matter of time before she would swing on gallows the way Thena did. Think back to everything Lord Jason has proposed that has helped the poor or the working class of Wildemere. Did he not make sound suggestions, and did not the people benefit? How could you be a party to murder of innocent people?" demanded Ephratha.

Robert looked at his daughter sternly and replied, "When they let an innocent woman and her unborn child die, there is no longer any excuse for them." Lydia looked at Robert in disbelief.

"This is what you honestly believe happened? That Thena let her best friend die? Robert, you are so blind! Thena did everything in her power to save Leanna. She worked tirelessly through those last hours. She was frustrated and upset because there was nothing she could do. Thena did not let Leanna die. There was nothing that could be done to save her!" replied Lydia. Robert turned and looked at his wife.

"How would you know anything about it?" he asked coldly.

"I was there Robert. I helped Thena through that whole ordeal," replied Lydia.

Ephratha stepped toward her father. She let Jared's hand fall away from her. She blinked back tears as she spoke. "You can still ask forgiveness for this act, father. You can choose to start again with a fresh mind, and see people for who they are. Do not let the ignorance in Nereheim poison the sound judgment I know exists in you," said Ephratha.

Robert felt his eyes blaze at her words. "I will not ask forgiveness when I know I have done what is right!" he roared.

"Then I suggest you leave North Agea quickly sir. You will find the company of the populace most disagreeable. For many are of the Craft," said Jared coldly.

Ephratha looked at her husband to be. She saw that Jared did not intend for her father to stay for their wedding if this was how he felt about those of the Craft. She lowered her eyes to the ground and turned to her father. She felt a fresh wave of tears flow from her eyes.

"I never thought I would see the day when I would be ashamed to be called your daughter. Sadly, that day has arrived. You have betrayed my best friend's parents and killed the innocent people they employed. Please leave and never return," said Ephratha quietly.

Robert looked shocked, but he quickly resumed his stony gaze. "Come Lydia, we are leaving. I cannot stay in this evil place," said Robert.

Lydia stood where she was, staring at the palace floor. Throughout the exchange between daughter and father, she felt her heart break. She began to realize that she no longer knew the man she shared a household with, and no longer wished to.

"Lydia let us go!" Robert shouted.

"No," Lydia replied. It was quiet, but with force and conviction. She looked up at once into her husband's eyes.

"I will not return to Nereheim ever again. I am ashamed of my home, and those who kill innocent people out of spite or ignorance. I will stay here in North Agea and be next to my daughter for her wedding."

Robert looked at Lydia and let out a roar as he turned and stormed out of the throne room. Ephratha embraced her mother when he was gone. Jared came to her as well. "You will be welcome to stay here as long as you wish," said Jared to Lydia.

"Thank you. It may take me some time to find suitable work," said Lydia. She brushed the tears from her eyes and said boldly, "Let us go, there is a wedding to plan, and I have something for you."

* * *

Lydia followed Jared and Ephratha to the room where her things were brought. With some difficulty, she lifted a large chest onto the bed.

"I brought a few things for you from home," said Lydia as she opened the chest. She pulled out a long black cloak with white fur lining the hood. "I knew you left in haste, for you would never leave this behind." She handed the cloak to Ephratha.

Ephratha smiled as she hugged it to her face. "It was made for me by my great grandmother. She made it years before she died, instructing my mother to save it for my sixteenth birthday," said Ephratha to Jared.

"This is what you requested. I knew the book even before I finished your letter," said Lydia. She handed Ephratha a small, but thick leather bound book. The parchment pages were almost a rich amber color with age. Ephratha took the book, her eyes sparkling as she did so.

"This book has been my guide, my companion, my teacher and my comfort for so many years," she said quietly. Ephratha turned the book to its side. As her eyes scanned the binding, her breath caught as she saw the triangular shape of three circles forming the triquetra.

Jared noticed the look on her face. "Is something wrong?" he asked. Ephratha shook her head and pointed to the symbol on the binding of the book.

"It is so odd how a little understanding changes everything. I never noticed the triquetra on the book until today. Do you suppose this book was created by someone of the Craft?" asked Ephratha.

"Anything is possible. You have taken a step into a much larger world," replied Jared.

Lydia had taken a few other things from the trunk as the two spoke. She now looked to Jared. She took a solid bar of gold and put it in his hands. "This is your dowry. There are twenty bars in all," said Lydia.

Jared looked down at the gold bar in his hands. He smiled and placed it back in Lydia's hands. "I understand only too well the custom of dowries. I do very much appreciate the effort you have made to bring this to me, but I must decline this gift. Ephratha is a treasure hidden in a field, and I have happily sold my heart for her. I will not accept money and turn our love into an arranged marriage. I propose that you keep this gold. Now that you are living in a new land, your life will begin again. Buy new lands, and manage them as you managed land for your husband. For I have no doubt that you will prosper here in

North Agea," said Jared. He hugged Lydia and then Ephratha. "Take some time together before dinner," he said as he walked from the room.

Ephratha sat on the bed next to her clothes and watched her mother unpack another trunk that was left. "I do not know what I shall do with the trunk for your father. In his rage, I am sure he has forgotten it," said Lydia.

"I am sure we can send it back another time," replied Ephratha. Lydia quickly put away her things in a beautifully carved bureau next to the bed.

"Mother, there is something I need to ask you," said Ephratha.

"What is it?" asked Lydia. She came and sat on the bed next to her daughter.

"How did you know Jason and Thena were of the Craft?" asked Ephratha. "That night when we stayed with Joel and Leanna, you knew; Joel and Leanna knew. How is that?"

"I do not know how Joel knew. Perhaps Jason felt he could confide their family secret to him. For me, I could tell almost from the moment they arrived in Wildemere. They were both so wise and resourceful. Things they said and wisdom they used came from the sacred book of YAHWEH," said Lydia.

"How did you recognize these things?" asked Ephratha. Lydia smiled and rose from her seat. She opened her trunk once again and pulled out a very old leather bound book. She handed it to Ephratha. She looked and saw the figure of the triquetra embossed on the cover. There were no words for a title. The figure itself was all that was needed. Ephratha's eyes grew wide as she looked at the book. "Mother, where did you get this?" asked Ephratha.

"It was from a special friend. His name was Ferdinand. I was probably thirteen years old when I first met him. His parents were silk merchants and came to live in our village. It was a small place just outside the port city of Burnea, so we saw many such people. Ferdinand was a quiet boy, but very inventive. He would carve intricate patterns in pieces of fallen tree branches. Or sometimes he would sketch a rare plant or tree. He saw me following him one day and asked me to sit with him. He would tell me fantastic stories of the travels he had been on with his family. He would also read from a book that he would carry. The things in that book I had never heard before. Ferdinand would ask me what I thought this author was trying to say. We talked for hours about things of that nature.

One day he finally confided in me that he was of the Craft and that he followed the teachings of YAHWEH. 'These are the teachings we have been discussing' he said to me.

I was afraid of what this could mean, of course. Stories of those of the Craft flew around villages even then. However, Ferdinand was such a gentle boy. I knew he could never hurt anyone with his knowledge. I even told him so once. He told me, 'People choose to be evil or good. There are those who only want to destroy or enslave those around them. I only wish to help.' I have never forgotten that.

For two years we kept our friendship a secret, much like you and Nafaria hid your friendship. Then one day, when we met in our place on the hillside, Ferdinand pulled me to him and kissed me. It was a kiss full of warmth and passion, and lasted for what seemed hours. Then he burst into tears. He told me that it was a custom for those of the Craft to marry within the Craft, to pass on the gifts YAHWEH entrusted them with. He was told the night before he would be leaving the next morning to meet his betrothed. He did not even know who she was. He told me how much he loved me and wished he could marry me. My tears fell as hard as his did that day because I knew I was losing my greatest friend. I was losing the first man I fell in love with.

He handed me his book, the one he always read to me and told me to follow what was written. 'This wisdom is the best gift I can think to leave you with. You will never have power to use incantations, but you can learn to be wise,' he had said. Never have I forgotten those words. So I read, and I even prayed that YAHWEH would help me understand his truth.

When I was seventeen I was finally betrothed to your father. He was so handsome, witty, and full of adventure. When we married, I told him of ideas I had for managing our land, and he encouraged me to try them. Soon your father entrusted me with all the household affairs because everything I did greatly benefited the family. I never did tell him the secret of my success.

I loved your father so much, but as Nereheim changed, so did he. I became frightened of the things he would say. Over time, he became someone I no longer understood."

Lydia took Ephratha by her hands. "You have been given a special gift to have a husband who respects what he does not fully understand. He will treat you well," said Lydia. Ephratha felt tears fall from her eyes as she hugged her mother.

* * *

Malcom and Nathaniel stood at the ferry in Burnea, waiting to cross the Anenderes into North Agea.

This body of water never failed to fascinate Nathaniel. He was enchanted by the poetic legend of the bell. The water itself was a mighty thing to watch when there was a storm. It was also a peaceful body when the sun was shining and the wind was calm. When he was a child, the faces would whisper of hope and encouragement to him. He was truly enchanted by the Anenderes River. Even today, when all his hope felt lost, he looked out at the waves and felt peace.

He woke from his reverie and followed his father onto the boat with their horses. He stood at the side looking out to where the shore of North Agea would appear.

"Nathaniel, you have been silent since we left Wildemere. Tell me what is on your mind," said Malcom.

Nathaniel sighed. "I feel as though the future is lost father. I tried so hard the past few years to find her. I searched with every incantation you ever showed me. I looked for potions that would help me see her. I even sought out others of the Craft to show me greater things so that I could find her. It was like she disappeared from the earth. Then, we finally do find Jason, Thena and Nafaria, only to arrive too late to help them. She has always been my life, father. I hoped for so much, but it feels like my dreams have slipped through my fingers like sand," replied Nathaniel.

Lara Giesbers

Malcom put his arm around his son. "This is a grave disappointment for me as well. I know the feeling you describe. It was how I felt the day I buried your mother. My heart broke in two with a mighty crack that black day. However, YAHWEH has helped give me peace and a hope for the future. My heart has mended, as I have watched you become a man. Though his way is not always clear, we can never doubt that YAHWEH knows what he is doing.

All is not completely lost. It is possible that Nafaria was able to get away. Perhaps king Lian has more news of the riots the lady spoke about."

"It will be nice to visit with Jared as well," said Nathaniel. He smiled slightly.

They continued toward Arioth after the ferry landed. Nathaniel was the first to comment on the amount of people on the road. "Father, does it seem strange that so many people should be going the same direction we are?" he asked.

"It does, but perhaps there is an explanation to satisfy us," replied Malcom. He slowed to a stop along the road beside a carriage. "Greetings, there seems to be a lot of folks traveling today. Is something special happening?" asked Malcom to the carriage driver.

"The people are most likely traveling to Arioth for Prince Jared's wedding, tomorrow. The king has generously allowed the citizens of North Agea to the festival at his castle after the wedding in honor of his son's marriage," said the driver.

"Thank you for your news," said Malcom cordially. He turned to Nathaniel. "I think we should make ourselves presentable when we reach Arioth. I would love the honor of congratulating Jared," said Malcom. Nathaniel nodded, but stayed silent. He was happy for the news of Jared's wedding, but still sad that his own journey to receive his betrothed had turned into a failure.

"Come son, let us rejoice with those who rejoice[29]," said Malcom softly. Nathaniel looked at his father and nodded his head. They

[29] Romans 12:15

continued on toward Arioth surrounded by the great throng headed the same way.

* * *

The sun shone brightly as Robert hastily galloped back toward Nereheim. He felt anger boil his blood to a rage at the way the events turned when he was reunited with his daughter. She had pleaded with him to ask forgiveness and learn to have respect for the people he knew to be murderers. When he refused, she made it very clear he was never to return to her. These people: witches, wizards, sorcerers, those of the Craft, whatever they chose to call themselves, were evil and poisoned the minds of his family against him. He would take his wrath out on these people and his fury would be felt to the ends of the earth.

Robert continued to gallop on, these thoughts burning in his mind as he reached the bank of the Anenderes River. He slowly made his way to the dock to wait for the next ferry.

It was fast approaching dusk as Robert led his horse off the ferry and through the crowds of people who thronged the cobblestone streets of Burnea. The endless sea of faces was nameless until he finally did see one he recognized. He saw Joel with four others from Wildemere meticulously searching the crowds, shops and alleyways. He finally reached them, but Joel had his back turned. Robert laid his hand on Joel's shoulder. He turned quickly and looked him in the face.

"Lord Robert," he said with some relief.

"Are you looking for the daughter of Jason Mauldon?" asked Robert.

"We were going to search the city, and then head into North Agea," said Joel.

"She is in North Agea, at Arioth, the castle of the king," replied Robert.

"She is at the king's castle? However will we reach her there?" wondered Joel.

"The prince is set to marry my daughter. A great celebration is sure to take place. Who is to say that with so many people present that tragedy may not strike?" asked Robert slyly.

"How soon?" asked Joel.

"I am certain you will have time to reach your destination," replied Robert. Joel put a hand on his shoulder.

"Thank you," he said.

* * *

It was dark as Joel and his company walked their horses onto the ferry. Joel kept his thoughts his own as the boat glided away from Nereheim toward the unseen shore of North Agea. His thoughts were interrupted, as the horses became restless. There was murmuring all around him. Joel leaned over to a stranger sitting next to him.

"What is happening?" he asked.

"The horses sometimes get restless when passing these waters at night. There is a legend that tells of faces in the water. Sometimes, you see them, and they speak to you," replied the stranger.

"How many times have you traveled this river?" asked Joel.

"Many," replied the stranger.

"Have you ever seen these faces?" asked Joel. He started to become uneasy about this trip. The stranger shook his head.

"I never have, though I have spoken to others that claim they have. It is only a legend," replied the stranger.

Suddenly, there was a loud shout from the front half of the boat. Joel watched as the people became excited and looked over the edge of the boat.

"The faces, I see the faces in the water!" someone shouted.

Joel, looked, and there he saw a sea of faces in the water as well. His shock was doubled when he recognized Jason and Thena in the water. His face turned ashen as he stared into the water at the face of the man he killed. His lips parted and formed the word *please*.

Joel continued to stare at the water long after the faces disappeared. He felt a tap on his shoulder. It was the stranger he was speaking to.

"Did you see a face in the water?" he asked. His voice quivered as he waited for Joel's answer.

"Yes," he whispered.

"Did it say anything to you?" he asked again with that same anxiousness.

"I believe he said, 'please'," replied Joel. He wandered away from the stranger to ponder what he had witnessed.

* * *

Michael sat up in bed, covered in sweat. He gave out a cry so loud that Lillia was instantly awake. She sat up to find her husband covered in sweat and gasping for breath. He was still shaking.

"Michael, what is wrong?" she asked, her voice alarmed.

"I had a dream. My father passed to me his gift of premonition. Joel is going to kill Nafaria," said Michael. He quickly got out of bed and went to his clothes. He laid them over the chair that was pushed up next to his writing desk in the corner. As he glanced out the window, he saw that a full moon was out, but it was still very dark.

"Michael, where are you going?" asked Lillia.

"I need to find my sister. She must be somewhere in North Agea. I thought I saw a large colonnade that she was standing in. The royal castle of Arioth is known for its colonnade. Perhaps she is there," replied Michael.

Lillia sat on the bed, a blank expression on her face. Then slowly she realized what his words meant, and she became frightened.

"NO! You cannot go!" shouted Lillia emphatically. He looked at her with great sadness.

"Lillia, I must go. This has been shown me as a warning. I must help her," replied Michael.

"Listen to me. You have just escaped the man who killed your father. If he sees you, he may kill you as well," said Lillia.

"I must take that chance," replied Michael.

Lillia got out of bed, and put her arms around Michael. "This is madness. I will not lose you to blind revenge. Let us talk to father and see if there is a more reasonable solution," said Lillia.

"There is no time!" shouted Michael. Lillia looked at him coldly. Her cheeks were completely red.

"Time will have to be made. We have a home now, Michael, and I will not see it destroyed for the sake of revenge!" Lillia shouted in return. There was no mistaking the conviction in her voice. Michael resigned himself to her request.

"Let us go quickly then," replied Michael. Swiftly he walked out of their bedroom with Lillia close behind him.

A short while later, Michael paced the floor of Lord Reinard's great room as he told his father in law about the dream he had and what it he thought it meant. Lillia sat in her favorite chair and stared at her husband, tears in her eyes and streaming down her face. Reinard himself sat staring at the fire, his fingertips pushed against each other, silent while Michael spoke. One of his servants continued to keep the fire burning, adding a log when necessary. Finally, it was his turn to speak.

"Lillia is right, you know. You cannot go. You have duties as a husband now that I will not allow you to abandon. You cannot go," replied Reinard.

"But father-" Michael started to interrupt his father in law but Reinard interrupted him. "However, I will do this. Nafaria must be warned, this I agree on. I do not believe you yourself would ever make it there in time. Lillia would not permit you to go without her, and two cannot travel as swiftly as one. Peter is my best rider. He is strong, and he handles his horse well. His horse is the fastest in Nereheim, I would wager. We will send Peter with a message to give only to the king of North Agea. He will know what to do," replied Reinard.

Michael looked at Reinard with great relief. What he proposed was very thoughtful and very wise. If Reinard entrusted this task to Peter, he must be quite capable indeed.

"I agree, it sounds like a wise decision," said Michael. Reinard nodded his head toward the man stoking the fire.

"Philip, wake Peter. He is to dress immediately and prepare for a journey to North Agea. I have an urgent message for the king," said Reinard.

Peter walked into the great room within fifteen minutes after Philip left the room. Reinard rose from his seat and handed him a sealed roll of parchment.

"Only the king of North Agea is to receive this from your hand. It is of vital importance that he follows the instructions within. Ride swift, do not stop, unless absolutely necessary, and be safe. You are the only one I trust with this task," said Reinard.

Peter looked at Michael who clapped him on the shoulder. Lillia looked exhausted and as if she had been crying all night. He looked back at Reinard. "It will be as you say," replied Peter. He quietly left the room. The moon was descending in the sky as Peter rode out of the manor toward North Agea.

* * *

The morning of the wedding, Ephratha stood before the looking glass in her room. Her blond curls were swooped into an elaborate style upon her head. Gold thread was woven throughout her hair, making it sparkle when the light caught it. Her dress was pure white and flowed around her. The neck was beautifully embroidered and revealed her ivory neck. She looked stunning, but still felt uneasy as she looked into the glass. She absentmindedly touched her hair when she heard a voice behind her. "Do not worry, you look absolutely perfect." Ephratha turned as her mother entered the room.

"I do not feel perfect, mother," replied Ephratha.

"It is normal to feel nervous on your wedding day. You are about to become a wife," said Lydia. Ephratha smiled weakly.

"A wife I am ready to become. It is becoming princess that frightens me."

Lydia took her hands and cupped them around Ephratha's face. The warmth gave Ephratha comfort. "You will make a grand princess. Follow your heart and continue to grow in wisdom. Let Jared lead you and you will find that all will fall into place."

"I am grateful that you are here, mother. I know it is hard, but I am glad you have chosen to stay," said Ephratha. Tears moistened her eyes and fell on Lydia's hands. She pulled her daughter into her arms.

"There is nothing in the world that would keep me away from you on this day," replied Lydia. Ephratha smiled.

"Have you any words of wisdom for me?" she asked.

Lydia thought for a moment. "Remember that love covers over many wrongs[30]. Learn to forgive your husband. Start your marriage in honesty and keep it always this way. Follow these, and your marriage will have great success," said Lydia.

"I shall heed your advice," replied Ephratha.

Nafaria swept into the room in a beautiful jade dress. Her dark hair was pinned to her sides, and left to flow down her back. She looked so much like a china doll to Ephratha. Her eyes widened when they met hers.

"Ephratha, you look grand," replied Nafaria. Ephratha took a deep breath and exhaled.

"Mother says the same. I hope I can get through this grand event with my sanity intact," replied Ephratha.

"You will be marvelous," said Nafaria.

"Your ever-present confidence still continues to give me great courage," replied Ephratha.

"Good, it is almost time for it all to begin," said Nafaria as she smiled her broadest smile.

Down the great hall and into another wing of the castle, Jared sat in his room gazing out the window. Philip entered the room quietly and stood watching him. Jared was perfectly still, except for an occasional twitching of his eyes as he sat looking out the window.

"Is there anything wrong, Jared?" asked Philip. He felt unsure as to whether he should have said "your highness".

At first, Jared did not answer. His gaze remained fixed on the blue sky. He finally sighed and said, "It is the oddest of ironies that I now face," said Jared as he looked toward Philip. "I always thought that becoming king would be the most terrifying thing that could happen. Now I find I am afraid of taking Ephratha as my wife. She is worth more than the entire treasure king Solomon ever acquired. What if I cannot do her justice?" asked Jared.

---

[30] 1 Peter 4:8

Philip stepped closer to him and stood next to where Jared sat. "The only injustice you could ever do Ephratha is not acting on your feelings. I have watched you with her. Your love is so evident that not a single person who has seen you will question whether you have made the right choice. The way you look at her is with a great and needful longing. She knows this, and you will be so happy together. You two are absolutely perfect for each other. The way you look at Ephratha reminds me of how I feel about Nadia. I cannot breathe without thinking of her. You will make a good husband, Jared. You have already let the wisdom of YAHWEH guide you to find a woman of great and noble character. Let his wisdom give you courage as well," said Philip.

Jared looked up at Philip with tears in his eyes. "I cannot let Ephratha down. I could not bear the thought of hurting her," whispered Jared.

Philip put his hand on Jared's shoulder. "You will not ever do that. If you continue to think of her first and let YAHWEH guide your steps, you will never let her down."

"Thank you for your strong advice. I am so grateful you could be here," replied Jared.

"I am grateful to be here for you. I owe you so much for being a friend to Nafaria. We owe you much for keeping her safe," said Philip.

* * *

Jared stood at the altar in the front of the grand cathedral of North Agea. It was the most spacious place and was perfect for his wedding day, but it was also the most peaceful. It was here that Jared first learned the respect due the great being those of the Craft revered. He felt closer to this mysterious YAHWEH here than any other place. He knew the sacred writings enough to know that YAHWEH was no respecter of grand buildings built to honor him. Or perhaps impress him? Was man so proud of his accomplishments that he felt that he could build a place majestic enough for such a great and powerful being? No such place could be fashioned by human hands.

No, Jared knew the truth, but he felt the tranquility of this ancient cathedral reach out its fingertips to soothe his anxious heart. He waited at the altar for the one that just entered the cathedral and lit the room with her beauty.

It was at that moment that everything around him disappeared. There was no vast crowd waiting expectantly for him to say the words he felt for his lovely bride. His friends were no longer present. They were the solid foundation that had built relationships and helped him understand what it was like to be a friend and want to be a friend to his one and only true love. Even their families were invisible to him, the people that showed him how to love unconditionally and challenged him to be more than he ever thought was possible. He only saw her, drifting toward him in a flowing white gown, her golden hair shining like the sun. His eyes clouded with tears and began to flow down his face. At this one moment, he was alone as this vision of loveliness came to him. He could see the tears in her eyes as well, as she reached up and dried his eyes with her delicate ivory hand.

Jared took her hand in his and gently kissed it. He closed his eyes, breathing in the fresh lavender scent that seemed to be created for her alone. He felt his heart pound so loudly; he thought it would come through his chest. His chest heaved, but it did not seem to take in air. He could hardly believe this creature before him was to be his for the rest of his life.

As he opened his eyes again, he could see that he was no longer alone. The cathedral was once again filled with loyal subjects, the closest of friends, and all his family. He whispered a prayer of thanks to YAHWEH for these great blessings on this day.

Jared felt his hands shake as he took her steady hands in his and walked toward the man who would bind them together forever. She looked up at him and smiled through her tears, happy to be led toward her marriage by this man she knew she would love forever.

Ephratha gazed into Jared's eyes and felt tears form as she watched how freely his fell. He was not ashamed to be so full of love that he would hide his true feelings for her. He was not ashamed to let her see that she was the center of his world. He thought of her as the pearl of great price, but Ephratha knew that a man as noble as Jared was just as hard, if not impossible, to find. However, it was possible, was that not what Nafaria had said the sacred writings taught? All things were possible with YAHWEH[31]. He had the power to do more than she could ever dream. As she looked into Jared's eyes, and watched his tears flow down his face, she made the decision to dream big.

Jared looked at her and cleared his throat. "Ephratha, there is something that I wish to say to you today before you marry me. I am not a perfect man, but what I am is yours forever. There will never be another woman for me for as long as we both live. I cannot be more grateful to YAHWEH for sending you into my life. I promise to always honor and respect your opinion, your intelligence, and your creativity. You have a beautiful heart, and I am so happy that you have chosen me to help guard it. I love you."

Ephratha could barely speak as she listened to his words. She felt her heart pound louder and faster as she listened to the way he described how he felt toward her. She looked into his green eyes and found the courage to speak.

"Jared, my life has been changed forever since the day you first laid your eyes on me. From the very night we met, you have proven yourself to be wise, courageous, witty and charming. You have filled me with such great hope for a future I never thought I could have. You have shown me that all things are possible. I want us to have the courage to dream big dreams for each other. Together we will face our challenges and conquer our fears. I will love only you for the rest of my life."

They turned toward the priest and listened as he said the words aloud that they would repeat to each other. Ephratha placed a solid gold band on his finger and gently kissed his hand. Jared took her hand and after placing the golden ring on her finger, he kissed her hand as well. They were joined together in front of family, friends, countrymen, and YAHWEH himself. He hoped he never had to be separated from her. His tears began again in a fresh wave, as he gently stroked her cheek. He whispered in her ear, "You are the most important treasure in my life." He closed his eyes as his lips touched hers and he felt the warmth of her

---

[31] Matthew 19:26

breath in his mouth. Her sweetness was intoxicating and now it was his for the rest of his life. His treasure and no one would take it away.

Jared opened his eyes and she smiled up at him, the entire cathedral erupting in cheers. They turned to face the crowd with wide smiles and tears.

* * *

In honor of Jared's wedding, the king opened his castle to his subjects in the greatest act of hospitality he could think of. The entire castle was alive and filled with laughter, music, dancing, and of course, food and wine. The celebration continued as the sun set and the first stars began to peek out of the purple sky. Music could be heard from every corner of the castle, on every floor. People moved from room to room, and stopped to congratulate the prince and new princess of North Agea.

Nathaniel left his father to wander through the castle and see what could be seen. He promised to come congratulate Jared after a while. He was still distracted by everything that happened on their journey. He needed time to forget his disappointment and change his mood.

His brilliant blue eyes flashed as he watched the young men and women around him. He watched the revelers curiously, as he did all people. What drew people to each other in the first place? Was it better to be able to follow the heart and risk rejection or to be betrothed and have the choice taken from yourself? Nathaniel pondered this and felt tears form in his eyes again. He hoped to have both in Nafaria. She was a woman his father adored and approved of; and she was the central crux of his heart. Had YAHWEH decided, like the great ancient Enoch, that she was too pure and too innocent for this earth? Had he spirited her away before he had a chance to really love her?

He could not bear to think such things, and he certainly could not bear facing Jared at this moment. He did not begrudge Jared his happiness, not in the least. However, he could not appear before him to congratulate him until his heart had its moment to mourn. Tears slowly trailed down his face as Nathaniel stood in the shadows allowing just that.

Nafaria grew bored of the formalities in the throne room. She whispered to Ephratha that she wished to step out into the fresh air. She flitted like a butterfly from one room to the next, enjoying the music, entertainment and merry making. Her smile was wide and radiant as she headed outside onto the colonnade.

Joel moved through the crowds of people careful not to alert anyone to his presence. He looked for Nafaria as he went, staying in the shadows. At long last, his quest for vengeance was going to be complete. Once he killed Nafaria, he could be at peace. He would no longer need to curse Jason for letting Leanna die. He would be free. As he moved in the shadows, Joel caught sight of Nafaria as she walked outside along the colonnade, heading for a quiet place, with fewer people.

Nathaniel stirred from his thoughts, to see a beautiful girl with midnight black hair slowly coming down the colonnade. She looked so radiant and pure in the jade green dress she wore. Her dark hair flowed down her back, and her face was so innocent; like the face of an angel. He was compelled to follow her through the colonnade toward a quiet place where she stood watching the stars.

Nafaria stood as far from the crowds as she could get, so she could catch her breath. She danced with Coleman until she finally excused herself and went to be with Ephratha. However the formalities of the throne room that Ephratha was obligated to face bored her quickly. She decided to come and look at the stars and take in the fresh air. The stars were numerous and twinkling brightly.

She looked into the sky and thought about what lay ahead. Ephratha and Jared were now married, and she had found her brother. What was she to do now? What plan did YAHWEH have for her? She would look for Malcom and Nathaniel next and let them know she was here.

She could hear the fall of footsteps on the pavement growing louder as they came nearer to her. They broke her thoughts, but she continued to look at the sky. She finally sighed and said, "Coleman, I do not wish to dance right now, find another maiden to sweep off her feet."

"I am here for vengeance, witch, not dancing," a harsh voice snarled.

Nafaria snapped her head in the direction of the voice, her eyes growing wide with fear. Joel stood before her with a menacing look in his eyes.

Coleman wandered down the colonnade looking for Nafaria. Jared's warning had not deterred him in the least in his affections for her. He may never be able to win her hand in marriage, but he could dance with her. He would spend as much time as he was able with her. He sighed, regretting for the first time in his life that he was not able to marry one of the Craft. He never cared much for those of the Craft. They always seemed so preoccupied with their books and arcane ways. Nafaria was different. She was innocent, and charming, and loved being in public. She enjoyed the time in the castle as if she had never had the opportunity to be around people. He wished he could convince her that he could make her happy. That he would love her more than anyone of the Craft ever would. He wished he could convince Nafaria to think about it.

His thoughts were broken by the loud clopping of a horse coming through the castle gate and slowing down near the part of the colonnade where the stable was. Coleman's curiosity was piqued as he saw a young rider quickly dismount. Solomon was there to greet him.

"Greetings, stranger, I trust that you will be able to join the festivities though you seemed to have missed the wedding!" said Solomon in his loud hearty voice. The stranger seemed very agitated. He looked at Solomon and said, "Sir, I need to see the king at once. I have an urgent message for him from my master."

"The king is very busy this evening, but I am sure I can get the message to him. Why not go and be refreshed?" asked Solomon as he held out his hand for the parchment the young stranger carried.

"That is not possible; I need to see the king at once. His guest from Nereheim is in grave danger," replied the stranger.

Coleman heard the stranger's last words as he came upon them. "Solomon, what seems to be the trouble?" he asked.

The young rider turned to face Coleman, a pleading look in his eyes. "I need to see the king. I have a message he must see at once. It concerns a young woman the prince came home with from Nereheim. She is in danger," said the rider.

Coleman's expression became grim. "Follow me quickly," he replied.

Peter followed Coleman through the crowd and into the throne room. They walked brusquely up to the king, the queen, Jared and Ephratha. Peter held out his message to the king. He bowed low and said, "Your majesty, my Lord Reinard Sallen of Nereheim sends you this urgent message."

The king took the parchment and broke the seal. He unrolled it and read the brief message. As he did so, a look of horror crossed his face.

"There is a man here trying to find Nafaria to kill her. Where is she now?" asked the king as he stood to look around the room. She was nowhere in sight.

"She said she was going outside to get some air," said Ephratha. Her face was completely white and her stomach tightened. She jumped up and rushed through the throne room, calling her name with Jared and Coleman running behind her.

Joel rushed at Nafaria, spinning her around as he grabbed her. His arm clutched her neck and she could not scream. Her breathing became a shallow gasp. She thrashed around, but Joel was too large for her to escape his grasp. He pulled a knife from his cloak. A thin film coated the blade. Its metal glinted in the light of the moon that now shown.

"This blade is dipped in a poison made from hemlock, wolfsbane, and black locust. It kills quickly enough, but with great pain. Though you will not suffer as long as Leanna did, you will suffer pain enough," snarled Joel.

"Stop!" Joel heard a voice shout in the night air. He turned to see a young man walking swiftly toward them. "I will not allow this treachery," said the young man. Joel brought the knife blade to Nafaria's neck, hovering near her skin.

"My quarrel is not with you, friend. Go your own way and let me have my prize," said Joel.

"I cannot allow you to spill innocent blood," he replied.

"She is far from innocent! Her blood is what I require for the death of my wife!" shouted Joel.

"You cannot hope to bring back your wife if you kill this girl. Blood for blood, it does not work that way. What good will come if you trade the blood of this girl for that of your wife?" asked the young stranger.

"Leave me to my business, I will have my vengeance on this witch!" thundered Joel, as he ignored the question completely.

Nathaniel looked at the young woman closely. Her eyes were deep, pleading. There certainly was great beauty there, and knowledge beyond her young appearance. He was struck by the steadiness of her gaze. She was quite beautiful and somewhat familiar to him. Where had he seen those eyes before?

With a flick of his finger, Nathaniel watched as the knife Joel held suddenly thrust into the air. A smile crossed his lips as Joel cried out and let go of Nafaria in an effort to control the knife. He clutched it with both hands, but it still advanced blade first, to his throat. Joel sank to his knees still struggling with the knife.

"You will give up your quest to kill, or be killed yourself. Which will it be?" asked Nathaniel coldly.

Joel gritted his teeth and struggled with the blade. It came closer, and nearly touched his skin. His forehead was covered in sweat as he fought in vain to control the knife.

"No! You must not! He was my father's best friend. This is not the way it should be!" shouted Nafaria.

Nathaniel's concentration broke long enough for Joel to drop his knife. He rose quickly to his feet and disappeared into the night.

Nathaniel turned his gaze to Nafaria, his eyes blazing. "Why did you do that? He was about to kill you!" shouted Nathaniel.

Nafaria came cautiously toward Nathaniel. She took a deep breath and said, "The way of vengeance is not the path my father taught me. I choose to leave vengeance to YAHWEH."

Nathaniel looked at her carefully. She seemed so innocent, so trusting. "What is your name?" he asked.

"I am Nafaria Mauldon from Nereheim," replied Nafaria.

Nathaniel widened his eyes. His heart quickened and his breathing was labored. He quickly sucked in air to keep his head steady. Tears once again welled in his eyes. "Your father was as wise in the Craft as he was powerful," said Nathaniel. He then brought her close to him and wrapped his arms around her.

"I have searched so long for you, little one," whispered Nathaniel.

Nafaria's eyes grew wide, and she looked at him closely. "Nathaniel?" she whispered. He smiled and held her close to him again.

The gentle child he loved dearly had grown into the graceful woman standing before him. Her dark hair flowed around her. Her eyes, those large blue eyes that spoke of wisdom and knowledge, also showed so much innocence and purity. She was an angel who was too good for this earth. This young woman he searched so long to find had grown into the most delicate and lovely creature he could have imagined. His gaze settled on one of her hands. On her smallest finger was a tiny silver ring, with a heart in the center. It was a delicate piece, but looked perfect on her hand. He recognized it at once. He swallowed as he composed himself enough to speak.

"I remember when I gave you the ring you wear. It was on your tenth birthday," said Nathaniel quietly. He smiled at her.

"We received your letter, and I waited impatiently for you to come. I thought I had lost you before we had a chance to meet again," said Nafaria quietly.

"We arrived too late. Your manor was burned, and there was a pyre that was smoldering next to the fountain. When I saw the pyre, I feared you were lost," said Nathaniel in a choking voice.

"I burned my father before I left Nereheim. Ephratha and Jared witnessed my mother's execution," Nafaria said.

"I know. Father and I met a woman in the Town Square of Wildemere who told us what happened," replied Nathaniel. He pulled Nafaria away from him and put his hands around her face. "You have grown into such a beautiful young woman, Nafaria. I am so grateful I found you before you found yourself married to someone here in North Agea," he said with a smile.

Nafaria laughed and smiled through her tears. "I intended to come find you and your father after the wedding. There would never be anyone else I could ever imagine myself with," said Nafaria. Nathaniel gently kissed her forehead.

"Nafaria!" a young woman's voice rang through the courtyard. It was full of panic.

Nathaniel and Nafaria looked down the colonnade and saw three people running toward them. A young woman in a white gown with a frenzied look on her face was in the lead.

"Ephratha!" she called to them.

Ephratha heard her name, and looked in their direction. Relief spread across her face as she slowed to a stop before them. She panted as she struggled to regain her breath. Jared and Coleman stopped behind her. Ephratha threw herself around Nathaniel and Nafaria.

"I was so worried for you. The king just received a message from a man in Nereheim who claimed someone was here to kill you!" cried Ephratha.

"What? Who sent the message?" asked Nafaria.

"Lord Reinard Sallen," said Jared. "Does that name mean anything to you? Was someone here?"

"Joel tried to kill me, but Nathaniel saved me. He escaped just moments ago," said Nafaria as she clung to Nathaniel.

Jared stepped forward and put his arm on Nathaniel's shoulder. He smiled at him. "My friend, I wondered why you did not come with your father. He said you needed a moment to find your heart again. It seems that you have succeeded," he said.

"My heart's desire has been given me this night," replied Nathaniel with a smile.

"I am Ephratha," said Ephratha stepping forward. "You saved my greatest friend from a death she did not deserve. I thank you from my heart." Her eyes filled with tears as she shook his hand.

"I am grateful that Nafaria has found such true friends," replied Nathaniel quietly.

"Let us join the celebration. My father will be worried until he has word that Nafaria is safe," said Jared. The group turned and walked back up the colonnade.

They returned to the throne room and found the king and queen. They were both relieved when they saw Nafaria was with them. Lydia rushed up to Ephratha and hugged her tightly. Then she did the same to Nafaria. "What happened?" she asked, her voice ringing with concern.

"Joel was here, mother. He followed Nafaria here to kill her," said Ephratha.

"Did you catch him?" she asked.

"No, he had already fled when we found Nafaria and Nathaniel," she nodded toward them.

"He will not return here. He is gone," replied Nathaniel.

"Then tonight is truly a night of celebration," said Lydia as she smiled at Nathaniel.

"Nathaniel, there you are!" Malcom appeared before the group. Lydia was startled when she looked at him.

"You look familiar to me sir. Do I know you?" she asked.

"We met in Wildemere, my lady, at the apple blossom tree," said Malcom in a gentle voice. "My son has found his truest love, and Jared has married a precious jewel. Tonight is indeed a night of celebration, as you have said."

Lydia smiled at him as the music continued to fill the evening air.

The next day, Peter left Arioth with a sealed message for Michael. Nafaria left specific instructions that Peter deliver the message to him alone. He was to respond with haste if he could join her at Arioth.

Peter rode swiftly through the countryside and waited to cross the Anenderes River. His horse was steady and very fast, but he wished for a winged horse at this moment. He could not wait to bring this great news to his new friend.

He rode through the night and late the next day he arrived in Denholm Glen. He went straight to Michael's manor and found him pacing the floor in the library. Lillia sat near the fire, watching him. It seemed that neither was able to sleep well, if at all, in his absence.

Michael looked up at him as he walked through the door. Lillia stood and walked over to Michael, her eyes on him as well.

"Is she safe?" Michael whispered.

Peter handed out the sealed parchment in reply. Michael took it and broke the seal with shaking hands. He slowly unrolled the paper, and tears formed in his eyes. Lillia looked at him, horror etched on her face.

"Michael?" she gasped.

Michael blinked his eyes frantically, to chase back the tears. He recognized his sister's careful, but flourishing script. He read aloud,

> *My dearest Michael,*
>
> *I am grateful for the warning you sent, to alert me of the danger. An attempt by Joel was made on my life, but he failed.*
>
> *Nathaniel Stone saved my life. We wish you to come to Arioth to be a part of our wedding ceremony. It will be a quiet affair, but I want you to be there. Philip and Nathaniel both send their best wishes and we all anxiously await your presence.*
>
> *Nafaria*

Michael looked at Lillia, his eyes alive with delight. He laughed and pulled her into his arms, hugging her tightly. "Come, we have a journey to take!" he exclaimed.

* * *

The circle is complete, Nafaria thought as she stood on the porch outside her room at the castle. The sun was rising gloriously in the sky. The air was warm, and she felt it caress her face as she stood there. Her gentle smile spread across her face. Then a laugh sprang from her throat as she thought of this day and what it would hold. She skipped back into the room and began to undress. She was going to be very busy this morning if she was to be ready by noon.

Michael walked with Nathaniel through the courtyard of Arioth. Nathaniel's nervousness showed in the briskness of his pace. No matter how he tried to stroll, he ended up moving swifter than he wanted. This was not lost on his companion.

"Was there something on your mind, Nathaniel?" asked Michael. Nathaniel stirred from his thoughts.

"I am so glad you came, Michael. It has been great to see you and Lillia again. She has grown into a precious woman. I should have suspected you to marry her," said Nathaniel with a wink. Michael smiled.

"Philip said the same thing. Lillia was my life in Denholm Glen, such as it could be for a boy. When my father told me he had to send me away, it was the only place I wanted to go. There was no way to escape my heart. She has kept it safe since we first knew each other," said Michael quietly. Nathaniel shook his head.

"I do understand how you feel. To choose to marry outside the Craft is your decision, not mine. If Nafaria would have been Reinard's daughter, I might have made the same decision," said Nathaniel.

He bent over and picked up a twig from the ground, examining the few leaves left on the branch, as he stood upright again. He finally threw it back on the ground. "I have searched for your sister since I was thirteen years old. I used every means available to me, and I could never find her. Father searched for Jason through ordinary means as well, but I never gave up until I found her. I know only too well the power of a heart's desire over a person. Now I breathe deeply, knowing that I have found her, and after today she will be my wife. I find I am more frightened of that prospect than I was of finding her dead. I want to be a good husband, but what if I am unequal to the task? I love her so much. I cannot fail," said Nathaniel quietly.

Michael smiled confidently, putting a hand on Nathaniel's shoulder. "You have certainly grown in maturity over the years, my friend. Let her confidence in you give you the strength to be the husband you desire to be. As long as she loves you, you can never fail."

Nathaniel smiled back at his friend. "Thank you for spending this time with me, Michael. I promise to take care of her."

Ephratha walked into Nafaria's room. The lavender dress she wore clung to her figure with grace and elegance. Nafaria turned and smiled as she looked at her friend. "You truly are made to be a princess," said Nafaria.

Ephratha blushed. She came forward and wrapped her arms around Nafaria. "And you, my friend, were made to wear that dress. You will bewitch Nathaniel to be sure, when he sees you," replied Ephratha.

"It is so strange that today, the greatest one of my life so far, I feel at peace. I am not anxious or afraid. I am ready," said Nafaria.

Ephratha laughed. "You are certainly better able to handle this than I was!" she exclaimed.

"Well, we are only going to meet a small circle of friends in Queen Clara's rose garden. You had a cathedral of people watching you," said Nafaria.

"That may be so. But you have not seen Nathaniel since you were ten. Do you not feel any fear at all for the unknown?" asked Ephratha.

"The sacred writings say not to worry about your life because each day has enough trouble of its own[32]. I choose not to worry about the unknown. YAHWEH will handle it," said Nafaria with a smile.

"Well, if that is your decision, I suppose it is time to meet your destiny," said Ephratha. She took Nafaria by the arm and led her out of the room.

Ephratha, Nafaria, Lillia, and Lydia made their way outside to the rose garden where the wedding party awaited.

Philip stood smiling as he took his sister's hand and led her to her betrothed. He moved her to the front of the small assembly where Nathaniel and Michael stood waiting.

Her breath caught when she laid her eyes on him. His eyes widened when they met hers as well. He stood there waiting as she drifted toward him. His brilliant blue eyes filled with tears as he reached out his hand to touch hers. He lifted it to his lips and kissed it gently. "From this day forward, my life is yours," he whispered. She smiled at him as they pledged their love and fidelity under the bright sunlight.

The celebration for Nafaria and Nathaniel lasted until the late afternoon sun began its descent and the day started to think about evening. While everyone ate, drank and danced, Nafaria could not take her eyes from her new husband. Nathaniel never left her side and

---

[32] Matthew 6:34

watched her just as intently. It was as if he was plotting the next move for their evening together.

She became nervous as she thought about their first evening together. Nafaria realized that she and her mother never really discussed what went into a physical relationship between a man and a woman. Thena probably always meant to talk about it once she was betrothed, but the time never happened. Then with all the tragedy and the way she fled, it was the last thing on her mind. Now, she stood at the brink of a deep chasm, and was afraid at what lay at the bottom. She drew in a deep breath and closed her eyes, willing herself to be calm while it was still daylight. She would confess her ignorance to Nathaniel when they were finally alone. She smiled as she opened her eyes to see Nathaniel standing before her, peering into her face.

"Is everything alright?" he asked. There was a shadow of concern in his eyes, but he smiled sweetly.

"Just wondering what the night will hold," she said quietly.

"Love, my lady," he replied in the same quiet tone, as he kissed her lips gently.

Malcom watched his son and new daughter in law with great satisfaction. He felt that all the deeds done in Nereheim had come full circle. Jason's children were all safe, and each was wandering their own path. He knew that Jason would be very proud if he was standing next to him at this moment, watching the lives of his family unfold before him.

"Is all well, Malcom?" asked a gentle voice.

He turned to see Lydia standing beside him. "All is very well indeed," replied Malcom with a smile on his face.

Lydia smiled as well, as she watched all four of the happy couples laughing and dancing together. "Today is truly a day to be grateful for. My daughter is now married, and will be enjoying her new family. It is now time for me to set my sight to other ambitions," said Lydia.

"What is it you will do now?" asked Malcom.

"I will leave in the morning with an escort of the king. I will search out land to purchase and build a new home," replied Lydia.

"You must let me know when you settle," replied Malcom.

"Unless something really strikes my fancy, it will not be for a while. I wish to see this new place I now call home," replied Lydia.

"I wish you luck in your journey, but for today, will you allow me a dance?" he asked.

"I would be most delighted," Lydia replied with a smile.

The day drew to evening and all the king's guests enjoyed dinner. Though the meal was just as heavenly as Nafaria had come to believe all the king's meals should be, she could feel her nerves getting the better of her once again. Nafaria drank an extra glass of wine to help steady her composure. It seemed to work, she felt less shaky.

Nathaniel watched her, with interest, as she sipped her wine. He leaned over next to her and whispered in her ear. She smiled, and he gently kissed her cheek.

* * *

The stars twinkled brightly, as Nafaria stood out on the terrace enjoying the warm breeze that blew in the night. In a few more hours, the temperature would start to decline, and the night would be cooler, but for now, she enjoyed the warmth on her skin.

She was dressed in nothing but a sheer gown that fell to her feet. The dress was pale blue with thin straps and a low neckline. It was so sheer, her naked body shone through it in the light of the moon that was now rising. Her nerves began to waver once again as she stood looking at the sky. She knew she had nothing to fear, and was excited for what the evening held, but she was still nervous anyway. She pondered this strange irony as the sound of footsteps became evident behind her.

She turned and walked into the room as Nathaniel came to her. He wore no shirt, only a loose fitting pair of linen pants. He carried a flask in his hands and two glasses. She focused on his face, but found her eyes drifting to his perfect muscular chest. She had never seen a man without a shirt before, and was fascinated by the muscles she had never seen. His body seemed tense and ready for what lay ahead.

He put down the glasses and uncorked the flask. He poured the liquid into each glass and handed one to Nafaria.

"What is this?" she asked.

"It is an old family elixir for nights just like this. It is my hope that we will consume so much of this liquid that we will know the recipe by heart," Nathaniel replied. A mischievous grin flashed across his face.

Nafaria lifted the cup to her nose. Its smell was rich, full and sweet. She took a sip and felt it soothe her throat. She took a few more sips and felt her body tingle. She smiled as she continued to drink.

Nathaniel watched her as she drank the liquid. He could see the outline of her breasts beneath the pale blue gown she wore. His heartbeat quickened as he turned his attention back to her eyes with a hungry stare.

"This is delicious. I can taste the milk thistle, but I cannot place any other ingredients," she said.

"We can talk about the recipe in the morning," whispered Nathaniel. He caught her up in his arms and plunged her onto the bed.

He kissed her lips, gently but with a passion that quickened Nafaria's heartbeat. She looked at him as he continued to gently kiss her neck and shoulders.

He saw the fear in her eyes and slowed his kisses. He lay down beside her and rested his head on his elbow. He let his free hand caress her face. He found teardrops that he gently wiped away. He kissed her cheeks and asked, "What is wrong?"

"I am afraid," she whispered after a moment.

"What are you afraid of?" he asked. He looked at her tenderly and let his hand drift down the outline of her chest.

"I do not know what to do. What if-", she whispered after a moment, but could not complete her sentence.

"What if?" he asked gently. His hand cupped her breast lightly.

"What if I do something wrong?" she asked. Her cheeks blazed so red she felt the heat rise from them as she blushed.

He smiled and pulled her closer to him. He chuckled quietly as he kissed her lips again. He twisted one of his hands into her soft hair.

"Do you think I am completely fearless? I want you more than anything. I want to feel your skin on mine, to create heat, and see your body completely. I have thought of nothing else all afternoon. However, I am not devoid of fear," replied Nathaniel.

"But you know what to expect, do you not?" asked Nafaria.

"With love, there are no wrong answers," replied Nathaniel. He kissed her neck once again.

Nafaria felt the straps of her gown gently glide off her shoulders and down her arms. She looked into his eyes and let her body feel all the passion she was made to feel on this most precious and passionate night.